The Shadow of the Daughter's Ring

Andrea Millard

This edition first published in paperback by
Michael Terence Publishing in 2024
www.mtp.agency

Copyright © 2024 Andrea Millard

Andrea Millard has asserted the right to be identified as
the author of this work in accordance with the
Copyright, Designs and Patents Act 1988

ISBN 9781800947771

No part of this publication may be reproduced, stored
in a retrieval system, or transmitted, in any form or
by any means, electronic, mechanical, photocopying,
recording or otherwise, without the prior
permission of the publisher

Cover image
Copyright © Igor Igorevich
www.123rf.com

Cover design
Copyright © 2024 Michael Terence Publishing

Michael Terence
Publishing

For Juliet
Who I tried to figure out the mystique.

Contents

Synopsis 1
Foreword 2
Prologue: One Day at Secondary School 3
1: The Spanish Holiday 5
2: The Midnight Séance 29
3: Recollection 33
4: Heart's Desire 53
5: The Dedication 67
6: A Christmas Consolation 77
7: Spanish Bliss 90
8: Bridesmaids 101
9: Wedding Highlights 108
10: A Summer Drive 122
11: Sweet Innocence 135
12: The Thunderstorm 139
13: The Godson 146
14: The Rosary 149
15: Riding Accident 154
16: Jennifer Rides Out 164
17: Repent or Damnation 166
18: A Midsummer's Ball 190
19: Christopher's Deep Memories 215

20: The High Season	230
21: The English Rose	256
22: Jennifer Fell Off her Horse	265
23: Jennifer's Trauma	267
24: Jennifer's Days of Being Housebound	269
25: Preliminary Rounds. Dressage. From Runner-up to Winner	271
26: Nobbs and Nells (Tamley & Hedley)	273
27: A Seasonal Peace at Christmas	279
28: A Religious Talk	281
29: Jennifer's Friends Call at Her House	284
30: Jennifer Stays at a Close Family Friend's	287
31: Dream House (A Beautiful Retreat)	289
32: Jennifer Visits a Gipsy Friend at a Caravan	292
33: Jennifer's Bitter Blues	295
34: Jennifer Goes to the Stables to be Alone with her Horse	297
35: Jennifer's Family Friends Come to Her House	298
36: Late Grandmother's Spirt in a Pretty Summer Garden	299
37: Jennifer's Request	302
38: Dream Rider (Horseman Pride)	303

Synopsis

Christopher is concerned about his sister, Jennifer. A disturbed teenager growing up but a formidable one!

Christopher loves his sister. He is possessive of his sister.

Jennifer's grandmother gives her granddaughter her ring. Jennifer wears this ring with great pride. Jennifer treasures it.

With fondness Jennifer remembers her grandmother and grandfather too!

Despite everything, life in general, Jennifer realises this ring she possesses is her most valuable jewel, more valuable than all her jewellery possessions.

Christopher experiences life with his beloved sister. His experiences together with his sister are his happiest times and fondest memories.

In life his mother is a dabbler. His sister and he from spiritual darkness see the light and subsequently become converted!

Foreword

All the friends who know Jennifer are fond of her. They all have such a nice, sweet camaraderie amongst them. Jennifer is a well-loved and pampered Granddaughter.

On Jennifer's birthday she receives a gift, a ring from her beloved Grandmother. This ring is a sapphire and diamond platinum ring. On this beautiful ring, the sapphire is mounted in a cluster of fine diamonds.

This ring is Jennifer's favourite jewellery, her most favoured possession.

Jennifer has a possessive obsession for jewellery and jewels. Jennifer's obsessional possession for diamonds, jewellery and jewels is an obsession. An obsessive female's obsession. Jennifer a female is obsessed by it.

Jennifer learns the craft of it. It's a customary family practice. A strange and mysterious daughter who engages in seances with either members of her family or a witch's coven. Once Jennifer's secrets in her past…

Prologue

One Day at Secondary School

A pupil going to her form room attended Registration as usual. In the Classroom, Jennifer sat down on a chair at the table. The pupil sat near the end of the table quite near a member of her form who was sitting at the opposite end of the table. Jennifer was cold.[1] Her cheeks were flushed, her hands numb.

After registration had ended, Jennifer attended her next period. During those morning lessons, Jennifer was moody, quiet, lazy and idle. Jennifer was in a bad mood.

At break time, she saw another member of her form standing opposite at an entrance to a departmental Block, A Department.

This clever pupil stood by the entrance pretending to play a violin, using both his arms and hands.

Jennifer in a moody state ignored this sign again!

Much later, during the course of the school day, this pupil attended her other periods. These were both long lessons.

During these lessons, she was hardworking and brilliant. The pupil did in fact enjoy her lessons and her classwork as usual. That afternoon, the pupils engaged in their classwork.

Sometime later in the afternoon, the pupil skived off the rest of her remaining periods.

Jennifer went home from college much earlier than usual. The schoolgirl ran to get her bus. The pupil took her bus to get home.

On Friday night, Jennifer's friends stayed with her at her home. At precisely midnight, Jennifer, a Witch dressed in a beautiful slinky black dress then with expectation decided to join her friends for a

---

[1] Her schooldays in a history classroom were freezing (cold).

seance. Her few friends belonged to a Witches Coven. That midnight they all engaged in a seance together.

This was Jennifer's first experience as a pubescent teenage daughter soon becoming a leader!

Mystery Teenager

The husband and wife stood by the French windows, opposite the balcony. From their view of the gardens, it overlooked the beautiful gardens. The lady and gentleman caught sight of a beautifully dressed guest surrounded by an entourage. Seemingly they all made a fuss of her. The guests were fond of her. They adored, admired and revered the lovable guest. This stunning-looking female guest was a mystique and an enigma! The guest wore a beautiful black evening dress. She was bejewelled and adorned with jewellery.

"Who is she? Isn't she damn strange!" said the gentleman perplexed.

A strange countrywoman guest appeared along the country gardens. An enigma and mystique. This guest was chic, debonair and enigmatic, mysterious and bewitching. Some of the guests had never seen this stranger before tonight in a beautiful, enchanting garden. With a thrill, a delight they watched a fountain emanating powerful jets of water.

Watching and looking at the mystery guest appearing and vanishing with her mother and her chaperon and private chauffeur assigned to Jennifer for them to attend this gala function, it made such a thrill of a difference to their lives! Their independent daughter was a responsibility. Jennifer possessed sweet charm appeal and a personality which was irresistible. Jennifer was engaging. Vibes of irresistible qualities. With definite certainty, her beauty an irresistibleness. She captivated them all, these family guests invited today, without doubt. Her captivation a guest's fascination!

1
The Spanish Holiday

The airliner departed from London to Malaga, Spain. All the passengers got off the airliner.

Christopher and his sister Jennifer and their parents got on the crowded airport bus which transported all the passengers to a terminal of the airport.

These passengers went through Passport Control and Customs and Excise. Some of the passengers also bought at a duty-free shop.

Christopher, Jennifer and their parents collected their luggage. They waited together near an entrance to the airport.

The driver from the hotel came and led them to the minibus which was parked outside the busy airport with many taxis there. The minibus driver opened the sliding door. He put their luggage in the minibus where there was ample room.

The driver drove to a hotel which was across the other side of the island.

The scenic island was quite beautiful. A typical Spanish paradise.

Christopher felt enervated and dehydrated. He sweltered from the heat. His parents were cheerful and exuberant.

The radio on distracted Christopher. His attentiveness lacked alertness. It spoiled his enjoyment of the island drive. It had a certain number of coastal and island beauty spots. It was a fabulous adventure beyond Ibiza and the other Islands, Balearics, where tourists, islanders and holidaymakers went for their holidays. It was currently the most popular tourist attraction and destination in this region. This Spanish Island.

Here was where the Iberians, Spanish, Islanders, Germans and holidaymakers went for their holidays. In large numbers they flocked over here. Enjoying the nightlife.

The minibus reached the luxury hotel. Parking outside the hotel in its grounds. The professional driver took out their luggage and put it down on the ground.

Christopher, Jennifer and their parents took their luggage. They entered the hotel. On the ground floor they went to the reception.

Mr and Mrs Staples checked in for their reservation. The receptionist led them to a lift. Suddenly the lift door slid open. They entered an empty lift. They went to the floor where the busy receptionist showed them to their hotel room.

Christopher went to his hotel room. He looked around. He admired his luxurious hotel room for the very first time. With curious excitement he stepped out onto the balcony. There he watched in the distance women sunbathing by a luxury poolside. Some of the sunbathers had glistening wet bodies and dripping wet hair. A few others had damp hair. Most of the others had dry hair.

Christopher caught sight of the women sunbathing by the poolside. All the sunbathers lying gracefully on sun-loungers appeared to be Europeans.

Christopher seemed to be quite embarrassed watching them. He ogled them when looking at their tanned figures. In embarrassment, Christopher went back indoors. He left the patio door ajar. Nervously, he drew the curtains, covering up the windows. He sweltered from the sun beating down. He perspired and dehydrated. He cooled down in the shade and from the air-conditioning.

Suddenly Christopher was disturbed by the sound of loud knocking at the hotel door. He was distracted as he hesitated to go towards the door. Standing at the door was his pretty sister, Jennifer.

Jennifer came in and looked admiringly at his hotel room. Inspecting it with such approval.

"Your room is big. A big double bed. You've got a balcony too!" said Jennifer.

"Would you like a tea?" asked Christopher.

"Yes. Please," answered Jennifer.

Jennifer pushed open the sliding door wider. Jennifer went out onto the balcony. Sweltering from the heat. She looked out from

The Shadow of the Daughter's Ring

the balcony. From high above the balcony. Jennifer stood while admiring the view.

After observing and making observations, Jennifer came back indoors. Jennifer sat down at the table. She felt weary, tired and sleepy, suffering from jet lag.

Christopher put on a kettle. He made Jennifer a cup of tea. He put a dash of UHT milk and sugar in a teacup. Christopher stirred the sweet tea. Christopher handed a teacup and saucer to his sister sitting cross-legged at the table. He noticed the noticeable ring on her ring finger, the sapphire and diamonds sparkling. Jennifer noticed how her brother looked at it with envy. Jennifer showed off her ring proudly. It was her most favourite ring. She approved of the platinum sapphire ring set with a cluster of diamonds.

"It's sentimental!" exclaimed Jennifer proudly. "My grandmother gave me this ring."

"It's lovely," remarked Christopher.

"Will you drive me to a séance next week?" asked Jennifer.

"I'll think about it."

"Oh, go on! You said you would. You haven't changed your mind, have you?"

Christopher assured his doubting sister.

"I will drive you there. Really there's no need to worry. I said I would."

Christopher touched his sister's shoulder. He raised his tone of voice in assurance. In confirmation he did confirm it, acknowledging his favour, he intended to do for her. Reassuring his sister of any doubts she still may have had regarding the uncertainty of her travel arrangement.

Jennifer's sweet smile brightened him up. She reached out and touched her brother affectionately. In affection, reminding her brother she still loved him!

"You know that I'll do anything for you," concluded Christopher sweetly.

"Well. I like to see you try."

"I do hope our holiday does live up to expectations," wished Christopher.

"By the look of it, I think we will have a splendid time," assured Jennifer.

Christopher fantasised about having a wonderful holiday. He wondered if his expectations would be fulfilled.

"I do hope so," said Christopher.

"I don't know about you; I am going to my room to get some sleep."

Jennifer flicked her hair with some obsessive narcissism. In her usual way. Her hairstyle customary in a modern style and trend.

Jennifer got up and left his hotel room. Going along the long corridor. Going back to her hotel room on the same floor.

Christopher sweated. Christopher took off his trousers. He got into bed and lay down in a position which felt comfortable. His bed was sun-drenched from the sweltering heat.

Christopher rested. He could not sleep. He felt too hot and tired. He tried to get used to the strange surroundings by trying to get rest.

About an hour later, Christopher got up. He put on his trousers. He made up his bed. He smoothed up the creases of the bed sheets and duvet cover. He picked up the light continental quilt and spread it out evenly.

Christopher was disturbed again when he heard a loud knock at the door. He wondered who it was disturbing him at this time. He groomed himself. Then he opened the door. His sister stood outside the door. He unexpected this unarranged and unorganised arrangement by his sister. It was an intrusion.

Jennifer looked really gorgeous with her make-up on which did accentuate her features and high cheek bones, especially the rouge in particular.

"Mom and Dad aren't coming. They want to spend more time together," said Jennifer loudly.

They both went out of the hotel room. Christopher and Jennifer walked down the long corridor. They both went to the nearest lift

The Shadow of the Daughter's Ring

on their floor. They went in a lift. At that time there were only a few people in the lift going down.

Christopher and Jennifer took the lift to the ground floor. They walked past the seated area and reception. Going out of an entrance. They looked around the hotel grounds. Admiring the incredibly lovely grounds, the brilliant colours of all the flowers and the loveliest plants which shone in the blazing sunshine.

They wandered off in another direction. They came to a swimming pool which members of families used. On the beautiful lawns, exhibitionistic and provocative female sunbathers lay on sun-loungers. They sunbathed themselves. Did they make an exhibition of themselves? Exhibitionists! Their bodies tanned from sunbathing. Their suntan a dark tan.

Christopher and Jennifer walked back the other way passing properties used for vacation rental by holidaymakers and private tenants.

They walked past the hotel and restaurant and headed back down the long path which led towards the beautiful beach. The fence ran down to the other end. It fenced off the beach. At these isolated parts of the beath it was rocky and stony and uninhabited.

Further down on the beach, families came to spend the day. Everywhere else there were sunbathers and holidaymakers on the beach. It included children playing and making sandcastles.

Christopher and Jennifer walked down the sandy beach along the shore. Admiring the beautiful blue and azure sea. Surrounding them everywhere were sunbathers and loungers. There were the Spanish and Iberian beauties in bikinis and swimsuits.

Christopher had an obsessive fascination for a few sunbathers. These beauties were narcissistic while sunbathing, attracting attention. He became aroused and excited at the sight of their figures. Also, those who proudly paraded with cool nonchalance.

Walking side by side with his sister, Christopher admired the sight of the sunbathers' bodies lying on blankets and on the sand. Some of them were lithe, petite and curvaceous, voluptuous sunbathers.

Christopher was enervated from walking on the sandy beach. He felt tired and exhausted.

Christopher and Jennifer turned back. Going back the opposite way, heading back to the hotel in the distance.

They both rounded off the evening by staying the rest of their time in the hotel.

They ate at the restaurant. Coming across different diners and their families. They dined at reserved tables which were candlelit. All the diners were entertained by a pianist.

Christopher stayed the remaining time in his hotel room alone. He still suffered with jet lag. He lay down on his bed, resting and relaxing in comfort in his quiet hotel room. From the moderate air-conditioning and the breezy freshness of the air from the open windows, it was pleasing to his comfort.

Christopher saw hardly anything of his neglectful parents. His parents preferred their own company to anyone else's. He saw less and less of Jennifer. Jennifer preferred to be by herself.

Christopher decided to go to bed earlier than usual. He took a hot shower. He used the luxury toiletries provided by the hotel. Then he went to bed at an earlier time. Recovering from jet lag and tiredness. From his expectations he was excited about his holiday. He was so excitable.

Early next morning Jennifer came to Christopher's hotel room. Jennifer knocked on the door. Christopher already dressed answered the door, expecting his sister to come. Jennifer felt weary and enervated. Was it because of the time difference and Spanish climate?

Jennifer sat down at the table in the shade. Christopher put on a kettle. He made a tea and a coffee. Sitting down at the table in the corner. Jennifer cooled down in the shade. Jennifer yawned. She stretched out her arms.

"It's going to be another lovely day. I can't wait. Are the Spanish religious? Are the Spanish Catholics? There are many churches dotted around here. I've lost count of how many churches I saw. I am a witch like my mother. It runs in the family. I have a black, green-eyed cat called Tammy. I have a séance coming up soon. I would like you to drive me there."

"Jennifer, you shouldn't worry. It's OK. I'll drive you there," assured Christopher.

Christopher handed Jennifer a teacup and a saucer. Jennifer stirred her sweet tea. She sipped her tea. She liked her tea. Jennifer drank up her tea.

Jennifer was feeling giddy. At once she left his hotel room. She went back to her hotel room, further down the long corridor at the other end.

Jennifer lay down on her bed to sleep.

Christopher walked onto the balcony and up to the balustrade, parapet, where he stood and overlooked the swimming pool in the distance.

He sweated and dehydrated from the radiant shining run. The radiance blazing. From high above he admired the view. He envied the attractive women sunbathing along the poolside. He desired one of them more than any other women. From oglers they attracted attention. The sunbathers desired to be the centre figure of attraction! In excitement, sexually attracting.

A few of the sunbathers saw him standing on the balcony, but none of them showed any interest whatsoever.

Christopher got frustrated and humiliated by looking at the tanned sunbathers. He suffered with an inferiority complex and even had suicidal contemplation!

He desired their attractiveness. The women's sex appeal! Despite being titillated and tantalised from the sight of sunbathers.

Christopher walked past his father who was lying on the bed resting. He hurried out of the hotel room.

As he reached the poolside, a group of women got up from the loungers and hurried inside the hotel.

Christopher had a tantrum but calmed down moments later.

At the bar he sat down at the table. He ordered a beer. Observing the holidaymakers. At a table nearby he envied the honeymooners and romantic married couples revelling and chatting.

Christopher gulped down his glassful of beer. Drowning his sorrows. Then left the crowded bar with no intention of returning at present. Maybe tomorrow night for possible nightlife.

Christopher napped for two hours, then he went into the sauna.

He soon got bored of doing nothing and just fidgeting during that short time. He felt faint from the temperature of the hot steam rising. He sipped a bottle of still mineral water which he had taken in with him. As he sat still, he thought about the women that he had seen earlier today. Hours ago. He envied their sexuality. Their sensualism. He wondered how they indulged in eroticism for hours. He thought of it as being a female pursuit.

He left after a while and walked barefoot to the swimming pool. In the sun the water shimmered, reflecting casting shadows.

He dived in and was refreshed by its rippling coolness. He swam at a steady pace up to the children who were playing. He had more interest in the playful children than the sunbathers tanning and exposing themselves. The sight of it may have distracted him. Making him wildly excited!

In an excitable state, Christopher became overjoyed at the children playing. He wanted to join in and play with them. How would they react towards him? He did wonder at how some of the children appeared to be pleasant, nice and energetic and playful. He tolerated their boisterousness and felt rejuvenated whilst playing with the youngsters. The smaller, younger children were rather friendly and showed a liking towards him. He became deeply fond of them. He enjoyed the company of children. Their enthusiasm and zest for life, but also, he was aware of how cruel and nasty children could be with their taunting and teasing. On quite a few occasions he had encountered nasty and bad children. He experienced it. Their bad behaviour. He was wary of children's torment. The older ones were temperamental, horrible and nasty as well as naughty. The foreign children were quieter and happier.

He perked up at the European children allowing him to join in, with some of them splashing water at each other. He enjoyed the excitement. Enjoying having fun.

The Shadow of the Daughter's Ring

As time passed, he became tired from the scorching heat. He might have stayed longer if it was not for the bad behaviour of the unpleasant older children who taunted and teased. He regretted not staying with the playful children longer. He was afraid of the violent, aggressive ones who obviously disapproved of him intruding on them.

Christopher soon lost interest in them. He swam away and reaching the other end of the swimming pool he got out quickly. He was afraid of them. Their aggressiveness and unpleasantness.

The following afternoon Christopher went out to the swimming pool again. He was still feeling enervated after going to a nightclub last night. (During the course of his holiday, on a few nights, he enjoyed the Spanish nightlife, going to beach bars, restaurants and a cabaret.)

Christopher was relieved that Gerald's family hadn't invited any guests today. On previous days his villa had been full of guests imposing on and intruding on him.

Christopher heard the children screaming and shouting in the swimming pool. He was tempted to join them once more. He wondered how they would react towards him on this occasion, yet again. He was terribly nervous that they might lose interest and afraid of the youngsters who may dislike and desert him. He expected the older children to be quite unfriendly and unpleasant. He dreaded how they might shamefully treat him, but today he was hoping for a better situation. A pleasanter friendship?

Christopher felt calmer and more relaxed as there were grown-ups present. He felt cool and calm when stepping into the swimming pool. He cooled down in the rippling water. He felt refreshed and revitalised while swimming.

Later he joined in with the children, ducking them in the water and splashing about. He seemed rather surprised at how the youngsters were still fond of him.

Christopher was dismayed at how some of the older children, teenagers, shunned him. They taunted and teased. Some of them did like him. They smiled and gestured at him by acknowledging his pleasantness and pleasantry.

Today the older children were nice, pleasant, playful and well-behaved. (Their parents told them off and reprimanded them for misbehaving. The little children were punished for being naughty and the teenagers for bad behaviour.)

Christopher gained an hour of enjoyable pleasure playing with the children. He had a natural way and understanding with the children. His relationship with them grew better. It was the best thing he could have done and of course nothing else gave him greater joy and pleasure.

Suddenly Christopher was aware that he was being watched and observed. He became self-conscious and diffident.

He quickly got out of the swimming pool. His wet body dripping wet with glistening drops of water. He wrapped a towel around him.

He hurried indoors. Going back to his hotel room. He quickly showered and got dressed.

He rejoined Gerald out on the terrace. It was blazing with sunshine, sun-drenched from the radiant sun. The blaze blinding and it bedazzled from the resplendence of the dazzling sunshine, its shiny reflections.

Christopher heaved a sigh. He sat down on a chair. Resting in comfort.

"The little children love to play. They don't have any objections to me joining them. The older ones are sometimes hostile, unfriendly and difficult. As days have passed, their behaviour has been getting much better."

Gerald lit up a cigarette.

"You're a natural with children. You really are. Give them a chance. You surely don't expect it to be easy," Gerald added.

Christopher was contemplative and reflective. He glanced at the older children playing together.

"They're harder to please," commented Christopher.

"If they do let you play, then you should play. Otherwise, I suggest you leave them alone."

Christopher was terribly humiliated at being told what to do. His indecisiveness of not making any friends was apparent.

"I won't bother with the older ones. I do love the little ones. They're cute."

"They're naughty. You'll cope," grinned Gerald.

Christopher looking around, mentioned something else.

"Where is the neighbour?" enquired Christopher.

"She's never in. Never even in the country. Globe-trotting as usual," replied Gerald.

Gerald glanced over at the villa next door.

On another day Christopher went out with all the children again. The older ones refused to play. Some of the younger children had brought bicycles. Christopher spent his time watching them cycling around the front drive, terrace and patio area. He wanted to join in the fun. He felt that he would miss out if he didn't pick up a discarded bicycle which remained lying on the ground.

Christopher rode someone else's bicycle. He borrowed it. Adjusting the gears accordingly. He practised riding the bicycle. He had no difficulty balancing on the bicycle. He managed to ride it effortlessly. He had such effortless grace, riding and pedalling the bicycle. He had such fun from riding it. It was a boy's excitement!

He hoped that the owner of this bicycle did not object to him borrowing it without permission.

He took the liberty as it belonged to one of the boys. He joined the boys who cycled. One of them riding his bicycle was being reckless and careless as he almost collided accidentally with another cyclist.

A few of the children rang their bells as they cycled by.

Christopher was charmed by the sound of the bells ringing. He remained alert at the cyclists. From the oncoming bicycles approaching him in his direction. His eyes blinded from the dazzling sunrays reflecting on the shining handlebars. It was scorching from the heat.

Christopher followed a group of boys who cycled around the neighbourhood. They stopped outside Claudette's villa. Christopher was curious to take a look at the neighbour's house.

Christopher got off the saddle. He put both feet down on the ground. He took interest in the neighbour. He wanted to go to her villa and ring the doorbell. He could at least find out if anyone was in and perhaps get the chance to identify the person close-up. He kept riding the bicycle near the front drive. There he loitered with the other neighbourhood children.

Suddenly another boy ran in front of him. The little boy obstructed his way. Christopher sympathised. He did not reprimand him for his carelessness. He gestured to the tough boy. He smiled by touching the boy on his shoulder gently.

Christopher returned the bicycle to whom it belonged. The boy the bicycle belonged to took the bicycle and walked off home with it. The boy belonged to a gang. The boy's brother appreciated his thoughtfulness.

Christopher walked back on foot whilst the others cycled back towards Gerald's villa where they dispersed and went back home. The rest of the gang kept away from trouble.

***

That afternoon Christopher and his father went into a bar. They stood among the crowd and queued up. They both waited until the barman served them. They took their drinks and sat down at a table.

Christopher cooled down in the air-conditioning. He observed everybody else in the bar. He felt jealous of the blissful honeymooners and married couples in love!

His first impression of the revellers and merry makers was that they were rapturously happy as they raised their glasses to make a toast.

Christopher could not figure out if they were practising Catholics. He also noted that the Spaniards and Iberians were rather pretty women. One of the men standing there was quite handsome and one of the husbands, a married man, rather good-looking. Talking to his merry, romantic wife.

"Why are they so happy, and we're not?!" retorted Christopher.

"The only explanation is that they are blessed!" remarked Father.

Christopher noticed their facial expressions. He swooned, looking at their lambent Iberian eyes and their charmed smiles.

"I never want to go back home," whispered Christopher.

They left the crowded bar. They both went back into the hotel room. Christopher walked out onto the balcony and stood still to enjoy the view. He wore trendy sunglasses and was able to relax with ease. As no one could see his eye expressions, he glanced at the lithe women still sunbathing and watched the children playing in the swimming pool. He took off his sunglasses. He was blinded by the glare. Then, blinded, he looked away quickly as an alert sunbather caught him watching, ogling.

Christopher was aroused from desiring the curvaceous sunbather. Michael, his father, joined him out on the balcony. He leaned on the parapet balustrade and looked down at the crowded poolside.

Christopher wanted to join in the fun. He desired pleasurable excitement. He gained joy from watching. The children were boisterous, playful and mischievous. They were playing together and having fun.

Christopher and his father stared at the sunbathers relaxing in comfort and indulging in luxury. Suddenly Christopher became restless. He decided he had to get out and do something as he was fed up with just watching and observing the sunbathers. He felt tantalised and titillated. Christopher fidgeted, unsure what to do now. Pacing up and down the balcony. Sweltering in the heat. He went back into his hotel room where it was shady and cool. The air breezy.

"Let's go to the beach?" urged Christopher.

They both left the hotel room and strolled down the corridor, taking the nearest lift to the ground floor. They passed through the foyer and went out of the grand hotel. They walked a distance until they reached the glorious beach. At this time of day, it was crowded, full of holidaymakers.

Christopher marvelled at the beautiful sandy beach and sunny weather.

"Isn't it a lovely beach? What a lovely day!" exclaimed Christopher joyously.

"I am pleased you like it. It's the very same place your mother and I used to come to when you were a child," recalled Father.

Christopher pondered on his memories. Remembering the photographs in the old photo album.

"Let's go on," insisted Father.

They kept walking down the beach. Leaving a long trail of footprints in the golden sand.

Christopher thrilled at the sound of the electrifying sea – and tide. He sighed in joy.

The wind whipped up his hair against his cheeks. He flushed. They both approached sunbathers, occupying a secluded spot. They had no intention of intruding on their privacy.

After a while, they stopped walking. They rested on the dry sand. Relaxing sluggishly.

Christopher grabbed a handful of thick sand and threw it. Making a wish as he did so.

Christopher and his father got up. They straightened up. They trekked further down the beach along the shore. Cooling down as they strolled.

They approached Mallorcans along the way as the locals and inhabitants flocked frequently to the beach. Their trek seemed endless and enjoying their walk, they had the endurance to go on for miles. They reckoned there were hardly any people who walked along these remote parts of the beach. They found it to be beautiful all over. It was the most popular resort in the coastal region.

They perspired and dehydrated from the scorching sun beating down. They walked further and further into the sea.

Suddenly Christopher became distracted as three scantily clad women ran past him and dashed into the sea. The sight of their

The Shadow of the Daughter's Ring

voluptuousness appealing. Attracting his attention. Christopher looked at them dashing into the sea. He watched the attractive women running. One in particular was a buxom tanned woman wearing a semi-transparent sundress which was drenched. Revealing her exposed curvaceous body underneath. He spotted one of them wearing a bikini and sarong. The woman burst out laughing. The other two were also in good humour.

He desired to pursue all of them all the way in the sea. As the waves swept over, they tumbled into the water.

His father grabbed hold of his son. He vigorously pulled Christopher out of the sea. Christopher fantasised that one of the women rescued him. Swimming to save him from drowning. None of them could even be bothered to pay attention.

Christopher reacted with disappointment. Christopher desired to be loved and adored! He resented the provocative women. How the females tantalised and titillated. Paying no attention to him.

"Let's go back?" gasped Father.

They both turned back. They began their long trek back to the resort. Going back took shorter in duration.

***

The following afternoon, Christopher and his father went into a restaurant. They expected their family to turn up at any moment. When they did come to the restaurant, the waiter showed them to their table. They sat down at a table. They both waited for their family to arrive at the restaurant.

Christopher and his father were seated at the table. Simultaneously, they both got up. Christopher and his father greeted, welcomed and embraced them. Every member of their family.

They each ordered beverages from a menu. Moments later the waiter came with their drinks. The waiter opened a bottle of mineral water and a bottle of wine, rosé. The waiter poured it into glasses. Then, deciding, they each looked at the menu and everyone chose what they wanted to order.

The waiter took down each of their orders from the menu. Sitting at the table, they waited some time before the waitress came back to served them their meals. The diners ate their meals.

"Are you happy?" asked Christopher.

"Yeah. It's been wonderful so far. I can't wait to go out and about," grinned Jennifer.

"Don't gobble your food. Where are your manners?" reprimanded Mother.

"Mom, you're embarrassing me!" wailed Jennifer.

Christopher sympathised with his sister bursting with anger. He was wary of his mother's temper.

Jennifer quietened down. The sulky teenager spoke to no one else except Christopher whom she conversed with.

After dinner they went back together to a suite where his parents sat out on the shady balcony whilst Christopher enjoyed some time alone with his sister.

Christopher remembered the last time they met he had confronted Jennifer about some stolen money and jewellery!

Christopher remembered that Jennifer had problems with bullying. She encountered bullies at state school. He wondered how Jennifer coped with her problems, her ordeal. She somehow overcame it!

Christopher worried about Jennifer. He hoped her problems with bullying would be resolved. How would she overcome her trauma? Her traumatic experience?

"You haven't told me. What happened about the bullying?" enquired Christopher.

Jennifer became embarrassed as Christopher mentioned it. Jennifer blushed.

"I don't want to talk about it," said Jennifer uneasily.

Christopher showed concern for her suffering with bullying. He could offer her some advice.

"I want to help you if I could in this matter. You mustn't keep it pent up," sympathised Christopher.

"Miss told me everything will be alright. There's nothing to worry about. I am sure now. I now can get on with my life," assured Jennifer.

Christopher seemed reassured. Were Jennifer's problems resolved? He did not worry about his sister anymore.

Christopher and Jennifer became quiet as soon as their father interrupted them by saying, "Let's toast."

Christopher got up and joined his parents and sister out on the balcony. They each took a glass of champagne from their merry mother.

"Happy birthday!"

"Many happy returns!" they said merrily.

The revellers celebrated their mother's birthday. They revelled in birthday celebrations.

Christopher and Jennifer enjoyed their treat, a glassful of champagne. The chilled sparkling champagne quenched their thirst. They were refreshed from drinking a glassful of frothy champagne spilling over.

Their over-indulgent parents indulged in another glass of champagne. Drinking the remains of the bottle of champagne between them, satisfying their over-indulgence.

The people had a clear view from the poolside of their over-indulging. Christopher and Jennifer became aware of them being watched. At once, they left the suite. Walking through the corridors, Christopher took Jennifer back to her hotel room.

"Sometimes I hate my mother. I can't stand her. I can't live with her," said Jennifer angrily.

Christopher sympathised at how Jennifer seemed deeply unhappy.

"I know how you feel. I understand. I feel the same way," said Christopher sympathetically.

As they reached Jennifer's hotel room, they both enjoyed the privacy of being alone together.

Christopher sat down on a chair. He watched television on remote control. Christopher watched British television. A British network.

A short time later, Christopher became distracted as Jennifer stood blocking his view by standing in front of him. Jennifer had dressed up and was wearing her make-up. A pretty girl.

Christopher smelled the scent of her perfume. He marvelled at the sight of his sister, a teenager, grown-up and twirling gracefully. Distracting him from watching the television screen. Jennifer standing still. Attracting his attention. She shook her hair in a feminine trait of hers.

"Let's go out?" said Jennifer impatiently.

With reluctance, Christopher decided to go out with Jennifer.

They headed out of the busy hotel. They made their way towards the half-empty poolside. Enjoying the peace and quiet of the surroundings.

During the evening, it became much cooler in the shade. At this time, it was much quieter and shady. They lay down on loungers and relaxed side by side. Jennifer exposed her shapely legs. Raising the hemline of her sundress. With intentional provocativeness. It was in a sort of provocative nonchalance. Showing off the suntan of her beautiful, tanned legs.

"I don't want you to be decadent. I want you to be a good girl. A good Catholic," said Christopher unashamedly.

"Do you object to me exposing myself?" frowned Jennifer.

"You're not indecent. You're just growing up," remarked Christopher.

From the poolside luxuriousness there were several sunbathers tanning themselves. They sunbathed for hours.

Christopher and Jennifer were unconcerned and uninterested in anybody else. Relaxing together in the coolness of the fresh breeze. They both enjoyed the quietude and tranquillity of the luxury poolside. Their privacy was not invaded that summer evening.

***

The Shadow of the Daughter's Ring

The following afternoon, Christopher and his father joined their family on the beach.

Federick, a stout, bearded old man, sat on a deckchair.

At Christmastime, Federick dressed up as Father Christmas. Federick amused and entertained the children. Grandfather smoked a pipe and watched all the children playing. Altogether the children joined up to make a big sandcastle.

Jennifer and her mother sunbathed together. Their bodies darkly tanned from exposure to the sun. Their family either talked or sunned themselves.

Jennifer lay on a tartan blanket. She closed her eyes. She dozed off.

Christopher could not resist touching his sister provocatively. The temptation he had unresisted. Christopher stooped down and gently touched Jennifer on her bare back. Disturbing her on purpose.

Jennifer roused from her nap. She glared from having been woken up. Jennifer seemed to be in a bad mood. The provoked teenager temperamental. She developed from puberty from growing up.

"I am back," smiled Christopher.

"Don't do that! What is it?" yawned Jennifer.

Christopher glanced at his wristwatch.

"It's late."

"Where's Grandpa?" mumbled Jennifer.

Christopher looked up and noticed that his grandfather had gone back with his family to the luxury resort. Christopher sympathised with his unsociable grandfather. He recalled Grandfather grumbling about the heat. It reminded him of the tropics. The Caribbean. How Grandfather grumbled about the hot weather in the tropics. The unbearable tropical heat. The sultry air and oppressive humidity.

Christopher knew that his grandfather could not stay out in the radiant sun too long. It was too hot.

Christopher told Jennifer, "He's gone to get his nap."

"I love Grandpa. I don't know what I'd do without him," said Jennifer pensively.

"I love him too. We all love Grandpa," smiled Christopher.

Christopher and Jennifer worried about their grandfather. They were both deeply attached to him. They both loved to hear the stories Grandfather told them.

They walked off and stopped further down the beach. There they saw a group of children making a sandcastle. They took a closer look at it. They stood close-up while admiring it. They were both impressed by the sandcastle. Watching the children make a sandcastle. The big sandcastle made an impressive sight. Towers, battlements, flags and a moat running around it filled up with water.

All the children who made the sandcastle took pride and gained enjoyment and complete satisfaction from completing it to perfection.

"All of you stand together by your sandcastle," gestured Christopher.

All together, the children moved and stood proudly by their completely finished sandcastle.

"Grandpa would love this. All this hard work. It won't be forgotten," said Christopher appreciatively.

Adjusting the lens, Christopher captured it on camera. All the photographs of all the children standing beside their sandcastle. These actual photographs captured their unforgotten memories. The children making a sandcastle. They greatly admired the impressive sandcastle. The sight of it impressed them.

Christopher offered to take more pictures of the children standing proudly by their made sandcastle. All the children ended up refusing to have their photographs taken by Christopher. Instead, all the children who helped to make the sandcastle did allow their parents to take photographs of them standing by their sandcastle in proud admiration.

Today was quite significant because it was one of the boy's birthdays.

The Shadow of the Daughter's Ring

All together, they celebrated his birthday, including friends and families, relatives and relations. The birth celebration lasted only half an hour.

Also, this sandcastle was judged and considered to be the best sandcastle made today on the beach. Incidentally one of the photos given to Grandfather reminded him of his summer holiday.

Christopher and Jennifer smiled broadly at the children, then walked off leaving them with their families. They wanted to spend more time with them. They felt saddened at not seeing any of them ever again! (They got deeply upset at missing the foreign children.)

They both thought highly of the respectful, well-behaved children. They missed their company. Did Jennifer become attached to any of them?

Standing still, they waved goodbye. Some of the children who walked off with their parents had turned around, acknowledging them both with a wave goodbye!

They avoided their own family who were sitting further up the beach. They decided to set off in a different direction. They perspired and dehydrated from the blazing heat. Their clothes saturated with sweat. Their hands clammy and their eyes blurred.

They felt weary from walking even a short distance. So, they turned and stopped at a nearby café. They sat at a table outside on the cobbled street.

Cooling down in the shade, they ordered freshly squeezed orange juice. The charming surroundings were enchanting. (The picturesque little village idyllic on picture postcards.)

Afterwards they walked the rest of the way back to a resort. There they parted company and went to their own hotel rooms. They took a nap and got up hours later. (At that time the Spaniards took a siesta.)

Sometime in the evening Christopher and Jennifer met along the corridor and together called at Grandfather's hotel room. His son opened the door. He greeted them and welcomed them in. They heard screams and shouts of the great-grandchildren playing. Grandfather told them to pipe down. The grandchildren quietened down. Grandfather gestured and showed them to where his bed was. There the grandchildren were all in bed. Grandfather sat and read them a story. Christopher and Jennifer paid heed to Grandfather reading a story. They saw the children's faces lighting up with joy as they listened with attentiveness. Reminding them of when Grandfather told them similar stories which were familiar when they were children!

***

The next day, Christopher called at Gerald's villa where he expected his mother and sister to be paying a visit. Christopher hugged his relative. He took joy from his warm welcome. He patted Gerald on his back, showing his deep appreciation.

"I would like to thank you for coming out with me," thanked Christopher.

"That's alright. You can do me a favour some other time."

"Ask me anything you want," said Christopher obligingly.

"Sally and Jennifer are out in the back," said Gerald calmly.

Christopher joined his mother and sister who both lounged out on a terrace. Jennifer was engrossed in reading a magazine while her mother dozed off. They both had a dark tan which looked noticeable close-up. (From hours of sunbathing, they had a glossy, darkish suntan. From gratification their sensuousness of it was appealing.)

Christopher stooped down and touched Jennifer's arm lightly.

"Hi!" said Christopher.

"What is it?" murmured Jennifer.

Sally woke up as her daughter was aroused from her nap.

"Chris, darling. Is that you?" said Mother hoarsely.

His mother reclined on the lounger. Raising her body in a position by moving forwards. Sally kissed her son on the forehead.

"I do hope you have a good time!" said Jennifer.

Christopher dreaded going to the wine bar tonight. He already sensed disappointment yet again.

"I do hope so. Are you sure you don't want to go?"

"No. I'll stay here with Mom," Jennifer replied.

The Shadow of the Daughter's Ring

His mother brushed a speck of dust from his black shirt. Christopher blushed as his mother made such a fuss.

"My boy! My good boy!"

"Be good," insisted Christopher.

Jennifer put her arms around her mother. Jennifer intended to stay in. Jennifer spoke no more about conversational topics and matters.

"Shall we go?" interrupted Gerald.

"Let's go."

Christopher and Gerald embraced Jennifer and Sally. Then they both left to go out. They walked to a parked car and got in. Gerald drove to a luxury wine bar. It was crowded with locals, tourists and holidaymakers. They indulged in drinks.

***

Meanwhile, a neighbour, Claudette, looked out of a window. The alarmed children who cycled caught sight of the neighbour, a French woman, staring out of the window at them. They saw her statuesque figure and recognisable face. The unafraid boys yelled out at the top of their voices. They cycled away into the distance.

The boys told the members of the gang. The gang reported it to the adults.

***

A long time later, Christopher and Gerald reached the bar. As time passed by it became crowded. The atmosphere was electrifying. The music blaring out. Queuing up, they bought beer and toasted each other merrily.

"To life in Mallorca," they exclaimed.

The revellers engaged in merriment. Christopher gulped down a mouthful of beer. He tried to lose his inhibitions. He was too shy, anxious and self-conscious, but still tried to mingle with the crowds. He watched the locals who seemed to be cheerful and exuberant.

Christopher spotted a group of Spaniards talking. One of them a talker, a chic woman. The flamboyant woman wearing a red dress appealed to him desirably. He desired the raving beauty! He could not overcome his shyness. He felt nervous.

Quickly, the Spaniard, the Spanish woman, was surrounded by her friends. Within moments, Christopher was within out of reach of the voluptuous (Spaniard) woman standing.

Soon the wine bar got too overcrowded. The ratio of men to women was 1 to every 5.

Quickly, Christopher and Gerald left the overcrowded wine bar. They decided to go home.

Christopher felt frustrated and humiliated. He did not make any impression whatsoever on anybody.

2

The Midnight Séance

Very late at night, Christopher arrived at the mystery house. Jennifer got out of the car quickly. She looked at the address on her card. The full address was slightly different with an abbreviation. The host. The person's name abbreviated.

"You stay here. I shan't be long," said Jennifer impatiently.

Christopher stayed seated in the driver's seat. During this time, he waited for Jennifer. In the shining light.

Jennifer went into the house. Going upstairs. Going in one of the upstairs rooms. She attended a séance at midnight.

The wind blew the net curtains and the lights flashed on and off. Jennifer was appointed and anointed. Jennifer was an oracle! Another member of the coven was a medium. The other one was a clairvoyant and another one, a leggy sorceress. Another witch interpreted it accordingly. It was a clandestine arrangement with the witch's coven at the midnight hour. All of them wore rings on their fingers.

After the séance ended, the lights were switched back on. The bright lights shone in the darkness. There were shadows and reflections. Suddenly, a black cat with glossy fur crawled out of an open window. The cat vanished from sight.

The other members of the witch's coven were somewhat satisfied with Jennifer. The youngest witch. They all allowed her to go without imposing any restrictions on her. Jennifer was free to go. She ran out of the top room. She ran down the stairs. She ran out of the house back to the car parked in the front drive. She ran to the car.

Christopher stirred from the sudden movement. Christopher wound down the window. He spoke out.

"Why do you do it?"

"Shut up! Get going!" snapped Jennifer.

Christopher got impatient from waiting. He started the ignition. He reversed the car out of the drive. Driving down the lane before accelerating faster and faster. The acceleration a turbo boost or fuel injection?

They reached home hours later.

Jennifer got out of the car first. She ran to her house.

She inserted a front door key in the lock. She unlocked the front door. She left the front door open. She ran upstairs to her bedroom. She kicked off her slip-on shoes. She stripped off. She turned on the taps. She ran the bath with running water. She put luxury bath salts in the bath water. She got in the bath. She bathed and soaked her skin. She enjoyed having a hot bath in the early hours of the morning. She took great pleasure in the soothing relaxation of the bath. Jennifer relaxed with comfort and indulged in luxury. She engaged in eroticism and erotomania.

Meanwhile, Christopher stayed in the lounge. He sat down on the armchair and rested from his long drive back home.

Drinking a nightcap, he thought of Jennifer. How she dabbled in the occult. It did result from peer pressure and bad influence. Christopher was in conflict with his beliefs. He could compromise no longer.

Christopher used to attend a Catholic school. (From the Catholic religion, Catholicism. The pupils were Catholics. For instance, Irish! And a Pentecostal church.)

Christopher used to be a regular churchgoer until he backslid!

Since having a crush on a girl. She fell in love with someone else. She dated her boyfriend.

Within a short time, Christopher went to bed. He forgot to say goodnight to Jennifer, his sister.

Getting up early in the morning, Christopher got dressed. Wearing his casual clothes. He went downstairs to the lounge. His mother made him breakfast. Christopher sat down at the dining table and ate scrambled eggs on toast and drank coffee.

Jennifer came downstairs wearing a dressing gown. It was tightly tied around her waist. Her beautiful breasts finely rounded indeed. Jennifer was bosomy.

"Who were those involved?" asked Christopher.

"What do you mean? The séance last night?"

"Yes. That's what I mean."

"They were people whom I knew," said Jennifer vaguely.

"You shouldn't do it," objected Christopher.

"I am a witch. I do things like a witch does. I am a witch like my mother," said Jennifer proudly.

"They are practitioners. They are interested in the paranormal."

"Don't question me. Don't preach to me," protested Jennifer.

Jennifer regained her composure. She showed off her ring with pride.

"This ring has been kept in possession by my generations!"

Jennifer went into the kitchen. She made herself a cup of tea, then went back upstairs to go back to bed.

Christopher objected to his sister who dabbled in the Magic Arts. Christopher tried to preach to his sister, but Jennifer did not listen to her brother preaching to her.

Alone in the lounge, Christopher sat down on the armchair. He relaxed while resting. Remaining seated, comfortably. He dozed off after being very tired and sleepy. Getting a lack of sleep last night. His beliefs and faith protected him from magic spells and incantation.

Christopher awoke. He was unaware of the time which had elapsed. He sensed the presence of Jennifer standing in front of him. He smelled the scent of Jennifer's ravishingly pure perfume. Jennifer was dressed up, ready to go out with her friends.

"Hi! Jennifer, it's you. Did you raise anyone from the dead? Did you call out their name?"

"We did invoke their spirit. We tried to raise them from the dead."

"Are you going out?" asked Christopher.

"Yes. I am going out. I'll see you later tonight."

Jennifer touched Christopher on his shoulder.

Much earlier, Christopher had written a note which his sister had read in the kitchen on the kitchen table:

Jennifer. Why aren't you innocent like the others?
Why do you play with darkness?

At once, Jennifer left the house with her group of friends who called around to get Jennifer. All together, Jennifer's nice and peculiar friends got in a car. They were driven to their friend's house.

One of them had been warmly invited to spend the night. A few others had agreed to stay longer. Those ones agreed to the arrangement which had been organised in advance. All the rest had gone home. They disapproved of staying out too late at night. Of course, they were wary and cautious of any danger which awaited them.

3
Recollection

In the dining room Christopher sat at the dining table. His sister sat opposite. Jennifer sat facing her brother. Christopher picked up a teapot. (It had a tea-cosy on it.) He poured the tea into a teacup.

"How many sugars?" asked Christopher.

"Two please," replied Jennifer.

Christopher handed a teacup and saucer to Jennifer.

"What's the matter? Why are you crying?"

"I miss the fifth and sixth formers. I won't ever see them again!" cried Jennifer.

"You're upset. You're feeling heartache. You'll get over it."

"No. I won't. I miss them!" blubbed Jennifer.

Christopher saw Jennifer cry. Her tears ran down her face. In this situation he was unable to comfort his sad sister crying. Christopher gave her a tissue.

"Wipe your tears."

"I love them. I shan't see them ever again. I know it. I just know it," sobbed Jennifer.

"You have your memories."

"I won't forget them," cried Jennifer.

"I do understand how you feel. I did once experience it myself, leaving school."

"You do understand. You do have some empathy," said Jennifer acknowledging him.

Christopher changed the subject.

"There's something I would like to ask you."

"What's that?"

"Why is it that you flinch whenever I stand behind you?"

"I can't explain. I don't know why exactly," said Jennifer uneasily.

Christopher figured it out.

"It's a fear, isn't it?"

Whenever somebody stood too close to Jennifer, Jennifer reacted with fear! She had a spontaneous reaction. She had a nervous disposition. It was a phobia!

"Oh! You are clever," praised Jennifer.

"It must have happened earlier in your school days when you were bullied. Tell me, what did the bullies do to you?"

"It was horrible. They taunted me, pushed me about. They called me names and made fun of me," recollected Jennifer.

Christopher tried to console his sister. Jennifer was feeling sadness! He was deeply sympathetic.

"Your mom tells you to go to church. It may well be the best thing for you."

"I don't want to be forced to go to church. I will go when I want to," said Jennifer defiantly.

"Don't you go to the chapel at school? Don't you like church?"

"There's a mass held at the end of term. As far as church is concerned, I'm not sure if I like it. The pastor says a few words. The congregation are friendly. They are strangers. The service is long. I try to worship. I just don't believe. Does that make me un-Christian?" said Jennifer contemplatively.

Christopher thought about it. He responded calmly, "You say that you are an unbeliever. Why don't you go to church? You may find comfort in the Lord," urged Christopher.

"I'll say my prayers. One of these days I may go to church. Let's see, hey!" said Jennifer apathetically.

Christopher still felt rather tired and enervated from having got up too early in the morning. Now he wanted to relax during the weekend. Intending to enjoy his time of leisure.

"I'm going back to bed," yawned Christopher.

"I'll be babysitting," sulked Jennifer.

Christopher got up and went out of the dining room. He went upstairs to his bedroom. He went in his bedroom. He got undressed and got into bed. He rested for a few hours. Then woke up precisely at midday. He got out of bed. He got dressed in his smart clothes.

Suddenly he heard children's screams and shouts from outside. The screaming and the shouting came from out in the garden. Listening to the reverberating and echoing sound of the girls' screams and boys' shouts.

His privacy was invaded as Jennifer knocked on his door.

Christopher answered the door. Expecting his sister.

"Are you coming down?" said sister.

"I am coming."

Jennifer left her brother by going towards her bedroom near the top of the landing. Going downstairs, Christopher made his way into the garden. Already out in the garden were his mother, grandfather and the children's parents. He greeted them all with affection. Christopher was pleasant, friendly and nice. They were pleasant and welcoming to Christopher.

Some of the children were engrossed in painting, drawing and reading. The others played hide-and-seek.

Jennifer joined her brother out in the garden. Christopher and Jennifer walked away from the pre-occupied children doing painting, drawing and reading. They were amused by the amusing children's laughter. They both walked up to Grandfather standing still. Grandfather walked unsteadily with his walking stick. The elderly gentleman gasped out.

"Grandpa, what's wrong?" asked Jennifer.

"I feel giddy," gasped Grandfather.

"Come and sit down," demanded Jennifer.

"My Godson!" muttered Grandfather.

"What on earth is the matter? What are you concerned about?" asked Jennifer.

"Please. Look after my Godson," demanded Grandfather.

Jennifer intended to fulfil her promise and obligation.

"We promise. We will look after him," said Jennifer assuredly.

"We will both take care of him," said Christopher reassuringly.

Grandfather was concerned about his Godson. Christopher and Jennifer reassured him.

Christopher and Jennifer put his arms around their necks. They helped him to sit down on a garden chair where there was the garden table.

"Can we get you anything?" asked Jennifer.

"A sherry!" replied Grandfather.

Christopher feared the worse about Grandfather's health worsening. Grandfather became pessimistic about his future. He regarded his grandfather as truly special. He got upset thinking of him being deceased.

Christopher remained quiet while listening to Grandfather's gasps. He put his arm around his grandfather. Christopher deeply loved his grandfather. He showed concern for him. The sympathiser was deeply sympathetic.

Jennifer came back with his sherry.

Christopher watched with concern as Grandfather gulped down a small glass of sherry which did revive him. Despite his bad health, Grandfather was in a good mood and of course in high spirits.

Grandfather was a jolly and merry old man. He was full of wisdom, mellow and philosophical in his outlook.

Christopher hugged his grandfather. He loved him.

"Don't move. Stay seated. Don't overdo it," said Jennifer sternly.

They talked to each other for a long time.

About three o'clock, Christopher and his grandfather got up and walked down the garden, where the children sat all together at the garden tables.

Christopher's mother and a few of the children's parents attended to them. All the hungry children ate to their hearts' content. They recognised Federick at once as being Father Christmas! The stout old man with the beard was recognisable.

"Will Father Christmas come this Christmas?" they asked.

"Oh! Will he give us presents?"

The Shadow of the Daughter's Ring

Christopher wondered what Grandfather's response would be.

Federick put his arm around each of the seated children. He spoke to them affectionately. He dearly loved them so much.

"Santa Claus won't forget you. He will be with you this Christmas. I promise you," reassured Federick.

One of the boys spoke up.

"I don't believe in dumb Santa Claus. He doesn't give me anything."

Federick spoke out.

"Tim. Santa will give you Christmas special priority. You will have more presents this year."

Federick intended to cheer up the deprived boy.

Tim cheered up. He licked the fresh cream around his mouth. The little boy believed Federick. The boy hoped his Christmas seasonal wishes would come true!

Christopher and Jennifer watched as the excitable children all reached out to touch him tenderly. Showing their deep love, respect and gratitude to Federick.

About quarter of an hour later, their parents came to pick up their son or daughter from the tea party to take them home.

Christopher helped Jennifer and his mother clear up the tables. They disposed of all the paper cups, paper plates, plastic cutlery and uneaten food into sacks. Christopher tied up all the sacks and put them in the dustbins.

Christopher walked back indoors. He waited for Jennifer in the lounge. Expecting his sister any minute. Christopher thought of Grandfather. He stood and admired a portrait of his great-grandmother.

Suddenly Christopher was startled as his sister touched him on his back.

"Does it look different in the light?" remarked Jennifer.

"Isn't she a beauty!" marvelled Christopher.

Admiring the portrait. The stunner.

Jennifer tried to tie her hair in a chignon hairstyle.

"If I do my hair this way, I would certainly look like her," said Jennifer vainly.

"You do resemble Anastasia. My dad seems to think she was an aristocrat."

"I think that too. If I put my hair up like that and wear a beautiful gown, do you think I could look like a lady?"

Jennifer pretended to be an aristocrat. She put on airs and graces.

Christopher unanswered. He objected to her pretentiousness. Assuming she was an aristocrat! Pretending to be one.

Christopher and Jennifer sat down on a settee. Needing a rest after helping to clean up. They relaxed together while sitting down. Listening to the sound of the grandfather clock chime as well as ticking and the rhythmic sound of a pendulum swinging back and forth.

Christopher handed Jennifer a photo album.

"Why don't you have a look? See what you think."

Jennifer half-heartedly looked through it.

"There are no photos of Grandpa as Father Christmas and none of him being with the children!" remarked Jennifer.

"It's such a shame there are no photos of Grandfather being Father Christmas," frowned Christopher.

"I'm not sure why. Perhaps he's superstitious about having his photo taken," said Jennifer pensively.

"Is he camera shy? Grandpa makes a perfect Father Christmas," commented Christopher.

"He's magic! He's got the right personality," exclaimed Jennifer.

"Did you suspect that Federick was Father Christmas? When you were younger?"

"I think so. He's an awfully kind man. A good man. Always merry!" answered Jennifer.

"It's getting late. I had better check on James," said Christopher impatiently.

Jennifer was overjoyed at her cousin intending to stay the night. (James had been invited to spend the night. It was due to a previous invitation arrangement by James' mother.)

Christopher and Jennifer got up. They both went upstairs. They both entered a bedroom. They both caught James playing with a train set. James stayed up and gained enjoyment playing with it.

"Get to bed. It's past your bedtime," demanded Jennifer.

"Can you read me a story? Please. Uncle said he would. He promised me," grumbled James.

"I'll read to you," assured Jennifer.

Jennifer tucked James into bed. James was cosy and snug in bed.

Christopher stood watching Jennifer as she sat on the bed. She told her cousin a bedtime story. At once the little boy's face lit up. He became excited listening to a fairy tale. Of course, James would have been much happier had Grandfather or Uncle told him one of their stories. In preference.

Due to tiredness, Christopher had lost interest. He left Jennifer alone with James again.

Christopher went back downstairs and out into the large garden. There he found lying on the garden table several children's drawings and paintings. They had dried up in the heat.

Christopher looked at them. He rather liked them. Did he dislike any? He was impressed with their ability to draw and paint. A few of their drawings showed whimsical images, imagery of Father Christmas. One of the pretty delightful paintings had drops of water on the paper. One of the little girl's tears had trickled down on it.

Christopher was concerned about Grandfather. Now he was in a happy and jolly mood.

That Friday night, Christopher stayed in. He retired much later than his usual bedtime.

***

A few days later, Grandfather passed away in his sleep.

Everybody had expected their beloved grandfather to die. Grandfather had been unwell for a long time. It was only a matter of time before Grandfather died!

Their families, relations, relatives and friends deeply mourned for Federick Crummings.

The funeral service was held at the crematorium. Then afterwards everybody attended a banquet in the church hall.

At the Staples' home, Christopher sat on an upholstered armchair while Jennifer slumped on a settee, resting on the embroidered cushions.

Christopher got up and moved towards the dining table. He held the handle of a teapot. He poured tea into the teacups. Christopher handed Jennifer a teacup and a saucer.

Christopher thought of the magic teapot which was reminiscent of a story Grandfather once told him. It was taken from a collection of Grandfather's favourite stories. (This book of short stories was unpublished.)

"I love Grandfather. I miss him so much," murmured Jennifer.

"I miss him too."

"I have so many memories and recollections of Grandfather," said Jennifer wistfully.

"Grandfather loved children. He did make sad children feel happy. He always favoured the neglected and deprived children. He did make certain their Christmas was a really happy one!" recollected Christopher.

"He would give out gifts. All the children loved and adored Father Christmas," remembered Jennifer.

"They would come especially to see Santa Claus."

Suddenly the doorbell rang.

Christopher got up and answered the front door. He greeted Mary and James. Mary dropped off her son and left to go to work.

James wanted to play. He was in a playful mood.

Christopher led James to his sister who kissed the little boy and made such a fuss. Jennifer was deeply attached and fond of James.

"Who's a big boy! Haven't you grown?" remarked Jennifer.

"Can I go to the park? Mommie takes me to the park," whined James.

Jennifer patted James on his head.

"Not now. Later."

"Can you read me a story? Mommie always does."

Christopher looked at James' dark eyes. He thought of Grandfather. He was obliged to fulfil his promise as well as obligation.

"I shall read to you."

James sat still with his hands clasped. James paid attention as Christopher read out aloud. James cheered up while listening to Christopher telling a story. Christopher's voice and persona were reminiscent of Grandfather's storytelling. It may have been almost a miracle!

The sunrays shone. The sun beat down and penetrated the windows. Sweltering from the heat. This house sun-drenched inside.

Later in the afternoon, Mary returned to pick up her son and drive him home.

***

The following afternoon, Christopher waited for his sister outside the school gates. It was a few minutes past 3.30 p.m.

The crowds and crowds of schoolchildren streamed out of the gates. All the pupils dispersed while heading in different directions. The pupils wore a beautiful school uniform. It was a delightful stunning sight. All the throng, all the crowds and crowds of schoolchildren leaving school while going home.

Sitting in his car, Christopher waited impatiently outside the school grounds. Within close proximity to the playground in the distance.

Jennifer appeared among a group of schoolgirls. Going to a car parked near the road. Jennifer left her group of schoolmates. Jennifer quickly got in a parked car. From the road there the crowds of schoolchildren and pedestrians walked by.

Christopher drove his sister home to his parents' house a few miles away.

"How has your day been?" asked Christopher.

"It's been a good day," replied Jennifer.

"How have you settled down? Any more bullying?" questioned Christopher.

"No. Thank God! No more pain. No more hurting. No more misery," said Jennifer triumphantly.

"How have things been with you?" asked Christopher.

"All bullies should be suspended or expelled!" said Jennifer bitterly.

"I quite agree. Now is the time."

"This year I have taken lots and lots of notes in my classes. Then it will be revision and finally exams," said Jennifer gruffly.

"Don't do everything all at once. Don't cram. Do break it down into bits," advised Christopher.

A short time later, Christopher and Jennifer arrived at their house. They both got out of the car, then both went indoors. It was cooler in the shade.

Arriving at the house, Mary came to pick up her son in the afternoon after work. In the meantime, their playful nieces played together out in the garden. With joy, James ran as soon as he saw Christopher and Jennifer in the garden.

James ran to them. Christopher and Jennifer stooped down to embrace James. They both greeted and welcomed James. They both adored the little boy. James's angelic face lit up with joy.

"Can you read me a story? Read me one, oh go on, please!" implored James.

Christopher and Jennifer grumbled about tiredness. How they both felt tired and unenthusiastic about reading. Jennifer has a passion for reading.

"I can't read. I am tired. I've had a hard day. All I want to do is sleep right now," mumbled Jennifer.

"Not just now. I've been at work," moaned Christopher.

The Shadow of the Daughter's Ring

Their father came home. He came out into the garden. He had finished work early today.

"Dad, can you read to James?" asked Jennifer.

"Oh! Yes! Alright then!" replied Father.

Christopher became irritable. They all went back indoors. They sat down together in the lounge. Christopher sat opposite his father and nephew. Christopher became irritated at his father reading out a story. At first, he listened half-heartedly to the story, then eventually began to enjoy listening to his father telling his nephew a story. The story itself enthralled and inspired him.

James enjoyed listening to a fable. He was engrossed in concentrating on the fable. Christopher got up and went into another room. There he enjoyed his privacy in a quiet room. Christopher dozed off while resting on the armchair alone in the living room.

He woke up when he had been disturbed by the sound of a door slamming.

Jennifer entered in the living room. She recuperated after taking a nap for an hour.

Christopher thought of his sister being thoughtless and inconsiderate at times. He disapproved of her selfishness and thoughtlessness. His sister had a lack of consideration for others. Jennifer hated pupils, especially bullies at school! She still bore grudges.

"Can you be quiet?" snapped Christopher.

"I am sorry," apologised Sister.

"Now, there are two envelopes on the mantelpiece. Can you please get them?"

"Here they are," smiled Jennifer.

"One for you. One for me. Mom looked after them."

Simultaneously, they tore open their envelopes. They both read their invitation cards.

"An invitation to a fancy ball," proclaimed Jennifer.

Christopher was rather enthusiastic about it. The prospect of the Masquerade enchanting and amusing. An exciting spectacle!

"It should be good. It should be fun, darling," grinned Christopher.

"What am I going to wear? What should I dress up as?" said Jennifer unsurely.

Christopher looked forward to the fancy dress. The enchantment of the Masquerade greatly excited him. Christopher was amused. He burst out laughing. An amusement!

"You have got plenty of time to think about it. You'll go as my great-grandmother, and I'll go as Father Christmas!" laughed Christopher.

"I like it. That's a good suggestion. It really is. I can pretend to be someone else. In my dreams, I'll be an ancestor," smiled Jennifer.

Afterwards, brother and sister had supper together, then they went upstairs where they both went to bed.

***

On Saturday afternoon, Christopher spent time out in the garden. He put his camera down on the garden table. He sat down while waiting for Jennifer. He soon got tired of waiting for Jennifer. He felt tired. Christopher spent today dozing. Only waking up when Jennifer disturbed him while he was fast asleep.

Christopher got up. He felt irritable and moody.

"Here I am. Now, how do I look?" asked Jennifer.

Christopher took joy at seeing Jennifer dressed up.

"You look beautiful!" Christopher exclaimed joyously.

Jennifer had applied make-up to accentuate her features. She used her perfume sparingly. The fragrance had a unique exquisiteness. She wore a white gown and diamond earrings and necklace and gold bracelets. Jennifer had done her hair. Her hairstyle in a great, beautiful chignon.

"Do I look like an aristocrat?"

The way Jennifer was dressed up for the fancy dress was in anticipated preparation for the Masquerade. She was dressed up like a beauty queen at a pageant. That remained her second choice. It was intentional. She had a motivational incentive to dress up again in fancy dress.

"Jennifer, you truly look like a lady," remarked Christopher.

Jennifer was obsessed at looking like Anastasia! Their great-grandmother. Her striking resemblance photogenic.

The neighbours looked out of the window. Watching the beauty queen parading. The neighbours looking at the masquerader were gravely concerned about the strange teenager. Jennifer was inclined to have behavioural problems as well as being a temperamental teenager!

Christopher took many photographs of his nonchalant and ostentatious sister posing. She struck an attitude. Her attitude was graceful and elegant.

***

Christopher and Jennifer arrived at the stately home. Christopher parked in the driveway, which was full of parked cars.

They got out of the car. They joined the other guests who were masked. All unrecognisable in the pitch-dark night.

Christopher was disguised as Father Christmas, while Jennifer masqueraded as an aristocrat!

They entered through the main entrance, then followed the masqueraders into the ballroom which quickly became crowded.

In the background, an Elizabethan-dressed orchestra played. The orchestra assembled on stage.

Christopher noticed everybody looking at his masked sister. He watched his extroverted and nonchalant sister unmask herself, revealing her identity for the very first time tonight. Now she appeared to be no longer an enigma!

The captivated masqueraders revered the unmasked belle!

The masqueraders could have idolised and worshipped her!

They had never seen anything so divine and pious!

The belle an amazing sight!

The masqueraders were agog as the nymph gave unhesitating commands.

Due to feeling tired, Jennifer glowered. She felt unsteady on her feet.

"Get me a chair so I can sit down. It's been a long drive. Too long. Get me and my brother a glass of bubbly."

Two masqueraders obeyed her commands.

The masqueraders came back with glasses of champagne and two dining chairs.

Jennifer and Christopher sat on the chairs. They each took their glass of champagne. They drank a glassful of champagne.

Jennifer enjoyed being pampered. Christopher was rather pleased at being attended to. He and Jennifer had been given priority. Christopher appreciated his privilege even more than Jennifer who was insatiable, ungrateful and unthankful.

Jennifer had delusions of grandeur.

The hosts came up to the invited guests. Christopher and Jennifer introduced themselves despite masquerading in their disguise!

Barbara and her husband, Charles, both welcomed them. It turned out to be a memorable function.

Other members of their families were also amidst the crowds of masqueraders. Christopher did not say much to any of them because of feeling terribly self-conscious and wary that strangers were listening to their conversation while staring at them.

Christopher dreaded being threatened with intimidation and violence. He suffered from paranoia. He feared being attacked and assaulted. The imagery of Father Christmas was provocative, amusing and comical. Did it arouse provocation?

At this present moment Christopher did not have any concerns, fears or worries about his sister. He was assured about her safety.

Christopher preferred having his own privacy. He objected to any intrusion. He tensed up about mingling with large crowds of masqueraders. They both avoided the crowds and crowds everywhere. They both insisted on having their own privacy. They ended up going somewhere else quieter and unfrequented.

"Would you like to come out with me to get some fresh air?" asked Christopher.

"Yeah. I would like to come. Hey! I could do with some peace and quiet."

The masqueraders slipped away and headed down the hall, where they stopped to take a look at the big portraits, landscapes and a seascape on the walls.

Suddenly a group of masqueraders approached their direction. Going forward one of the masqueraders clenched his fist aggressively.

Christopher flinched. He quickly moved away from the masquerader.

Christopher was afraid of being attacked. He walked on ahead. He quickened his pace. Avoiding the masquerader down in the hallway.

Jennifer seemed to be aware of what was happening. Jennifer stayed calm. She looked at them and also those passing by down the hall. The few masqueraders were charmed and captivated by her engaging smile and persona! The masqueraders smiled back at the nymphet while approaching and going past them.

Christopher praised Jennifer for her boldness. He personally thanked her for taking the incentive and protecting him. He was amazed and astounded at her calmness and nonchalance.

Jennifer was unafraid and uninhibited. She made an exhibition of herself!

Christopher tried to open a couple of doors. He found each one locked. They both walked further and further on. There they came across hosts standing beside a doorway.

Barbara and Charles saw them. They acknowledged them both. The friendly hosts' greeting welcomed them in.

Jennifer and Christopher dithered on entering the library.

"Federick loved books. He never stopped reading," grinned Charles.

"He was a bookworm. Reading and storytelling were his passions," replied Christopher.

Christopher and Jennifer followed the hosts around the library. They both stopped when they came to bookshelves near the end of the library. They watched Barbara take a big leather-bound book from the shelves. Barbara gave permission to access the Reference section.

"What's the subject?" asked Jennifer.

"Occult," answered Barbara.

Christopher shuddered. Jennifer was used to this subject. Her friends and peers were witches. Jennifer belonged to a witch's coven (a Magic Circle). Every single member of this witch's coven were all schoolgirls!

Christopher wanted to go home. He was not interested in this subject. He may have been fearful! Regretting his invitation to the fancy dress.

"Do have a look. Take out any book you like," urged Barbara.

At this time, Christopher and Jennifer were both uninterrupted and not interested in taking out a book of their choice. They lost interest while looking for a book from the bookshelves. They pretended to look at the books since they were uninterested and unenthusiastic about choosing one.

From the various bookshelves Christopher took notice of the different categories A-Z. The various sections.

Christopher hesitated at choosing a subject. He ended up choosing a book from Christianity.

He preferably wanted to get a Bible, but it was unavailable. He put the Christian book back in alphabetical order.

Jennifer took a travel book out about Spain. She required information about Valencia, as she had a passion for Spain. She had a fascination for the country. (She was also fascinated with the Canary Islands, Canaries and Ibiza.) She had an obsession for the nightlife there. She was obsessional about dance music – and trance. An obsessive delirious raver!

"The banquet will be held in the dining hall. Do ask if you are unsure, if you don't know where it is," said Barbara politely.

"We'll be there shortly," said Christopher nervously.

Christopher and Jennifer waited until the hosts left the library before they resumed talking again. They tended to whisper in the presence of other masqueraders. They were less tense and nervous of being alone together again. After all, the Staples were librarians by profession! This strange place confused, perplexed and bewildered them.

Jennifer sat down at a table. She rested in the silence. Christopher lost interest in reading a book. Any book of Christianity. Jennifer with keen interest browsed through a travel book.

"Can we go home soon?" said Jennifer anxiously.

Christopher insisted on staying there until the Masquerade finally ended.

"Since we're here, we'll stay till it ends," insisted Christopher.

"Don't wander off! Do stay with me," pleaded Jennifer.

"I won't leave you!" said Christopher assuredly.

Brother and sister had such love for one another. They were quite happy to be just in one another's company.

They both got up from their chairs and walked towards the bookshelves.

Christopher took a travel book from Jennifer. He put it back in the travel section. The shelves there. There were more books on travel than any other subject.

They both left the library and followed the signs which led to the grand dining hall. In there they enjoyed their banquet. In the company of banqueters.

The masqueraders and banqueters adored, idolised and revered Jennifer. They deeply loved her! Treating her like a member of the aristocracy. 'Lady Lovell.'

Christopher and Jennifer left the dining hall. They followed everybody else to the ballroom where the guests were dancing.

Christopher felt amused at the bizarre spectacle of masqueraders dancing. The Masquerade an amusing enchantment. The flamboyant masqueraders dancing. Their colourful costumes and choreography.

Christopher danced with his mask on. He was an unrecognisable masquerader. He was uninhibited in dancing since he was in disguise. (His identity revealed when he unmasked himself.)

Every masquerader wanted to dance with the masked masquerader. The enigmatic nymphet.

Christoper waited for a partner, but no-one wanted to dance with him. He took offence from each person's refusal to dance. He got upset when they refused. He intended to enjoy himself, amuse himself.

Jennifer exchanged partners. She ended up dancing for the rest of the night!

After a few hours, Christopher demanded to depart.

"Come now. Let us leave."

"So soon! Can't we leave later?" objected Jennifer.

Christopher spoilt his sister's enjoyment.

"Let's go out in the garden."

Another masquerader wanted to dance with her. Jennifer refused to dance. Her refusal offended him. The mysterious masquerader got upset. He took umbrage at her refusal.

"Your name? What's your name?" the masquerader repeated.

"I must dash!" said Jennifer haughtily.

Jennifer ignored somebody else making advances. She turned in the direction of her brother. The masquerader danced alone by himself.

"Let's go somewhere else. It's so loud and noisy in here," said Christopher loudly.

Jennifer felt exhausted from dancing. She disappointed many others who waited to dance with her. All the partners she refused to dance with were all unrecognisable masqueraders.

Christopher and Jennifer followed a jester and a minstrel. They recognised them without their disguise. These masqueraders were the same ones who had brought the chairs and drinks for them earlier. They had appreciated their warm welcome and hospitality.

Sidney and Timothy walked quickly ahead. Avoiding everybody else.

Christopher and Jennifer followed them. They quickened their pace to catch them up. They both wanted to speak to them to personally thank them.

They reached the beautiful garden. There were many acres of grounds full of topiary. Everywhere garden lights shone brightly in the pitch-black darkness. A labyrinth could be seen in the distance. The shadowy outline of it they could make out in the distance. It was an enchanting sight.

Christopher and Jennifer were bewitched by the autumn night and enchanted at the Masquerade.

They followed the two masqueraders down to the end of the gardens. They went past masqueraders, partygoers, fancy-dress-goers and lovers holding hands.

At the end of the labyrinth Sidney and Timothy parted company. Sidney walking off in another direction. He mysteriously disappeared out of sight in the darkness.

Christopher and Jennifer stopped walking forwards as soon as they both reached the labyrinth. A mystery enchantment.

They both ventured in together.

"It's late. We can't go in," grumbled Christopher.

"What about Tim? We can't leave without thanking them," protested Jennifer.

"We can't get involved," said Christopher cautiously.

"Will he be alright in there? I'm concerned. Should we go after him?" said Jennifer worried.

Christopher and Jennifer waited at the enchanting labyrinth. They shouted and called out his name. Remaining calm when there was no response. Uncommunicative. Sidney, the silent masquerader.

Minutes later, a figure appeared from out of the shadows. They both reacted with great joy at seeing the masquerader emerge from the labyrinth.

Suddenly the masquerader came towards them. Approaching nearer and nearer.

Christopher and Jennifer embraced Timothy. Jennifer kissed him passionately on his cheek. Appreciating his considerateness!

At midnight, a spell was broken!

Timothy began to love again!

They felt agoraphobic while walking back to the stately home in the distance. At that time everybody else was either waiting to be picked up or leaving to go home.

As they left, Christopher and Jennifer said goodbye to all the emotional guests leaving and departing.

Quickly, they left the entrance. They walked down the driveway to get to their car parked there. They both got in the car.

Christopher drove off. Within moments the car reached the country lanes. The cats-eyes lit up in the pitch-darkness. There they saw police cars on patrol. Patrolling the area. They both took notice of the police patrolling.

Christopher set off. The journey going back home was long.

4
Heart's Desire

Christopher heard Jennifer playing her clarinet. Jennifer was disciplined at her practice. An obsessive disciplinal.

Christopher went back in a study. He idled away some time by looking at a women's glossy magazine. Particularly the women's fashion section.

Christopher desired the voluptuous models wearing dresses and outfits.

Last night Christopher had a nightmare!

Momentarily, Christopher had been distracted. He was preoccupied, looking at the chic models. Then he resumed work. The desk was piled up high with encyclopaedias. He first looked at the Reference book, then at the relevant encyclopaedia, trying to find relevant information about: The Last Supper, Crucifixion, Resurrection, and Ascension.

After Christopher made some notes, he put back a set of encyclopaedias in alphabetical and chronological order on the shelves of the cabinet.

Jennifer distracted her brother's attention. With a sister's love she touched her brother on his shoulder.

"Have you found out anything?" asked Jennifer.

"So far I have found out about the Eucharist," replied Christopher.

"Is that Holy Communion?"

"Yes. It's related to the Last Supper."

"What's so significant about it? Why is it so important?"

"It is a religious ceremony in which you honour and worship Christ. The bread being his body and the wine his blood. The Holy Sacrament."

"That's typically the sort of thing which happens in church usually," said Jennifer matter-of-factly.

Christopher learned about Christianity. Not only just about Catholicism. Additionally, he also read the Bible. He was enlightened from reading the scriptures. He was illuminated as a result of it. He read it due to constant fear which he experienced in his life!

"Once, a priest answered my question. He said to take Holy Communion," added Christopher.

"What on earth for?"

"Against magic," blabbed Christopher.

"All these books. Where do they all come from?" asked Jennifer.

"Some of them personally belonged to our grandfather," replied Christopher.

In the large study, the bookshelves and cabinets were filled with hard-cover books and paperbacks galore.

Michael, his father, kept Grandfather's collection. His books had sentimental value. Federick was a professional librarian by profession.

The study smelled of old books. A distinguished rich leather smell from ancient times.

Going out of the study, Christopher and Jennifer went out into the garden. There they found their father engrossed in doing gardening. They both walked sluggishly to a garden table. Standing still on the paved slab-stone, they both felt dehydrated and thirsty.

Christopher picked up a glass jug of freshly squeezed orange juice. Simultaneously, they both gulped down the fruit juice made from several juicy oranges. They were refreshed from drinking a glassful of fresh orange juice.

"I am sorry. It's not from Valencia," apologised Christopher.

"It tastes so good. Really. Is it from Seville oranges?"

"No. It's not from Florida juice. It's Jaffa," confirmed Christopher.

Suddenly the doorbell chimed.

The Shadow of the Daughter's Ring

Christopher hurried to answer the front door. He was expecting Mary and James to arrive. He greeted and welcomed them both in. Christopher rejoiced at seeing them together. He led Mary and her son out into the garden. He stood and watched fondly as his sister lifted James off his feet and swung him around gracefully, then put him back down gently on his feet. The boy balanced while standing in a balanced position on his feet.

"James. My sweet boy!" exclaimed Jennifer joyously.

"I'll be going now. I'll pick James up tomorrow," smiled Mary.

"Are you going to marry again?" asked Jennifer.

"Good heavens! No! I am divorced!" expostulated Mary.

"Won't you date?"

"James is my responsibility," said Mary proudly.

Christopher led James's mother, Mary, indoors. Then he showed Mary out of the detached house.

Christopher had a deep sympathy for Mary as she was a single parent raising her son, James.

Christopher stood by the doorway. He said goodbye to Mary, then waved goodbye to the parent.

Going outdoors, Christopher stood on a doorstep. He stood and watched Mary get into her car before driving away.

Christopher went back indoors. He closed the front door.

Going to a room, Christopher wanted his privacy. He wanted to be alone. He felt rather tired.

In the living room he sat down on an armchair. After a while he dozed off, only to be woken about an hour later by Jennifer who was reading a story to James.

Christopher was disturbed at hearing his sister's loud voice. He insisted on having silence during his time of relaxation. Christopher left the living room. Leaving Jennifer alone to read to James a story.

Christopher stayed in his bedroom for many hours.

At the stroke of midnight, Christopher was reading his Holy Bible. Suddenly he heard a noise. It sounded like someone fumbling and clattering in the dark.

Christopher was disturbed by the sound of the noise. He got out of bed. He found a torch. He switched on a torch. He quietly went downstairs.

Christopher went out of the patio door. He went out into the garden where he shone a torch into the darkness. A powerful beam shining.

Christopher breathed in the fresh air then walked further and further down into the garden. He wondered if his sister had been sleep-walking? After all, she was such a strange and disturbed teenager!

Going ahead, Christopher saw his sister standing near a tree, smelling a rose. Jennifer was swaying her hips gracefully and dancing barefoot. She appeared to be lost in a reverie. Jennifer wore a gold crucifix and a lacy nightdress. Her very long hair cascaded down to her hips.

In the pitch-dark, Christopher shone a torch at his sister.

Jennifer blinked from the dazzling light reflecting. Jennifer looked beautiful! A voluptuous teenager. His sister. The girl a teenage beauty!

"What on earth are you doing out here at this time of night?" grumbled Christopher.

"I can't sleep. It's a beautiful night. I could dance in the moonlight," sighed Jennifer.

Christopher and Jennifer shivered in the nippy air. Christopher took off his dressing gown and gave it to his sister gentlemanly.

"Now put this on or else you'll catch a chill," said Christopher considerately.

Jennifer put on his dressing gown. Jennifer tied it up tightly around her waist. Her breasts covered up. She did not expose herself any longer.

"I was thinking of Grandfather. I am still in mourning," said Jennifer hoarsely.

"You're still in a state of shock," replied Christopher.

The Shadow of the Daughter's Ring

In the moonlit night, Christopher and Jennifer walked around the garden together. They were bereaved, mournful and melancholic.

Walking around and around the pitch-dark garden, there they could both see their way from the garden lights shining. They both became calmer and peaceful and quieter. Going around and around the garden in circles. They exhilarated from being alone together. They romanticised gazing up at the starry skies. They each had romantic notions of falling in love due to the enchantment of the romantic atmosphere. There, out in the peaceful surroundings, they both were deliriously romantic when they looked up at the starlit skies. In a daydream!

Going back indoors, they both went to bed.

The next day, Christopher got up late. Oversleeping till midday. He got dressed. Wearing casual clothes.

Now Christopher knelt down and prayed. Half-asleep, he tried to concentrate on saying a prayer. He rose to his feet. Then went downstairs into the living room where Jennifer at present lay across comfortably on a comfortable settee. She indulged in a glass of wine. It tasted fruity. Jennifer was tipsy and giddy from drinking a glassful of wine. Christopher refused to drink. He does have abstinence.

Christopher encouraged Jennifer to drink alcohol in moderation. He disapproved of his sister drinking. Their father, Michael, had a drinking problem. He drank excessive amounts of alcohol. He had alcoholic tendencies. Their father was inclined to drink regularly at a pub. When sober, their father was calm and quiet. In a drunken state, he was in hysterics.

Later that afternoon, the parents accompanied their children to Peter's birthday party.

Most of the parents dropped off their son or daughter here. (One of the parent's daughters were identical twins.) They soon departed without any further delay.

Christopher welcomed all the excited, happy children arriving at Peter's birthday party. The children went out into the garden to play.

Meanwhile, Jennifer attended to the little girls. One by one, they each sat down on her lap. Jennifer made fine plaits in every girl's hair. Every girl's hairstyle was beautiful. The elegant girls each had impressive elegance in dress, style, mannerisms and etiquette.

"Let's play hide and seek?" they shouted.

"Yes, let's play."

"No hiding in the house. It's out of bounds," insisted Christopher.

Christopher agreed to play hide and seek. He was the one chosen to count up and look for everybody hiding.

Christopher stood by a tree. He counted loudly while all the boys ran off and quickly hid in hiding places. When he had finished counting, he looked everywhere for them. He soon found those ones hiding behind a garden shed, bushes and shrubbery.

Some of the children soon got tired of playing this game. One of the boys running caught his shirt on a rose bush. The prickly thorns ripping his shirt on a rose bush.

A few of the others came out from hiding. They gave themselves up. The other ones not caught agreed to surrender. Those others did surrender conditionally as a result of them being caught hiding by Christopher.

Sometime later, everybody went indoors to the dining room, where they all sat down at the table.

Peter's mother came in and brought in a birthday cake lit with candles.

Peter seated at the table blew out all the lit candles in three or four deep breaths. He made a wish!

Everybody applauded and cheered.

Peter spoke. "Thank you for all your presents. I would like to remember Mr Staples. I miss him. We all miss him dearly. I remember the Christmas when he was Father Christmas. He gave us lots of gifts," stuttered Peter.

Everybody was mournful, pensive and wistful and speechless at remembering Mr Staples. They all had wonderful memories of

The Shadow of the Daughter's Ring

Father Christmas! Attending to the children. Santa Claus gave out gifts!

Christopher patted Peter on his head. He gave his condolences. Jennifer also consoled Peter and the other children eating. She was rather endearing speaking to them. Her sentiments deeply moving.

About three quarters of an hour later, Christopher and Jennifer went into the spacious living room. The whole room was empty. All the furniture removed for the party.

Christopher and Jennifer joined the energetic and excited children. They danced to the music being played by a DJ. It blared out of the speakers. Disturbing the neighbours.

Christopher wearied from dancing. He was deafened by the blaring music. As soon as Christopher got tired of dancing, he left the hyperactive children. He went outdoors. He needed to be alone for a short time at this present time. Therefore, to keep away from those individuals who intended to intrude on his privacy. With calculated intent.

Due to being paranoid again, he avoided everyone who imposed on and obtruded on him.

He walked alone to the end of the garden. Passing along the way many guests, mainly groups of children walking by.

There he looked at the bloomed and blossomed roses. The sight of the wet budding rosebuds sparkling in the sunlight.

He sniffed at the rose-scented air. The fresh gloriousness of the natural scent of all the roses which emanated out naturally.

Going on ahead, Christopher stopped walking when he reached a tree down the garden. He lay down on the wet grass. His costume became damp and got covered in mud and grass stains.

Christopher cooled down from the blown gust of wind. He stirred as he heard someone tread on a broken twig which snapped from the weight of a foot treading on it.

Approaching towards him, in his direction, he saw Peter and Sean going towards him. Walking ahead from the others who lagged behind.

Christopher got up on his feet. He straightened up as they both approached him.

"There won't be any presents this Christmas. Will there ever be another Father Christmas like Mr Staples?" asked Peter wistfully.

"I do hope so. Isn't Father Christmas magical!" replied Christopher.

"On Christmas Eve, I shall wait for Father Christmas. Hopefully he will put presents in my stocking," said Peter.

Christopher thought of it as wishful thinking. He had memories of his childhood at Christmastime. A Christmas reminiscence.

As the group of children joined up with the others, Christopher became quiet. He had nothing else to say.

Minutes later he rose from the ground and followed some boys going back to the house.

More and more parents soon arrived to pick up their sons. Their arrival was expected.

Christopher neglected James. Grandfather's Godson!

Going instead upstairs to his bedroom as he was still disturbed by hearing the loud music blaring out of the vibrating speakers.

Christopher lay down on his bed and rested in the dark. Christopher was half-awake as he imagined the reflections to be a Guardian Angel! The reflections in the shadows…

***

The following afternoon, Christopher spent time in a study as he browsed through a girlie magazine.

Christopher looked at the centrefold with such interest. Desiring the gorgeous brunette posing in the nude. He envied the young model's beauty. He seemed quite obsessed about her. He admired her beautiful figure and was aroused by her voluptuousness.

As he looked at another model, he had an obsessive desire for the voluptuous model's blondness! Her beauty as well as the fair model's figure!

Last night he had a dream! A vision that he should stay single under the circumstances. If he got married, he would probably end up being unhappily married or divorced! A divorcee?

Christopher soon became tired of his male fantasies. He got pretty fed up with looking at the pictures in the glossy magazine. He threw the magazine in the bin.

Christopher remembered the Masquerade fondly and with some regret. He remembered how no one had danced with him. He felt that the opposite sex had spurned him. All the females had refused to dance with him. They had detested him. They spurned him for dressing up as Father Christmas!

Christopher drowned his sorrows. He drank a can of lager.

Christopher got depressed. He drank another can of lager. He mourned for Grandfather.

He felt unloved and unwanted at the Masquerade. He pondered on the fancy dress. He had an amusing time. Dressing up for the fancy dress was an embarrassing situation!

Suddenly Christopher heard footsteps. He heard persons coming. At once, he hid the rest of the cans of lager out of sight.

Jennifer and James entered the study.

"Will you be kind and read James a story?" asked Jennifer.

Christopher lost concentration on reading a book.

"I can't read. I can't stay awake!" moaned Christopher.

"Have you been drinking? I can smell your breath. Where is your self-control?" tutted Jennifer.

Christopher did admit to drinking. He was aware of his hypocrisy. He got embarrassed at being exposed by his unprovocative sister.

"I have been drinking. Really, I ought to be setting an example. I am ashamed of myself," said Christopher ashamedly.

Jennifer sympathised with the hypocrite.

"You must stop drinking. You'll be an alcoholic. Jesus forgives sinners!" said Jennifer sanctimoniously.

Christopher tolerated her sarcasm.

Jennifer retaliated.

"You certainly know about the truth. But do you actually obey it? For instance, the Ten Commandments!"

Christopher objected to being scolded by his sister.

"Don't lecture me. Not in front of James, please."

Again. I am reminding you. You must learn from your faults."

"Will you stay? Or will you go?" gasped Christopher.

"I will read to James," smiled Jennifer.

"Why don't you read here? There's nowhere else to go. Besides it's quieter," suggested Christopher.

Christopher got up from a swivel chair to allow Jennifer to sit down. Her legs exposed from the slits of her skirt. James sat on an easy chair next to Jennifer.

Christopher became claustrophobic seated from a lack of space as they were crammed in together. Christopher got up. He moved towards the bookshelves. Christopher took a children's book down off the bookshelves. He opened it, then gave it to Jennifer. She read out loud. Her voice reverberating in the study.

Christopher concentrated on listening to Jennifer reading out loud.

At this time James had forgotten about his father. James was engrossed in listening to Jennifer reading a fairy tale. It was one of his personal favourites.

Afterwards, Christopher, Jennifer and James went out of the study. They all went into the garden. They walked slowly to the garden table positioned in the middle of the lawn.

On top of the garden table there was a drawing of Father Christmas. It was reminiscent of Grandfather masquerading as Father Christmas. It fully captured the essence of a seasonal Merry Christmas!

**

On Sunday morning, Christopher parked his car in a multi-storey car park, then took a lift down. He made his way out of the shopping centre. He walked down the crowded high street. He crossed over the busy road, then turned right to go down to the

The Shadow of the Daughter's Ring

Pentecostal church where he waited outside near the entrance for Mary and James. Waiting outside the church, he watched the car park fill up. He remembered in his childhood he never attended Sunday School. He never had the opportunity to attend Sunday School. At that time there were only limited places available and also a crèche was provided.

Christopher may have been discriminated against. He was a discriminated and disadvantaged infant!

Mary accompanied her son James outdoors. All the parents who came out of church were unaccompanied and unattended by their sons and daughters. The other parents talked among themselves.

Christopher was happy at seeing them both together. He greeted them both with joy.

"Good afternoon!" exclaimed Christopher.

"I am worn out," yawned Mary.

Christopher stooped down and hugged James.

"How are you? What did you do today?"

"I learned about Nebuchadnezzar," stammered James.

"You're learning new things about the scriptures."

"He's a good boy. He's my baby. My love. My sweet boy!" exclaimed Mary proudly.

Christopher respected James's mother's endearing sentiment. He looked at the other children who came out of the building to rejoin their parents. All the children rejoiced in the Lord!

Their spiritual parents took their son or daughter home.

Christopher, Mary and James left the church car park. They walked up to the high street and headed back to the multi-storey car park. From there Christopher drove to Mary's bungalow, Rosewood, where they arrived a short time later.

Reaching the bungalow, they got out of the car and went inside. In there they hung up their coats and jackets on a rack. Then went into the cosy lounge.

"Take a look at the photos. I will make some tea," grinned Mary.

With interest, Christopher looked at a photo album. He saw photographs of Mary's husband. Christopher respected Frank.

Despite their unhappy marriage ending in a divorce, he still regarded Frank as a family friend.

Mary held a tray when coming back into the lounge. She put it down on a smoky table.

James took a small carton of blackcurrant juice. He sipped out of a long straw.

Christopher sipped his hot tea. He nibbled at a biscuit.

"Will you settle down and marry again?" asked Christopher.

Mary predicted her future.

"Oh! No. I won't marry. I'll stay single. I'll have friends. I won't fall in love again."

"How do you feel about your ex?" asked Christopher.

"A good question. I am glad I am divorced. It was becoming a marriage of convenience," said Mary emphatically.

"Are you positive you won't wed again?"

"It's unlikely," replied Mary.

"Is Frank happy since he's married again?"

"You should ask Frank that. His wife is expecting a baby."

Christopher stood and looked out of a picture window. From there he saw a large garden. He admired the view of a pond and a fountain, from which a fountain gave out jets of water. He thrilled, listening to the sound of the water running. The crystal water sparkling.

Christopher and Mary were irritated by James as he began to read out loud. He tried to attract attention. Mary got annoyed at her son. The parent pulled a book out of her son's hand.

"You're obsessed. Can't you do something else?" snapped Mother.

Christopher rose. He smartened himself up.

"I'd better get back."

"Won't you stay for dinner?" asked Mary.

Christopher declined the offer of an invitation.

"Thanks – but no. My aunt is cooking me a roast."

Christopher embraced Mary and James. His goodbye was emotional! Then he left the bungalow and drove home.

Reaching home, Christopher went straight to bed. He rested for most of the afternoon. He got up then got dressed. He went downstairs into the living room where he sat down on an armchair. He relaxed comfortably in comfort for a short time.

Suddenly Christopher became startled as his father burst into the room.

"Can you go and pick up Jennifer now and take her home? She's at Annie's house."

Christopher glanced at his wristwatch. It was 10.30 p.m. It was late at night.

Christopher agreed to pick up his sister. He had a moral obligation to do so. He got up and left his house. He got in his car. He drove to Annie's home.

Sometime later, Christopher arrived at the semi-detached house. He parked his car outside the semi-detached house.

Out near the kerb, Christopher got out of the parked car. He opened a wrought iron gate. He walked on a path. Going towards Annie's house. He rang the doorbell. He stood by the front door. He waited for his sister.

By the doorway Jennifer kissed Annie then came out of the house wearing her stilettos. Jennifer's footsteps echoed on the path.

"Thanks for coming. I truly appreciate it. I can't go home on my own. I've got my stilettos on," said Jennifer uneasily.

"Now that I am here, there's no need to worry," reassured Christopher.

Jennifer shook her hair. Her beautiful hair had been done in the same hairstyle as Anastasia's. Standing out gracefully by the pavement and by a kerb, Jennifer looked so beautiful with the streetlamps shining in the night reflecting on her hair. The lamp lights shone.

"Tonight, I am Anastasia!" said Jennifer jubilantly.

Both sister and brother looked at each other with a smirk. Jennifer's mischievousness like a child's! A mischief of a little girl who misbehaved!

Christopher and Jennifer got in a parked car along the kerb. Christopher drove off taking his sister back home.

Jennifer's tension eased. She relaxed. Appreciating how her brother cared for her by taking the trouble to give her a lift home.

5

The Dedication

On Saturday at noon, Christopher remained all alone at home. He liked being alone. He did enjoy his privacy. He relaxed without the burden of anyone bothering or disturbing him.

Christopher put a CD in the CD player. He pressed play. He listened to the trance music playing. This complementation.

Using a remote control, he turned the volume up high. The music blared out of the speakers. It reverberated in the spacious lounge. Around the high-ceiling, wooden beams and décor.

Christopher sat down on an armchair and rested for hours. He meditated in the silence.

Afterwards, he rose to his feet. He straightened up and smartened himself up.

Christopher stayed in today. Resting and relaxing at the weekend. It had been his sister's birthday yesterday. This evening her family intended to celebrate Jennifer's birthday! Her mother had made preparatory arrangements for this birthday party weeks in advance.

Later in the evening, Jennifer's friends arrived at the detached house. At present the driveway was full of cars parked there.

Christopher looked out of a bedroom window. He caught sight of Jennifer's friends. Anne, Cathy and Julie spotted Christopher standing while looking out of a window.

They acknowledged Christopher with a broad smile and graceful gestures. Christopher was overwhelmed by the friendly girls' attention.

Christopher came downstairs.

Quickly he answered the front door. He greeted all of them, including Sophie, another friend of Jennifer's. They all greeted Christopher. On arrival, Christopher welcomed them in.

Christopher had completely forgotten a few of their names. He remembered Jennifer's best friends. He had forgotten their names.

Going downstairs Jennifer hurried to greet and welcome all her friends arriving. Jennifer joined her friends.

Christopher embraced his beloved sister and kissed her with deep affection.

"Happy birthday!" brother exclaimed happily.

"Come and take a look at my presents," smiled sister.

Christopher looked at all the unwrapped birthday presents piled up on top of the table.

"Did Father Christmas give you these presents?" said Christopher sarcastically.

"I wish he had. When I was a child, I sat on Father Christmas, alias Grandfather's, lap. He would cuddle me and give me lovely gifts," recalled Jennifer pensively.

"I gave Jennifer make-up," pointed out Anne.

"I ended up buying her toiletries," smiled Julie.

"I got her jewellery," grinned Catherine.

Jennifer kissed her brother. Her brother favoured her, especially the way his sister had showed her appreciation.

"I do hope you liked it," said brother.

Jennifer thanked her brother with kindness, touching his hand. Then sprayed perfume sparingly onto her wrist. She sniffed at the scent.

"Thank you for the expensive perfume. Chanel is my favourite."

Christopher smelled the scent of her perfume. The fragrance irresistibly ravishing indeed.

They all left Jennifer's bedroom and went back downstairs to join everybody else out in the garden. There everybody gathered around. They decided to play a game.

"Let's play Blind Man's Bluff," they decided.

Christopher was chosen to be 'it'.

Jennifer, his sister, the birthday girl, tied a scarf around his eyes. With his eyes covered up, he was entirely in darkness.

The Shadow of the Daughter's Ring

Christopher got dizzy from his sister spinning him around and around. He heard the girls' giggles and screams. He felt dizzy. He kept his balance.

Moving around the garden, he struggled to catch anybody. They were far too cunning and agile while moving and moving around him. Moving forward with his arms outstretched. All the girls surrounded him. Surrounding Christopher in circles. Christopher got quite confused at hearing the sound of their voices speaking out all at once. Calling out his name in spite. Moving around the garden.

Christopher felt agoraphobic. Again and again, Christopher became frustrated at not catching anyone. He reached out and tried to catch someone but missed by a few inches! He lost his balance and stumbled.

Christopher heard the girls' hysterical laughter. Christopher got embarrassed from his tumble. He struggled to get back up on his feet. With his arms outstretched, he moved and moved around while he reached out to get someone. He made another attempt to catch somebody. Moving about with both his arms outstretched, he tried to catch the nearest person but failed yet again. They kept a few yards away from him.

All the girls ran around him in circles, graceful in movement. They each escaped his grasp every time. They frustrated him with their quick pace. There was no way he could catch any of them. He knew that most of them participated in gymnastics, ballet and music classes at school.

All the girls enjoyed themselves by having fun. The girls gained pleasure from humiliating a grown-up. A few girls did sympathise with Christopher.

Christopher was wary of the others who would misbehave and be spiteful brats.

He tried to chase to catch a person running around. He soon wearied from running aimlessly around the garden with his arms outstretched.

Christopher became frustrated. He stopped and stood still. He gave up.

All the girls running around and surrounding him, called out his name in a spiteful way.

Finally, Christopher decided to use his intellect. He changed his tactics. He stood still and conserved his energy. He waited for the right moment to reach out and grab someone close by.

Fortunately, he caught a girl who formed a circle. Christopher squeezed the girl tight and heard her scream. Christopher took off the blindfold and appeared triumphant and surprised at who he had caught. He smiled with joy and relief, taking pride at the girl's innocence and striking prettiness. Julie a skinny redhead with a flushed face. Then Julie bent down and took off her shoe. Julie emptied out the tiny bits of gravel from her shoe. Julie put her shoe back on her foot.

Everybody stopped playing Blind Man's Bluff. As soon as a person got caught, the game stopped momentarily.

They clapped their hands and gathered around.

"It's my turn now," insisted Julie impatiently.

In exhaustion, Christopher lay down on the moist grass. He gasped for breath. He declined to play the game anymore. He rested on the lawn lazily. Recovering from exhaustion.

Christopher watched his sister tie a blindfold around Julie's head. Jennifer vigorously spun Julie around and around. The game continued. All those playing Blind Man's Bluff ran off, with Julie going in pursuit of them. The girls' screams and shouts reverberated in the wind.

Lying on the lawn, Christopher paid attention for a little while, to Blind Man's Bluff.

Christopher soon became uninterested in the game. As soon as Julie caught someone else, the game had stopped now once more. This game had finally ended.

It seemed that everybody had had enough of playing Blind Man's Bluff.

Christopher's mother came out into the garden holding a tray.

Everybody standing took a glass of orange juice. They quenched their thirst by gulping it down. They were refreshed from drinking a chilled drink or appetiser.

"Can I have your attention, please?" said Sally loudly.

Everybody stopped talking at once.

They gave Jennifer's mother their undivided attention. Sally resumed speaking.

"Can everybody go in now, please. It's time to eat. It's time for my daughter to celebrate."

Everybody walked back indoors.

After warming up from the central heating, they all went into the dining room which was full of birthday decorations and balloons galore.

Everybody sat down at the dining table which was laden with party food. They wore paper hats and tucked napkins around their necklines.

Meanwhile, Christopher stayed in the kitchen for a short time. He sweated in the hot kitchen. He cooled down with an extractor fan on full power.

Mrs Staples lit all the candles on the birthday cake. Mrs Staples picked it up and carried it to the dining table, with Christopher and members of his family following.

The revellers sang 'Happy Birthday!'

Already sitting down at the dining table, Jennifer positioned herself gracefully. She leaned forward and blew out all the lit candles after doing a few breaths. Jennifer made a wish!

Her friends cheered and applauded. They remained seated while insisting Jennifer made a speech.

Her brother reached out and patted his sister gently on her back, encouraging his sister to speak.

Making a gesture, Jennifer rose and spoke out eloquently.

"I would like to thank you all for coming and for your lovely presents. I wasn't going to have a party this year. Last year was a very difficult time for me. My mum and my friends suggested that I should celebrate my birthday by having a party. I am awfully glad you are all here. So far it has been a memorable and enjoyable birthday. My one regret is that my grandfather is not here with us. He will be sadly missed!" said Jennifer mournfully.

Everybody respected Jennifer and approved of her short speech. They all knew her grief affected her deeply. Christopher was especially sympathetic to Jennifer's suffering! Her sorrow in particular. Jennifer still mourned for her late grandfather!

Jennifer's mother sliced the birthday cake and served every person piece of birthday cake each. Everyone like the rich, sweet birthday cake.

Christopher responding to their requests served them with another slice of birthday cake. All the children and teenagers tucked into the food. They all had an appetite. Most of the sandwiches and other delicacies were gobbled up.

Christopher poured out drinks for the children. These ones were once pampered by Father Christmas when they were youngsters! Now they appreciated the hospitality. Some of the others took it for granted. Unfortunately, two of the girls were deprived, neglected or abandoned. These ones did enjoy every minute of it. It was a delightful treat which of course satisfied both of them.

A short time later, Christopher joined everyone else in the living room. A professional DJ had finished setting up the sophisticated equipment and accessories, testing out the sound. Sometimes the DJ spoke or remained quiet while playing selected music of his choice.

Christopher joined in and danced with his sister while amongst her friends. Those dancing had been impassioned at listening to the music blaring out. The sound of the room reverberating.

They danced while looking at each other with such emotional love. Laura danced well. A fine versatile dancer. All those dancing were certainly impressed by Laura's dance routine and choreography. Laura was leggy and tall. Laura attended her ballet lessons regularly. She was one of the best dancers in her class, so was unsurprising. Laura was the centre of attraction with her dancing.

The Shadow of the Daughter's Ring

At present, Christopher had enough of dancing. He came out of the living room. He felt deafened from the blaring music. He followed his sister and Katherine, Anne and Julie into the sitting room.

These few girls wanted to be alone with Jennifer. They disapproved of his presence. He was intruding on their privacy.

Christopher was displeased at being ignored again. Resenting a few of them. He just stood still on the other side of the room.

"It's quiet in here. I can now relax in peace," said Jennifer hoarsely.

"You've had a good time. You've also had a wonderful birthday," commented Anne.

"It's been a birthday to remember. So much love!" smiled Katherine.

Christopher moved around the room. In a sideboard and cabinets, he looked close up at various objects. The fragile ornaments, antiques, sculptures and statuettes. Christopher left untouched anything fragile. He was cautious of his mother's bad temper, how his mother reprimanded her son for breaking anything fragile.

Christopher looked at the wall opposite. He stood still and looked at himself in a mirror. Stepping back and standing away from the mirror, he took another look at the mirror. He caught sight of the reflection of Jennifer's statuesque-ness. She was standing behind her brother. Facing directly the mirror ahead of her.

Suddenly their mother came into the sitting room holding a tray. Sally put it on a table.

Christopher then walked out of the sitting room, stopping as Jennifer obstructed him deliberately. She grabbed hold of his arm. Jennifer firmly squeezing his arm passionately.

"Don't go! Come back. Join us in a toast," urged sister.

Christopher smiled joyously at his sister's change of heart!

He walked back to the crowded sitting room where everyone in there picked up a glass of champagne. All together they made a toast!

"To Jennifer. Happy birthday! Sweet sixteen!" they said merrily.

Jennifer acknowledged all the revellers with a charming smile.

Christopher had never ever seen his sister as happy as this before. Christopher cherished the moment of his sister's bliss!

Jennifer was beatific and overjoyed. Jennifer was overwhelmed with bliss at being all together with all her friends. Hearing the music playing and being with her close friend Anne made Jennifer elated.

Anne's father was a distributor for a major record company.

Christopher gathered up the glasses. He put them on a tray.

"Will you play something for us? You said you would. Go on! Why don't you play us something," prompted Geraldine.

Jennifer, Stella, Anne and Gabrielle agreed to play a piece.

"We'll keep our word. Give us five minutes," assured Jennifer.

Everybody went into the living room. They stood and gathered together, watching with excitement as the girls played their instruments. They performed well. Anne and Gabrielle currently played for the school orchestra and Jennifer attended her music lessons.

Christopher recognised the tune being played. Remembering his sister practising it at home. Everybody applauded the girls' performance.

Jennifer, the birthday girl, gained adoration and constant attention from everybody. They all loved her!

Christopher slinked out of the sitting room. He headed down the corridor, stopping along the way to look at a few paintings. The few oil paintings and also watercolours had quality. There was an appealing strikingness in almost every painting.

Christopher was a dilettante. He had an interested passion in aestheticism. The librarian accustomed to public exhibitions in libraries. His late grandfather was a connoisseur and aesthete.

Christopher went into the glass-paned conservatory. He was surprised to find no one else already in there. He sat down on a wicker chair. He relaxed in the silence. The luxurious surroundings were so much quieter and shadier than anywhere else.

There were many plants everywhere in the conservatory.

After a while, Christopher got up from the wicker chair. He walked to the windows. He stood by exotic plants. Admiring the lovely plants, soon realising he had forgotten the Latin names of the plants. He stood by the glass windows while enjoying the view.

He did try to fathom the mystery of the Creator, God's creation!

He still seemed perplexed at the purpose and meaning of life!

Christopher came out of the conservatory. Cooling down from the draught from an open window and a door ajar.

He went out of a side door, then made his way into the garden. He walked past a group of girls who smirked and sniggered at him. The girls were pretentious and disrespectful.

Going further and further down along the garden, he passed by another two girls. Both girls smiled at him. One girl was plump and the other one lanky. Both of them deeply respected Christopher.

Christopher remembered both of their names. Shirlie and Kelly. From his memories. He also remembered when Father Christmas had pampered them both on two occasions at Christmastime.

Christopher kept walking through the garden. It had lovely lawns, flowerbeds and big trees.

In his direction Christopher approached Jennifer and another group of her friends who were standing beneath a tree down at the bottom of the garden. In the glowing pitch-darkness.

"Meet me back at the house," ordered Jennifer.

Some of Jennifer's friends willingly obeyed her. Her group of friends left and made their way back to the house.

The others stayed longer in the big garden. In the glowing moonlight. In the shadowy reflection a group of teenagers stopped by a big tree. Those teenagers ignored Christopher when going back. Christopher appeared to be deeply unhappy, unloved and lonely. In the dark, Christopher trailed behind the group of girls going back to the detached house in the distance.

Going towards the house, Christopher reached a back door. He found his sister waiting for him out by a doorstep. Jennifer proudly showed off her birthday present. A platinum sapphire ring set with a cluster of diamonds. In the shining light Jennifer's diamond ring sparkled.

Christopher embraced his sister. He kissed his sister on her cheek affectionately.

Christopher stepped over his sister, gracefully sitting down on a doorstep with her hands near a doormat. He then left without intending to say goodbye. He came in the house. He ignored everybody else. He was unsociable. Avoiding the guests. All of Jennifer's invited friends at the birthday party.

Christopher stormed out of the house. Quickly, Christopher got in his car and drove off.

Earlier in the night, Christopher had consumed alcohol. As he drove off, he was wary of a police patrol car accelerating past at a very high speed. He sighed in relief when the patrol car speeding past had gone.

Christopher calmed down and relaxed when reaching his aunt's house. He was relieved to get there.

6

A Christmas Consolation

On Christmas Eve, Christopher stayed at home while his family went Christmas shopping. This was the very first Christmas without Grandfather!

Christopher deeply mourned his grandfather, especially at Christmastime. He deeply loved his grandfather.

Christopher wrapped up a Christmas present. It displeased him immensely as it was not beautifully wrapped up compared to the other Christmas presents. Christopher wrote on a little card which was tied around with a red string: *To Father Christmas who has gone forever.*

Christopher put the Christmas present down with all the other gifts which were stacked up beneath a Christmas tree. The Christmas tree lights switched on. Flashing on and off.

Christopher got up from his knees. He walked towards the window. He stood and looked out of the window. He was far too disappointed at the bad weather. It never ever snowed at Christmas. This murky and rainy day certainly did not capture either the spirit or atmosphere of Christmas!

Christopher fantasised about Christmas this year. He dreamt of a snowy Christmas. A typical white Christmas.

Christopher had Christmas fantasies. His expectations of a wonderful Christmas unfulfilled.

Christopher sat down on a chair. He looked at photographs of a Christmas holiday in Lapland with the entire family. It showed poses with a merry Father Christmas. This particular photograph showed when he had been showered with gifts. He looked at those photographs of a snowy forest of enchanting beauty. He also looked at the other ones. The photographs of his families huddled up in a luxury log cabin. These may have been memorable days at Christmas. A festive, quiet and peaceful Christmas holiday.

Christopher did not participate in many leisure activities. During that time, he spent most of his time with his beloved grandfather. He enjoyed being alone with his grandfather.

The living room was adorned with Christmas decorations. All the Christmas cards were hung up on a strong, long piece of string from one end of the room to the other.

Christopher received a small number of Christmas cards, mostly cheap ones. Christopher was becoming older, wiser and mature spiritually. Did he fully understand the spiritual significance of Christmas?

He had lost the enjoyment of Christmas. The children tended to enjoy Christmas even more than anybody else. Full of excitement, the children still expected surprises and treats from adults. Even so, the children had all been deeply affected by Federick's death. Some of them had lost the spirit of Christmas and lacked enjoyment of the exciting pleasures of Christmas. Most of the children still became thrilled and excited by Christmas!

Christopher sat down on an armchair. He felt warmed up and snug sitting in front of the fireplace. The firelight flickered in the dark, casting shadows which appeared in the far corners of the room near the unopened windows and a lampstand.

"What did you buy?" asked Christopher.

"I treated myself. I bought clothes, make-up and perfume," replied Jennifer.

"Let's see," gesticulated Christopher.

Jennifer sprayed her perfume onto her wrist. The scent of her perfume aroused him. He took delight in smelling the fragrance. All the creams, lotions and a suntan lotion which Jennifer put on her face and hands and body respectively. Every product each had their own different perfumed smell specially. Jennifer used luxury brands.

Jennifer leaned forward gracefully.

"Tell me. Have you noticed anything about me?" asked Jennifer.

The Shadow of the Daughter's Ring

Christopher stood up and looked at his sister close-up. In particular her strikingly pretty face and slender figure. He noticed the considerable difference in her make-up. Her eyeliner, eyeshadow and kohl accentuating her features. Her thick eyelashes had been applied with black mascara. Her high cheekbones with rouge and her sensual mouth with lipstick. Applying different make-up on her features made Jennifer look amazingly stunning. It enabled her.

"You look completely different. So really stunning," complimented brother.

Christopher went into the lounge. Jennifer helped Aunt Beth cook in the kitchen. Christopher felt lazy. He had no intention of helping by doing any chores or housework.

He switched on the television. The television programmes on the channels uninterested him. He got bored of it. Christopher switched on the radio. He soon got bored of listening to the radio programme. All the conversationalists, intellectuals were having a debate.

Christopher smelled the aroma of the food cooking, particularly the roast. The seasoning of the spicy stuffing and turkey.

Christopher still grieved for Grandfather. He revived himself by drinking a little sherry.

"Dinner is now ready," said Aunt Beth kindly.

Christopher stayed in the dining room. He stayed seated. When his family came into the dining room, Christopher got up. He walked unsteadily to the dining table at the other side of the dining room. He was tipsy. He sat down at the dining table with his whole family. The family stayed seated while waiting for Christopher.

Together they all raised their glasses and made a toast.

"Merry Christmas and a Happy New Year!" they said merrily.

All the revellers were merry. They engaged in merry making.

Almost the whole family talked while they ate their Christmas dinner.

Christopher had an appetite. He kept quiet. He wasn't as loquacious as the rest of the members of his family present.

Christopher felt queasy at eating now. He tended to be unsociable. He felt unwell.

"Excuse me. I am going to lie down," groaned Christopher.

"Any dessert?" asked Aunt Beth.

"Aren't you well?" asked Mother.

"No. Thanks. I really must lie down. I don't feel well," moaned Christopher.

Having excused himself, Christopher got up from a chair. He pushed his chair back under the dining table. Christopher felt nauseous as well as suffering from indigestion. He left the dining room. He went upstairs to his bedroom alone. He dashed in and ran. Christopher threw himself on his bed. He lay down on his comfortable bed. He rested in the dark for a long time.

Suddenly Christopher heard his sister calling out at the top of her voice. Jennifer knocked loudly on the bedroom door.

"Christopher. Are you awake?"

Christopher was annoyed at being disturbed by his sister. He got up and switched on a bedside lamp. He glanced at the alarm clock.

"Come in," said brother hoarsely.

Jennifer entered her brother's bedroom.

"Do you fancy going out for a walk?" asked sister.

"Do wait for me downstairs. I'll get ready," answered brother.

Jennifer left the bedroom. She waited downstairs for her brother at the bottom of the stairs. Standing gracefully with her arms folded lady-like.

Christopher combed his tangled hair. He changed his stained shirt and creased up trousers. Going out of his bedroom. He joined his sister who was sitting on a bottom stair waiting for him.

Christopher and Jennifer put on their coat or jacket. Together brother and sister went out of the house. They passed through the neighbourhood and then headed around the block the long way around. Going down near the end of the road. They both loitered in the grounds of the church. Neither of them attended this church. They paid attention to the church. They both were cheerful, joyful and relaxed.

Listening to the organ playing and hearing the choir boys singing. Their heavenly voices resounding.

They both walked out of the church grounds. They continued going around the block. They completed it taking less and less time to get back home.

***

At midnight, Christopher woke up. He got out of his bed. Wearing his pyjamas, Christopher tiptoed downstairs. He sneaked into the living room. Closing the door quietly behind him. There he saw in front of him, all the brilliant, dazzling Christmas lights adorning the tinsel, glittering Christmas tree, flashing on and off in automatic sequence.

Christopher knelt down by the Christmas tree. He looked for his Christmas presents which were stacked up under the Christmas tree.

He found a few Christmas presents which had his name clearly written on the Christmas cards. Everyone tied cards on a string attached to his Christmas presents.

Christopher ripped open his Christmas presents. He appeared to be dissatisfied and discontented with every gift he received from his family, relatives, relations and friends.

Christopher had such wonderful memories of Santa Claus. He had a flashback of Father Christmas who had pampered him when he was a child on Christmas Day.

He had not forgotten about his beloved grandfather. He mourned for his grandfather.

Christopher wiped his tears away with a tissue. Remembering Grandfather as Father Christmas.

Christopher felt deeply mournful.

Now Christopher had a much better perspective of life!

He cherished his memories. He remembered once his grandfather on Christmas Eve Day gave him a bear-hug and treated him to gifts.

Christopher was lost in a trance-like state gazing at the tinsel glittering on the Christmas tree. He became lost in a reverie. He appeared to be lost in a trance! He may have been enchanted at the magical Christmas. The joy of Christmas, exciting and wonderful. The Christmas enchantment overexcited him like an excitable child.

Christopher yawned. He was feeling tired, half-awake and sleepy too. Christopher went upstairs back to bed where he fell asleep and dreamt until dawn.

***

During the morning of Christmas Day, the overexcited grandchildren at once opened their Christmas presents. They each received a selection of assorted milk chocolate too.

Subsequently everyone else and families opened their Christmas presents. They all seemed rather satisfied and contented by what they had been given for Christmas.

The Staples family expressed their gratitude. Showing love and appreciative thoughtfulness to one another. They exchanged passionate hugs and kisses.

Christopher walked out with Tara and Sebastian outdoors. Going in the garden.

Tara dressed up as a ballerina wearing a tutu while Sebastian wore a Batman costume and a mask. Tara did handstands with graceful ease while Sebastian ran around, yelling at the top of his voice. His cape blowing in the wind. Wearing his black gloves. He clenched his fist. With his right arm he swung. He punched. Sebastian was an aggressive boy playing a superhero! (His favourite comic character. Sebastian has a passion for reading comics. It remained his enjoyable interest.)

"No presents from our Father Christmas," moaned Sebastian.

"Grandfather always gave us presents," sulked Tara.

Christopher sympathised with the sad, mournful grandchildren.

"Father Christmas has gone forever. He will never come back," said Christopher sadly.

Tara stopped doing her gymnastic routine.

The Shadow of the Daughter's Ring

"No more Christmas. No more presents. No more sweets," grumbled Tara.

"I have given you enough sweets already," scolded Christopher.

"Sebastian has eaten up all my sweets," blamed Tara.

"No, I haven't. Don't lie," expostulated Sebastian.

Christopher remained in a good mood. He decided to offer them a treat.

"No tell-tales. Don't squabble. If you're both good, I will give you both sweets."

Tara and Sebastian cheered up as Christopher assured them of giving them even more sweets. Tara and Sebastian expected the sweets required. Giving them either a surprise or treat would intensely delight both of them.

Tara and Sebastian appreciated their thoughtful cousin's kindness and pleasantness.

Christopher left the grandchildren to play alone together in the garden. He was concerned about Sebastian and Tara. Sebastian and his niece Tara were subdued children. At present their deep grief affected them deeply. Both Sebastian and Tara were bereaved and mournful.

Christopher went back indoors to join his family in the lounge. He sat down on a footstool. He listened to their conversation when his nephew spoke to him.

"How is work?" asked Andrew.

Christopher blushed and moaned with discontent.

"I am a low-paid librarian. I could do with an increase in pay. I am usually exploited. I do work as hard as any of the others. Yet they earn far more money than me. Isn't it unfair! It's the same damn monotonous thing," grumbled Christopher.

"Never mind," said Andrew unashamedly.

"I guess. There is room for improvement I suppose."

Christopher was embarrassed at talking about it. The members of his own family and friends bragged. One of them boasted about his job. His recent promotion in personnel. The other one boasted about his voluptuous wife.

Christopher envied the married couple's blissful marriage and jetsetter's lifestyle. Christopher coveted at times. He was covetous of every husband and wife owning luxury holiday homes abroad. He envied everyone else's success and their status.

Aunt Beth came into the lounge. Aunt Beth interrupted their conversation.

"Dinner is now ready," said Aunt Beth loudly.

Everybody listening had stopped talking. The families and their friends got up and went to the dining room. They entered the room.

As they all sat down at the dining table, Christopher spoke up. Usually at mealtimes he could not get a word in edgewise.

"Tara and Sebastian don't eat too much. There will be sweets later. You won't forget," reminded Christopher.

"We won't make pigs of ourselves," smirked Tara.

Sitting at the dining table, everybody ate their Christmas dinner, followed by Christmas pudding enriched with brandy.

Christopher disliked his Christmas dinner but liked his Christmas pudding. Christopher remained quiet as the others conversed. Christopher felt irritated by his chatty families and invited guests talking. Remaining seated in a fidgety, restless state, Christopher impatiently asked to be excused.

"Please excuse me. I would like to leave please," said Christopher politely.

Now Christopher was allowed to go. So, he rose and at once left the dining table quickly. Going out of the dining room. He went into the quiet study. Totally alone, Christopher sat down on a swivel chair. He looked at a holiday brochure. Spending his time concentrating on reading about Spanish holidays. With great interest, he looked at the colourful pictures of the hotels, pool sides and restaurants and sandy beaches.

Christopher was eager to book a package holiday at a travel agent. He was quite interested in a particular luxury hotel to spend his vacation.

He flicked through the brochure. He saw a picture of a voluptuous sunbather climbing up the steps after the bosomy woman in a bikini had got out of the swimming pool. Going in the surrounding poolside.

Christopher was distracted as his sister came into the study. Jennifer stood in a graceful position directly in front of her brother. Jennifer's arms folded gracefully.

Christopher sat comfortably on a studded leather armchair. He was engrossed in reading a holiday brochure.

"You haven't really spoken much," said sister.

"All this overindulgence is so bad," said brother disapprovingly.

"Isn't Christmas a time to celebrate and rejoice?" retorted Jennifer.

Christopher frowned and tutted.

"Now Christmas is far too commercialised. Its whole meaning and significance of Christmas forgotten. It's a damn mockery. Shouldn't there be more emphasis on the religious aspect of Christmas?"

"Are you planning to go on holiday?" asked sister.

"I'm just looking. I haven't made any decision yet," pondered Christopher.

"I do want to go on holiday myself. Mom says she can't afford it," sulked Jennifer.

"Be nice to her. I am positive Mom will change her mind."

"I do hope so. I can't go on like this," said Jennifer miserably.

Christopher comforted his sister as she burst into tears.

"Grandfather has gone. Now Father Christmas will never be coming back," cried Jennifer.

As their families came in the study, Christopher and Jennifer released each other simultaneously. The brother and sister felt inhibited at being deeply emotional as they consoled one another.

"Are we intruding?" said Laura.

"No. You're not. I was just about to leave," replied Christopher.

"Where are you going?" asked Laura.

"I've got indigestion. I'm going to lie down now," groaned Christopher.

Christopher's aunt entered the study. His aunt cautioned Christopher for being too unsociable. He was intolerable.

"Where's your manners? It is disgusting you're antisocial."

Christopher ignored his angry aunt. Avoiding his families. He hurried away. He went upstairs alone to his bedroom, where he lay down on his bed to get rest. He rested for a long time.

Suddenly Christopher was disturbed by hearing his sister playing her instrument. He got up and rushed out onto the landing. He stood by the balcony. Listening to his sister playing her clarinet for a few minutes. The music resounded down the long, narrow corridor.

Christopher was impressed at her ability to play her clarinet well. He loved to hear his sister play. (Jennifer practised her clarinet regularly. She had an aspiration to be a professional clarinettist and had obsessive desires.)

Christopher often encountered and praised his sister for how well she played her clarinet. Christopher was thrilled at listening to his sister playing her clarinet. Christopher was overwhelmed with great joy. Christopher was feeling rather happy and joyful again.

Christopher went back into his bedroom. He lay down on his bed and rested again. He pressed a button on his wristwatch. The light lit up in the dark. The luminous digits lit up in the dark.

Later Christopher got up and went downstairs. He sneaked into the dining room. There he waited for Tara and Sebastian. Christopher now expected to meet both children there. Christopher was overjoyed at the two of them who came in.

Christopher pointed at the dining table. The dining table was already set. It was laid with a plain white tablecloth. It had several boxes of assorted chocolates. An assortment of biscuits, all sorts of sweets, fruit juices and soft drinks.

Christopher saw the children's joyful expressions as they both took a handful of chocolates and sweets each.

Tara and Sebastian put them in their pockets, then went out of the dining room.

Soon afterwards other members of his family entered the dining room. His family indulged in eating chocolates, sweets and biscuits. The family gathering together. All the family talked amongst themselves. Some of them holding their drinks. A glassful of appetiser.

Christopher spilled his drink as his father hugged him.

"Merry Christmas! I love you, son. Come here! Give me a hug. Do cheer, Christopher. Grandfather loved you. We all deeply miss him. I do have regrets. I think we all do," said Father consolingly.

Christopher remained ambivalent at his father. Christopher was overwhelmed by his father hugging him. He held in his hand an empty glass dripping. His father held his son passionately. His passionate father patted his son on his back.

Christopher walked away from his father. He spoke to the others. They did grieve for Federick and were deeply upset at the loss of their loved one.

Soon his family and their friends began to leave the house. They got in cars and drove off.

Those guests that stayed behind longer were husbands with their wives.

Christopher envied the wives who were happily married. He coveted one of them in particular. Clara, a luscious secretary who exposed her cleavage from her unbuttoned blouse. Her tanned legs appeared out of the slits of her black skirt.

Clara ignored Christopher. Speaking to her handsome husband. The wife put her arms around her husband. Christopher became offended at being ignored and shunned by Clara.

Another wife, a provocative businesswoman, avoided Christopher. Going out of the room with her arms around her husband.

Also, Clara left the room with her husband. Fulfilling her obligation to engage in her commitments and responsibilities.

"Good riddance!" said Christopher to himself.

Christopher thought two of the wives, Englishwomen, snubbed him. Christopher walked off in disgust and left the crowded dining room. Christopher quickly went out of the side door and into the back garden.

He wanted to be alone again. Avoiding everybody again. He did elude those guests intending to intrude on him as well as obtrude and impose on him.

Approaching more and more guests coming towards him in his direction, Christopher appeared to be unsociable. He remained quiet. Christopher walked ahead down the garden. At present he kept away from everybody else walking through the garden. Christopher came towards the flowerbeds and borders. There he noticed that even more gnomes had been added to the collection. Most of these gnomes belonged to Grandfather. Grandfather's obsessive possessions were his favourites.

Walking alone around the garden, he avoided the guests invited to his home. He was quite uninterested in the festivity. Some of the guests who did stay behind engaged in Christmas celebrations indoors.

Going around the garden, he spotted married couples kissing passionately as well as walking hand in hand around the garden.

Christopher felt envious of the romantic, blissful couples and lovers.

Going walking around the garden, Christopher objected being intruded on. He dreaded his privacy being invaded.

Christopher avoided the married couples and lovers who did intrude on him. He hurried away back down the garden. He went back towards the side door. He found the door locked. In anger he barged into the door, hurting his shoulder. In pain Christopher went around to the front of the detached house. The driveway was half full of parked cars.

Christopher walked to the front door standing in the shining house lights outside. Christopher fumbled for a bunch of keys in his trousers pocket. He took out a bunch of keys from out of his pocket. He inserted his house key into a lock. With his house key he opened the front door. Christopher entered his house. He closed the front door.

Going towards the stairs, he smiled at the guests who were standing together while talking amongst themselves at the bottom of the stairs. The guests there were crammed up together in a confined space.

Sitting on the bottom step were two girls. Their beautiful legs graceful. Christopher moving forward slipped through both teenagers sitting together at the bottom step.

Both girls moved their bodies aside gracefully. From moving up their seated position graceful.

Christopher squeezed through their bodies on either side of the bottom step. He sneaked upstairs. Going to his bedroom. He locked his bedroom door. Going to his drawer, he took out from his top drawer many photographs. Lying down on his bed, he looked at a photograph of his beloved grandfather.

Christopher had Christmas memories of his elderly grandfather.

Christopher reflected on this photograph. He felt deeply sad. He mourned for his grandfather.

7

Spanish Bliss

One day in February, it poured with rain. It pitter-pattered onto the windows and on the skylights above. Christopher warmed up from the heat of the radiators. From the automatic thermostat the temperature rose.

He opened the top window. He cooled down from the blown nippy air. Feeling the heavy raindrops splashing on his wet face.

Christopher felt queasy after eating his dinner some time earlier. He slumped on the armchair. He relaxed while seated comfortably in his restful position. He lounged in the silence.

A few minutes later, Christopher was disturbed, hearing the sound of the front door slamming. The front door rattling.

Jennifer entered the lounge.

Christopher saw his sister's joyous expression and broad smile. Jennifer looked beatific from coming home from school. The pupil was well-loved and adored by pupils at school. Since last year, her state showed that Jennifer was a disturbed pupil growing up. Although this pupil had recovered from being bullied, she still suffered with psychological fear and trauma.

Christopher saw the happy look on his sister's face. His sister filled with joy.

"What are you so happy about?" asked Christopher.

"Guess what? I received Valentine cards from my admirers," smirked sister.

Christopher disapproved of admirers who did each wrote Valentine cards anonymously to Jennifer. He discouraged his sister from actually having any relationships with the opposite sex. The brother was obsessively possessive of his sister.

"What is your New Year's Resolution?" asked brother.

"Quite simply to live happily ever after," replied sister.

"Isn't that used at the end of fairy tales? Isn't that ever so philosophical?"

"What's your resolution?" asked sister.

Christopher intended to impose on his relative.

"I'd like to live in Mallorca. To stay with Gerald at his villa," answered brother.

"That's a good resolution. That can be achieved," remarked sister.

"It would be a dream if I could live there or stay," smiled Christopher.

Jennifer agreed to the offer of an invitation which her relative made for her to stay at his villa.

"I really would like to stay. That would be truly wonderful. So romantic," said sister dreamily.

Christopher and Jennifer ended up keeping their New Year's resolutions. Of course, their resolutions did not change or alter.

Everybody else made their resolutions too. They kept theirs. Their profound resolutions were interesting.

Christopher left his exhausted sister alone by herself.

At this present time, he stayed in the lounge. Sitting on an armchair watching television for a few hours.

Christopher became uninterested in watching the remaining programme on television.

Christopher decided to go to bed. At present his bedtime spent tonight was about half an hour earlier than previous nights spent in bed. Christopher spent the night reading a war novel. It was his favourite author. Reading novels remained an obsessive interest of his. Christopher had a passion for reading.

***

That summer, Christopher went on holiday with his father.

At the airport, Christopher and his father got into a taxi. About forty minutes later, the taxi reached the village square. They both got out of the taxi. His father paid the taxi fare. He tipped the taxi driver.

They both found the proprietor unexpectedly waiting for them in the square near a bar and café.

The proprietor greeted both of them.

Near the steps there was a church located in the far corner. The lights reflected in the shadows.

The proprietor carried their luggage up to the very top of the steep steps. Christopher and his father followed, carrying theirs.

They all reached the top of the steps. In the dark, the house lights were shining. They turned left and walked down a path. Passing by townhouses on either side. They entered into a townhouse which was situated near a corner. From the surroundings all the bright house lights shone in the moonlit night.

They both put their luggage in their rooms respectively. At this time of night, both Christopher and his father were tired from jet lag and from travelling. Also, they were both hungry.

"Is there anywhere you can suggest where we can eat?" asked Michael.

"Yes. There's a restaurant nearby. I strongly recommend it. Come! Follow me. I'll show you," said the proprietor kindly.

During the night, they all went out of the townhouse. Christopher and his father followed the proprietor who kindly accompanied them to a restaurant down at the very bottom of the unending long road.

Reaching the restaurant, the proprietor left them.

Christopher and his father entered the restaurant. In the shining lights they both went up to the top of the stairs to get to the restaurant upstairs.

A waiter showed them to a table. Sitting at a table in the restaurant, Christopher admired the panoramic view of the mountain tops. Christopher admired the panoramic sight of all the mountains in the distance.

Christopher was charmed by the enchanting ambiance. With his curious observation, Christopher looked at the blissful English girls sitting at the next table. The three teenagers talked while eating their dessert in the late hours of the night.

The Shadow of the Daughter's Ring

Another waiter came with their drinks. Sparkling mineral water and freshly squeezed orange juice. Unfortunately, at this late time of night, virtually all the food on the menu was at present unavailable, so they both decided to order the same vegetarian dish which was now only on the menu.

"Isn't it romantic here. It's ideal for a honeymoon," said Father.

Christopher fantasised about having a romance. He had fantasies of his exciting pleasures.

"It's such a charming village. It's renowned for being the prettiest village in Mallorca," added Father.

A petite waitress came back with their meal. Christopher and his father were both hungry after their travel today. They both gobbled up their food.

After paying the bill, and also tipping the waitress, they both got up from their table and left the restaurant. They both walked back to the townhouse. It was now very late at night. After their flight and from travelling, they both still suffered with jet lag.

Going back up the road, they passed by imposing buildings and properties. They both admired the charming surroundings. They breathed in the fresh air.

Some minutes later, they reached the townhouse. Michael unlocked the doors. They both entered in the townhouse. They went upstairs, remembering their way to get to their bedrooms.

Christopher and his father left each other. Both of them were emotional when saying goodnight.

Christopher felt tired and sleepy. He stayed awake. He went in a bedroom. It was a big bedroom. He ended up staying in that same bedroom for ten nights.

The windows had wooden shutters.

Christopher got undressed. He went in the bathroom. Immediately he took a hot shower. He used a bathroom towel. He dried his wet body. He put on his pyjamas. Going back to his bedroom, he got into bed. The Spanish night was sultry.

Christopher got up late the next morning. He opened the shutters. The glare blinded him. He got dressed and went downstairs to have his breakfast in the kitchen. The kitchen was modern. On the marble table tops Christopher saw glass jars of marmalade. This marmalade was home-made. A Spanish speciality.

Christopher tasted the marmalade. He rather liked the taste of it. The marmalade had a sugary zest.

Afterwards he spent time looking around the townhouse. The townhouse had been refurbished, furnished and decorated. Every room was cosy and luxurious. On first impression he liked the townhouse. It was located in a lovely spot within reach of the square and bars. He found it to be dingy, dull and dark inside.

Christopher went back to his bedroom. He rested for hours. Sitting on an armchair. Relaxing in the quiet bedroom.

During the morning Christopher and his father went out of the townhouse. As they walked along a nearby street, they both watched a chic lady walk away to rejoin a camera crew who were filming slightly further ahead. It was being shot in a beautiful location by a professional cameraman.

Christopher and his father were greatly surprised at finding filming taking place here.

Christopher felt uneasy in case they were intruding on the set.

They both remained calm and relaxed as they were both allowed freely to pass by the film crew filming.

After a certain time had elapsed, all of the film crew took a break.

They both walked further down the road, stopping by the steps for a while. It was a steep climb up to the top where other premises were noticeable.

They passed a church, then they went down the steps, until they reached the square. Sitting in the square and bars were tourists and villagers.

Michael went into a supermarket alone and bought groceries while Christopher waited outside, looking at the postcards on the racks. He spun every rack slowly around and looked at the various postcards of Spanish regions, tourist hotspots. The beautiful pictures of the loveliest locations in Mallorca and Menorca.

The Shadow of the Daughter's Ring

After his father had finished shopping in the supermarket, they both went back to the townhouse where they refreshed themselves. Earlier in the daytime, they had been moody due to hunger and being thirsty and from lethargy after waking up.

Later, they both went out again, out of the townhouse. They admired the sight of all the beautiful hanging baskets everywhere. They looked at the beautiful flower arrangements.

Walking down the hill, they reached a longer road. There was traffic.

They both stopped and stood waiting to cross over the road. Crossing over the road, they marvelled at the view of the mountains in the distance.

"Isn't it beautiful!" exclaimed father.

Christopher and his father stopped strolling when they came to an estate agent. They stood looking at the luxury properties: villas, fincas, townhouses on offer in the market. They coveted the most expensive properties and luxury ones. Standing there, they both felt so humiliated and miserable at being unable to afford any of the properties on offer which were currently available on the market.

"These ones are well over a million euros!" pointed Christopher.

Christopher standing while looking at the shown properties on offer. He appeared to be disappointed, miserable and unhappy.

"Son. We could never afford it. Where on earth can we get such money from?" said Father disappointedly.

They walked off in another direction. Going somewhere with unfamiliar surroundings. They explored the sleepy village. They ended up following a trail which led for some way down until they came to a signpost. From there, they decided to turn back to go home. (Following the trail led to another part of a village and other trails where there was another different village leading further and further on.)

***

The following morning, Christopher and his father set off to follow a different trail which led to a railway station where they boarded a tram. Sometime later, the tram reached a harbour where there were restaurants, bars and boutiques.

Christopher's first impression was that the jet set and millionaires resided or came to this popular tourist resort during vacation. Christopher had seen all the catamarans and yachts in the harbour. All the white vessels shone with brilliance in the dazzling sunshine. Christopher blinded by the glare.

They both sweltered in the blazing sun.

They sat down on a bench, facing the harbour which especially appealed to tourists and day-trippers.

"It's so hot," grumbled Father.

Christopher sweated in the heat. He marvelled at the hot sunny weather.

"It's a beautiful summer's day," Christopher exclaimed joyously.

"This place is ideal for boat trips and walks."

"It's nice and quiet here. It's typically Spanish."

They both got up. They went to a bar and sat down at a table. At this present time, sitting outside there were only a small number of people.

A waitress came and served them. Christopher drank a glassful of Coca-Cola with ice which melted. His father had rum and raisin ice cream and a glass of freshly squeezed orange juice.

Enjoying relaxing in the shade, they both cooled down under the sunshade. The sun beat down. It made casting shadows and reflections.

About half an hour later, they got up and left the crowded bar to go and have a look at the shops, boutiques and markets.

Christopher and his father looked at the clothes, ornaments and souvenirs. They were both uninterested in any of them.

They joined up with the throng of tourists, holidaymakers and day-trippers waiting for a tram. As the tram arrived, all the passengers got on board and sat down on the seats. Within moments, the entire tram was crammed up with a large group of German tourists and a European contingent.

They both felt claustrophobic huddled up while being seated. Their sitting position uncomfortable.

Christopher put on his trendy sunglasses. As the tram travelled to Sóller. Christopher saw sunbathers afar on the beach as well as at the resort.

From Sóller, they took a taxi back to a village. The taxi had stopped at their request. They both got out of a taxi. They walked up a road, then up a steep slope, following a path till reaching a bend where they came to a flight of steps. They climbed up the concrete steps until they reached the top, then turned left and followed a track. They entered by a gate which led to a finca.

***

Two days later, Christopher and his father went to a railway station, where they waited for a train with all the commuters. Arriving on time, Christopher and his father got on board a train which took them from Sóller into the city of Palma.

They went out of the crowded underground and into the Tourist Information Centre. They mingled with the public. They queued up and waited their turn to be attended to. Christopher asked for a map, requesting for an indication of directions. A uniformed advisor marked their whereabouts on it.

Christopher grasped the geographical location. Michael enquired about the travelling alternatives of leaving the city of Palma.

They went out of the automatic sliding doors and walked past shops while looking for museums, art galleries and other places of interest and tourist attractions that were shown on the map of Palma.

They entered an art gallery and walked around while looking at all the paintings from the exhibition. The dilettantes admired the paintings. They both had an acquired taste for the paintings of townhouses, fincas and their rather beautiful flower arrangements.

Amongst the other paintings, they really liked the ones of the fields and meadows. After they had finished looking at the exhibition, going out of the art gallery, they went to a shopping centre where there were tourists, shoppers and holidaymakers. They came across a group of Spanish Catholic schoolgirls. A few of them bought cakes and confectionery. Further on they passed by another Catholic schoolgirl. She was from Valencia. Her Valencia dark eyes beautiful! These features of hers were her loveliest compared to her other attributes.

Christopher was smitten at the fine Catholic schoolgirl. In particular her Valencia eyes which were amazingly stunning. Her eyelashes had black mascara and also applied black eyeliner. This Spanish schoolgirl wore a pale blue blouse with an emblem on it and a grey skirt.

The sun beat down on the schoolgirl. She had been dazzled by the blazing sunshine. The sudden appearing schoolgirl a miraculous figure!

Walking further on, Christopher and his father passed by bars, cafés and restaurants.

Suddenly a carriage went past, down a cobbled street. The sound of hooves echoed on the concrete ground, a horse trotting.

They kept walking, leaving the main tourist areas.

They became calmer and quieter going further down the streets in the city region.

Walking a long distance, they soon reached the cathedral, which was located in busy, agoraphobic surroundings. The ambience of a historic nature indeed. There, near the grounds of the cathedral, were tired black horses resting in the blazing sun. Christopher sympathised with all the beautiful black horses which were beautifully groomed.

They entered the cathedral with the throng of tourists and sightseers. They paid for their admission. Then went for a tour around the cathedral which was undergoing restoration at present.

Walking around the cathedral, they looked at the stained-glass windows and rose windows and at the chapels of the saints. At the pulpit, the worshippers were prostrate while praying. The sightseers and tourists used their cameras to take photographs. The Catholics paid a visit to the cathedral. Amongst some of the visitors there may well have been divine intervention, regarding conversion of a sinner, repenting. The Catholics have devotion of worshipping their

The Shadow of the Daughter's Ring

saviour. The worshippers took joy, peace and comfort in worshipping. The prayers sat down to pray or knelt.

As the cathedral got increasingly crowded, Christopher and his father decided to go. After sightseeing and paying a visit to the cathedral, they both went out of the sliding doors and returned to a station where they sat and waited for a bus. As soon as their bus came, the small number of passengers waiting got on board. Every passenger each took their ticket and sat down on the seats in the bus.

A long time later, Christopher and his father got off at Sóller, then waited for another bus which took them back to their village.

It rained during the evening as they both went walking back to the townhouse.

***

On Tuesday afternoon, Christopher and his father entered a hotel which had been converted. They walked past the reception. At present the receptionists on duty were unapproachable.

They walked around while admiring the luxury hotel. They both cooled down from the air-conditioning. They both trespassed in the hotel.

The sun shone through the large windows, its dazzling sunrays blinding them. Covering their eyes from the blaze, they looked away from the glare.

They went upstairs and took a look around. They went in a bar, dining room and storeroom. At that time there was nobody around so they relaxed and calmed while being alone together.

Moments later, they went out of a door to go outdoors. They went outside into a beautiful garden (it was really the loveliest garden in summer).

Outside, in the hotel garden, the paying guests sat at garden tables, enjoying one another's company. The time they had spent together they enjoyed themselves. Those other individuals also there in the garden did seem to enjoy themselves.

They walked around the garden, admiring the garden at summertime. Everywhere in the surroundings, in the garden, all the flowers bloomed. Its brilliant colours blaze. A beautiful natural sight.

Both trespassers were tired of walking. They walked towards the garden table and sat down. The two of them facing and looking at the mountains ahead in the distance. They admired the view. It was truly breathtaking, wonderful natural scenery. They marvelled at the peace and quiet. They admired the loveliness of the natural surroundings.

"It's so peaceful here. It really is. Isn't it beautiful!" exclaimed Christopher.

"I love it here. I wish I could stay here forever," sighed Father.

"We do fly back tomorrow. I don't wish to return," frowned Christopher.

"We really should come back. Another time perhaps?" suggested Father.

Christopher and his father relaxed in the Spanish hot sun, dehydrating in the scorching heat. Despite them trespassing here, they did not have any more anxiety.

They both enjoyed their short time together here before leaving the hotel to get back to the townhouse a distance away.

8

Bridesmaids

One midsummer's day, Christopher and his sister sat together on the settee while in the luxurious living room. They both ate biscuits and drank a hot chocolate drink. Both brother and sister relaxed together while enjoying comfort.

During the day, no one else intruded on them or came in apart from themselves. At that time, they had enjoyed each other's company without any intrusion, enjoying their pleasure of relaxation and luxury indulged.

Christopher relived his experience of his holiday. He may have been unconcerned and neglectful towards his sister.

"Do I have to repeat myself? You still haven't told me about your holiday," grumbled Jennifer.

"What is there to tell?"

"You can begin by telling me your best moments."

"There's nothing to say," paused Christopher. "Well, there is one thing, I guess. The bus going along the hairpin bends was dangerous and hair-raising. We came across bend after bend."

With curious interest, Jennifer listened.

"It sounds as though it was scary," remarked sister.

"It was a frightening experience, one which I would not like to experience again. That's all I can remember. It sticks in my mind," Christopher paused. "What is it you're so happy about? Get that smirk off your face."

Jennifer wanted revenge.

"Those bullies are not coming back. I just hope they failed their exams," said sister spitefully.

"You're vindictive. You're obviously happy about it. You're revengeful."

"Oh, indeed I am! I want vengeance," said Jennifer unashamedly.

Christopher admitted his ignorance.

"What on earth did they do to you?"

Jennifer folded her arms. She was rather calm at answering.

"They bullied me. They teased me. They called my mum names. They made fun of me."

"Are the bullies school leavers?" asked brother.

"I damn well hope so. I bloody curse them," said Jennifer angrily.

"That's un-Christian," reproved Christopher.

"They shouldn't have bullied me. They shouldn't get away with it."

"Can't you forgive? It does say in the Holy Bible to love your enemies."

"Don't preach and lecture to me," snapped Jennifer.

"You're stubborn. That's your problem," remarked Christopher.

Christopher said nothing else in case he provoked his sister to anger.

Jennifer changed the subject.

"Are you looking forward to the wedding this weekend?" said Jennifer.

"Not really. Although Joe is a good friend of the family."

Jennifer praised herself. She was conceited.

"I am a bridesmaid once again. You should see me dressed up. I am special. Really so. Isn't it wonderful!"

Christopher respected his sister and her eager keenness to be a bridesmaid. Jennifer was obsessed at being photographed by a professional wedding photographer.

"Hopefully everything will be alright on the day," said brother uncertainly.

Later that night, Jennifer engaged in a séance. She was intent on gaining revenge on her enemies.

At midnight, Christopher walked into a pitch-dark room. He disturbed Jennifer and her friends. He disapproved of the clandestine practice of the witch's coven.

Quickly, Christopher left the pitch-black room. He had no motive or obligatory intention to report it!

***

On Saturday morning, all the invited wedding guests attended a wedding ceremony in a church.

Christopher sat next to his father. Christopher was an invited guest who attended the wedding.

He was envious of Joe getting married to his beautiful bride.

Christopher listened to the organ playing then the voluptuous bride walked down the aisle, followed by the three beautiful bridesmaids holding the bride's wedding gown. The taffeta.

The bride joined the bridegroom in the presence of the vicar. The bride and bridegroom said their wedding vows.

Christopher looked on with jealousy as the bridegroom and bride exchanged their wedding rings and husband and wife kissed passionately for the first time. Both husband and wife were deeply in love! Looking at each other with such great love. The newlyweds then rushed out of the entrance where the cheering crowd, guests and well-wishers stood in two long lines while throwing confetti.

They newlyweds held each other's hands while they both hurried to a Rolls Royce straight ahead, parked in the grounds. The newlyweds quickly got in the Rolls Royce which whisked them off.

***

Later, all the wedding guests arrived at the church hall for a banquet.

Christopher felt tired and enervated. Christopher wanted to go home. He was unenthusiastic at attending the banquet. (At present he was a stranger. He hadn't known any of the strangers and guests arriving.)

Jennifer enjoyed doing her natural poses. The professional photographer favoured her amongst the other bridesmaids. The wedding photographer ended taking a few photographs of the three bridesmaids who stood together while holding posies when posing with the married couple and the members of their family. (Other photographs included the extended family.)

Christopher seemed to be camera-shy. He wanted to be excluded from the wedding photographs. (At first, Christopher declined to be photographed by the professional wedding photographer. Jennifer insisted on her brother being included in the wedding photographs.)

Finally, Christopher was photographed for a wedding photograph in the church amongst everybody, all the wedding guests, including friends, families, relations and relatives.

For a short time, Christopher avoided the wedding guests. He made an excuse when he rejoined all of them when going back to the church hall.

Someone did ask him why he refused to join in for the wedding photography taken earlier on in the day.

The guests stood in groups while talking to each other. Then they all sat down and eagerly listened to Joe give his wedding speech. Joe, a married man, stood up while Trish, his wife, remained seated as she still clasped her hands.

"My wife and I would like to thank you all for coming to our wedding. It has been a pleasure inviting you. We would like to take the opportunity to personally thank our families for their love and support. Special thanks to Charles for organising the wedding for me, including the catering as well, and John, Lorraine, Jane, Tim and Christine too, as well as many others. It has been a wonderful day. A memorable wedding. One which me and my wife will never ever forget. Trish and I will see you all soon when we get back from our honeymoon in the Seychelles," said Joe happily.

All the banqueters began to eat all together. Enjoying their banquet as well as the gathering.

Christopher got up from his chair. Moving to another table, he walked over to the three beautiful bridesmaids eating a slice of wedding cake.

Christopher disturbed his sister who was relaxing with the beatific bridesmaids.

"Where have you been?" asked sister.

"Not far. I was on my own."

"As you can see, we're enjoying ourselves. Aren't we?" smiled Jennifer.

One of the bridesmaids remarked on the banquet.

"Good grub. It's really nice."

Christopher remained deeply contemplative about his sister.

"One day you too will fall in love and get married!"

"Any objections? I am not in love. I will always be a bridesmaid forever!"

Christopher felt pity for himself.

"Who's going to marry me? No-one will ever want to marry me!"

Jennifer had deep sympathy for her unmarried brother.

"Isn't it really good to be single? You're free to do anything you want without being restricted."

Christopher was ashamed of being unmarried. He did dread being unloved by the opposite sex! He avoided those guests who seemed to be quite happy. Especially the newlyweds who were in love!

"Marriages now end up in divorce," stated Christopher.

"That's quite true. The statistics do prove that. Have you eaten anything?"

"Oh, yes. A few sandwiches and a glass of bubbly," smiled brother.

Jennifer ran her finger on a rim of a glass.

"I like it. It's awfully good."

"How was the wedding photography? Were you all photographed?" asked brother.

"We were all in the right frame of mind. The photographer was well-pleased with us. He remarked that we were all professional," boasted Jennifer.

"Jolly good. I am pleased."

The three bridesmaids were pretty delighted at the photographer's remarks. The professional photographer had favourable impressions of them. The wedding photographer showed considerable favouritism to every bridesmaid who was intent on a modelling career.

The bridesmaids looked elated as they sat at the dining table near the corner in the blaze. They sweltered in the heat. Their cheeks flushed and their darkly tanned skin darkened from a suntan.

Christopher reacted when Joe, a married man, leaned on him as Joe touched Christopher firmly on his shoulder. Christopher respected Joe. Admiring the family friend.

"We haven't yet spoken. I am sorry about that. I've been too busy," apologised Joe.

Christopher put his arm around Joe.

"Do have a happy marriage. Trish is right for you. You have been busy. Now you can relax."

"Trish and I will be leaving soon to go on our honeymoon," smiled Joe.

"I do hope you have a wonderful time. Do let me know how you get on," said Christopher amiably.

"We're looking forward to our honeymoon. I just can't wait to get on the beach. To have a beach party," said Joe happily.

Joe rejoined his seated wife waiting for her husband.

The wedding guests talked away.

Christopher wanted to be alone again. He decided to avoid all the guests.

Going out of the entrance. He came outdoors. Going outside he came to the church grounds and gardens. He met along the way a few guests wandering around.

The Shadow of the Daughter's Ring

Going past the church, along and around the surroundings. There he spent time alone. As he engaged in deep spiritual contemplation. Christopher reflected on his unmarried life.

Christopher went back to the church hall. He rejoined all the guests in there. All the wedding guests spent time together for hours and hours. All the wedding guests socialised and mingled with everybody. The guests were chatty or quiet and reserved and with well-wishers too.

As time elapsed, it was time to leave, and all the wedding guests began to leave the church as soon as the newlyweds had gone. The newlyweds were driven away by a uniformed chauffeur wearing gloves. The experienced chauffeur drove off in a new Rolls Royce.

The romantic married couple looked forward to their honeymoon.

The married couple had high expectations of their holiday.

The dreamy honeymooners fulfilled their expectations by going on holiday abroad.

9
Wedding Highlights

About a fortnight later, Joe and Trish invited the Staples to their home.

In the lounge, Christopher, his parents and sister gathered together.

Joe and Trish, the married couple, showed them the recording of their wedding. They all watched the plasma screen.

All except Christopher were filled with joy. Christopher, a well-wisher, was still envious of the wedded couple. Joe and Trish were deeply in love!

The husband and wife were both wealthy stockbrokers.

From a different angle, a camera zoomed up close on the seated guests watching the recording of a wedding. It was the wedding day highlights.

"Oh look! It's you, Chris. You look glum," said Mother loudly.

Christopher looked away in embarrassment. He felt sheepish in the presence of everybody watching the highlights of the wedding recording.

Christopher remembered the wedding day. (He had been given priority as a wedding guest. He had not appreciated his privilege. A few others had been privileged.)

Christopher's memories of the wedding day made him of course envious and miserable.

Remembering the wedding of Joe and Trish, it reminded him of the husband and wife's wedding bliss. He also witnessed the three bridesmaids' happiness!

"It was a long day. I was exhausted," recalled Christopher.

After watching the recording of the wedding day highlights, Jennifer spent time looking at all the wedding photographs.

Christopher sitting next to his sister watched her take a look at every photograph. Many of the photographs showed the newlyweds' wedding bliss and their honeymoon happiness!

Jennifer concentrated on looking at many photographs. Christopher seemed to be uninterested in the photographs as his fascinated sister passed them to him.

Jennifer pointed to one photograph in particular.

"Hey! That's me!" said sister arrogantly.

Christopher looked at a few photographs half-heartedly. Again and again, he appeared to be uninterested in looking at the photographs at this present time. Christopher looked at two of the photographs. He admired the really beautiful bridesmaids, all of them, each looking so natural together. All the bridesmaids were naturally photogenic.

On the wedding day itself, Christopher had been proud and respectful of the well-behaved bridesmaids. (During the course of the wedding day, every bridesmaid had been on their best behaviour! One of the bridesmaids was adorable!)

Christopher looked at Trish the moment the married businesswoman spoke.

"This photographer is the best," praised Trish.

"He is professional," remarked Christopher.

"The ones of me and the bridesmaids are lovely. Don't you think?" said Trish proudly.

"The photographer snapped. He was well-pleased with us," said Jennifer modestly.

"I believe you do have the potential to be a model," remarked Trish.

"Oh good! Do you think so?" smiled Jennifer.

Christopher conversed for the sake of it.

"Will you have any kids?" asked Christopher.

"Oh! Yes, of course. I would like to raise a family of my own," replied Trish.

Afterwards, Trish and her husband showed them around their luxurious large house. While they looked around at their house,

Trish suggested that the Staples were welcome to stay at their house, Rose Valley, in the near future, as soon as Trish and her husband settled down at their new house. The newlyweds had to get used to their new married life together in today's society.

The Staples appreciated Joe and Trish's warm welcome as well as being appreciative of husband and wife having invited them around to their new house now several times. This country house had been recently refurbished, furnished and decorated.

Christopher felt envious of the millionaire's lifestyle. He coveted their million-pound country house.

After they had stayed for a few hours at Rose Valley, they all left together shortly afterwards to make their long journey back home to Kent.

***

A few weeks later, the Staples stayed the weekend at Barnhurst. Mr and Mrs Harvey invited the Staples family to come round.

Christopher was polite as he expressed his thanks.

"Mr and Mrs Harvey, thank you for allowing us to stay here," said Christopher appreciatively.

"You're welcome. We do enjoy all your company," smiled Mrs Harvey.

"It's a pleasure. Isn't Barnhurst a fine place!" said Father.

"It's our home. We do our best to make it comfortable. We do get satisfaction from knowing that people love our home," said Mrs Harvey proudly.

"We are very happy that Jennifer comes to stay with us. Jennifer helps out in the stables. She is good with horses and is a good rider. It is a pleasure to work with her," grinned Mrs Harvey.

"My daughter loves horses. It's her joy in life! She always looks forward to staying here," said Mother happily.

A housemaid came in the living room carrying a tray. Everybody came forward. They each took a glass of port from the tray. They all toasted together and drank it up.

"To good health and prosperity," exclaimed Mr Harvey.

Mr Harvey drank it up in a gulp.

They felt revived from the tipple.

Christopher and Jennifer got up from the settee. Then they both left the manor house.

Christopher walked with his sister to the stables. In the stables Christopher watched Jennifer put a saddle onto a horse. She fastened the straps.

Christopher joined Jennifer who walked out with a horse from the stables into the yard. They walked together while heading down the fields, going past a paddock where there was a small number of horses galloping.

As they reached the horse-jumping course, Jennifer mounted the horse. She rode while her brother lagged behind.

Jennifer joined a few riders who were waiting for her.

Christopher using a stopwatch timed Jennifer, his sister, as she began horse-jumping around the course. At present, Jennifer was horse-jumping over fences and fences, faster and faster.

Jennifer completed the full course without knocking any fences down. It was a perfect clear round, but a slower time than her previous personal best time.

Christopher stopped the stopwatch.

"Jennifer, your time was slower than your personal best. Your previous one. But you did manage a clear round. Well done!" praised brother.

Jennifer patted the horse.

"I am not good enough," said Jennifer despondently.

Trotting forward, Jennifer joined the other riders on horseback who were waiting for her.

Minutes earlier, the impressed riders watched Jennifer do a round of horse-jumping around the whole course.

Amongst the few horse-jumpers they remained undecided as they tried to decide the order of participation.

One of the riders on horseback gestured. She said out loud, "Who's going to go first?"

All the riders were eager to participate. The older, experienced rider took the initiative to decide the running order.

"Meg, you go first. Then Clarice, you go next," said Moira.

One by one, the horse-jumpers jumped over the fences around the course. Two of them knocked down fences. Only one fence was knocked down during their round of the course.

Another horse-jumper managed to do a clear round in quite a fast time.

Christopher applauded the pleased horse-jumper. The other two horse-jumpers were bitterly disappointed at being eliminated at this stage of this round.

"Helen, it's just you and me now. I'll go first," said Jennifer emphatically.

Helen approved of the challenge.

"Alright. You go first."

Christopher stood and timed Jennifer first while watching her horse-jumping. The horse-jumper jumped over several fences around the course. As Jennifer approached the very last fence, the horse's hoof clipped one of the bars. Miraculously, it somehow stayed on without falling on the ground.

Expecting the last horse-jumper to enter, Christopher timed Helen next. This time Helen managed to get another clear round. At the end of the round, Helen's time was rather slower than her previous times.

At last, Christopher declared Jennifer the winner!

Helen finished up as runner-up!

They had all been unaware of Mr and Mrs Harvey watching them show-jumping.

Helen congratulated the winner first, then after Meg and Clarice congratulated Jennifer who evidently felt triumphant at herself. The triumphal rider clenched her first up in the air in triumph, holding tightly the reins in one hand as the horse trotted forward.

The other riders rode off ahead, going back to the stables.

The Shadow of the Daughter's Ring

There the stable girl waited for the riders to get back. The few riders dismounted from their horses. The stable girl held the reins and took every horse back into the stables.

Jennifer felt pleased with herself.

Jennifer trotted back along the fields. She stopped when she reached a paddock where she joined Mr and Mrs Harvey who were both waiting for the rider.

"You're a promising rider. Why don't you enter for a tournament? Haven't you yet considered that option?" suggested Mr Harvey.

"I'd love to be able to do showjumping and dressage," wished Jennifer dreamily.

"You should compete," urged Mr Harvey.

"It's a pity that you don't enter tournaments. You do have ability," said Mrs Harvey sympathetically.

Jennifer felt demoralised and disappointed at being unable to compete in show-jumping tournaments. (Jennifer loved horses. She had a passion for riding. She had an interest in equestrian events.)

Jennifer agreed to compete if the opportunity arose to enter a show-jumping tournament or dressage.

"I would compete if I could," said Jennifer.

"Do think about it and we will talk about it another time," smiled Mr Harvey.

Christopher and Jennifer walked away. Jennifer held the reins of her horse as they walked down together to the fields until they both reached the scenic, natural beauty spot far away.

By the trees, Jennifer and Christopher sat down together on the hot, dry ground. It was sweltering from the heat. Overhead, in the treetops, the radiant sunrays were dazzling, blazing and blinding.

Relaxing, they both cooled down in the shade and from the fresh coolness of the gently blowing breeze.

From her calm nature, Jennifer stretched out to stroke a horse which was tied to a tree nearby in the cool shade. The coolness of the shade cooler there.

"I would really love to own one of these damn fine horses," said Jennifer dreamily.

Christopher sitting in the dark shade under a tree was deeply contemplative as well as reflective.

"It's good to have dreams. Maybe one day your dreams will come true," said brother optimistically.

"I hope so. I do hope so. It's rather quiet and peaceful here. Isn't it lovely!" remarked sister.

Christopher marvelled at the ambience.

"It's wonderful here! So quiet and peaceful!"

"I come here whenever I get the chance. I can't resist its appeal," said Jennifer excitedly.

"I forgot to ask you. Are you going to take part in the fox hunt?" asked brother.

Jennifer objected to the controversial blood sport.

"I am not getting involved. I will probably meet up with all of them. You can come if you like and keep me company. I am an animal lover myself. I am against all animal cruelty," protested Jennifer.

"It sounds controversial. I would like to come if that's alright," insisted Christopher.

"Oh! Good. You can keep an eye on me. The Harveys are expecting me," smiled sister.

"In these parts fox hunting is a tradition here, isn't it? Does the ban still stand?" asked brother.

"The Harveys seem to think so. This tradition has lasted for generations," replied sister.

They both had unspoken thoughts about the further controversies of the blood sport. (In this region fox hunting remained a popular tradition!)

They both ended their conversation about the controversial matters which arose from fox hunting.

Christopher and his sister got up from the moist ground. Jennifer untied the reins of her horse. The horse neighed. Taking her horse, they both walked together while going back the other way, reaching the fields in the far distance. They both watched the teenage riders take it in turns to jump over the fences on the course.

They reached the stables. The stable girl took the horse from Jennifer. The stable girl attended to the horse by taking it back into the stables.

Christopher and Jennifer both went back into the manor house. Christopher spent the night and his sister Jennifer over-indulged in the comfort of luxury in the boudoir.

***

On Sunday afternoon, Christopher went to meet Jennifer at a haunt deep in the countryside. He met along the way on a beaten track a horsewoman. Mrs Harvey gestured and smiled at Christopher, a walker. He walked alone on foot on a track. The rider rode off. Going back to the stables.

Christopher walked further and further up the track. He approached a wooden signpost in the middle of a fork in the track.

Christopher met his sister, a rider, waiting on horseback along the track. Brother and sister were both punctual. They both had arrived early. (The time of their meeting was much earlier than previously arranged.)

Simultaneously, brother and sister glanced at their wristwatches. They both waited in anticipation for the fox hunters and a pack of fox hounds and huntsmen to pass by. At present his sister Jennifer refused to take part in the fox hunt. She declined to get involved in it.

The fox hunters had earlier given their approval to allow Jennifer to join them in the fox hunt.

Jennifer was cautious of fox hunting. She was wary of the circumstantial consequences that she might get arrested by the police or be perhaps intimidated by protesters, campaigners and activists marching in protest. Jennifer wanted to avoid confrontation with the police force, protesters, campaigners and animal rights activists.

Jennifer took precautions by declining to join the fox hunters in their fox hunt today.

Christopher and Jennifer moved away and stepped aside, watching all the fox hunters ride off following a pack of fox hounds sniffing the scent.

They both disapproved of fox hunting. Jennifer objected to the blood sport. (One of her friends, a student, was a campaigner. On a regular basis, she campaigned for the blood sport to be banned!)

"Let's leave! I don't want to stay here any longer," grumbled Jennifer.

Along the route they both came across the fox hunt again. All the fox hunters and huntsmen on horseback. Going onwards ahead, they again met Mr Harvey, a huntsman leading the fox hunt.

Jennifer respected Mr Harvey's decision to allow her to ride a thoroughbred. She had pleaded with Mr and Mrs Harvey, especially the squire. Mr Harvey allowed Jennifer to ride one of their horses.

Christopher and Jennifer heard a bugle in the distance and fox hounds barking. Suddenly a pack of fox hounds came through the trees, sniffing a scent along the trail, followed by huntsmen on horseback.

Christopher stood back out of their way. He disrespected the aggressive, obnoxious and cruel fox hunters and huntsmen riding past.

Suddenly, a huntsman stopped and dropped behind.

"Are you coming?" asked Mr Harvey.

Jennifer, pressed for a decision, had declined to join them and to take part in the fox hunt.

"I won't be coming," declined Jennifer.

"Good day!" saluted Mr Harvey.

Christopher and Jennifer turned back.

While going the other way, following the track back, they both took the opposite way back.

As soon as they got back to the manor house, they relaxed and rested together in the lounge.

Amongst their family present, they discussed fox hunting. The controversies of the blood sport which arose were debatable.

Jennifer, a controversialist, did object to animal cruelty during fox hunts. She advocated that this blood sport should be banned!

They all debated the blood sport. They argued the case for and against fox hunting. In the end, most of them concluded that the blood sport ought to be banned!

The following day, Christopher left Barnhurst with his family, except for Jennifer who spent a few more days at Barnhurst.

Christopher slept in the car during his long journey home.

***

One night, there were flashes of lightning and peals of thunder. A thunderstorm. Brother and sister sat in front of the fireplace, with the lights switched off, the firelight flickering in the darkness. They both warmed up from the heat of the fire.

Christopher got up and walked towards the window. He felt fearful of the storm.

Jennifer arose. She moved towards her brother. She stood next to her brother. Jennifer spent a while at looking out of the window. Standing still with her arms folded gracefully. Jennifer remained calm, unafraid and unperturbed.

A flash of lightning lit up the skies with peals of thunder.

"I won't be able to sleep tonight," sighed sister.

"Oh, you will. You won't have any problems in sleeping," assured brother.

Suddenly the peals of thunder drowned out the sound of the doorbell ringing.

During that moment of silence, they both heard the sound of the doorbell ringing. The sound of the chimes resonant in the house.

Christopher rushed out of the room. He hurried to the front door. Quickly he answered the front door.

Christopher greeted Mary and her son James who were both drenched from being out in the torrential rain. James sniffled from the nippy air and cold weather.

Christopher welcomed Mary and her son to come in out of the pouring rain.

"You're soaked. Come in before you catch your death of cold," gestured Christopher.

Christopher thoughtfully took a package from Mary. He accompanied Mary and her little son into the living room.

At present there Jennifer waited for them to come in. Jennifer greeted Mary and her son. She welcomed them with joy.

"Thank you for coming. It's a pleasure to see you. It's awful weather," greeted Jennifer.

"I have collected it. I have brought you what you wanted," smiled Mary.

Jennifer was pleased. Receiving this portrait excited her. The teenager was highly excitable!

Christopher gave his sister a heavy item. In excitement, Jennifer unwrapped the packaging of the portrait. She held it firmly while admiring a portrait of herself for the very first time. In obsessive narcissism! A self-love of oneself. Jennifer had a proud narcissistic obsessiveness of herself!

"It's me! Isn't it beautiful!" exclaimed Jennifer proudly.

Christopher took the portrait from his sister. He lifted it upwards. They all stood together and admired the beautiful portrait close up.

"Where is it going to go?" asked sister.

"Don't worry. We'll find somewhere to put it," reassured brother.

Christopher held the light-framed portrait and walked with it to the other side of the room, standing still by the wall on the opposite side. He was still undecided as to where to put the portrait.

Mary made that decision and pointed to a spot on the wall.

"Let's put it there," said Mary decisively.

Christopher took a hanging painting down from the wall. With decisiveness, Mary again pointed to the exact spot where the portrait should be hung on the wall.

At once, Christopher removed it and replaced it. Christopher hung the portrait on the wall.

The Shadow of the Daughter's Ring

The three of them stood together and looked at the portrait. They admired the portrait of Jennifer.

"It's a lovely portrait. You look so natural and innocent," remarked Mary.

Most of them stood together while looking at it with further deep admiration. Except for James, a little boy, who appeared to be uninterested in looking at the new portrait. James was far more interested in his sweets rather than anything else on his mind.

Jennifer, with deep gratitude, embraced Mary with affection.

"Thank you very much," said Jennifer gratefully.

Christopher approved of Mary's favour.

Jennifer again expressed her gratitude.

"I am really grateful. Thank you," thanked Jennifer.

Christopher politely offered, "Would you like a drink?"

"I would like a sherry, please. For James, my son, nothing. I will give him a drink before he goes to bed," answered Mary.

"Jennifer, please get Mary a sherry," demanded brother.

"Yes of course," responded sister.

Jennifer obeyed her brother while going out of the living room.

From his mother the attention now focused on James, her son. Mary took the fringe out of her son's eyes.

"My son is tired. He's being such a brave boy. He is scared, no doubt of the thunder," said mother.

"James is a good boy. He loves his stories," said Christopher fondly.

Mary told Christopher of her intention. Of course, Mary reminded Christopher again of the arrangement with regard to the invitation of her son.

"I will drop off my son next weekend if that's alright. I will confirm this with my phone call," said mother cheerfully.

"Jennifer has said that she will babysit," confirmed Christopher.

Mary stood by the fireplace while warming herself up. She rubbed her hands together.

"It's lovely and warm in here."

In obedience, Jennifer did what her impatient brother told her to do. Jennifer came back in the living room holding a small glass of sherry. She brought it to Mary.

"Drink this. It will make you feel better," insisted Jennifer.

Mary was grateful to Jennifer. Her pleasantness a trait of the nice girl. Mary took the small glass of sherry. Mary drank up the sherry. Mary was revived from drinking the tipple.

"We'll be going now. James, now say goodbye," admonished mother.

"Goodbye!" uttered son.

With childish sweetness, Jennifer said goodbye too. Her girlish affection quite emotional!

Christopher and Jennifer led Mary and her son out of the detached house. Christopher closed the front door. He walked away from his sister who went upstairs. Jennifer retired.

"Goodnight," said sister.

"Goodnight," replied brother.

Christopher walked down the corridor. He was deafened by the peals of thunder. He was blinded by the flashes of lightning which lit up in the pitch-dark room. Christopher heard heavy raindrops splashing on the roof above. He came in the room. Walking towards the portrait facing ahead on the wall opposite.

He saw the portrait light up in the dark. He stood close to the portrait hanging up on the wall.

With intense delight, Christopher admired the portrait which lit up in the pitch-darkness from the flashes of lightning.

This same portrait reminded Christopher of his great-grandmother!

Jennifer had the same ancestral resemblance and striking likeness of her great-grandmother. Jennifer resembled her great-grandmother. She did look like her great-grandmother.

Christopher moved close to the portrait opposite. He stood admiring the portrait further.

The Shadow of the Daughter's Ring

Christopher shuddered from the thunderstorm. He was afraid of being alone in the pitch-darkness. At present the thunderstorm was frightening.

10

A Summer Drive

Last night Christopher came home very late at night. He got into bed at a quarter to midnight. During the night, Christopher slept peacefully throughout the night. Christopher overslept. At this present time, Christopher slept till midday. Christopher got up. He got dressed. He went downstairs. In the kitchen he made himself two slices of toast. He thickly spread butter on the toast. He ate his breakfast and drank up his nice cup of tea. After, he relaxed in the cosy lounge. At daytime the sun shone through the windows. The blaze dazzling and blinding. The radiant sunrays penetrated through the sky roofs over above.

He took a daily newspaper from on top of the table. He browsed through the newspaper. He flicked through the pages of the newspaper. Christopher was aroused at looking at a provocative model posing in a pretentious unnatural way.

Turning over another page of a newspaper, he soon became uninterested at the nonchalant model's titillation. The female's eroticism!

Losing interest in something else, the critic's column, he read about another page of a newspaper. This time he read about a film star's amassed fortune at the box office.

Christopher was envious of the film star's international success and his recognition.

Christopher felt rather humiliated and discontented with his life. His lack of success and failure in his work, education, and the lack of status etc. (In his position, job, there were no opportunities for promotion as an assistant librarian!)

Christopher was dissatisfied at being a low-paid employee.

Going out on the terrace, there he saw his sister basking in the sun. Her body suntanned from sunbathing herself for hours from excessive exposure to the sun and its radiance. The summer sublime with its gloriousness.

The brother admired the beauty of his curvaceous sister. The teenager growing up precocious and sophisticated.

Jennifer lying gracefully on the sun-lounger had gazed up at her brother standing in front of her. Jennifer looked at her brother's glum expression.

"What on earth is the matter?" asked sister.

"I am a librarian. There are no prospects," grumbled brother.

"Well. I am a poor Fifth Year," exaggerated sister.

In the cool breeze, Christopher smelled Jennifer's suntan lotion which she had rubbed over her body a few hours earlier. With self-love and self-admiration of herself. She had an obsessive narcissism for herself and for the pubertal transformation of her body. Jennifer was growing up. Her body transformed from puberty as a result from adolescence. Her big, full breasts of a pubescent girl. The gorgeousness of her bronze suntan ravishingly appealing to Christopher's senses.

"Today is exactly a year since my grandfather passed away," reminded brother.

Christopher's mournful sentiment moved his sister. It touched deeply his sister's heart.

"Oh! It is! Gosh! How time flies," replied sister.

Christopher saddened from thinking of his memories. The past last years of his grandfather's life alive!

"Grandfather said never give up on your dreams and to take care of his godson. That was Grandfather's last request. That was his last wish," recalled Christopher pensively.

Christopher looked at James, the little boy wearing shorts and long socks and lace-up shoes. Christopher was deeply fond of James.

"I loved Grandfather. I really did. He was like a father to me," said Jennifer fondly.

James got up from the garden chair. He fully completed the colouring of a page of a colouring book. He left the colouring book open on top of the garden table. James was excited. He was eager to show his colouring book. (At the last weekend Christopher and Jennifer paid their undivided attention to James colouring a page of his colouring book.)

He ran towards Christopher and his sister Jennifer.

"I've done it!" interrupted James rudely. James interrupting the conversation between them.

Christopher and Jennifer then paid attention to James who was rather impatient to show them both what he had coloured in his colouring book. They looked at James' colouring book on top the garden table. James proudly showed them. James pointed at it with pride. He had coloured it well. He used colouring pens. The colours were brilliant.

"Now colour the next page," prompted Jennifer.

James seemed quite half-hearted and unenthusiastic at colouring another page of his colouring book. James was uninterested in spending more time on colouring the next page of his colouring book. So far, the pages of his colouring book were beautifully coloured using colouring pens and pencils. James refused to do colouring of another page in his colouring book at present.

"I don't want to colour. Why don't you read to me? Oh Chris, why don't you?" moaned James.

Christopher was uninterested and unenthusiastic at reading to James now at this present time.

"No, James! Not now!" moaned Christopher.

Jennifer intervened. She agitated her brother.

"Go on! Read to James. You said you would. Didn't you. You haven't read to James for some considerable time," urged sister.

Christopher changed his mind. He agreed to read to James. He did realise he had to fulfil his promise and obligation to James, Grandfather's Godson!

"James. I will read to you," agreed Christopher.

At this present time, Christopher sat with James in the lounge. The dazzling sunshine radiant. It shone through the windows. The scorching sun from the drawn curtains and half-open windows. The lacy net curtains blown in the wind. The spacious lounge brightened up from the daylight and sunlight.

Christopher opened a children's book. There he continued to read on at a page from where a book marker was placed. He continued to read from a page of a book where his mother had last stopped reading at that page last night.

Christopher read out to James. He concentrated on reading.

After about half an hour later, Christopher strained his voice. His voice became hoarse. The sound of his strained voice become hoarser. Christopher struggled to read out to James aloud. His deep strained voice was hoarse.

Presently, Christopher stopped talking. Losing his will to read. He closed the book.

James moaned and grumbled at Christopher when he had stopped reading to take a break.

"James. I am sorry. I can't read on. I can't read anymore. I have strained my voice," apologised Christopher.

James was unsympathetic to Christopher who strained his deep voice. Christopher's voice sounded hoarse. James was rather more concerned at Christopher not reading to him. James grumbled at Christopher.

"Christopher, you're not reading to me. You said you would read to me."

Christopher was ashamed of neglecting James.

"Stay here. I'll get Jennifer," said Christopher hoarsely.

Christopher got up from the settee immediately, quickly going out of the lounge. He looked for his sister. His sister wasn't anywhere present downstairs. Christopher went upstairs. He went to his sister's bedroom. Standing outside the door. There he knocked loudly on her bedroom door.

"Come in," said sister.

Christopher entered in his sister's bedroom.

"Can you please read to James? I have strained my voice. I can't read anymore. Oh! Can you read to James please? I would really appreciate it is you can," said brother impatiently.

With grave concern, Jennifer listened to her brother's request.

"Alright," agreed sister. "I will read to James."

Together, Christopher and his sister went downstairs. They both rejoined James in the lounge. Christopher sat down on the armchair positioned in the corner of the room. His sister Jennifer sat beside James. Jennifer picked up a book from the table. She opened the book where the book marker was in the page of the book. This was where Jennifer decided to continue to read on. Jennifer sat down and read out aloud to James.

James listened intently to Jennifer reading out. He was intrigued by the story. Jennifer's soft voice was expressive and deeply emotional and clear.

Christopher soon lost interest in Jennifer reading out to James. He slipped out of the lounge. Jennifer was too engrossed in reading. She concentrated on reading well. At this time, Jennifer was unconcerned whether her brother was intent on neglecting James at present.

Christopher went out of the side-door. Going outdoors into the garden.

Christopher walked out onto the mowed lawn. It smelled of freshly cut grass. At present, his father spent time doing gardening. One of his father's interests was gardening.

Christopher's father stood by the edge of borders and flowerbeds. There from the rose bushes he tended to the roses which sparkled from raindrops.

Christopher became tired of walking around the garden. He decided to rest. He sat down on the garden chair somewhere in the garden. He rested lazily. He sweltered from the blazing sun shining.

Christopher sweated and dehydrated from the glare. Christopher was blinded by the radiant sunrays. He closed his eyes while sitting on an uncomfortable garden chair.

Quite soon, Christopher became restless. He fidgeted. His legs shook and he tapped his feet. Christopher opened his eyes. He got up. Christopher picked up the garden chair. Going forwards, he moved it further down the garden. He put it down. He sat down on the garden chair again. In boredom, he daydreamed. Christopher was engrossed in daydreaming. The daydreamer fantasised of having ecstasies!

With realisation, he became quite familiar with regarding everything else on his mind. Christopher had awareness of his surroundings. Suddenly he heard voices in the garden. Jennifer and her father engaged in a conversation.

Christopher was distracted hearing them clipping with both using shears. Christopher got up from the garden chair. He joined his sister who began to walk anywhere around the garden. Jennifer greatly admired the blooming roses as well as the blossoming rosebuds. Jennifer saw everywhere all around the garden many rose bushes with prickly thorns as well as all the beautiful deep colours of all the roses. Jennifer sniffed at the scent of the roses in the breezy freshness of the air. She took great delight in the rose-scented air. Smelling the natural scent of the roses. Admiring the natural gloriousness of it. Jennifer walked around the garden while looking at all the various colours of the roses and the large number of rose bushes surrounding the garden everywhere. The breathtaking sight of all the sublime roses took her breath away.

As Jennifer walked on the lawn, she almost trod on a pitchfork lying on the grass accidently. The dangerous garden tool could have caused a nasty accident.

Christopher reacted spontaneously by picking up the pitchfork from the lawn. He lost grip of the handle of the pitchfork as his sister in anger, retaliation and from a reflex and spontaneous reaction, snatched it from her brother's grasp.

Jennifer with such strength threw the pitchfork at the garden fence. Over there was a loud noise as the wood split due to impact. A thud! The wooden fence damaged as it splintered the wood.

"Bloody thing!" shouted Jennifer.

"Are you alright? Are you hurt?" asked brother.

"I could have had a bad accident," yelled Jennifer.

"You're not hurt?" asked brother.

"No, thank goodness!" gasped sister.

Christopher's tone of voice was affectionate.

"Thank God you're alright!"

Christopher, showing concern for his sister, reached out and touched her affectionately.

Christopher moved forwards towards the garden fence. At once, the father had stopped pruning the roses. In a hurry, he came up to his son and daughter. With concern, the father wondered what had happened!

Christopher retrieved the pitchfork. It had a dent in it.

In a temper, Jennifer stormed off back indoors, closing the door behind her.

Showing concern for his daughter, the worried father wondered what the reason for his daughter's tantrum was.

"What happened?" wondered Father. "Why did Jennifer go?"

Christopher responded, "Jennifer nearly had an accident. She almost trod on a pitchfork on the ground. Thank goodness my sister didn't. Jennifer does have a bad temper. My sister ought to control it," explained Christopher.

Christopher had unexplained yet Jennifer's behavioural problems. Her tantrums!

The father and his son together went towards the garden shed at the bottom of the garden. He put the pitchfork inside the shed. All the different garden tools in there were stored in neat order.

Christopher closed the shed door. He put a padlock on the shed door. With a padlock key, Christopher turned the lock in the padlock.

Going back, Christopher and his father went indoors.

At this present time, Christopher and James sat together in the living room. They both waited for James' mother to call at the house to come to pick up her son.

Christopher spoke highly of James' enthusiastic interest in books.

"You are a bookworm and are fine at reading. It's really impressive. Tell me, how on earth do you read so many books? I am impressed. There are too many titles to choose from," praised Christopher.

They both stopped talking as soon as they were disturbed by the doorbell which rang. The sound of the chimes resounded.

Christopher and James both went to the front door. At once, Christopher answered the front door, expecting Mary's arrival. The parent arrived at the house to pick up her son James to drive him home.

Christopher stepped out of the house. He stood on the doorstep, smiling and waving goodbye while watching Mary and her son get in the car.

Mary drove off out of the drive. With Mary's foot pressing down on the accelerator, the car accelerated down the long road. Mary drove to get home.

Christopher went inside the terraced house with a terraced roof. He closed the front door. Christopher went back into the living room where he spent moments alone by himself. He stood and admired a portrait of his great-grandmother. The great-grandmother stood gracefully in the background wearing a gown. The great-grandmother stood while posing in a natural elegant manner. Her expression, in particular her nonchalance, the lady's great beauty had a prepossessing attraction!

Christopher walked out of the living room, avoiding his parents and the company of their friends who had just come in. His parents had invited their friends to their house.

Christopher in anticipation, expecting guests, had smiled at them. He walked off in a hurry. He felt faint while going upstairs. He also felt sleepy, languorous, and tired. His heart beat faster and faster. His blood pulsated in his veins.

He went to his bedroom. He stayed in his bedroom. He enjoyed the quietness of being alone by himself. He lay down on his bed. He rested for hours. He recuperated since that time.

He woke up when the alarm clock rang at 10 p.m. He stretched out to the bedside table. He switched off the alarm clock. He got up from his bed. He got dressed. He smartened up. He went downstairs. He went into the kitchen. He put on the kettle. He made himself a cup of tea. Going into the lounge, Christopher relaxed while sitting in the cosy lounge.

After relaxing in silence for a quarter of an hour, he switched on the television. As time drew near, the classic film started. Christopher watched the suspenseful film. He was engrossed in the suspense of the heroine. It probably was one of his most favourite films. Certainly, it was one of the best films he had ever seen in his life!

That night may have been one of Christopher's best nights of his life! (That midsummer in comparison to past summers was wonderfully unforgettable . . .)

Christopher was feeling pretty emotional and tearful from watching the thriller.

After the film ended, Christopher went to bed in the early hours of the morning. At the first light of dawn, he awoke up from his deep sleep. He roused from his sleep. At that time of dawn, he heard the beautiful dawn chorus.

***

On Sunday afternoon, Christopher his parents and Jennifer, his sister, enjoyed a picnic at a beauty spot. (The family's last picnic together was at a picnic site last summer.)

They all used to come to this haunt when they were youngsters. Grandfather used to bring them all here after a short summer drive.

By the trees, they all sat down in the shade and together they ate their picnic food. Cooling down in a shady spot. The foursome enjoying their privacy together while sharing their food with one another. Two of them relished the delicacies.

"It hasn't changed much over here!" munched Mother.

"I used to remember when my father brought me here," said Father pensively.

Jennifer daydreamed while lying down gracefully on the ground. Jennifer twirled her finger around the strands of her hair. Her locks had highlights. She romanticised dreamily.

"I do really love it here. This happens to be one of my most favourite places. I used to come down here when I was a child," nibbled Jennifer.

Christopher marvelled at the beauty spot. He took joy from the quietude.

"It's really quiet and peaceful here. It makes such a change. At work, you're either overworked or you have no privacy being at home. Coming here is great. It's a place to relax."

"Grandfather loved it here. It used to be his favourite place," remarked Mother.

"He did indeed love this place. My grandfather used to come here with Annabelle. Of course, the old photos do bring back memories," said Christopher wistfully.

Jennifer remembered the past.

"Our grandfather will always be in our hearts. He is forever in our memories. We shan't ever forget Grandfather," said Jennifer sadly.

"As long as we shall live. We shall always remember our grandfather," gestured Mother.

"Father Christmas lives on. His legacy lives on forever," mourned Father.

Christopher recalled every memorable Christmas in the past. He reflected on Christmas with his family and the great joys of Christmas and seasonal bliss as well. In tribute, he remembered Father Christmas with such great fondness. (Christopher was one of the lucky children who did receive a gift from Santa Claus. At the time, he was the happiest boy at Christmas!)

"Christmas will never ever be the same again without Grandfather. It has lost its Christmassy magic," said Christopher unashamedly.

"Federick loved Spain. That's where his heart was. He did desire the señorita!" recalled Father.

Christopher and Jennifer got up from the ground. They both went out into the fields where Christopher picked up a tennis ball and threw it hard to his sister to catch it. Jennifer caught it with ease and threw it back.

Standing a short distance away from each other, Christopher and Jennifer kept on throwing a tennis ball to each other. Every time,

Christopher kept dropping the tennis ball, while Jennifer caught it well with such ease. Jennifer caught the tennis ball effortlessly. Jennifer was skilful at netball. Her skills evident from her footwork. Jennifer's reflexes were spontaneous.

Christopher, a spoilsport, threw a new tennis ball hard over his sister's head deliberately.

Jennifer reacted by jumping high to try and catch it. At this time, Jennifer was unable to catch it.

Christopher smirked at his sister as she failed and struggled to catch it.

Jennifer and Christopher played catch together. They both enjoyed playing. They threw the tennis ball and caught it most times.

Christopher kept dropping the tennis ball. Christopher had failed to catch the tennis ball on many times.

Jennifer was a good catch. Jennifer was very good at netball.

Christopher was embarrassed and humiliated at dropping his catch. He enervated at playing catch. He soon got tired from exertion. Christopher perspired from the radiance of the sun shining.

As soon as Christopher got tired of playing catch, he walked away from his sister. Approaching the fields further and further on, Christopher stopped there somewhere. He waited for his sister who lagged behind to catch up. From there they walked together back to the beauty spot. As they reached the trees in the distance, their father was waiting for them to walk back together to the shady spot.

The father wasted no time in using his camera. He took a photograph of his photogenic daughter.

Jennifer, in eager anticipation, had posed naturally by standing near a tree in the shade, holding her hat down firmly on her head.

Jennifer did another pose. Jennifer shook her hair. It was so naturally beautiful! With graceful elegance, she moved position again as she struck an attitude.

"Go on! Take a picture of me. Wouldn't you say I am photographic material?" said Jennifer boastfully.

Her father gestured to his daughter standing in the shade under a tree. Christopher in a calm mood. He watched Jennifer pose naturally in a lady-like fashion. She looked rather beautiful wearing her dress. She twirled an umbrella around gracefully. Christopher encouraged his father to take photographs of Jennifer. His beloved daughter!

At first, her father disapproved of his daughter's arrogance and pretentiousness. Jennifer smiled too much and pouted her lips. Her father disliked Jennifer's girlish poses. He objected to his daughter's posing. Jennifer now posed in a different manner. Her natural poses became like a model's!

That day, the father ended up taking rather fine photographs of his beloved daughter. After their father had finished taking photographs, they all sat down in the shade again under the shady trees. From there cooling down from the breeze and in the shade. The sunless spot darker and cooler in the shade.

Christopher and Jennifer and their parents took their time to relax in the shade. They spent about an hour longer over here. They all admired the natural scenery of the surroundings. Enjoying the peace and quiet as well as the solitude. They enjoyed their time of leisure and recreation. They all relaxed together in the coolest spot.

The sun shone down. It made shining reflections there in the shadows by the trees and everywhere else in the playing fields area. The radiant light reflected in the shadows.

After an hour, time passed. Jennifer and her mother cleared up and neatly packed everything away in wicker baskets.

The enjoyable picnic was a treat. On their day out, having a picnic was pretty delightful!

Jennifer and her mother carried their wicker baskets. They walked together quite a way back to the car park. In the daytime there were only a few cars parked in the car park at that time of day.

Michael opened the hatchback door. His teenage daughter and wife each put their wicker basket inside the boot.

They all got into the hatchback.

Michael turned an ignition to start the engine. Michael drove away back home late that summer afternoon. The heat was sweltering. Today's weather was hot and sunny. The air itself sultry.

Today the summer drive back home was far quicker than when they had first arrived to get here to the picnic area.

11

Sweet Innocence

One hot sunny day Christopher drove to Anne's house. He parked his car in the front drive. He got out of his car. He spruced himself up. He walked up to the front door. He intended to pick up his sister at the arranged time which they had previously agreed between them. Apparently, it was a mutual arrangement between brother and sister.

Christopher stood outside the front door. He hesitated to ring the doorbell as he could hear the sound of the grand piano being played. It resounded in the blowing wind. Christopher listened admiringly to the piece. Admiring the pianist playing. After a few minutes of listening to the music, Christopher used a door knocker to knock on the front door about three times.

Mrs Lowe, Anne's mother, answered the front door. Christopher entered the house. Mrs Lowe, expecting Christopher greeted and welcomed him. Christopher was charmed by Mrs Lowe's engaging irresistibleness. He smiled at Mrs Lowe. He followed Mrs Lowe into the living room. At present her daughter Anne was playing the grand piano. It was her regular practice. Christopher stood near the grand piano and the seated pianist who presided at the grand piano. He admired Anne playing the piano well. The musician avant-garde.

Anne had been distracted as Christopher entered the living room with her mother. Despite the distraction, Anne somehow managed to concentrate on her practice regardless.

Mrs Lowe and Christopher went past the pianist and grand piano where the drapes lay beautifully over it.

"Jennifer is out in the garden," said Mrs Lowe politely.

Christopher followed Mrs Lowe who led him away towards outdoors. Going outside in the garden. They went out to the poolside. Mrs Lowe called out to Jennifer who ignored her. Jennifer treated Mrs Lowe with complete disregard. At this present time Jennifer swam away from the others in the swimming pool. Jennifer reached a far corner of the swimming pool. Jennifer stayed at a corner of the swimming pool. She stood still. She remained motionless at the claustrophobic corner, suffering from claustrophobia. She gasped out. She spent moments standing still there in a corner.

She took her time to recover, to thus regain her breath. Jennifer had not noticed her brother at being present there. She was unaware of her brother's presence (with Jennifer's mind deep in thought, Jennifer had completely forgotten about her brother who had come all this way just to pick her up.)

Christopher was standing along the poolside watching all the girls swimming together gracefully in the swimming pool. Their wet tanned bodies glistening in the sun-reflected water.

Christopher gaped at four of the girls swimming. Christopher was stunned, admiring the teenage virgins' purity and their beauty.

Christopher became rather impatient waiting for his sister to get out of the swimming pool. In disobedience Jennifer stayed longer in the swimming pool without really having any intention to get out. She still wanted to stay in the company of her friends.

Mrs Lowe stepped forward towards the edge of the swimming pool, keeping her balance, moving steadily. Mrs Lowe losing her patience called out again to Jennifer.

"Jennifer. Get out! Your brother is here to pick you up."

Jennifer was unresponsive as she unanswered. Jennifer obeyed Mrs Lowe this time. Jennifer swam to the other end of the swimming pool. Everywhere there were girls' bodies in the ripple of the water. Jennifer swam away from those swimming towards her. Jennifer had lack of space to move about freely when she tried to swim away. As a result, from claustrophobia Jennifer could not move about any further or swim anywhere else.

From directional positions their bodies remained in claustrophobic restricted space from deep water. From the deep end those ones, swimmers, occupied spots there and also over there at a shallow end. The shallowness there less and less deep. In the swimming pool. The depths much further on down there. The deep water remained deeper and the deepest.

Jennifer reached the very end of the swimming pool. She quickly got out of the swimming pool. From Jennifer glistening drops of water were dripping from her suntanned body. Jennifer climbed up the steps to get out. From the radiance of the sun, the sunlight reflected on the shiny steps which shone in the blaze.

At present, Christopher stood near the steps. Christopher waited for his sister.

"It's time to go," said brother impatiently.

Jennifer stood with drops of water dripping from her body and wet hair. She put on her bathrobe.

"I'll get dressed. I won't be long," gasped sister.

"Do hurry up," said brother impatiently.

Christopher and Jennifer went back indoors. Christopher came into the sitting room. He sat down on the armchair. During that time, he waited for his sister.

In the bathroom Jennifer showered and dressed. She wore different clothes. She put on a beautiful gown. Jennifer came out of the steamed-up bathroom. She went down the corridor. She went into a bedroom. She used the same bedroom where she had spent last night. Jennifer looked in the dressing table mirror. Jennifer applied her make-up. Jennifer had a narcissistic obsessiveness for herself.

***

A short time later, Jennifer rejoined her brother in the sitting room. Christopher was amused at how his sister again appeared to be dressed up, masquerading as her great-grandmother!

His theatrical sister had dressed up in the exact same way as her great-grandmother. Jennifer even looked like her great-grandmother.

As Christopher and Jennifer went out of the sitting room, they saw Mark, Anne's older brother, approaching them. Mark gaped at Jennifer. Mark thought Jennifer looked beautiful and glamorous.

Mark was amazed at Jennifer, how miraculously she'd transformed into the same likeness of her great-grandmother!

Mark took notice of Jennifer's change of identity as well as her appearance and difference in her image!

Jennifer looked unrecognisable dressed up. Mark unrecognised Jennifer dressed up. Jennifer's applied make-up and beautiful hairstyle was unusually different this time. For most of the time it was customary, her make-up, hair and her fashion obsession.

Christopher had noticed the complete difference and transformation in his sister's appearance as she masqueraded as her great-grandmother.

"Aren't you going to show me out?" smiled Jennifer.

Touching Jennifer, Mark was courteous again. Mark held Jennifer's arm as they both waled together towards the front door. At present, Christopher felt tired and lethargic. He lagged behind the pair as they both hurried out of the house. Mark held tightly to Jennifer's arm as they went together to the car parked in the drive. There they found Anne and her friends already waiting for them to come outside.

Christopher and his sister both got into the car parked in the drive for all this time to the afternoon. At this departure time, Anne and the rest of Jennifer's friends reappeared with Anne's other friends standing together in the drive.

Watching the car go past. They all waved goodbye to Jennifer, their friend.

Jennifer seemed to be quite upset and passionately emotional! Was Jennifer elated too from dressing up as her great-grandmother?

Jennifer received admiration from all her friends who cheered.

Christopher concentrating on his driving had unnoticed his sister's deep emotion. It was an emotional farewell and a quick departure.

They all moved out of the road, from oncoming cars approaching, some of them standing on the kerb while watching. The others went back into the drive of the house. They all had revered Jennifer. Admiring and adoring Jennifer. An enigma! The enigmatic passenger being driven home.

12

The Thunderstorm

One Saturday morning, Christopher sat down on the armchair, relaxing in comfort, sitting in a restful position, whilst his sister was fidgety, restless and fearful. Christopher was alarmed at his troubled sister.

"What's the matter?" asked Christopher.

Jennifer hesitated as she responded.

"My friend's house was burgled last night!"

Christopher showed grave concern for his afraid sister.

"Aren't you going to tell me what happened?"

"My friend Julie dined out with her family at a restaurant. Then when they got back, they found that their house had been burgled. The French windows in the extension were broken into and all the bedrooms were ransacked. All of Julie's mother's jewellery has been stolen," added Jennifer.

Christopher got up from the armchair. He walked over to the settee. He sat down next to his sister. He put his arms around her. He comforted her, showing his love.

"Don't be afraid!"

"All my mum's valuables gone!" mumbled Jennifer.

Christopher tried to comfort his sister. He was unable to console her. Jennifer was feeling apprehensive about the house being unsafe. Jennifer became paranoid. Jennifer was suffering from paranoia.

"Let's check the locks, the doors and the windows," said Jennifer apprehensively.

Christopher thought it was wise and sensible to take precautions.

Frantically they went together around the house. They both took the time to double-check all the locks on the windows and doors were locked.

They took measures to double-check again and again every lock on every window and door.

Christopher also warned his sister against wearing too much jewellery. He cautioned his sister, reminding her of the common dangers.

"Do take those rings off your fingers and don't wear too much of anything else. I don't want you to get robbed. This is serious. Do take note of what I do have to say. I am concerned for your safety."

Jennifer usually disobedient. She pleased herself. Jennifer admitted she was unashamed of her habitual obsession.

"I do love jewellery. You know for a fact I do. I can't stop wearing it. It's an obsession of mine," said Jennifer unashamedly.

"Why don't you put some of it in the safe?" suggested Christopher.

"That's really sensible," replied Jennifer.

Christopher and Jennifer came out of the living room. They went into the study.

In Christopher's mind, he remembered the combination. Christopher entered the combination of the safe to open it. Jennifer took her rings from her fingers. Jennifer gave a few rings of hers to her brother who then put Jennifer's jewellery into a jewellery box. He closed the safe.

"What's the combination?" asked sister.

Christopher told his sister the combination.

Jennifer required the disclosure. Jennifer memorised it. She took note of it, writing it down at the back of her pocket diary.

Jennifer stayed downstairs whilst Christopher went upstairs to his bedroom. He went to bed to get a rest.

About a few hours later, Christopher came back downstairs. He went in the study, locking the study door behind him. Christopher walked to the safe at the front of the study. In his mind he memorised the combination. He entered again the combination. He opened the safe door. He took out a jewellery box to check on Jennifer's jewellery: a diamond ruby ring, a platinum ring and a sapphire diamond ring set with a cluster of diamonds. The diamonds sparkling. Christopher put everything back into the jewellery box. He closed the lid.

The safe also contained petty cash and money, banknotes, valuable documents and other valuables.

Christopher counted his money. He found that some of the banknotes had been stolen!

He double-checked the banknotes, counting up his banknotes again. He calculated the full amount. Christopher was maddened at his money being stolen!

Christopher burst into the living room to confront his sister. Christopher stood and faced his sister. He yelled.

"Did you take my money? You have taken my money!" accused brother.

Jennifer unresisted her temptation to steal her brother's money. With her brother confronting her, accusing his sister and making false allegations against her. Jennifer denied her brother's accusation.

"I haven't taken your bloody money! Why don't you take a look in my handbag? That's all the money that I have."

Christopher thought his sister lied! Christopher could not prove that his sister was a liar and a thief!

Christopher opened his sister's leather handbag. He took out a purse. He opened it. He counted up the money. He was ashamed of himself for accusing his sister of theft. He put back the old banknotes in her purse. He closed it and put it back in her handbag. Christopher zipped up Jennifer's handbag.

"I know. Let's go upstairs and take a look at the neighbourhood," suggested Christopher.

Christopher took his sister to his bedroom. He handed the binoculars to his sister. Jennifer stood by the window. She drew back the net curtain. She looked through the binoculars. She adjusted the lens. The focus of the lens was clear and close-up.

Christopher was looking through the telescope. Christopher adjusted the lens. They both had a look through the telescope. They watched the neighbourhood for a short time. They both took notice of everything, including the vicinity.

They were both vigilant at looking out of the telescope. From their observations, there were nothing suspicious to report.

"See? There's nothing to be alarmed of. The neighbours are all law-abiding citizens. There haven't been any break-ins around here. It's a middle-class neighbourhood and it's quiet. A safe place," reassured brother.

Jennifer agreed. "Yes. It is quiet and safe around here."

Jennifer was afraid and fearful. Jennifer had fears of a teenager growing up.

"I am scared to stay alone at night. Do I really have a choice in the matter?"

"Let's go out into the garden and double-check anyway," said brother.

Christopher and Jennifer went out into the garden. They both took a look at the garden fence surrounding the whole garden. They took notice of the neighbours' houses, including the elevation, extension, conservatory and roofs.

"Without doubt it's safe here," said Jennifer assuredly.

"Yes. All peaceful and quiet."

They both went back indoors.

Jennifer spent time as she double-checked the locks on the doors and windows again. Everywhere was locked. Jennifer had no cause for concern nor did her brother who double-checked the doors and windows again to his approval.

"My parents have gone away for the weekend. I shall be alone at night," shuddered sister.

Christopher was concerned for his sister. He had no intention of leaving her alone at home.

"I'll stay with you tonight. Don't be afraid," reassured brother.

"So, you don't expect me to stay here alone. Do you?" shrugged sister.

The Shadow of the Daughter's Ring

"Our mom is a little neglectful at times. It's not her fault. It's just the way she is."

"I love my mom. I am expecting her to check up on me," said Jennifer.

"You're safe here at home. You're protected here. No burglar can get in," said brother assuredly.

Jennifer shuddered. "Are you sure? I don't want an intruder to kill me!"

Christopher reassured his sister again. Jennifer's fear subsided.

"Don't worry. You are safe here. Don't be afraid."

"I am going to lie down and rest," groaned Jennifer.

Jennifer felt tired, lethargic and sleepy. Jennifer went upstairs to her bedroom to get some rest.

Christopher stayed downstairs in the lounge. Using a remote control he switched on the television. He got bored as he flicked through the channels. He was uninterested in watching any of the programmes on television. With a remote-control Christopher pressed a button. Christopher switched off the television. He put it on the table.

Christopher rested his head on a cushion. He relaxed sitting on the settee. He heard outside the wind blowing and the sound of the leaves rustling in the trees.

Christopher nodded off.

A long time later, Christopher woke up when his sister awoke him.

"Supper is ready," said sister loudly.

Christopher was appreciative of his sister cooking for him. Christopher had not eaten since breakfast. He appreciated that his sister took time to cook for him. He could smell the food cooking and the aroma.

Christopher sat down at the dining table. He ate his supper and drank a glassful of orange juice.

"It's nice. Aren't you going to eat?" asked brother.

Jennifer had a lack of appetite.

"No. I'm not hungry. I'll eat later."

After Christopher had eaten his supper, he joined his sister in the sitting room. The brother and sister stood together and looked out of the windows, observing everything in sight. They saw a housewife pushing a pram along the pavement and a cyclist going down the road and a girl taking a dog for a walk around the block.

Christopher and Jennifer both sat down together on the settee. They conversed for some time. It was a reminder of security and prevention of crime. After they had stayed up longer, they both went to bed at night-time.

During the night, there was a terrifying thunderstorm.

Suddenly Christopher woke up when he heard the sound of glass shattering. He got up. He put on his slippers and went downstairs He came into the kitchen. He picked up a torch with a torch strap hanging behind the door.

Christopher turned around while facing his sister who stood by the side door. Jennifer held a torch. The dazzling torchlight shone in the pitch-darkness.

"What was that?" said Jennifer apprehensively.

They were both terrified of the storm.

Christopher unbolted the side door. They both went outside into the garden. They both held their torches. The bright torchlight shining in the pitch-dark.

They both reached the greenhouse which was situated near the rear of the garage. Christopher and Jennifer shone their torches ahead. They saw that a tree from the next-door neighbour's garden had fallen on the greenhouse. The greenhouse had collapsed.

They both trod carefully on the lawn. Everywhere there were shattered panes of glass and debris all over the lawn. Christopher and Jennifer were both vigilant, treading carefully on the lawn. Christopher held his sister's arm, stopping her from stepping forward. Christopher holding her back.

They both shone their torches at the shattered greenhouse. From the shining torch beam, they had awareness of the extensive damage caused by the storm.

"Watch out! Don't go any further. Watch out for broken glass," warned Christopher.

The wind was howling. They were frightened of the thunderstorm. Jennifer was trembling with fear.

They both hurried back in the side door. Christopher closed the side door. He bolted the door. They both went back to bed. They both had insomnia. The storm kept them awake. Jennifer, an insomniac, was terrified of the thunderstorm. The insomnious teenager twisted and turned in bed. Jennifer changed and moved positions. Jennifer had a sleepless night.

13

The Godson

During the evening, Christopher sat next to James at the dining table. On top, it was piled up with books. At this time James was enthusiastic and interested in spending time reading. (James usually read when his mother dropped him off at Jennifer's house. Occasionally, Jennifer, a babysitter, did babysit.)

James occupied his time as usual. He was engrossed in looking at a storybook with beautiful colourful pictures.

Christopher took a paperback from a pile of books. James became distracted as Christopher flicked through a novelette, admiring the illustrations. (It featured the different atmospheric sceneries and great characters.)

"You will love this one. You should read it," recommended Christopher.

James glanced up. "Which one is that?"

Christopher told James the title of the book and the name of the author.

"I would like to read it," replied James.

"It's your age group. I recommend it," said Christopher.

"Are you reading any spooky ones? They give me the creeps," asked Christopher.

James lifted up the storybook. He took a closer look at it.

"I like to read comics," said James.

"Do you still sleep with the lights on?" asked Christopher.

In response, James responded, "I used to be scared of the dark. I put on a lamp."

"Are you scared of thunderstorms?" asked Christopher.

"I can't sleep. I am scared," mumbled James.

"These storms do scare the hell out of me too," admitted Christopher.

"My mum comes and tucks me in and kisses me goodnight."

"Have you read any of these books?" asked Christopher.

James knocked a pile of books down. A few books fell off the dining table onto the carpet.

Christopher bent down and picked up a few books from the carpet. He stacked up the pile of books.

James put the storybook back down on the dining table. The shiny, polished dining table gleamed.

James pointed to his most favourite storybook. "I like Father Christmas."

"That's out of season. We're in mid-summer," said Christopher.

"I miss Santa. I never did have the chance to say my goodbye!" said James mournfully.

"Federick loved you very much. He was fond of you. You were his favourite child," remarked Christopher.

Christopher and James went outside in the garden. They both imagined a snowy Christmas. They remembered the past. They relived their experiences. They both had wonderful Christmassy memories of Father Christmas!

They stopped as they came towards a border and beyond a flowerbed. James stood still with Christopher standing behind him.

"Close your eyes."

The little boy obeyed and closed his eyes. Christopher twirled James around and around. James became dizzy at being spun around and around. James becoming dizzier from spinning around and around. James felt dizzy from spinning in circles. He spun around and around while being unaware of his surroundings. He dizzied. James stopped spinning. He stood still on his feet. He kept his balance. He somehow stayed on his feet. He almost did fall over.

James opened his eyes. He felt dizzy and unsteady on his feet. James imagined Father Christmas entertaining dwarves, elves and children.

All the grown-ups were forbidden in this magical enchanted land.

Father Christmas sat on his sled. He gave out gifts to all the excited children.

"Come, children! Come all! Let me tell you a story."

The children gathered around. They listened to Father Christmas telling them a story. They listened with great joy. They were amused at Father Christmas's storytelling. Santa's voice resounded in the deep forest.

James' reverie ended from the distraction. Suddenly, from a treetop, birds fluttered before the birds flew away.

Christopher and James staggered before going back indoors. James went up to bed.

Christopher expected to meet his sister Jennifer later that night. His sister stood and looked at herself in the mirror and then paraded ostentatiously in front of her brother wearing her new clothes. Her fashion like that of a secretary. A white blouse, jacket, slinky black skirt, black stockings and black shoes. Jennifer looked lovely from being dressed up.

She told her brother that she was preparing for the next morning by attending an interview at Personnel, at a department store.

"I've got an interview tomorrow. It's a sales assistant position. I do hope I get it," said sister optimistically.

"I really do hope you get the job," said brother.

Christopher and Jennifer went walking together towards the portrait hanging on the wall opposite. The lights reflected on the portrait.

Going ahead in the direction facing them where there was the wall straight opposite, they stood still together while looking at the portrait, admiring the portrait.

"You are a beauty! Just like your great-grandmother!" complimented brother.

14: The Rosary

In the conservatory, the sun shone through the glass windows. Christopher and Jennifer sat facing each other, dehydrating and sweating in the heat. Jennifer sat on a wicker chair. She fanned herself, cooling herself down. Jennifer got tired of fanning herself. She put the fan down on the ground. She took out from her pocket a rosary. She held in her hand a dangling rosary.

Christopher sweltered in the blazing sun. The radiant sunshine was blinding and dazzling. The scorching sunrays shone through the glass-paned windows. The conservatory sweltering. The conservatory full of plants and houseplants in pots everywhere.

Christopher used a bottle opener. He removed a cap off the beer bottle. He poured the bottle of beer into a glass, the froth spilling over the glass.

Christopher indulged in another glassful of beer. He became tipsier from drinking.

Jennifer was pessimistic about her future. She sulked.

"I just hope my life doesn't end up in a tragedy," said sister.

"Say your prayers. Be a good Catholic," advised brother.

"Now that I am a big girl, do you think I am still rebellious and stubborn?"

"You don't listen! You're stubborn! You still disobey," admonished brother.

"I have my reasons," said sister.

Christopher saw Jennifer's expression.

"Why the smirk?"

Christopher expected an explanation from his sister. Jennifer refused to comment. Jennifer had gained revenge. She heard a rumour that at least one of the bullies had been beaten up.

"What?"

"Is there anything you want to tell me?" asked brother.

Jennifer kept personal matters confidential.

"No comment."

Christopher noticed a difference in Jennifer's attitude.

"That's unlike you. You always talk to me about things."

"If you don't mind, I don't wish to talk about it. The least said about it, the better it is."

Christopher sensed a change in his sister's mood. Jennifer was placid, cheerful and unperturbed sitting in the radiant sunshine. Her sitting position comfortable, then, after a short time later, Jennifer uncrossed her legs gracefully. Jennifer moved position of her graceful legs. Jennifer marvelled at the glorious natural weather.

Christopher looked at his sister with such love. Jennifer shook her head. Her hairstyle looked exactly like her great-grandmother. Her hair so beautiful!

Christopher distinguished between his sister and his great-grandmother. Jennifer had the same likeness as her great-grandmother. Jennifer's resemblance like her great-grandmother.

Their father walked into the sun-blazing conservatory. The father interrupted his son and daughter talking.

"Jennifer. Are we ready to take photographs? You can add these to your portfolio."

"Most of my photos won't ever get looked at," said Jennifer negatively.

"These will. I assure you," assured Father. "These ones will be special."

Christopher encouraged his sister to get photographed at once.

"You should do it when you have the opportunity. Father has film for the camera. Now why don't you?"

Jennifer agreed to be photographed. She allowed her father to take photographs. Jennifer pleased herself as she had the opportunity to engage in obsessive narcissism. She had an obsession for fashion. It was a habitual obsessiveness. Jennifer had a tendency for exhibitionism. Jennifer got up and walked towards the other side of the conservatory. This spot in the conservatory was scorching hot in the sun.

Afterwards, Jennifer, Christopher and their father went out into the garden. They walked slowly to the flowerbeds. They smelled in the air the scent of roses.

Christopher picked one and gave it to the princess. Jennifer sniffed at the long-stemmed rose.

With quickness, the father liking his daughter's pose instantly reacted. A spontaneous reaction from the photographer.

"Don't move! Keep still! That's splendid. Out of my way, son!" gestured Father.

Christopher stood back immediately, allowing his father enough space to take photographs of his daughter. The father was absorbed in taking photographs. The pleased father was proud of his daughter. He hoped that his daughter would accomplish her objective as a teenage model. The father had high expectations of his daughter being a top fashion model.

The father finally took the last photographs of Jennifer sitting on a swing, swinging back and forth. All these fine photographs captured his daughter's teenage innocence and virginal pureness and Jennifer's girlhood fantasies!

Jennifer's expressions showed nonchalance as well as languor. Jennifer was cooly serene and beatific at doing her poses. Her elegant poses natural. Jennifer was so photogenic!

Since Jennifer's father divorced and got married again, Jennifer had become disturbed and a rather ambitious teenager. Jennifer bore a grudge with her father. Jennifer had intentions and an inclination to desert her father!

Christopher stood and looked at his sister swinging back and forth. The brother pushed his sister harder and harder on the swing a few times.

Jennifer raised her feet up, swinging faster and faster. Her long hair whipped up in the air. Her wind-swept hair blown.

Christopher watched his father take photographs of his daughter. Jennifer engaged in narcissistic exhibitionism. Christopher disliked Jennifer's provocative poses. He thought his sister's poses were too ostentatious and girlish. On one pose her childlike face looked pure angelic. On other poses Jennifer pouted her lips and her natural smile angelica.

The father was pleased with his daughter. He was very proud of his daughter. The father was satisfied with his photographs he had taken of his daughter. He put a camera strap to hang around his neck.

The father stayed outside in the garden with his son. His daughter went back indoors. Quickly, Jennifer went to her bedroom. Apparently, Jennifer was obsessed with her photographs taken. Jennifer spent time alone in her bedroom. She stood by the wardrobe. She engaged in narcissistic obsessiveness by looking at the reflections of herself in the wardrobe mirrors.

Christopher sat down on the swings. He remained still seated.

"My sister is happier. Isn't it good?"

Michael lit up a cigarette. He smoked.

"Jennifer at last has found something she likes doing. I am pleased."

"At wedding shoots my sister models as a bridesmaid. Isn't that marvellous? I do hope my sister gets more work," said Christopher proudly.

"My daughter has a keen interest in being a fashion model," smoked father.

"We are proud of our Jennifer," said Christopher joyously.

Jennifer came back downstairs and went out in the garden again.

Christopher became distracted as his sister called out to him. Christopher watched Jennifer coming.

Jennifer's sparkling brooch dazzling in the radiant sunlight. Jennifer looked smart in her new clothes, even when dressed casually. As Jennifer came nearer towards Christopher, he caught sight of Jennifer's jewel which sparkled. (On Jennifer's last birthday, her mother had given her daughter jewellery. It possessed sentimental value!)

Michael picked up a newspaper from the garden table. He sat down on the garden chair. From the newspaper the supplement dropped out of it.

"What's the point of it? We can't afford it," said son.

"Maybe one day we'll be able to afford our dream house. It's my wife's dream," said Father.

Jennifer fantasised her dream.

"When I get older, I want to own my own big house with a big garden," said Jennifer dreamily.

"You will marry a millionaire," predicted brother.

Jennifer stood near her father sitting at the garden table and her brother standing beside his father. Jennifer twirled a finger around her thick strands of hair.

"I wish I will meet Prince Charming and fall in love!" romanticised Jennifer.

As brother felt possessive of his sister, Christopher disapproved of Jennifer's romantic fantasies and marriage expectations!

Suddenly a doorbell rang. Anne and her band came through the house and came out into the back garden.

Anne switched on a stereo. She pressed the cassette recorder. The music blared out. The members of the band performed together. Anne on lead vocals and the rest of the band did backing vocals.

Christopher, father and sister watched the group perform. They approve of the recording. All of them clapping when finally, the track ended.

Some of the neighbours watched and looked on in amazement. To other neighbours watching, the disturbance was a nuisance.

15

Riding Accident

On another day Christopher drove to Anne's house. He parked his car in the driveway where there were others parked.

Christopher got out of his car. He walked towards the house to the front door. Standing by the front door, Christopher heard laughter and music. He stood still and rang the doorbell. He waited expectantly for his sister to come out of the house. His sister kissed and said goodbye to all her friends.

Christopher picked up his sister and drove home. Jennifer had declined to stay the night. Her friend Anne had invited Jennifer to spend the night at her house. Jennifer was unwilling to help in the cleaning up of the house and doing chores tomorrow morning.

Sometime later, at his parent's house, brother and sister relaxed together for hours and hours. They both perspired in the warm room, then cooled down from a draught. The wind blown through an open window.

Jennifer regretted leaving Anne's party early. Her departure was arranged.

"Why did I have to leave so soon? I know it was getting late. It was such a happy house. There's happiness and merriment. I tell you; you won't find that anywhere else. Also, there's love! So much love," moaned Jennifer.

"I was tempted to go in myself. It seemed a good party," said brother honestly.

Jennifer clicked her fingers.

"You missed dances. You missed the music."

"Everyone loved you! They really did," remarked brother.

"So, they did. I loved them too. It was an enjoyable party. I had a good time," answered sister.

"Did Anne perform?" asked Christopher.

"Oh yes! Anne did perform. It was the highlight of the night. Everyone loved her and applauded. She sang beautifully on the night."

Something else on Jennifer's mind gave her cause for concern. Jennifer reflected on a recent burglary in a suburb.

"This may sound silly, but is their house easy to break in?"

"I am positive their house is safe. No harm will come to them. Besides, Anne's family is religious," replied brother.

Jennifer reflected on Anne's religious family.

"They are blessed. You can see the blessings."

Brother and sister passed time as they talked away. As soon as it was bedtime, Christopher left his fearful sister alone downstairs. He decided to go to bed. Christopher went into his bedroom. He got in his bed to get sleep.

Some minutes later his sister burst into his bedroom. Jennifer was afraid.

"Are you awake?" said sister apprehensively.

Christopher was still awake in bed. Christopher moved position of his body, turning over to face his sister who was standing near him.

"What on earth is the matter?"

Jennifer trembled with fear.

"I am scared."

"What are you scared about?" asked brother.

"Will the burglar break in?" said sister fearfully.

"Jennifer don't be afraid. You're safe," assured brother.

Jennifer had doubts about her personal safety.

"Am I safe?" said Jennifer doubtfully.

Christopher tried to reassure his doubtful sister again.

"Don't be afraid. Say your prayers!"

Jennifer shuddered. She was frightened.

"Am I safe? Is it safe?" said sister fearfully.

"If you are still scared, why don't you lock yourself in your bedroom?" advised brother.

Jennifer listened to her brother's advice.

"I'll do that," mumbled Jennifer.

"Now go! Let me sleep."

Jennifer left her brother. She went out of her brother's bedroom. Jennifer shut the bedroom door. She came in her bedroom. Jennifer was still petrified. She locked her bedroom door. Jennifer locked herself in her bedroom that night.

***

Christopher put on his sunglasses. He walked out onto the balcony. Standing looking from an angle, he saw down below Gerald's attractive wife and her voluptuous daughter lying down together at the edge of the swimming pool. The bodies of the mother and daughter suntanned.

Christopher just stood there looking. The husband got up from the sun-lounger. The husband joined his wife in the swimming pool. The husband and wife both swam together a length of the swimming pool. The husband and wife were both deeply in love!

The curvaceous daughter remained lying down by the poolside. Gina's graceful figure stretched out, with both her palms resting down on the ground. The heat blazing hot. It was sun-drenched.

Christopher felt lonely at being by himself up in his bedroom. He went out of his bedroom. Then went downstairs. He found his way out to get to the back garden. Christopher walked to the poolside. He lay down on a sun-lounger. He perspired in the blaze. The glare blinding. His armpits and body sweated. His half-unbuttoned shirt saturated with perspiration.

Christopher enjoyed his freedom and free time here at Gerald's house. His UK residence.

Christopher hoped Gina took an interest in him. Gina was seemingly uninterested at taking notice of Christopher. Christopher felt offended by Gina who ignored him.

Gina was lying down gracefully in a comfortable position. Gina took pleasure at sunning herself. Her tanned body becoming a darker tan from suntanning.

Gerald left his wife alone in the swimming pool. He got out of the swimming pool and climbed up the steps to get out of the swimming pool. Gerald's body dripped with drops of water. Gerald, a family friend, joined Christopher by the poolside. Gerald stood beside Christopher who was lying on the sun-lounger taking some comfort from relaxation.

"Do take a look at this. Do tell me what you think," said Gerald impatiently.

Christopher took it from Gerald. Christopher looked at a property magazine. He looked at the Spanish properties which were divided into different regions.

"These properties are really luxurious indeed. I like the ones in Deia in Mallorca best," remarked Christopher.

"Those ones actually are favourites among foreign buyers."

Christopher envied Gerald who was a professional property developer, a good friend of his father.

"We do value your opinions, your preferences," thanked Gerald.

"Our dream is to live in Mallorca, to own a villa," dreamed Christopher.

"Our business is to sell properties."

Christopher felt envious of how Mr and Mrs Tanner owned luxury properties abroad.

Gerald's wife stood and dried herself with a bath towel.

"That's a sweet dream. Maybe one day your dream will come true," patronised Lorna.

Christopher became desirous, jealous and miserable. He felt frustrated and humiliated at his desires being fantasies!

Christopher felt depressed, moody and unhappy. Now he had to leave Gerald's house.

Suddenly his sister came out to the poolside. Christopher watched his sister dive into the swimming pool. Jennifer swam gracefully in the water. Her wet tanned body, skin glistening in the water. Jennifer's suntan a glossy bronze. Jennifer swam a length of it. She reached the other end of the swimming pool.

Christopher despised how Jennifer gained all the undivided attention of Mr and Mrs Tanner and their daughter Gina and how everybody made a fuss over her!

"Our children will marry those who work in the industry," boasted wife.

Christopher got tired of Gerald and his wife's boasting. He was fed up of Mr and Mrs Tanner's arrogance.

Quickly Christopher got up from the sun-lounger. He walked to the other end of the swimming pool.

Jennifer swam nearer towards her brother standing by the edge of the swimming pool. Jennifer cried out at seeing her miserable and unhappy brother.

"Don't be sad!"

Jennifer reached out and stretched out her hand to her brother who leaned forward towards her. Christopher held tightly his sister's hand. Christopher became emotional and squeezed his sister's hand passionately. He let go of his sister's hand. Christopher hurried off. He said goodbye to Mr and Mrs Tanner. The husband and wife were lying on sun-loungers drinking an exotic cocktail. Mr and Mrs Tanner tried to persuade Christopher to stay longer at their house.

"Why don't you stay? You're welcome to stay. You're going so soon," said wife.

Appreciating their hospitality, Christopher thanked both Mr and Mrs Tanner.

"Thank you for having me."

Christopher ignored Gina. Gina was engaged in sunning herself further in the hot sun. Her body tanned.

Christopher left Mr and Mrs Tanner's house. He got in his car and drove off home.

**

Mr and Mrs Harvey invited the Staples family to Barnhurst at the weekend. At present, in the kitchen, Christopher and Jennifer sat at the dining table.

Both brother and sister enjoyed their time off respectively. The Staples stayed the weekend. Enjoying Mr and Mrs Harvey's hospitality. The host accommodated members of the Staples family.

"How have you found it? Are you having a good time?" asked brother.

Jennifer enjoyed oneself.

"I am actually having a really good time. Really, I am. Barnhurst is such a lovely place. It's great. The food is good. The people are nice and friendly. The stable girl is sweet. All the horses are beautiful. The countryside is so lovely. It's the finest things of life."

After brother and sister ate their lunch, they walked together down to the stables where a stable girl attended to a horse.

Christopher walked all the way to the fields while his sister accompanied her brother trotting on horseback.

Reaching the fields, Christopher and Jennifer came across other riders who were taking it in turns doing showjumping.

Christopher took the initiative and used a stopwatch. Christopher timed each of the other riders. One by one.

Two of the four showjumpers managed to get a clear round while the other two were eliminated at these stages of the round. Regarding their times, it was either slower or faster, despite having knocked down obstacles.

Now it was Helen's turn next. The showjumper somehow managed to get a clear round. The showjumper's current time was faster than theirs. The amateurish showjumpers had been eliminated at this stage of the round. These amateurs were bitterly disappointed.

Meanwhile, Jennifer on horseback waited to go next. Jennifer was tense when waiting her turn next. Jennifer had warmed up in equestrian preparation. The equestrienne did wish the showjumper all the best as Jennifer prepared and waited for her turn next. Going next, Jennifer was the last one to go.

The showjumper knocked an obstacle down while jumping over obstacles. At this stage Jennifer completed the course in a slower time.

Christopher declared Helen the winner at showjumping. Christopher announced the winning time. All the showjumpers and riders congratulated the horsewoman, potential showjumper champion material. The other showjumpers who participated in doing showjumping. These amateurish ones were subsequently eliminated earlier at the earliest stages of the round. These amateurs had congratulated the winner. The riders rode off in bitter disappointment.

Jennifer moved forward to pat her horse.

"I am not good enough," gasped Jennifer.

"Don't give up. You require more practice. You do lack discipline," remarked brother.

"This horse does have a mind of its own. I can't control it. It won't obey me," grumbled Jennifer.

Neither of them recognised the strangers who passed by. They both assumed that this group of people were visitors.

Christopher and Jennifer headed back to the stables where a stable girl waiting attended to a horse.

Christopher and Jennifer went back to the manor house. After eating their supper with Mr and Mrs Harvey, Christopher and Jennifer and Mr and Mrs Harvey, all relaxed together in the drawing room.

A housemaid came in while holding a tray full of crystal glasses. Everyone took a glass of port. They all stood together and made a toast. They raised their voices.

"To prosperity and health."

They all sat down and began talking among themselves. The topic discussed was controversial. The controversialist stirred up controversy.

"Fox hunting should be banned! It is cruelty to animals. Are you going to fox hunt?" protested Jennifer.

Mr Harvey, a squire, appeared to be defiant. He adhered to the very same traditions as his ancestors, those past generations.

"Of course I will fox hunt. Why should I change my plans to suit you? And do differently," scowled Mr Harvey.

"No more cruelty to animals," protested controversialist.

Mr Harvey glowered at the protestor, campaigner. "Young lady, do I detect defiance?" retorted Mr Harvey.

"My sister is a campaigner for animal rights. She is an animal lover herself. She is just concerned, that's all. You've got to understand my sister's point of view," defended brother.

Jennifer, a campaigner, defended her cause passionately.

"I do care about the welfare of animals. In principle, I am against animal testing," said Jennifer unashamedly.

"Ahem! So, you are a campaigner? It seems to me you're passionate about your cause. I certainly won't argue my case!"

Mrs Harvey came forward to touch Jennifer gently on her shoulder.

"Jennifer, dear, you're welcome to stay the summer," smiled Mrs Harvey.

Mr Harvey rose. "It's time. Let's go in," he gestured.

Christopher, Jennifer and Mr and Mrs Harvey came out of the drawing room and went into another room where already seated were Mr and Mrs Harvey's grandchildren.

Jack Harvey operated a projector. The rest of them sat down and faced a screen in front of them. Since the children were present, this film, an animation, was suitable for younger viewers. During the evening, everybody watching the animation really enjoyed it.

***

The following afternoon, Christopher sat alone in the drawing room waiting for Jennifer to return. He soon got impatient of waiting for his sister. As arranged, he expected to meet his sister a 1.45 p.m.

Christopher paced up and down the drawing room. He wondered if his sister had forgotten about their arrangement.

Christopher passed time by looking at the framed paintings everywhere on the walls. He liked the landscapes most of all, then followed by the nature and wildlife pictures. Christopher wondered why his sister was late.

Suddenly Christopher heard voices and a door slamming. He was alarmed. Christopher wondered what had happened.

Mr and Mrs Harvey rushed in. The housemaid hurried ahead of them, and the blacksmith carried Jennifer in his arms upstairs and took Jennifer to her bedroom. The strong blacksmith put Jennifer down gently on her bed. Jennifer's body light.

Everybody gathered around and looked with concern at Jennifer lying on her bed in pain injured.

"Jennifer has fallen! I do hope she will be alright. Jennifer is shaken," said Mrs Harvey.

"Jennifer is bruised but not injured," assured Mr Harvey.

"Thank goodness it's not serious!" assured Mrs Harvey.

"Thank God!" praised Christopher.

"Now leave Jennifer alone," said doctor.

Obeying the doctor, Christopher left his sister at once. Christopher waited at the bottom of the stairs. He had anxieties!

In anxiety, Christopher paced up and down the hallway. He worried. He felt deeply concerned for his sister.

A short time later, the housemaid came downstairs. The housemaid told Christopher, "Now you can come up."

Christopher worried about his sister. Christopher again felt concerned for his sister.

Christopher hurried upstairs. He came in alone in his sister's bedroom. He came to Jennifer's bedroom. He came to Jennifer's bed.

Jennifer sat up in bed. She was pleased to see her brother. Christopher touched his sister's forehead, with his fingers moving the thick tresses out of his sister's eyes.

"You should be asleep. Are you alright?"

Jennifer felt such bodily discomfort. She ached from pain.

"I have aches and pains," moaned sister.

"Tell me. What happened?" enquired brother.

His sister recalled her last moments when she rode out with her friend.

"I went riding with my friend Helen in the countryside. Then all of a sudden, my horse bolted. I lost control of my horse. I fell off my horse. I just can't remember what happened after that," said Jennifer hoarsely.

Christopher gave his sister a rosary. Jennifer took it and held it in her hand. She twirled it around her fingers. The rosary dangled from her stretched out hand.

"I must ride. When I get better, I will ride again!" wished sister.

As soon as his sister fell asleep, Christopher left his sister at once to sleep in peace.

Jennifer's beauty sleep sound!

Christopher sighed with relief. He felt greatly relieved at his sister being uninjured and still alive after her horse-riding accident!

16

Jennifer Rides Out

Jennifer recovered from her horse-riding accident. (Supposedly, if Jennifer had died, her death would have resulted from misadventure!)

Going to the stable, there a stable girl waited for Jennifer outside the stable and yard. The stable girl stood still and held the reins of a horse. Jennifer smiled at the pleasant stable girl attending to and accommodating her.

Jennifer mounted her horse.

"Now go! Have the ride of your life!" said stable girl.

Jennifer rode out into the countryside. Jennifer felt free indeed. A relieved rider! She took control of her horse. Jennifer took great joy at her freedom. The horse galloped faster and faster. Soon Jennifer changed direction, riding out somewhere else unfrequented. Jennifer took a different route by following a trail, a fox hunting trail. (Jennifer a campaigner, a protestor, activist, who campaigned against blood sports!)

In these parts of the trail, it was remote and frequented by fox hunters with a pack of fox hounds going on a fox hunt.

Jennifer admired the nature.

Another track leading somewhere else led to a nature trail.

Jennifer certainly enjoyed her ride. Jennifer was used to the trail. The rider knew her way around the endless trail and a beaten track in other directions in these remote parts.

Jennifer enjoyed her freedom, enjoying her privacy of riding alone. She marvelled at nature and the natural environment. The environmental heartland.

Eventually, Jennifer emerged out onto the fields somewhere else. Jennifer took a shortcut and came out onto the country lanes. Jennifer on horseback trotted along the country lanes. Jennifer rejoiced. She praised God for her speedy recovery and for being able to ride. Jennifer recovered from her accident. She was riding better than ever. The rider rode well.

Taking another way, the rider followed another lane. The rider on horseback. Jennifer's horse trotting down along the lane. Jennifer headed back to the country manor deep in the countryside.

Jennifer got back to the stables. The cool stable girl stood waiting for Jennifer to get back. The stable girl took Jennifer's horse. Jennifer let the stable girl take charge.

Jennifer entered the manor house. In the cosy lounge, Jennifer sat on a lounge chair and relaxed as she rested.

Mr Harvey disapproved of Jennifer riding. Jennifer persuaded Mr Harvey to allow her to ride. Jennifer was very determined to ride her horse, despite Mr Harvey raising objections. She sighed in relief at going riding. She solaced.

Jennifer had a motivational urge to ride her horse. She accomplished her objective. Her goal!

Jennifer was very proud of having ridden out.

Jennifer gained fulfilment and complete satisfaction from riding out this afternoon, today.

17

Repent or Damnation

In the study, Christopher sat at an office table. He browsed through car magazines which he had a subscription for. (He also had a car annual which he was obsessional about.)

Michael, his father, sat facing his son. Michael explained his intention and motive.

"Mr Martins has made an offer to buy a set of books," said Father.

Christopher disapproved of the book collector making an offer to buy a set of books.

"Don't sell! These books are valuable. They belonged to your father," said son disapprovingly.

"At the moment I am not selling. Mr Martins is persistent," said Father assuredly.

Christopher again had disapproval of the persuasive collector at persisting in trying to make another offer to buy a set of valuable books.

"Mr Martins is a damn collector! He's looking for a bargain."

"My father has a certain number of valuable books."

Christopher tapped his fingers on the office table.

"With these encyclopaedias the world is at your fingertips."

Christopher and his father were unaware of Jennifer eavesdropping while standing by the door.

Jennifer entered the study.

"Don't sell! These are our grandfather's books. If you do sell, you will regret the decision, I assure you," objected Jennifer.

"I guarantee you; I shan't sell them. I will keep them," said Father assuredly.

The Shadow of the Daughter's Ring

The son and daughter were relieved that their father had made the right decision in keeping their grandfather's set of books. Christopher and Jennifer certainly knew their father was obviously tempted to sell the books at a high price.

"Do look up Equestrian, Palomino and Thoroughbred," instructed sister.

Christopher looked in a reference book. He selected a few encyclopaedias in alphabetical and chronological order, then wrote neatly the reference numbers on a piece of notepaper while telling his sister.

"Here you are. Do your research well. Don't give up! Keep riding. But do everything slowly, gradually and steadily. Don't be hasty. Don't lose your belief and self-confidence."

Jennifer was embarrassed at her failure! (Jennifer's horse-riding accident remained an embarrassment!)

"I will read up on it. I've had a riding accident. I feel as though it's back to the beginning again. As far as I am concerned, I have learned the hard way."

"Jennifer. Take heed and do listen to advice. Don't make the same mistake again. Do not be gullible and foolish," advised Father.

Christopher stayed in the lounge whilst at this time his sister practised her clarinet usually in her bedroom.

Their father went out to go to work at a firm.

Sometime in the afternoon, Jennifer's friends came around for a barbecue in the back garden. Her aunt helped her mother to grill the barbecue.

Christopher's aunt and mother alternated between them. Alternately, they both took it in turns to grill the barbecue and also to serve the food.

Christopher was acquainted with some of Jennifer's friends. He made the acquaintance of meeting them.

His talkative sister spent time with her friends.

A Jewish girl stood away from them. Christopher paid heed to the Israelite. Fatima relaxed by herself as she breathed, standing alone in the far corner, near the garden fence. Fatima was quiet, placid and reserved. Fatima joined her friends queuing. Fatima queued up, waiting for her turn to be served by Aunt Beth.

"What would you like to eat?" asked Aunt Beth.

"No meat please. I am a vegetarian," replied Fatima.

Fatima took from Aunt Beth a paper plate which had on it a vegetarian burger in a roll of bread.

Christopher, Jennifer and Fatima sat down together at the garden table. They all ate and drank together, including a few friends of Jennifer's who sat down on garden chairs at the garden table when joining them seated.

"Have you seen any horrors lately?" asked Jennifer.

"No, I haven't seen any spooky movies recently," replied Fatima.

Christopher showed interest in Jennifer's friend Fatima. He seemed fascinated with Fatima!

"What do you want to do when you leave college?" asked Christopher.

"I do hope to go to university," answered Fatima.

"Fatima wants to be a teacher or a nanny," said Jennifer.

As Christopher was a low-paid librarian assistant, Christopher in shame looked away from Fatima's stare whenever she spoke to him. Fatima possessed lovely dark eyes. She was such an exceptional student. Fatima showed remarkable brilliance. She possessed charisma! She was pretty certain of her future and optimistic as well as being an opportunist. Fatima's education was her main priority therefore to obtain her qualification.

The rest of Jennifer's friends joined them by sitting down at the garden table. A sunshade put up. The three of them rose and left straightaway.

Christopher, Jennifer and Fatima avoided everybody else as none of them at present were in the right mood to socialise with persons now. Two of them did agitate. These ones had worries, problems and troubles of theirs to cope with.

Christopher had been aware of his sister's bad mood. His moody sister was temperamental. Jennifer felt faint. She had a migraine.

"Excuse me, I must go to my room. I don't feel well. I really must lie down now," groaned Jennifer.

Christopher and Fatima showed deep concern for Jennifer. The two of them had been sympathetic to Jennifer.

The three of them went indoors. They went together upstairs to Jennifer's bedroom. They came in her bedroom. Jennifer lay down on her bed in discomfort. She felt faint, unwell and languorous. Jennifer suffered from fatigue and exhaustion. She also had angina. Her legs were throbbing with pain. Jennifer groaned. She lay on her bed. Her body ached from pain. She groaned in discomfort.

"Oh! My legs are stiff. Please, Fatima, pray for me," implored Jennifer.

Christopher wished to respect both girls' privacy. He decided to leave them both alone together.

"Shall I go?" said brother.

"No. Stay with me," replied sister.

Christopher watched Fatima put her hands on Jennifer's legs. Fatima, a miracle healer, prayed while firmly pressing on Jennifer's legs.

Christopher looked in wonder at Fatima as she treated Jennifer's legs. Fatima tried to heal the pain in Jennifer's legs which were throbbing with pain. He hoped something miraculous happen. Christopher had doubts about Fatima's healing power.

Fatima was pressing down on Jennifer's legs. Fatima applied pressure on Jennifer's legs. Her pressure points. Suddenly Fatima eased the pain and discomfort in Jennifer's legs. Fatima soothed Jennifer's pain by healing her. Jennifer recovered. She brightened and became sanguine.

Christopher was rather pleased at how his sister made a recovery.

Finally, he left them alone together. Standing at the bedroom door, he spent a few moments eavesdropping. Christopher listened to Fatima babble. Hoping Fatima was not a bad influence?

After a while, when Christopher eavesdropped, he was convinced that Fatima did not corrupt his sister in any way.

Christopher went back downstairs. He rejoined the others. He was quiet and reflective no longer in the company of Fatima and his sister.

Going into the kitchen, Christopher reacted with displeasure at his mother who pulled her son aside.

"Son. Please help me with the washing up. I've got so much work to do," grumbled Mother.

Christopher disobeyed his mother. He declined to do any chores. The son eluded his mother by going back upstairs. Christopher knocked on his sister's bedroom door. Jennifer called out to her brother to come in. He came into his sister's bedroom. His sister stirred and roused from her nap.

"You're awake. Fatima has gone. I do apologise for waking you," apologised brother.

"I must have dozed off," yawned sister.

The brother sat down on his sister's bed in an uncomfortable position. He took discomfort from sitting on his sister's legs stretched out towards him.

"How are you feeling?" asked brother.

"I still feel sleepy. Otherwise, I feel fine," murmured sister.

Christopher raised his tone of voice.

"Jennifer. You should be sensible. How many times have I told you about your riding! Your problem is that you're stubborn and reckless," cautioned brother.

"I won't ride again. I must surely regain my belief and confidence," breathed sister.

Christopher moved forward to his sister who sat up in bed. Jennifer rested on the soft pillows against the headboard. He touched his sister's shoulder.

"Get some rest. You are tired."

Christopher got up from his sister's bed. He touched his sister again affectionately. In deep affection. He called out his sister's name. "Jennifer! Jennifer! You're well at last."

Christopher came out of his sister's bedroom. There, standing at the bedroom door, were a few of Jennifer's friends who had come to pay Jennifer, their friend, a visit.

"How is Jennifer?" they asked. "Can we go in?" they asked. "Can we go in? Is Jennifer well?"

Not answering the girls' questions, he opened the bedroom door. He stepped aside to allow them to enter inside their friend's bedroom.

Jennifer was pleased at how her friends had come to pay her a visit. Jennifer did expect her friends to arrive. Jennifer in anticipation of their arrival.

A large number of visitors had come to pay their friend a visit. Jennifer seemed unsurprised at expecting visitors now. Jennifer cheered up when her friends brought her a bunch of flowers, posies and a bouquet of roses and a box of chocolates and fresh fruits.

Jennifer appreciated her thoughtful friends' kindness.

Under the circumstances, her friends stayed with Jennifer for only a short time until it was finally time for Jennifer's visitors to leave.

***

Next morning, Christopher hurried into his sister's bedroom. He found that his sister had already left at an earlier time in the morning. His sister had recovered. Jennifer had made a quick recovery.

Jennifer's bedroom smelled of her perfume. A rose-scented fragrance made in France.

Christopher saw around his sister's bedroom fresh flowers in a few vases. These were freshly picked flowers of a meadow spring. There were also a dozen white roses in an oriental vase. The drops of water sparkled on the roses from the watering.

It appeared Jennifer's friends had visited again their friend. They cheered up Jennifer and took her to their friend's house.

***

Christopher arrived on time at work in the library. He started work at 9.30 a.m. as a librarian assistant by doing his usual duties.

On the sixth floor, Christopher worked in the Bibliographic department. Christopher worked alone in the stock room. He opened new cardboard boxes. Christopher put all the brand-new books, hardbacks, onto a trolley, arranging the hardbacks in alphabetical order. These was a miscellaneous range of books from fiction to non-fiction.

After Christopher had done all the unpacking of new hardbacks from cardboard boxes, as well as sorting out hardbacks alphabetically onto a trolley, he took a break.

The employee took a lift to the first floor and made his way into the Reference section.

In there that's where the employee saw Fatima, Jennifer's friend, sitting at the table reading a psychology textbook.

Christopher, an employee, walked past library members at their local library. In this library the membership was full; it was the main library in the borough.

Christopher came up to Fatima who was engrossed in reading. The foreign student concentrated on her study of the subject. Christopher disturbed the student reading.

"Hello Fatima! How are you? I am so glad you are here," smiled Christopher.

"I am alright," replied Fatima. "How about you? How is Jennifer?"

"My sister is well. Thanks to you!" said Christopher appreciatively.

Christopher knew that Fatima's religion was Judaism. Christopher was ignorant of the Jewish faith.

Fatima spoke up. "Oh good! I like to help. My friend has really suffered. It's over! Thank God! Those bullies did not get away with it!"

Christopher realised the seriousness of it. He was aware of the bullies and how they were bullying Jennifer, a younger pupil.

"What was your involvement in all this?" asked Christopher.

"Once, my friend Jennifer came up to me in tears. Jennifer was in a right state. I stuck up for Jennifer. I protected her," answered Fatima.

Everywhere in the Reference section the employee noticed seated students sitting at tables doing their studies.

"Give my regards to your mother. Now I must get back to work," gasped Christopher.

The employee left the Reference section. The employee came out of an exit. The librarian assistant went down the steps, then past Security. Two security guards were on duty. One of the security guards was busy being observant and vigilant while doing the surveillance and the other alert security guard guarded the ground floor of the library every day.

The employee went from the ground floor and took a lift up to the sixth floor, the Bibliographical department.

The employee made his way back through an office and then into the stock room where the librarian assistant resumed doing his hours of work again.

After Christopher had finished his day working at the library, he left the library. Going from the high street, he walked all the way to the multi-storey car park a short distance away. From there, Christopher got into his parked car and drove off home.

A short time later, the motorist reached his house. There he parked his car in the driveway. At that time there was another parked car too.

Christopher's parents had invited a family friend.

Christopher inserted his key into a mortice lock. He turned the key and opened the front door. He entered his house.

In the kitchen he microwaved his meal. He opened the microwave. With a tea towel, he held firmly the hot plate of food. He brought it into the dining room. He put it down on a table mat. Christopher sat down at the dining table and ate his supper.

After he had eaten his meal, he took his plate and cutlery and went in the kitchen. He washed up his plate and knife and fork. Christopher turned on the cold-water tap. Running the cold water, he rinsed off the suds. Then he left it on a draining board to dry out.

Christopher felt tired, exhausted and sleepy. He could not stay awake any longer. Going upstairs to his bedroom, he rested for a couple of hours.

***

Christopher got up from his bed and got dressed. He went downstairs to join his sister in the lounge.

Christopher sat down next to his sister on the settee. He still felt tired and enervated as he tried to stay awake.

"How was your day?" asked brother.

"I had a good day. I did ride my horse but at a steady pace. I didn't do anything hasty," replied sister.

Christopher cared about his sister. He showed considerable concern for his sister. Christopher loved his sister naturally. He worried about her. Usually, he did favours for his sister. The brother had a natural love for his sister!

"Do be careful! I don't want you falling off your horse again. Don't be careless and reckless," cautioned brother.

Jennifer was cocksure of not falling off her horse again. Jennifer was quite certain of not having another accident again.

"I won't fall. I shan't. Not again. I am in control," assured sister.

"Do take care of yourself. Your legs are an important function," emphasised brother.

Jennifer bent down to caress her leg. "My legs are perfect. There is nothing wrong with them," said Jennifer vainly.

"I saw your friend Fatima in the library today. Fatima gives you her regards," mentioned brother.

"Fatima gets about. I also saw her when I went riding out today. She wore a hood. I recognised my friend Fatima. She waved at me and smiled. Fatima is a Godsend! She gave me her blessing," recalled Jennifer.

"Did Fatima actually bless you?" asked Christopher.

"Fatima did. It's in her nature."

"Do you still bear malice?"

"I do still bear a grudge."

"Christianity teaches love. Shouldn't you learn to love?"

Jennifer glowered. She reflected on her schooldays. She has reminiscence of it. She thought of the bullies at her secondary school.

"Don't you mean to hate!" snapped Jennifer.

"So, vengeance is sweet."

"Too bloody right!" said Jennifer bitterly.

"I am tired. I am going to bed."

Jennifer felt fit and well riding her horse today. Jennifer obliged to show her gratitude to her brother.

"Thanks! You have really helped me so much. I am truly thankful. You've given me so much support and advice."

Christopher was seemingly obliging towards his sister. He was relieved that his sister had recovered.

"I did what I could to help you. I was desperately concerned for you. When you fell off your horse, I was so worried about you. Thank God your fall wasn't that serious."

Jennifer realised how fortunate she was to be still alive! Fortunately, her fall off her horse wasn't a serious accident!

"I am lucky. It could have been worse," admitted sister.

He reached out and touched his sister affectionately. His deep tone of voice affectionate.

"Jennifer. I am glad you are well. It's a miracle you are still alive!"

Jennifer leaned forward and kissed her brother on his cheek. Jennifer's lips left traces of thick red lipstick smeared on her brother's cheek.

"You have been so kind and helpful to me. You care about me," said sister gratefully.

Christopher left his sister alone in the lounge. Jennifer, a contemplator, was preoccupied.

Christopher went upstairs to his bedroom. He went back to bed.

During that summer night, Christopher had a nightmare! He awoke during the course of the night. Christopher had a sleepless night. It was probably those old books, a whammy which cause him to have alarm. He lost count of how many books he had sorted out and shifted through. He removed these tarnished old books, hardbounds and hard covers, from the bookshelves. He put all the books on another shelf somewhere else. These old books kept temporarily stored.

***

The next morning, the librarian assistant worked in the Bibliographical department. After the employee had finished using the VDU, the employee took liberty to do something else which was inappropriate to work. He took some time to look at the latest up-to-date reference book. The employee did select a few encyclopaedias. The employee looked at various religions, excluding cults and sects. Christopher became familiarised with the subject of religion. Christopher learned about religious ceremonies. He took some interest in ceremonies and ritualism. It did somewhat fascinate Christopher, especially the rituals used in ceremonies in the past and present day. He also learned about Christianity, in particular the Holy Communion. (Spiritually, it's a defence, a protection against the Black Arts!)

After the employee had finished looking at the encyclopaedias, during that time he gained the required information necessary. Christopher was interested in learning about the Last Supper. He found the scriptural interestingness profoundly spiritual.

The employee put back the few encyclopaedias on the bookshelves. The librarian assistant resumed doing more work at the library. The employee resumed his work, doing the rest of his remaining hours left today in the library.

After work, Christopher drove home.

As he arrived home, Christopher grumbled at being overworked and underpaid.

Jennifer stood straight beside her brother and rested her hand on his shoulder. Jennifer leaned on her brother. His cheerful sister appeared to be sympathetic!

"Never mind!"

***

On Saturday afternoon, Christopher drove to Anne's house using a different route to get there as there was a diversion and roadworks in the main road ahead.

Christopher arrived at Anne's house. He parked his car in the driveway. Christopher got out of his car. He could hear instruments playing. Going towards the front door. He listened to the chamber music while he stood outside the front door. He preened himself before ringing the doorbell a few times.

Christopher waited for a while before Mark answered the front door. He smiled at Mark, a welcomer, Anne's brother. He thought Mark was good-looking (Mark had the makings of a male model), intelligent and debonair.

"Jennifer will be with you shortly," said Mark politely.

Going into the sitting room alone, Christopher sat down on a settee, listening to the string quartet perform. The acoustics resounded from an empty room used for practice.

Christopher was very impressed at how well the string quartet played.

He thought of Anne being an aspiring musician. Anne seemed to be promising, versatile and a sophisticated young lady! His sister was ambitious and precocious. Jennifer suffered from a split personality! Jennifer had a behavioural temperament. (His sister a virtuoso played the clarinet very well. Jennifer did her best to impress them with her virtuosity.)

Usually, Jennifer played her clarinet well. Her playing was rather impressive indeed. So admirable!

Many minutes later, Jennifer came into the sitting room. Jennifer expected her brother to come and pick her up.

"I'll just get my belongings. I do apologise for having kept you waiting," apologised sister.

"I've been waiting ages. How's Mark?"

"Oh! Mark. I am not in love with Mark. It's just platonic," tutted sister.

Christopher waited outside the detached house while his emotional sister embraced all of her friends one by one. Saying goodbye to them deeply saddened Jennifer, as one of them intended to leave her to go to university. Her anxious friend made educational preparation at university and at campus. At present her allocated accommodation was sorted out. Her friend had high expectations for her education.

Christopher and Jennifer got in the car. Christopher drove home via the diverted route. Driving his car, Christopher reached his house. His quiet passenger was his teenage sister whom he pick up and drove home. The pick-up arrangement made in advance.

On their arrival at their house, simultaneously they both got out of the car which was parked in the drive. Christopher was displeased at how his sister took it for granted. Jennifer did not appreciate her brother's thoughtfulness to pick her up and drive her home. The sister expected her obliging brother to do this willingly. By driving her around to different places and to pick her up and to drop her off at home or to her friends' houses.

Christopher and Jennifer went indoors to join their father who was waiting for his son and daughter to come home. In the lounge their father sat on an armchair. He wore a pair of spectacles. In another glasses case he had another pair of glasses. The thick lens had no tint. Their father was engrossed in reading a book.

"This is really interesting. You should read it when I have finished it. It does have the makings of a modern classic, I do believe," recommended Father.

Christopher stooped down to take a closer look at the book cover of this latest publication of the new edition of this new paperback.

"Perhaps another time," grinned son.

"I have sold some books," mentioned Father.

Christopher objected to his father selling Grandfather's collection of books which had been stored in cardboard boxes up in the attic.

Christopher glared. "Those books are Grandfather's. Don't you have any respect?" said son indignantly.

Jennifer joined in to object to her father for selling Grandfather's books which the Bibliophile collected.

"How can you do such a thing!" protested daughter.

The father disregarded his son and daughter's objection.

"I had to get rid of them. After all, there is no room to keep them all," defended Father.

"Nonsense! All you are concerned about is your inheritance!" said son reproachingly.

Their father, questioned about his motives, refused to talk about his affairs, the current matters concerning their father's inheritance. Their father refused to discuss it. Their father still kept it private and confidential until this present time.

"Whatever you inherit is none of my business. My grandfather had a great love for books. A bibliophile Storytelling was his interest. He was damn good at it, and being Father Christmas, of course, was his passion, to entertain children!" sighed daughter.

Christopher disapproved of his father for selling Grandfather's books. He did object to his father selling and how he tried to get rid of his grandfather's collection of books which were still in good condition.

Christopher thought of the bibliomania! His grandfather used to be a bibliomaniac. His grandfather's bibliographic obsessions and bibliophilist obsessiveness, including bibliophiles the librarian had the pleasure of working and spending time with and their bibliophilism!

The son and daughter were disgusted at their father's attitude! Christopher and Jennifer were intent on confronting their father. Both brother and sister remonstrated and raised objections!

In disgust, Christopher and Jennifer walked away. They avoided their father. They both had a disregard and disrespect for their father. Christopher and Jennifer went upstairs together. Reaching the corridor, the brother and sister left each other to go to their bedrooms respectively where they stayed until evening.

During those hours spent in their bedrooms, they rested and pondered on their father's personal reasons to sell their grandfather's books.

Going downstairs together, both brother and sister deplored their father. In disgust they avoided their father again. With both of them having the intention to elude their father again.

Meanwhile, in the lounge, their father was reading a newspaper. Earlier Michael had put down his book. He was becoming tired of reading fiction. The father became fed up with his son and daughter and how both of them had neglected him.

Going out of a side door, Christopher and Jennifer went into the rear of the garden together. They both felt disgust for their insensitive father. Christopher and Jennifer disapproved of their father's mentality.

The brother and sister stayed out in the garden together until finally a full moon appeared in the skies. The moon reappeared from the scudding clouds. The bright moonshine reflected in the shadows.

Christopher and Jennifer took a moonlit stroll out in the garden at night. Christopher and Jennifer strolled together around the garden.

Christopher and his sister saw ahead the opposite way. The reflections of the moonlight in the shadowy pitch-darkness. They both felt enchanted at the moonlit glow which reflected in the shadows.

Christopher and Jennifer irradiated and regenerated during the time they spent together. Christopher and Jennifer were contemplative, reflective and deeply spiritual from their contemplation, as they mourned for their grandfather tonight.

Going back to the house in the pitch-dark, they went in through the side door. Jennifer left her brother to go upstairs to her bedroom. Christopher stayed downstairs in the lounge. He picked up a travel book which his thoughtful sister had left on the dining table in the dining room.

Christopher appreciated his sister's favour which she had done for him. He had forgotten about a travel book which his sister had subsequently borrowed from a friend.

He got up from a chair. He picked up one of the holiday brochures on the dining table. He wrote a note to his sister Jennifer:

You might be interested in this. There is some information about Valencia. It is quite a popular holiday destination among holidaymakers and tourists.

Valencia is of course rich in history. It is historic. The Moors once invaded and conquered Valencia.

I hope you do find the information interesting.

From Christopher.

Christopher slipped a note in the very front pages of the glossy holiday brochure.

Christopher went upstairs. He came in his sister's bedroom.

"Can I come in?"

Jennifer did not answer her brother, since she had fallen asleep.

Christopher tiptoed towards his sister who was fast asleep in her bed. Christopher admired his stunning sister. He looked at a virgin sleeping. He stood facing her while admiring his sister's beauty. He gazed at the virgin's figure. The shapeliness of her beautiful body. Christopher gaped at his sister's purity. His sister's glow.

In the pitch-darkness Jennifer's nightdress was the most brilliant pure white in the moonlight. The moonshine reflected on the material of her nightdress. Jennifer's negligee was hanging up and hooked up high behind the door. The black silk negligee glimmered in the pitch-dark. The sheer material so glossy indeed.

Christopher cooled down from the wind blowing from the opened double French doors which were ajar. The gust blew the net curtains up in the air.

From his sister lying still in bed, her body position motionless, Christopher gained comfort as he had seen that his sister was well. Jennifer had fully recovered from her riding accident last week.

With joy, the brother left his sister at once. Christopher yawned when going back to his bedroom. With a landing light on and a light on in the corridor, the bright and dim house lights shone. The bright lights reflected inside his bedroom. Christopher's bedroom door was ajar. In the dimmed light Christopher got in his bed. Christopher slept the remaining hours until finally it was time to get up really early in the morning.

***

During the rainy day, Christopher was still alone in his bedroom, standing and facing the window, from his view from high above. It overlooked the back garden. Christopher's view from standing in a directional opposite angle, he watched his sister go out alone in the garden in the downpour. Today's weather was torrential rain. The downpour throughout in the daytime.

Jennifer's long hair was wet and darkened from the wetness. Her clothes sopping wet. Jennifer was drenched while standing still in the downpour somewhere in the garden.

Jennifer was in a deliriously good mood at present. Jennifer felt ecstatic and euphoric. She shivered in her condition!

The brother watched his sister act really strangely and odd. His sister looked disturbed! Why this strangeness in Jennifer's characteristic behaviour? Jennifer's clothes were soaked. Her wet hair dripping with raindrops. Her leather shoes squelched. Jennifer breathed. She exhaled. She shivered in the nippy air. She breathed in the fresh air. Her warm breath rose in the air.

At that time, the next-door neighbours observed the strange, disturbed teenager acting peculiarly. At her age, it was out of character.

Christopher came out of his bedroom quickly. He rushed downstairs to get to the side door. There Christopher waited by the already opened side door. Christopher stood waiting for his sister to come in the side door. Jennifer came indoors from the garden.

"Are you crazy! Jennifer, where is your coat? You will shiver in the freezing cold," admonished brother.

Jennifer defended her escapade.

"I had to be out in the elements, of course, be with nature," gasped sister.

Christopher thoughtfully helped his sister put on her black raincoat. With Jennifer's slinky raincoat on and tied up tightly in a bow, it was figure-hugging.

"Get in! You're soaked. According to the scriptures, will God ever flood the world again?"

Jennifer understood the scriptural passage.

"I once learned that at Sunday School. Those were the days It's pretty unlikely," answered sister.

Christopher closed the side door. He bolted the door and also locked it by turning a key in the lock.

The brother and sister went together through the house. They both entered the spacious living room.

Jennifer stood by the fireplace. Jennifer warmed herself up by a fire. She dried herself thoroughly.

Going out of the warm living room, the brother got a dry towel from the airing cupboard. Christopher hurried back to the warmed-up living room. He gave his sister a large bath towel. Jennifer used the towel and dried her wet hair dripping from raindrops.

Christopher felt tired and moody. He left his sister alone.

Jennifer took the time to dry out her wet clothes. She stood by a fire while warming herself. Jennifer dried out her wet clothes after standing by a fire for a long time. The heat from the fire dried out her damp clothes.

∗∗∗

On another summer night, Christopher and his mother both together entered Jennifer's bedroom. Jennifer's mother tucked her daughter up in bed.

Christopher left his mother alone with her daughter. Christopher came out of the French doors. He stepped out onto the balcony. He walked along the balcony. From the balcony, Christopher stood still as he leaned on the balustrade, admiring the view of the garden around the side of the house. The bright house lights enabled him to see clearly the garden beyond in the darkness. Christopher was enchanted at the moonlit night and from his pleasurable Christmas memories. All the Christmassy enchantment delighted Christopher.

Christopher relaxed in the silence, momentarily enjoying his time alone.

Christopher came in the French doors. He picked up a holiday brochure which he had left on an easy chair.

Leaving again his sister and mother to be alone together, Christopher said goodnight to them. He put a holiday brochure down on top of Jennifer's dressing table. The dressing table mirror made reflections of Christopher's own reflection. Christopher came out of his sister's bedroom. Christopher went back down the corridor as he returned to his own bedroom. At bedtime, Christopher got in his bed to go to sleep.

***

Early on a Sunday morning, Christopher climbed up a ladder to get up to the attic. In the dusty, stuffy attic, Christopher rummaged through old books which were stored in big cardboard boxes. He assumed that these old books were worthless and typical pulp. (Grandfather had an interest and an obsessive fascination for science fiction. This was Grandfather's favourite category among the other various categories in fiction. Grandfather used to have a liking for his favourite authors, for general fiction and also science fiction too.)

Christopher looked among the other boxes which contained hard covers and paperbacks. In another box, Christopher found Christmas decorations and an old scrapbook. He blew the dust off it. He opened the scrapbook. He turned over the pages. The paper was tatty. He flicked through it.

Finally, Christopher stopped at a page which he took interest in. Reading the tale of The Magic Teapot fascinated him. The extract had a quotation in italics. It was italicised. It had a whimsical illustration of a teapot with a tea-cosy, with cupcakes and assorted biscuits on a tea-tray set on a beautifully polished dinner table. It was laid with a beautiful tablecloth. There, near the dinner table, a tea-trolley at the corner. It was positioned close to a fireplace. A fire with burning logs in pieces was crackling. The firelight flickered in the shadowy dark living room.

As soon as Christopher had enough of taking the time to take a browse in a scrapbook, he ended up putting it back in a cardboard box. He covered it up with red tinsel glittering and other tinsel which glittered. The many deep colours of all the glittering tinsel were beautiful!

He put back the working Christmas lights and flex on top of it, sticking the whole flex inside of a stuffed box. He squeezed the flex inside the full box. With both hands, he pressed it down. Christopher cried when remembering how once his grandfather told him the same story when he was only a child. It was a charming and enchanting whimsical tale of Grandmother's teapot. The granny used her favourite china tea set. Granny's chinaware kept in the china closet.

Suddenly the doorbell rang again and again. The sound of the chimes was resonant.

Using his unbuttoned long sleeve, Christopher wiped away his tears.

Christopher got down from the attic. He climbed down a ladder to get down. Christopher hurried down the stairs to get to the front door. Quickly, he answered the front door.

Christopher's father came to greet Mr Holt. Michael led Mr Holt into the study. Michael and Mr Holt came in the study. Michael with his foot kicked away a door stop which was wedged under a door.

Christopher got annoyed at the intrusion of his uncle and a bibliophile. His privacy had been invaded again and again. Without delay, Christopher had to vacate the room downstairs because of the arrival of a guest and his uncle intending to occupy the room. Christopher came in the unoccupied room to find that his sister had gone out to dine at a restaurant later tonight with her friend Anne and her family.

At an earlier time of day, Jennifer had shown disrespect and disregard for her uncle. Her disapproving uncle apologised for upsetting Jennifer.

Christopher slammed a door in anger and annoyance. How Christopher hated his father!

Christopher felt fed up. He went upstairs alone to his bedroom. Christopher lay down on his luxury bed to rest. Christopher felt deeply upset, thinking of his grandfather. He mourned for his grandfather.

Christopher became haunted by his memories of Grandfather. His memory of Grandfather was bittersweet!

***

On Saturday morning, Christopher spent time as he decided to stay longer with his sister in the lounge. Brother and sister sat down on armchairs positioned opposite. The rest of the furniture was a three-piece suite. Jennifer and Christopher sat facing each other as they each drank a cup of tea.

Christopher spent time at relaxing. He was restful and peaceful. Christopher and Jennifer were quiet and untalkative.

Jennifer passed time away as she looked through a women's magazine. The women's fashion interestingly appealed to Jennifer. All the glossy pictures of the fashion models interested Jennifer. Every tall model's natural pose was ladylike, graceful and elegant. The chic models wore the latest fashion of the current season. The summer collection range this year.

Today it poured down with heavy rain. The heavy falling raindrops splashed and spluttered from an outside drain down a drainpipe. The drops of rainwater dripping. It spluttered on a drain.

Christopher took a nap while sitting on an easy chair. He took comfort from morning relaxation.

Later, Jennifer took pleasure from her self-indulgence. She enjoyed herself, enjoying the luxuries. Jennifer took pleasurable gratification of herself and from her obsessive narcissism. Jennifer's vainness a teenage obsession of hers. From Jennifer's adolescence and pubescence, she was becoming a beautiful grown-up teenager.

Jennifer dreaded her examination results, at receiving the notification of her examination results. She tended to worry about it. She was inclined to have worries. She did in fact fail her exams. (Jennifer had a tendency to fail her examination year after year. The candidate sat her examinations with examination failure!)

Sometime later, Christopher woke up from his nap. He reminded his sister about her washing on the clothesline.

"Jennifer, your washing. It will get wet. Do get it."

Jennifer had forgotten about it as Jennifer's mind had been pre-occupied with her thoughts.

Jennifer got up. Going to the back door, she unlocked the back door. She turned a key in a lock and went outside in the garden.

From inside the kitchen, Christopher looked out of the window. Christopher stood watching his sister quickly take off all the plastic clothes pegs from her wet clothes which hung up on the clothesline. Quickly, Jennifer put all the gathered-up clothes pegs in a clothes basket. Jennifer stuffed all her clothes in a clothes basket. Standing near the clothesline, Jennifer stood in the pouring rain. She became drenched by standing in the torrential rain. Her clothes were soaked in the pouring rain. She tilted her head back, the heavy rain falling on her face. Her faced flushed and her cheeks in a glow. Her long, wet hair dripping. Jennifer glowed. Her black shoes squelched in the wet grass.

Jennifer picked up the clothes basket. She hurried indoors. She put the wet clothes basket in the kitchen on the kitchen floor. Then Jennifer joined her brother who waited for her in the living room. A graceful Jennifer stood by the fire. She warmed herself up and dried herself. Jennifer's wet clothes dried after considerable time standing by the fireplace. The heat from the fire dried up her clothes.

With a clean towel, Jennifer dried her wet hair thoroughly. Her long hair was soft, silky and curly. Jennifer's hair was beautiful.

Christopher stood while admiring his sister's beauty. Jennifer's fresh-complexioned round face and cheeks aglow.

Christopher and Jennifer remained quiet. They both stood and waited for the doorbell to ring anytime now. They both expected Laura to call at their house. (Jennifer's friend Laura called earlier to confirm that she still intended to come at 3 p.m. today as expected prior to arrangement.)

Suddenly the doorbell rang.

"Get the door," demanded sister. "I am going up to change my clothes."

Jennifer expected her friend to come around. (Jennifer was only allowed to invite one of her friends at this time.)

Christopher hurried to the front door. He answered the front door. Laura entered in the house. Christopher welcomed Laura. Christopher smiled at Laura. The youngest one of Jennifer's friends. Christopher favoured Laura especially because her family worked in tourism. A few members of her family worked in a travel agent and for tour operators.

"Jennifer will be with you shortly. She is getting changed," said Christopher.

Christopher took Laura to the lounge. Christopher and Laura sat down together on the settee. Laura sat while waiting for Jennifer. A good friend of hers. Laura was fluent in Spanish and French. Laura had a flair for foreign languages. Laura's father was a tour operator.

"Do you know anything about Valencia?" asked Christopher.

"Yes, Valencia is historical. Centuries ago, it was once conquered by the Moors. It's quite a popular destination. The location is historical. It's enriched with Moor history. It's not really the most favourite and popular region of Spain. It may be unpopular in other aspects of it. Of course, here's where there is tourism," said Laura knowledgeably.

Christopher was impressed at Laura's impressive knowledge of Spain. Laura was knowledgeable about Spain as well as Spanish tourism in Spain.

"Perhaps you can suggest any other parts of Spain that are popular?"

Laura continued to impress Christopher with her knowledge of tourism.

"You should go to Mallorca or Majorca on holiday in these parts of Spain. These are beautiful parts of Spain. These parts and regions there are tourism. What I do like most of all personally are the beautiful Spanish beaches. To me it is personal! You should travel or go on holiday to the beautiful Spanish islands. For instance, Ibiza. I strongly recommend it. It's my personal choice. Over there you have the island lifestyle and island nightlife and night scene. The tourists and holidaymakers on vacation do flock here in numbers. One really should enjoy oneself after clients having to pay all that money to book their package holiday."

After changing her clothes, Jennifer came into the lounge. At once Laura stopped talking about her favourite hotspot, regional location and holiday and tourist destination.

Christopher got up. He touched Laura lightly on her shoulder in thoughtful appreciation (thanks).

Christopher came up to his sister. He pressed Jennifer's hand affectionately. He left his sister alone with her friend Laura.

Christopher came into the study. He checked if any books had been removed from the shelves. He noticed that none of the books had been taken or borrowed. Christopher sighed with relief.

A few days ago, Christopher had argued with his father about selling or getting rid of Grandfather's old books and those other books in good condition.

Christopher had concern and respect for Grandfather's books. Grandfather used to be ever so obsessional of his volumes.

Grandfather was a bibliophile. Grandfather used to be obsessed by his own books, he once possessed.

These favourite books of his used to be of sentimental value and his favourites, especially all his valuable collection!

18

A Midsummer's Ball

One rainy day, Christopher and Jennifer played a game of chess on the dining table in the dining room. During the game of chess, Christopher made a bad chess move which made him lose the game. As a result of this move, the opponent's black queen was captured.

Jennifer capitalised on her opponent's bad chess move by attacking her opponent with an impressive offensive. A positional formation of attacking white chess pieces which made her opponent's defence defenceless!

The blacks were exposed to attack and followed by the king being checkmated finally.

Within a sequence of whites making moves. (Jennifer concentrated on her tactical skill. Depending on how she played chess. Jennifer depended on her strategic chess moves.)

The black king had been checked and subsequently from the white's next move the black king had been attacked again. With constant check to the opponent's black king at moving position from check again and again. The opponent realised defeat was imminent. The blacks decided to resign!

The losing opponent finally conceded (at the chess game consequently being over) rather than to allow whites to continue to play until the black king's ultimate checkmate in the following next move.

"How about another game?" asked sister.

Christopher declined to play another game of chess because at present he was off form.

"No thanks. One game is quite enough," blushed Christopher.

"That was a good game!" remarked sister.

"You played well. You made some impressive moves," praised brother.

Jennifer was a promising chess player. She aspired to be a chess champion.

"I am not a grandmaster yet. I doubt if I will ever be one. I wish I was!" sighed sister.

Christopher got up from the chair. He pushed the chair under the dining table. From sitting down in a seated position for less than an hour, Christopher ached from cramp, suffering with stiffness and cramp in his legs. Christopher stretched his legs. Christopher moved around the dining room.

Christopher grieved for his friend Dean. He changed the subject.

"I woke up feeling sad. I couldn't stop thinking of Dean," said Christopher mournfully.

"What do you remember?" asked sister.

"Once, my sister rented a house up at the Strand. My sister invited me and my friend to a party. That night we made fun of the young nurses invited. My sister told us off. It was a miserable occasion! Later that same year, I so happened to be in a hospital ward that day. It was a hospital admittance in a ward. From the ward I was allowed and granted permission to go home. Leaving the ward to go home, I met Dean walking by in the hospital grounds. I never really knew Dean was dying of cancer!" said Christopher remorsefully.

Jennifer reached out to touch her brother with love. Her gentle touch was soft.

"I am really sorry. I really am. It's a terrible shock. I only wish things could be better," said sister sympathetically.

Christopher recalled his very last times with his departed friend Dean. His sad memories of Dean deeply upset him. Christopher's sorrow deeply affected him. Suffering from bereavement!

"I have regrets. I only wish I had spent more time with Dean. I neglected my friend. When Dean passed away, it was too late," sulked Christopher.

With condolence, Jennifer consoled her brother. Jennifer showed deep sympathy for her mournful brother.

"I am truly sorry. Truly I am, dear. What could I have done?"

***

James wiped his shoes on a doormat at the back of the house. James took off his small shoes. James obeyed the house rules made by Sally, Christopher's mother.

From outside in the garden, James came in the back door, shouting at the top of his voice.

"My picture! Look at my picture!"

The neglected boy was seeking attention. James ran in the lounge.

Christopher took a look at James' drawing which was nicely drawn in pencil. (James' other pictures were beautifully coloured in felt-tip pens, colouring pencils and crayons. James took the necessary time to do all the colouring of his pictures well.)

Jennifer attended to the neglected boy. Jennifer unzipped James' jacket. Jennifer took off the boy's jacket.

"Do remember Grandfather. Do remember Father Christmas. You must picture him with love. An eternal love!"

Jennifer held James' jacket. Jennifer left the living room. Jennifer hung it up on a coat stand out at the front.

Christopher felt that he had neglected James. He had to keep his promise to look after James. A promise witnessed by his observant sister. Christopher had to fulfil his moralistic obligation toward James (his grandfather's last wish that his godson ought to be taken care of and look after!)

"Later, James, I will tell you a story."

James smiled in delight. James was pleased at Christopher as he intended to read a story to him. James hurried out of the lounge. James went upstairs to a bedroom which he stayed in overnight sometimes.

James plays with his toys. He kept himself occupied as he enjoyed himself.

Christopher remained undisturbed as he sat down on an armchair alone in the living room. He was cosy, comfortable and warm when sitting in front of the fire. Christopher warming up from the fire. He warmed up from the heat.

Christopher rested. Within quarter of an hour, he had dozed off.

Approximately an hour later, Christopher woke up. During that time, he had neglected James again. He had forgotten about James since that time.

Christopher was startled as Jennifer burst into the living room, slamming the door behind her. Jennifer was ashamed of her brother. Jennifer confronted Christopher. She was cross at how Christopher continued to neglect James. With anger Jennifer grabbed firmly hold of Christopher's arm. Christopher felt his arm being squeezed by his sister. Jennifer pulled her brother to his feet. Jennifer agitated her lazy brother.

"Your damn promises! You promised you would take care of James. Why aren't you doing it? Why don't you make James' wishes come true? Shouldn't you be concerned about James' wellbeing? Now go and read to James!" scowled sister.

Jennifer was displeased at her selfish brother who wanted to idle away more time.

Christopher's conscience perturbed. Christopher changed his attitude toward James. Christopher seemed to show some concern for James. Christopher did obey his angry sister. His sister indignant.

In the meantime, James waited for Christopher to come. James was expecting Christopher to come up to the bedroom. James got tired of playing with his toys.

Christopher came in the bedroom. This time Christopher was already prepared to read to James. James was wearing his pyjamas and already in bed waiting for Christopher to read out a story. Christopher sat down on a chair from a position facing James.

James sat up in bed ready to listen to Christopher to read out to him from a book.

Christopher opened a children's book. He began to read out to James. It was James' favourite author. James enjoyed listening to

Christopher reading out aloud to him. James was fascinated by the bedtime story.

After Christopher had spent time reading to James, he had finished reading within about half an hour. He closed the children's book.

Jennifer came in the spare bedroom to tuck up James in bed. She kissed James on his forehead.

Christopher waited out along the corridor for his sister to finish attending to James.

Walking out together towards the landing, Christopher and his sister spent a short time talking to each other again up on the landing, before finally leaving each other to go to their bedrooms.

That late night they both went to bed respectively.

Tomorrow, it was the start of the summer solstice.

***

Early next morning, Christopher got out of his bed. Christopher got up. He stretched himself. He got dressed. He wore casual clothes. He came down the stairs. Going into the dining room, Christopher sat down at the dining table. He joined his moody sister who was sitting at the far end of the dining table. Jennifer reclined.

Their mother brought in their breakfast. Their mother put on two table mats a plate of two slices of toast and scrambled eggs and a bowl of cereal. The two cups of tea had already been made earlier. One sweet tea strong and the other one had three teaspoons of sugar.

Christopher and Jennifer had not spoken to one another. Jennifer remained tired due to lack of sleep last night. Also, Christopher had insomnia again.

Christopher and Jennifer ate their breakfast. At this time of the morning, Christopher had a lack of appetite, while Jennifer (suffering from anorexia on a few nights running) ate only a bowlful of cereal.

In the living room their mother took two envelopes (propped up against the wall) off the mantelpiece. Going back, Sally came into the dining room. Their considerate mother gave her son and daughter an envelope each.

Simultaneously, Christopher and Jennifer opened their envelopes. Inside was an invitation card. With interest, Christopher and Jennifer read their invitation card.

"You are invited to the annual Ball," they said loudly.

Christopher and Jennifer perked up. They were both delighted at their invitation from Lucy Sanders. They both appreciated their invitation. Their invitation card had fine calligraphy written in black ink.

They favoured and deeply respected Lucy Sanders. The host and linguist (a model and also personnel from a top modelling agency).

Jennifer was pleased at her invitation to the annual Ball. Her brother seemed quite surprised by his invitation. Nonetheless he expected this invitation because of personal favouritism by Lucy Sanders. Christopher wondered why Lucy Sanders bothered to invite him.

Jennifer had consideration for those ones uninvited. Jennifer took hers for granted. Lucy Sanders disappointed those ones by uninviting guests. Lucy disappointed those ones uninvited. It was the same ones at last year's annual Midsummer's Ball who were denied entry and again invitation.

Jennifer left her brother by going upstairs to her bedroom.

Christopher entered the lounge alone. He sat down on the armchair. He rested in comfort from his position. He stirred from his body movement.

Christopher thought of the Midsummer Ball. He dreaded the ballroom dances. Christopher's dancing was unimpressive compared to everyone else's. He knew nobody took any notice of him dancing. He looked forward to it to some extent. He hoped for a wonderful time at the annual Midsummer's Ball.

Christopher nodded off.

He woke up about an hour later in a deeply contemplative state of mind. Christopher reflected on his beloved grandfather. He mourned for Grandfather! His sad memories caused him deep sorrow. His memories of Grandfather were also tinged with happiness.

Christopher was denied bereavement counselling after the loss of his friend. He died of a brain tumour. Christopher was aggrieved. Christopher had bitter resentment till this present day. He also had a grievance with the authorities, as well as his friend's parents and their families.

On Friday evening, the chauffeur-driven limousine arrived at the grounds of a grand stately home. The uniformed chauffeur wearing his gloves parked the limousine outside in the grounds of a stately home. Already parked there were other convertibles, cars and vehicles.

A few guests got out of cars having arrived. The guests punctual on arrival.

Christopher and Jennifer got out of a limousine. They both walked together towards the entrance of the stately house. There waiting for them were a member of staff expecting the two guests arriving. The leggy, voluptuous brunette. An employer wearing a red suit and stilettos greeted Jennifer and her invited guest.

"This is my brother, Christopher. He is family," introduced Jennifer.

Christopher blushed. He smiled.

Christopher was shy from being introduced to a member of Personnel.

The employer gave the two guests a warm welcome. The courteous welcomer, employer, attended to Jennifer, an employee.

Christopher wanted to make a good impression. Christopher shook the welcomer, employer's hand.

"I am pleased to meet you," said Christopher.

Another employee, a member of Personnel, assisted to escort both guests.

"You must be the librarian. Jennifer has spoken about you."

Christopher blushed. He felt so humiliated. He was dissatisfied by his status at present.

The Shadow of the Daughter's Ring

The employer smiled. The greeter had an appealingly delightful charm and personality. The employer spoke.

"You two, do have a good time. I will see you both perhaps later."

The employee, the employer's colleague, a member of Personnel (Recruitment Administration), accompanied both guests inside the imposing stately home before eventually deciding to leave them together to attend to other punctual guests arriving.

Jennifer thanked personally the staff: employers and employees. Jennifer had an appreciative consideration for all of them.

The guests walked away by following the crowd going along on ahead onwards.

The chic, elegant employee rejoined the uniformed doorman out by the entrance again, by the double doors. Welcoming and greeting more guests arriving, Christopher and Jennifer joined other guests going in the ballroom. Quickly it filled up with crowds.

Christopher didn't know most of the guests. However, he recognised the ladies of Ascot. He now had seen them a few times. The first function Christopher had ever met them was a long time ago. He remembered the romance of one of them. These same chic ladies attended the masquerade last year (Christopher unrecognised the ladies. The ladies disguised masqueraders wearing masks. Christopher recognised their disguise when every masquerader unmasked themselves!).

Christopher and Jennifer stood at the back of the ballroom. Standing in the background where no one took any notice of them whatsoever. All of the gathered guests stood among themselves while waiting for this dance to finally end. At present most of the guests found a partner and got ready in anticipation for the next dance.

Jennifer danced with a millionaire businessman. Christopher asked an attractive woman to dance with him, but she declined. Christopher then asked another woman for a dance, but she also refused to dance with him. Both women found partners to dance with. The women ended up dancing with someone else. The men were far more handsome than their previous partners. The voluptuaries had a tendency to overindulge.

Christopher stood somewhere at the back of the ballroom floor, watching the pairs and couples dancing.

Apparently, all of them having an enjoyable time. He paid attention, looking at the amorous couples dancing. Christopher observed almost everybody there. He caught sight of their joyful and blissful expressions, at how the couples dancing looked blissful! Perhaps enamoured and enraptured.

Christopher regretted coming to the ball. He felt quite unhappy, unloved and unwanted at this time. He was humiliated by being spurned. He became embarrassed at how none of the women bothered to dance with him. Both women refusing to dance!

Christopher left his sister to dance. To enjoy herself!

Christopher came out of the double doors, following signs which indicated an exit and rooms available. Christopher followed a number of guests going outside. There, Christopher also headed out into the lovely gardens which were scenically and photographically picturesque. The photographic picturesqueness was in colour and monochrome.

Christopher walked toward a fountain. The jets of water flowed out of it. The crystal water sparkled in the radiant light. It reflected with resplendence.

Christopher stood near the fountain. The strong jets of water emanate out from a fountain. Christopher stood still in a position. He cooled down from the blown light wind.

Christopher became calmer, cooler and more peaceful listening to the sounds of jets of water flowing out of the fountain. Christopher admired the landscape. The scenery itself was pretty delightful.

Christopher walked further on and looked at the flowerbeds. All of the blooming flowers and roses and blossomy rosebuds of natural great exquisiteness. Also, in beds many plants and shrubs were growing.

Christopher caught sight of topiary on either side of the gardens and down towards the bottom of the gardens. (This scenic spot was one of the most photographed scenes and spots!) There also lush plants were growing and shrubbery in beds and borders.

Christopher walked by people wandering through the grounds and gardens.

Christopher went further and further down to the end of the gardens. There he reached a labyrinth. He became wonderfully enchanted. Christopher was lost in a deep reverie. He admired the sight of the natural scenery. Christopher ventured into a labyrinth, going further and further down in it. His initial adventure into the labyrinth was unintentional. Christopher explored beyond it.

Suddenly Christopher came across a damsel wearing a beautiful burgundy gown. Her fresh complexion peachy and ruddy. The chic woman ran past him at a fast pace. Her footsteps re-echoed. Her fair hair was being blown in the wind. Her thick hair whipping up against her cheeks in a glow.

Christopher tried to run after the startled young woman running away.

Christopher was flustered as he had lost sight of the damsel in distress!

Christopher gave up chasing her, running after her.

Christopher got lost by going the wrong way, by taking a different direction while going along through the labyrinth. He had forgotten his way. He lost his bearings. He became confused at his whereabouts. Christopher took a deep breath. He tried to keep calm and not panic. He became tired. His heart was beating faster. His blood pulsated through his veins. His legs throbbed from pain. He felt fatigue.

He stopped somewhere in the labyrinth. He stood still to recover. He regained his breath. He tried to regain his composure. He stayed calm. Despite having anxiety.

Then he decided to proceed back up through the labyrinth. Christopher concentrated on finding the right way. At taking the right directions back despite having difficulty at finding it.

From his confusion about directions and his confused mind, Christopher was baffled at the confusing way along through the labyrinth, made increasingly difficult by his own indecision of making a right decision to find his way back out of the labyrinth, along the way back to try and find his way to get out of the labyrinth.

Unexpectedly, Christopher found scattered confetti and a scarlet ribbon. He spotted a trail of confetti scattered everywhere. The scattering of handfuls of confetti thrown. Christopher was surprised at finding a new ribbon dropped on the ground and the scattering of confetti there. Christopher bent down and picked it up. In the cool air he smelled the scent of cologne of a young woman's perfume. It was a ravishing scent of a fine luxury brand of perfume.

Christopher stuffed the long ribbon in his trousers pocket. He thought it was a beautiful girlish thing for girls!

Christopher thereafter proceeded further and further back out of the labyrinth, becoming determined to find his way out and from everywhere else beyond.

Finally, Christopher emerged out of it. He became relieved at finding his way out. He sighed with relief.

Christopher walked back up in the agoraphobic gardens, passing by a romantic couple holding hands and a few guests walking by, taking pleasure of admiration of the beautiful gardens.

Christopher reached the stately home. He entered an entrance. He avoided guests intentionally in groups: twosomes, threesomes and foursomes, and those few individuals alone. Christopher intended to be unsociable again, avoiding a large number of guests and the company of employees.

Reaching the hallway, Christopher found a housemaid doing the dusting to all the antiques. Christopher disturbed the housemaid from doing the dusting. Christopher asked the housemaid,

"Please can you tell me where the drawing room is?"

At once, the housemaid stopped doing the dusting to the rest of the valuable antiques. All of the antiques were polished and shiny. The housemaid put the duster down. The accommodating housemaid attended to Christopher by showing the guest the way to where the drawing room was. The uniformed housemaid pointing in the direction to take the way to the drawing room.

Christopher thanked the housemaid just before she left to make her way back in the hallway. The fit housemaid overworked using a duster to continue dusting the antiques.

Christopher entered in the drawing room. He stayed in the drawing room. He stayed downstairs.

Already in there relaxing themselves, in the drawing room were only a few guests enjoying their relaxation. The moment a guest had been intruded on. One of the guests had burst out of the drawing room. This female guest, an aristocrat, objected to her intrusion. The other two guests remained longer in the drawing room until finally both of them decided to leave after being intruded on by a stranger. The stranger's intrusion invaded their privacy.

Christopher was alone in the drawing room at this present time. He enjoyed his privacy. Christopher sat down on a studded leather armchair. It was enriched with a strong smell rich from real leather. Christopher enjoyed his time alone and his freedom for himself!

Christopher was unrestricted from being uninhibited. He took the necessary time to rest and relax himself. He recuperated and recovered by sitting alone by himself in a spacious drawing room. He rested in the silence.

About an hour later, Christopher was unhappy and moody at being neglected by his sister and from being shunned and snubbed by guests.

Christopher took offence at two elegant ladies declining to dance with him and from the ones ignoring him on purpose. He was offended at a snubber avoiding him with deliberate intention to shun! (Hours earlier Christopher had pent-up anger. Now he had calmed down after having a rest.)

Christopher came out of another entrance. He went out into the gardens again. He tensed up from agoraphobia. He got tired of getting lost. He became panicky. He walked out into the gardens, out along the beautiful lawn.

Christopher walked past lovers and a newly engaged couple. The fiancé whose fiancée proudly show off her engagement ring to some of their friends who marvelled at it. (These guests were invited to the stately home. These ones received their invitation cards first. Their personal invitation a priority from the hosts. These ones appreciating their privilege. The privileged granted first priorities.)

Christopher proceeded walking ahead down the gardens. He walked past ladies of Cheltenham wearing hats, lying down on the grass together. (The new turf lay on the soil, ground.) These romantic ladies romanticised. One of them chewed a strand of grass in her mouth.

Christopher ogled the women. He had a desire, a fancy for the prettiest woman.

Christopher went the wrong way, walking about the gardens aimlessly. His aimlessness purposeless. He turned back and went the other way. Christopher headed back to the stately home.

Christopher entered by the main entrance. He entered a crowded reception room. He was aware of guests and snobs watching him. He wondered why he had been given the privilege of an invitation to the ball. Some of the privileged guests. especially the aristocrats, shunned commoners. All of the plebeians were detested!

Christopher avoided the talkative strangers who were standing together while holding glasses of champagne in their hands. Christopher felt sickened by these persons' attitude. One of them had seeming superiority.

Christopher walked off and looked at the happy and blissful couples going past. Their expressions of love strikingly noticeable.

Christopher walked down the hallway and spent some time looking at the paintings. One of the paintings was scenic and there were various landscapes.

Christopher soon became distracted as he heard footsteps and shrill voices in the hallway. A woman's chuckle. The woman amused herself.

With curiosity, Christopher glanced at the chic, elegant women wearing hats. He ogled one of them. He stared at another woman unamused at him who burst out laughing. Christopher at first unrecognised the woman with jet black hair. Looking at the woman close up, her raven locks, he recognised her. It was the same

The Shadow of the Daughter's Ring

woman who was one of the masqueraders attending the masquerade months ago.

Christopher watched the models wander down the hallway, then all of them went into another room by themselves where these models spent time together. At present everybody else had been excluded from them. The exclusion lasted hours. The other rooms remained locked. Presently out of bounds.

Christopher forgot which room. He saw two men playing cards, playing a card game. One of them shuffled a pack of playing cards and dealt out all the playing cards. Both men were engrossed in card playing.

Christopher went somewhere else.

Christopher had seen antiques, ornaments, sideboards and cabinets and furniture. DO NOT TOUCH.

Christopher took notice of the displayed behind glass taxidermy and caught sight of a stag's head with its antlers hanging on the wall overhead. He noticed the magnificent coat of arms generally on display to the public.

Christopher passed by in the sitting room. He saw guests smiling at him. He was charmed by their pleasantness and the charming ladies' sweetness! The guests were seated and standing.

Christopher realised they were the host's employees and personal friends of theirs.

Christopher left them because he was inclined to be untalkative and unsociable.

Christopher went into another large room. In there he noticed the aquarium. He became calmer and cooler whilst looking at the various goldfish.

Sitting down on a chair, Christopher relaxed in the silence. He ended up staying by the aquarium for a short time. During that time, Christopher soon got bored of doing nothing in there. Everywhere else in this gloomy room had dull and dim light. There also it was shadowy and shady with dimness and dullness in the aquarium.

Christopher got up from a chair the moment other guests intruded on him. These guests invaded his privacy. Christopher felt irritable. He was irritated by them for intruding on him.

Quickly, Christopher left the room, having justification for his leaving. Christopher got fed up with being constantly ignored and shunned by people. (To some extent Christopher did regret being invited to the ball!)

Christopher went past guests. Christopher went somewhere else. He got tired of looking around the estate.

Christopher felt hungry. His stomach rumbled.

He came into the drawing room again. Christopher found only two guests already in there. These different guests were sitting down and talking.

Christopher slumped down on an easy chair near the big sash window. It was overlooking the side view of the garden sidewards.

Christopher relaxed and rested in the presence of these two guests. The two professional photographers talked about wildlife photography. One of the photographers talked to his colleague about his photographic material he used in a photography book for publication.

Christopher listened to some of their conversation. Both photographers shut up the moment Christopher listened to their conversation (he paid heed as they had engaged in their conversational sensationalism), as well as listening to their photography conversation about a photographic still!

Christopher rested while sitting on the easy chair, admiring the view of the natural landscape and scenery, this scene at a vertical sideward angle.

Christopher became distracted by someone's movement. One of the photographers rose, leaving his colleague to go alone to a dark room, with his motivational intention to develop a print. Earlier the same professional photographer used up the remaining roll of film in his camera, these various photographs of professional models taken in monochrome and black and white.

Christopher got tired of waiting for the start of the banquet. He glanced at his wristwatch again and again. He got fed up with waiting. He fidgeted.

On the dot, as soon as it was time for the banquet, Christopher got up immediately. He went out of the drawing room, leaving the photographer alone by himself. This photographer decided to stay in the drawing room for a longer time with the intention of waiting for his colleague to get back. His colleague was engrossed in developing prints in the dark room.

Christopher entered the dining hall which soon became full of banqueters. Christopher sat down on a chair near a corner of the dining table to eat up his repast. Christopher felt refreshed from nourishment and drink. He was irritated by all of the banqueters' babble and their clatter. Supposedly, everybody appeared to be exuberant, happy and joyous.

Christopher felt humiliated, looking at the prettier models sitting at the dining tables opposite, on their best behaviour, attracting attention as an individual amused herself. Their cuticles had been treated at a beauty parlour. Every model's fingernails were beautifully manicured and nail varnished. Accordingly with every model's hairstyle the same or different or with a variation of hairstyle which was either similar to theirs or with differences of variations of models' hairstyles at salon or hairdresser. The models' hairdressing done by a professional hairdresser. A bisexual, lesbian!

At present the chic models took no notice of the invited guest. All of the models snubbed, shunned and ignored Christopher again and again until the very end of the ball that night.

Christopher disliked the provocative and unprovocative models. He was jealous of them. From his own impression of them. Most of the models ostensibly were businesslike (a few of them potential businesswomen in the making), snubbers and humiliators and ignorers.

Unashamedly, Christopher disrespected models, as he thought of modelling as a stigma of degradation! A degrading occupation.

Christopher felt humiliated by the ambitious and arrogant models. From his inferiority, he had apparent discontent. He was dissatisfied at himself. Usually at his status. In his present state, Christopher felt sullen, miserable and moody. He took displeasure at the banquet. He disliked it. (However, on a positive note, Christopher enjoyed the novelty. His experience was disappointing as a result of the invitation to a stately home.)

Christopher unappreciated his special person invitation by the hosts. Christopher felt perturbed and uncomfortable seated. He had to get out of there.

He got up. He excused himself. He was ill-mannered and rude, standing up and leaving the dining table. He hurried out of the crowded dining hall. Nobody whatsoever really paid attention to Christopher leaving to get out of the dining hall.

Christopher may have been unnoticed leaving the grand dining hall.

Christopher headed back outside into the gardens. He kept on walking down the gardens which were several acres long. Christopher proceeded on through the gardens. He finally stopped as soon as he reached the trees further down near the bottom of the gardens which was within reach of the labyrinth. This particular tree was a bigger one. Perhaps the biggest tree in the whole gardens?

Christopher found it was an inconspicuous spot out of sight. He felt worn out, lethargic and lackadaisical while remaining standing on his feet. He tried to bear his exhaustion. Christopher lay down under a spot of a tree. He rested while lying down in the cool shade. It was a cooler spot in the shade. His body stretched out. At that time the guests walking by were going past Christopher, a daydreamer. He was engrossed in daydreaming.

In a shady and sunny spot there, persons' shadows emerged. Their shadows appearing, reappearing and disappearing. All their shadows faded away.

Over by the shady spots of the berried trees there were shadows and reflections from the radiant light which faded. Somewhere in the garden there, guests' and persons' shadows appeared and then vanished from sight. Their silhouettes noticeable in the semi-transparent marquee.

The Shadow of the Daughter's Ring

Christopher got up after resting alone in a secluded spot far away from everywhere else. Christopher's trousers were soiled and creased up. His black trousers had mud and grass stains. The ground was damp and slightly muddy from the moist soil.

Christopher straightened up. He smartened himself up. He smoothed out the creases in his trousers.

Christopher turned back. Going back the other way. Christopher strolled all the way back to the entrance.

At present there, standing outside by the entrance waiting for Christopher, were staff from the top modelling agency. The employees and greeters. In reaction and response to their warm welcome and from their greeting, Christopher greeted the welcomers by showing his approval to them all. Christopher acknowledged them with a gesture and a sweet sentiment.

"You are so kind. You're the nicest people I have known from a very short space of time."

Christopher greeted the employees. One of them a voluptuous secretary. Touching Christopher on his shoulder, the pleased personal secretary smiled with sweet charm.

Another colleague of hers worked at Personnel. The employer an interviewer involved in recruitment and employment. It did certainly remain the employer's personal responsibility. Other employees worked for different agencies.

"Are you having a good time?" asked the secretary.

"So far it has been a good experience. My sister is having a better time than I am. It's a pity I am alone," replied Christopher.

A businesswoman wearing a suit, standing at the back, appeared from behind the employees. The experienced businesswoman spoke up.

"Has Jennifer neglected you?"

Christopher grumbled at his neglectful sister who was enjoying herself. Jennifer avoided her brother intentionally. Was it because of embarrassment? Or her superiority of being a centre figure of attention! Jennifer's attraction did attract them!

"It's typical! My sister has forgotten about me. It's awful! My sister is having a ball!"

Another employer defended Jennifer for her obsessiveness for pleasure and her intention to have fun. Jennifer did intend to enjoy herself.

"You mustn't deny your sister her privilege. Her right. Isn't Jennifer entitled to do whatever she likes?"

Christopher was displeased at how his sister continued to neglect him.

"My sister will live it up!" said brother unashamedly.

An employee coming forward in movement paid heed to Jennifer's brother.

"Aren't you going to dance?" asked the employee.

Christopher evaded answering the employee's question. The employee repeated herself and asked the same question again.

"Well? Aren't you going to dance?"

Christopher became humiliated remembering the provocative voluptuaries who had declined to dance with him. He felt humiliated by both women's refusal. He was embarrassed.

"I still haven't danced yet. Not even once. Who knows, I may dance later."

The secretary paying attention to Jennifer's brother encouraged Christopher to have fun. The materialistic personal secretary was unashamed of her obsessive hedonistic tendencies.

Christopher referred to the hedonist.

"Are you here for pleasure or business?" asked Christopher.

The buxom personal secretary responded amiably.

"As always, we're here for business. We don't get any pleasure. Do we? Really there isn't any. It's work as usual. It's promotion to be precise. It's been a good day," said the secretary honestly.

Regarding Christopher's invitation to the stately home, Christopher took the opportunity to thank all of them personally for his random invitation to the ball. He was appreciative of their consideration for him, especially the host for allowing him an invitation.

"I'd like to thank you for my invitation. My invite did come as a complete surprise," said Christopher appreciatively.

Christopher was pleased at his pleasing invitation, his invitation card.

The employer replied first in response to Christopher's appreciation of his invitation to the ball.

"Don't thank us. Thank the host!" said employer.

"Now we must go. We have to see Jennifer," said the secretary.

Christopher stayed outside while the smart employees, employers and businesswomen went indoors.

Those guests that came outdoors went walking around the gardens, admiring the gardens. It was beautiful summer scenery. This summer photography had been taken weeks ago before the start of midsummer. (The summer months prior to midsummer. These summer days had been the hottest weather at summertime. This season hotter than previous years' summers.)

In advance the public viewed the main attraction of the stately home and gardens.

Christopher was alone by himself again. The loner lonely again.

Christopher stood outside near the grounds of the stately home, watching everyone else. He observed people. Some of the people Christopher had met earlier. (On previous occasions Christopher met the same people again and again. Meeting them again another time was an interesting experience and also humiliating.)

Christopher knew some of the acquaintances already. Most of them Christopher recognised. These strangers may have been employees working for the National Sector of Tourism in the country. Probably for tour operators?

The guests together walked off ahead in the distance. He no longer caught sight of any of them going down the gardens. His view of them all unnoticeable.

Suddenly other guests came outdoors.

Christopher observed the others going out along the grounds. From another entrance, the others came out together. The older ones wandering down the gardens. Some guests took delight in admiring the afterglow scenery of the gardens. The sight of it was a breathtaking view. The glowing radiance of the sunset. The beautiful natural skies. The sublime sunset.

Christopher was preoccupied. He thought that there was nothing worthy to take notice of. Christopher lost interest in practically everything else.

Christopher went indoors. He found his way to the drawing room. At this time, it had ease of access.

Christopher entered the drawing room. At this present time the drawing room was becoming crowded with more and more guests. The other guests came in and out of the drawing room. Christopher wanted to sit down. He had been standing up for a long time. Now shaky, he felt rather unsteady on his feet. At present he found that there was nowhere to sit down. Anywhere else made no difference for him to relax at ease. He might find that he might be intruded on again.

Christopher felt tired, enervated and exhausted. He stood by a large window, looking out at the garden, admiring the view of the garden at a different angle from standing opposite in a straight position. Christopher caught sight of the natural scenery of the landscape in the distance.

Suddenly Christopher was startled as he felt a person's hand rest on his shoulder. The person leaning on him caused him discomfort. Christopher felt uncomfortable from remaining standing.

Christopher turned around and faced that person face to face. A suave gentleman spoke to Christopher. His deep voice husky.

"Ahem! Young man. Is Jennifer your sister?" hemmed gentleman.

Christopher looked at the smartly dressed gentleman holding a pipe. Christopher recalled seeing the same gentleman a few hours ago when he had first seen him. At the time of meeting new guests when he had first been introduced to them. The hosts addressing all the guests gathered together. It was a preliminary introduction!

Christopher acknowledged the gentleman in response. His interest in the gentleman fascinated him.

"Jennifer is my sister," replied Christopher.

"I was curious. I always see you with Jennifer," grinned gentleman.

"Do you know Jennifer?" asked Christopher.

"I am acquainted," answered gentleman.

"What is your name?" asked Christopher.

The chauvinist did not hear Christopher the first time. "I beg your pardon?"

Christopher stepped forward.

"What is your name?" repeated Christopher.

"My name is Clarence," answered gentleman.

Christopher stretched out his hand. He shook Clarence's hand firmly.

"Pleased to meet you. My name is Christopher."

Clarence's handshake was firm. Clarence squeezed Christopher's hand.

"It's a pleasure to meet you," smiled Clarence.

"How long have you known my sister?" asked Christopher.

Clarence calculated the approximate time. "About a year, I guess. Maybe longer. I am concerned about Jennifer. You mustn't let your sister get corrupted. Don't let anyone lead her astray."

To a degree, Christopher appreciated Clarence's concern for his sister. He did have respect in some sort for Clarence.

"I do assure you that it won't happen. When Jennifer gets older, my sister will be chaperoned. All of her friends love and adore her," said Christopher assuredly.

"Jennifer is special. You really must be proud of your sister," said Clarence gruffly.

"I am very proud of my sister. Are you here for business?" asked Christopher.

"Well sort of. My colleague, a photographer, has taken photographs of a male model wearing cricket sweaters. I am proud of the model. I like him," puffed out Clarence.

Christopher showed interest in his occupation.

"Are you a photographer yourself?" asked Christopher.

"When I had first started out, I was freelance. Then I got my lucky break working for a photographer," said Clarence modestly.

"Humble beginnings," remarked Christopher.

With impatience, Clarence glanced at his solid gold wristwatch.

"I am late. I must get going. I am meeting my friend," said Clarence impatiently.

Christopher assumed Clarence had made a commitment. Christopher watched Clarence walk away among a few guests going out of the drawing room.

Christopher thought of the chauvinistic gentleman as being a nice man.

Going upstairs, Christopher went for a wander along the corridors. Christopher had forgotten his whereabouts. Everywhere did seem unusually strange to him. Christopher expected to meet his sister any time now.

Suddenly a door opened. The elegant models came out of a studio. One of them was his sister, Jennifer. A fashionable teenage model. The professional photographer had finished doing his photography.

Jennifer, a photogenic model, had finished doing her photo shoot. Jennifer pleased herself after being photographed. Jennifer's photo shoot only lasted for a very short time. (This session shorter than usual.)

The photographer assigned for this particular photography intended to do it that way. The photography session which included a photographic background. Today's photography from the photographer went according to schedule.

Waiting in the corridor, Christopher joined up with his pleased sister. Christopher admired the striking beauties going past along the corridor. A few voluptuous models indeed looked admirably stunning. Christopher ogled them. Christopher felt humiliated as sone of them took no notice of him. Christopher rushed away, leaving his sister again.

Jennifer expected to meet her brother in the ballroom in the next hour, in about an hour's time.

The Shadow of the Daughter's Ring

Christopher went out alone into the gardens again for the very last time that night. The dazzling shining lights shone in the dark.

During the night at that time, there were guests strolling about together, enjoying the company of their colleagues. A romantic couple walking hand in hand at the time, enjoying their romance without having an intrusion of any persons to contend with.

Along the gardens somewhere, Christopher stopped within reach of the grand stately home. Christopher was within sight of it. It was photographically scenic, the gardens and the grounds.

Christopher rested on the lawn, with his hands clasped behind his head. He moved his clammy hands from behind his head. He changed position. Here supine while looking up at the starry skies. His positional supineness as he faced up at the skies above.

Christopher appeared to be in a romantic mood. He enjoyed his fantasies. His fantasies became delirious ecstasies.

About an hour later, Christopher got up lazily from the lawn. He stretched oneself out. Christopher looked at his watch. He timed himself, calculating the remaining time left. The minutes which remained left of an hour.

Christopher went in an entrance. From there he found his way to the ballroom. He took the right direction. Christopher went to where the ballroom was situated right down at the bottom, at the very last door. The white door was unnumbered compared to other numbered bedroom doors down the long corridors.

Christopher entered the ballroom, expecting to meet his sister waiting for him. Christopher became quite determined to dance tonight despite his inhibitions and feeling dejected.

He looked for his sister in the ballroom. He saw Jennifer standing in a corner by a wall near the door while waiting for her brother to come and get her.

Christopher smiled at his sister. He stretched out his hand which his sister took hold of, squeezing it tightly. Christopher ended up dancing with his beloved sister. Both brother and sister ended up only dancing once at this time, for only a few minutes.

Christopher cheered up. He enjoyed himself. Christopher took great pleasure from his dance, at dancing with his sister.

213

Christopher showed deep love for his joyous sister, appreciating how his sister intervened in the ball as a last resort.

Neither of them took any interest in anybody else dancing. At this time, it was so late at night. Both of them had forgotten about everyone else. Did they distinguish between the most favoured persons and the ones discriminated and neglected by the host?

Did they also differentiate between the most successful candidates and employees and those ones and applicants thwarted with departmental promotion?

Christopher and Jennifer were both preoccupied. They were unconcerned at everybody else, since they were oblivious of the couples and pairs dancing.

Afterwards, brother and sister left the ballroom together quickly. They both hurried out of the entrance. They both ran out onto the tiny gravel drive.

Christopher and Jennifer quickly got in a car. The car whisked them off fast.

The coy passenger seated in the passenger seat with her fastened seat belt. The passenger unexplained the circumstances.

Christopher and Jennifer got home at 1.22 a.m. The inaccuracy at the time of their arrival (at their house) inaccurate as everyone's time on their watches was either slow or fast.

After stopping off, the passenger was driven home next to her house miles and miles away.

19
Christopher's Deep Memories

One day, Christopher spent time alone in a garage. Christopher's mother, a driver in her car, had reversed out of the garage and driveway. The car pulled up out on a road before the driver put her foot on the accelerator to accelerate down the road.

Christopher stood near the front of the garage. Christopher remained in the empty garage for a short time. During that time, Christopher reflected on a deceased Mod!

Christopher's deep memories came flooding back. He felt deeply saddened by his sad memories. Christopher was deeply mournful and sad. He was overcome with sorrow!

Christopher stepped forward. He came out of the garage. Standing by an opened garage door. He smelled the smoky air exhaust fumes. The fumes built up of carbon monoxide.

He pulled down the garage door. He came indoors. He climbed the stairs. Going upstairs to his bedroom. Christopher stayed in his bedroom alone. He spent his time as he mourned for a Mod! A tall Blond Apollo! (The deceased's ancestors used to be involved in film sets, in film studios of various film productions of major film companies.)

"Open the door. It's me, Jennifer," said sister impatiently.

Christopher saw an envelope being pushed under the door. He picked up the envelope. With his other hand, he opened his bedroom door, allowing Jennifer to enter in his bedroom.

Christopher opened the envelope. He took out all the photographs from the envelope. Christopher looked at the photographs with such interest. He had joyful admiration for his sister. Every photograph of Jennifer was naturally photogenic. Her narcissistic poses so natural, elegant and feminine. Jennifer's imagery in the sceneries was photographic. Of course, Jennifer liked all her photographs. Jennifer seemed obsessed by her favourite photographs.

Jennifer was growing up into an older teenager engaged in narcissistic exhibitionism. Did Jennifer's photographs reflect her exhibitionism?

Christopher spent longer looking at the last photograph. He preferred the last one. This photograph was his most favourite one of his sister.

"These photographs are lovely. You're glamorous."

Jennifer perked up from her brother's remarks. Jennifer took all the photographs and a big envelope from her brother. Jennifer put several photographs back in an envelope. She took great pride from her photographs.

"These ones are so personal. I wouldn't show them to the world. Don't I look wonderful! Uh! I am Cinderella at the ball!" said sister figuratively.

Christopher was greatly impressed by all of the photographs. His sister was an impressive teenage model! The promising model professional.

"You're a natural. These photos are really fine," remarked brother.

"Hey! I have to admit I was over the moon," admitted sister.

Christopher reminded his sister to attend a Sunday Service at church. He encouraged Jennifer to attend one the sooner the better. From his experience, Christopher realised the dangers of being exposed. As a result of learning from his experiences, he was wary of people, public and society and authorities.

Christopher was an afraid citizen, while his sister was a brave teenager, a former pupil, a school-leaver, accustomed to spiritual warfare and spiritualism. (Jennifer was a member of a witch's coven and attended seances. Jennifer was an oracle of mediums.)

"Now, you must go to church. So why don't you? Why don't you come to church with me now? It doesn't have to be for long," insisted brother.

Jennifer was apathetic about going to church. Jennifer's interests preoccupied her mind.

"You go. I don't wish to go. I don't wish to see anyone right now," groaned Jennifer.

Christopher insisted that his sister should go. He pressed upon his sister to go to church. Christopher insisted his sister attended a Sunday Service at church. Christopher made Jennifer aware of his concerns for her. Christopher prompted his sister to go to church. Reminding Jennifer again of the need for church.

Jennifer listened to her brother. She obeyed him. Realising the consequential importance of sanctuary, Jennifer decided to join her brother by going to church.

Jennifer stipulated, "I will come. Not for long. Chris, it shan't be for long," repeated Jennifer.

Christopher and Jennifer both went down the stairs and out of the front door. They walked out onto the driveway. Christopher and Jennifer got into a car. Christopher drove to a back street within distance of the high street along the road by the kerb. Christopher parked his car by a parking meter. Christopher and his sister got out of the car.

Christopher walked up to the parking meter. A parking ticket printed out. He took out the printed parking ticket. He put a parking ticket onto the windscreen inside his car for the traffic warden to check it.

Christopher and Jennifer walked up to the top of the side road towards the high street. From there they turned left to go straight up the shopping street. Christopher and Jennifer continued walking up to the top of the shopping street. and high street. Reaching the end of the shopping street, they turned right to go down another road. They walked past a chain restaurant and pharmacy. From near there the shoppers were going through an entrance on the ground floor leading down to the busy shopping centre.

Christopher and Jennifer come to a church located in the high street. They both entered. Christopher wondered what denomination it was. He tried to differentiate between the denominations which he had forgotten about. It was either Anglican or Presbyterian.

Christopher and Jennifer went inside the church. There was an area for tables and chairs.

Those who had come to church that day were from the local community, churchgoers, or those from the public and also mothers with their toddlers in prams attended crèche. In the area of the seated area, there, near a door at the corner, there was an office and on the other end of it, a kitchenette. A helper served hot drinks, cakes and biscuits.

There, straight ahead, at the furthest end, was a door which led to two rooms which were occupied and a prayer room constantly used throughout the day by worshippers and Christians.

On a noticeboard pinned up were leaflets, pamphlets and a newsletter.

Christopher and Jennifer went towards the locked double doors which were directly opposite at a corner straight ahead of them. They both stopped and stood still, looking for the opportunity to use the chapel. They asked the caretaker standing by the double doors, holding a bunch of keys in his hand.

"Can we go in?"

The caretaker took notice of them.

The caretaker had seen him many times.

The caretaker unlocked the door and unbolted the other door. The caretaker opened the door, allowing them both to go in, without the caretaker imposing restrictions.

Christopher and Jennifer entered the nearly empty chapel. There in the chapel, in a confined space on one side of it, were stacked up chairs galore. The wooden floor was shiny and polished in that claustrophobic enclosed space which was piled up with the very many chairs stacked up on top. The restricted space was claustrophobic.

At present the caretaker imposed his restrictions on other people, refusing them entry.

Christopher and Jennifer each took a chair from the stack of chairs. They placed them down on the wooden floor somewhere in the chapel. It was yards and yards away from all the stacked-up chairs.

They were both dissatisfied with the positions of their chairs. The actual positional angle of it. They both rose. They picked up their chairs and moved to another position. They sat down on their chairs facing the presbytery.

Christopher and his sister relaxed together in the peace and quiet of the chapel, enjoying their privacy without the intrusion of anyone else wanting to enter. This modern church was a different denomination from the other churches that he used to go, to attend church services. The others such as the chapel and St Marks had a prie-dieu.

Christopher engaged in deep contemplation. Christopher meditated in the silence.

Jennifer wanting attention disturbed her brother's meditation.

Christopher lost concentration on his contemplativeness. For about five minutes, Christopher had been meditative.

Jennifer patted her brother on his back.

"Well, I am here. You didn't think I would come."

Christopher smiled at his sister. He moved sideways to reach out to touch his sister affectionately. Christopher looked at his angelic sister. His innocent sister a virgin! A pure teenager who was the purest of all the other virginal teenage girls!

"I am glad you have come with me. You did change your mind. Going to church isn't bad at all."

Jennifer felt restless and uncomfortable at remaining seated. She rose and stretched her legs. In the chapel Jennifer walked around on the wooden floor in circles. The spaces becoming claustrophobic. In the chapel it was cooler in the shade. His sister walked around the chapel while admiring the stained-glass windows reflecting the light. Jennifer's stiletto heels echoed on the wooden floor. She was deep in thought. Jennifer proceeded up and down the chapel.

"It's so peaceful here. Where else can you find peace as great as this?" sighed sister.

"I am pleased you have come to church. Don't you feel better for it? Coming here? Your mother does insist that you should," smiled brother.

Jennifer stood still with her arms crossed gracefully, ladylike. Her mannerism quite elegant (without exception Jennifer learned etiquette at charm school).

"My mom cares about me. All this pressure, it's dreadful. How do I cope?" paused Jennifer. "I do think my mother is right after all."

"My mom is superstitious. It's in her nature. She cares about you. Mom loves you!"

"Our mom is difficult. I know my mom loves me. I love my mom, too! At times we don't get on."

Christopher took an interest in something. Christopher looked at the wall again straight opposite. On it a chart of baptisms from the past up until the present day. The chart included christening of married couples' babies from the past till the most recent christenings. Christopher admired the calligraphy.

The radiant sunlight shone through the sky roofs. The fresh air circulated throughout the chapel. It was air-conditioned.

Christopher and Jennifer stayed together for another half an hour in the silent chapel, before leaving the church.

They made their way back to a side road to get to the parked car. At daytime it was full of parked cars at parking meters.

Christopher and Jennifer got in the car. Christopher drove home, getting back home in the afternoon.

***

One Saturday afternoon, there was a tea party held in the garden of the Staples' house. Only a small number of children had been invited to the tea party.

The children ate sandwiches, cupcakes, crisps, ice cream or jelly and peaches and drank orange squash.

Jennifer's mother Sally organised the tea party. It was a treat for the children. Expecting it this summer, this year.

Jennifer was a helper attending to the children. Christopher stood back while watching the children enjoying themselves. All the children took pleasure from their treat. They had such a good time together. One of the children invited to the tea party was James sitting at the garden table with all his friends.

Most of the children had an appetite, except for James who lost his appetite. James seemed to be serious while his friends were in a happy mood. With James' chair moved away from the garden table, Christopher listened with interest to Jennifer talking to amused and happy children. One of them interrupting, amused himself by telling a joke.

Christopher took notice of the godson sitting on a chair away from the garden table. James felt discomfort. He felt pain in his knee.

James left the garden table with the intention of avoiding his playful friends, intending to play among themselves out in the big garden.

James went indoors. Christopher observed James. He wondered if James had trouble.

In the lounge James sat on the armchair. He rested himself. James moaned from the discomfort of pain.

Christopher standing still nearby watched his sister roll up James' trousers. Christopher noticed the sight of a plaster on James' kneecap. Jennifer made a fuss over James. James, a sulker, kept quiet. Jennifer stooped down and gently rubbed James' kneecap. Jennifer tried to sooth the little boy's pain. James felt discomfort and stinging pain on his kneecap. A few days ago, his kneecap had a dressing.

"You must be careful when you are playing. Your mommy worries about you. You must stop running about. You're a silly boy," cautioned Jennifer.

Jennifer was fond of James. Jennifer loved James.

James regretted being disobedient and stubborn. His disobedience was regretful.

"Mommy is good to me. She lets me play."

Jennifer raised her deep soft voice. "Chris, can you read to James please? That would certainly cheer him up."

The hours earlier during the day, Christopher had rested in bed. He avoided the children, as he had been selfish, unthoughtful and from having an inconsideration for others.

"I'll read to you later. You'll be staying the night. I will read to you this evening," said Christopher.

James sulked and fidgeted.

Jennifer rolled down his long trousers. Jennifer hemmed up the bottom of his trousers to stop James' trousers from dragging under his trainers.

Christopher went outdoors, expecting to see the children out in the garden. On the garden table seated children did quite good drawings or paintings of pictures.

Christopher took notice of one of the pictures. This one was Father Christmas. A caricature of Federick.

Much further on in the garden, the few girls were engrossed in skipping.

Christopher going forward had watched them. Their quick graceful movements impressed Christopher. Every girl skipping soon got tired from skipping energetically. Every girl soon lost momentum when every time the skipping rope got caught between their feet when skipping vigorously. Every girl took it in turns to skip. Two of the girls each holding a wooden handle of the skipping rope while standing on the lawn on either side of each other, the strong skipping rope going faster and faster.

The two girls sang and chanted. Christopher watching was uncertain if both girls were singing nursery rhymes.

The last girl had stopped skipping. The girl gasped out after physical exercise and exertion. The girl rested, recovered and regained her breath.

One of the girls holding a skipping rope in her hand spoke in a soft voice.

"Would you like to have a go?"

Christopher hesitated, then nodded uneasily.

He decided to attempt skipping.

He got into position, standing still and waiting. The two girls held handles of a skipping rope, standing on either side while facing one another opposite. The skipping rope taut.

Christopher tried to skip. He could not skip. The few girls chuckled, laughing at the way he skipped. The girls found it rather amusing at how he tried to skip.

Christopher was embarrassed at how he made a spectacle of himself.

Christopher decided to give up. One of the girls showed Christopher how skipping should be done. The graceful girl showed Christopher how to skip step by step. Paying attention, Christopher watched the girl skipping gracefully. Christopher was impressed at how well the girl skipped. He admired the graceful girl skipping faster and faster, the skipping rope going increasingly faster and faster. The skipping girl had technical uniqueness and quickness at skipping. The girl moving quicker and quicker. The girl's gracefulness in her movement at skipping.

Out of all the girls skipping, Gill was undoubtedly the best at skipping. The youngest of the three girls.

Christopher smiled with joy as he walked off leaving the few girls. The girls were amused at how he tried to skip. The three girls were untalkative as they rested together while lying down on the lawn when romanticising or daydreaming. One of them in a reverie, in a dreamy state.

Christopher walked to the group of boys sitting at the garden table drawing and painting. Christopher decided to spend some time with the boys engrossed in painting and drawing. Christopher stood still and looked at one of the boy's unfinished drawings. The boy colouring his picture on a drawing paper. Christopher wondered who it depicted?

"Explain to me what this picture is," said Christopher.

The reticent boy explained.

"It is Santa. Who else?"

Christopher sympathised with the boy's heartache. He empathised with the mournful boy, how he was feeling. The sad boy mourned for Mr Staples, the old, bearded gentleman, an elderly Christopher's grandfather. The bereaved also grieved for Mr Staples including a small number of boys and girls.

The other boys took no notice of Christopher. One of the boys immersed deep in thought.

Christopher left the boys by going back indoors.

Christopher went into the unlocked study, going towards the safe at the front of the room. Christopher had memorised the simple combination. He turned all the digits of the dial. Christopher opened the safe and counted his money. He calculated that over two hundred pounds had been stolen.

Christopher thought he must have miscounted the banknotes when doing the counting up.

Christopher then took out a wallet from his pocket. He put the new banknotes in a money bag and a money box. He put it into the safe, then closed the safe. Christopher added to the amount which was now over two thousand pounds. He noticed Jennifer's valuable jewellery was still in the safe for security measure and purposes.

Christopher went outdoors, finding Jennifer outside in the garden with a few girls.

Christopher, losing his patience, questioned his sister. He confronted her with a purposeful intention.

"Did you take my money from the safe?" scowled Christopher.

Jennifer hesitated in answering.

"Keep your voice down."

Jennifer from her embarrassment hushed him up in the presence of observant girls. Jennifer felt uncomfortable discomfort. She flushed and blushed.

Christopher put his arm around his sister. He led Jennifer away. They both walked in the direction of the house.

"Did you take my money?" repeated brother.

"No. I haven't," denied sister.

Christopher accused his sister of stealing his money from the safe.

"You have taken it, haven't you? Tell me!"

Jennifer denied her brother's accusation. Jennifer was wrongly accused by her brother's false allegation.

"I will clear up. I haven't taken your damn money!" protested sister.

"Father doesn't steal. And you do know the combination."

"I don't know it. Anyway, I thought it had changed. You can't accuse me. You can't prove it! You do not have proof," remonstrated sister.

"Aren't you good with figures?" said brother.

Jennifer put both her hands on her swayed hips gracefully.

"I can differentiate between figures in maths and of course my own figure," said Jennifer sardonically.

Christopher burst out laughing. He laughed at his sister's wit.

"It's not funny. It's just not a laughing matter. It's serious. I am telling you."

Jennifer was obsessed with her valuable diamonds. She remained obsessional about her jewellery.

"My diamonds are still in the safe. I haven't yet taken them out."

"So they are," gestured brother.

Jennifer remonstrated against her brother's accusation.

"How can it be me? I haven't done it! I haven't taken it," shrugged Jennifer.

Christopher mentioned he had called his father a few hours ago. Christopher confirmed his communication as well as a short conversation with his father.

"I have asked our father if he has taken it. Our father hasn't taken it. You should really tell the truth. I am disgusted," glowered brother.

Jennifer remonstrated her case of her denial of theft.

"You're accusing me. Besides, I've got my own money from modelling now. Why on earth do I want your money when I have got my own money?"

Christopher was baffled at the amount of stolen money taken from the safe. Without certainty Christopher could not explain the subsequent theft from a money box.

"It doesn't make sense. Can you explain the stolen money?"

"Chris, look in my purse. Perhaps that will satisfy your doubt," scowled sister.

Christopher unzipped his sister's leather handbag. He took a purse out of Jennifer's handbag. He opened his sister's purse. In Jennifer's purse there were no banknotes, only lots of coins which accumulated after going shopping regularly, a number of times.

Christopher had a bad conscience. He sympathised with his sister at having hardly any money and no savings saved up.

Christopher closed his sister's purse. He then put it back into her handbag. He zipped up Jennifer's handbag.

***

Throughout the evening, the doorbell chimed again and again. A melodic sound resounding.

Quickly, Christopher answered the front door as parents came to pick up their children. Christopher, his sister and parents stood by the doorway, waving goodbye while watching them leave to get in their car.

Later, Christopher went upstairs holding a tray which had hot drinks and cookies on a tea plate. Christopher came into the spare bedroom. He put the tray down on top the dressing table. The dressing table mirror (facing straight opposite the window) made a dazzling reflection. The sunshiny radiance of the sunrays reflected on the mirror. The radiant brightness of it a gloriousness.

James spent the night in the spare bedroom where James usually stayed the night every Saturday. James munched his cookies and drank his hot chocolate drink. James wearing his pyjamas got in bed.

Christopher read James a bedtime story. His sister compelled him to do so. Christopher did not have a choice in the matter. Christopher continued to read from a page of a children's book where he had last finished reading. Christopher read James an adventure story.

James took enjoyable pleasure from Christopher reading to him. James was enthralled at listening to boys' adventures. James was excited at Christopher reading to him.

About an hour later, the little boy fell asleep.

Jennifer entered the spare bedroom. She came up to James who was asleep in his bed. Jennifer tucked James up in bed. She kissed him on his forehead.

Christopher took a tray from the dressing table. He came out of the bedroom with his emotional sister deeply passionate.

***

Early next morning, Mary picked up her son and drove home.

***

At the weekend, Christopher rested for hours until the afternoon. He joined his sister and her friends in the living room.

Jennifer, with her irresistible charm, entertained her friends. They were amused at the entertainment.

***

On Monday morning, Christopher rang up the library. His employer. He spoke to one of his employees.

Christopher made up an excuse, saying that he was feeling unwell today.

Christopher decided to take the day off. Christopher spent the day looking at holiday brochures. Christopher was interested in a package holiday. He remained undecided regarding the whereabouts of his destination. He thought about going to Menorca. However, he changed his mind in preference for Mallorca. He thought that Valencia was a less popular destination compared to other tourist regions, even though it was a historical place of interest.

Christopher was interested in other Spanish regions, particularly the locations of the paradisiacal islands interested him, especially the scenic paradise!

Christopher desired glamour and was interested in the Spanish nightlife. He was particularly interested in the five-star hotels with their balconies and highly luxurious swimming pools. These ones appealed to him in particular. He satisfied his intent at having romantic fantasies and carnal desires.

Christopher remained undecided at making up his mind.

In the regions the hotel rooms were available in regional parts of Spain. Everywhere else he looked at and read about. Keeping informed of these hotels was informative. Its information and pictures were appealing, inviting and tempting. The prices at this time were more expensive at the high season.

In his narrowest of choices, from the selection of hotels, Christopher finally made up his mind. He chose his option. Christopher made his final decision. Christopher ended up choosing Ibiza.

He booked his holiday at a local travel agent, without any consideration of telling his own family first about it.

Christopher went in the lounge. He spent time alone by himself. He sat down on an armchair resting in the silence.

Jennifer stormed into the lounge. She informed her brother of the situation of what her father had done.

"Father has sold Grandfather's books! He sold the lot!" informed sister.

"Has he? He hasn't, has he?"

"I am afraid so," confirmed sister. "The bloody lot."

In a rage, Christopher burst out of the lounge, leaving his sister. Christopher rushed upstairs, going to his bedroom. He stayed in his bedroom until his anger subsided.

Christopher pondered on his grandfather. Christopher was outraged that Grandfather's books had been sold without any consideration given whatsoever.

Grandfather used to have an obsessional attachment to his books. Grandfather was a bibliophile.

Christopher also had his memories of Christmas when Grandfather dressed as Santa Claus. He used to make sad and deprived children happy. All the rapturous and blissful children loved Father Christmas as he gave them each a gift to every boy or girl.

Christopher stayed in his bedroom for many hours. He hated his father!

That night, Christopher dreamt.

He had forgotten about his dream when waking up early next morning.

20

The High Season

During the summer, the Staples went on holiday to the Balearic Islands.

The day after their flight, Christopher rested, recovering from jet lag.

Christopher got out of bed. He got dressed. He familiarised himself with the strangeness of different surroundings. (Apparently everything was completely different in comparison to a week ago. Working in a department. Sitting at a desk. Using a VDU.)

Christopher walked out onto a balcony overlooking the view of a sandy beach in the distance. Christopher admired the view of it. The breathtaking scenery.

He lost his desire to swim in the sea. At his age now, Christopher became flabby and undesirable. He had inhibitions about showing his half-naked body in public.

He perspired as he stood out at facing the radiant sun. The shining sunrays blazing and blinding. His eyes blinded at the sunlight.

Christopher's untanned body, skin, was covered by the smart casual clothes he wore.

He came out of his hotel room. He took a lift to the ground floor. He walked past the elegant reception. At the reception, the busy receptionist attended to the immediate arrival of guests who checked in for their reservation at the reception.

In the seated area there were holidaymakers sitting down with their families. The oak table had lots of women's magazines piled up on it.

Passing by guests and holidaymakers, Christopher came out of an entrance of the resort. Christopher walked further on, going towards a beautiful beach. Christopher walked along the beach. On the beach, countless sunbathers lounged on the sands, some on sun-loungers beneath sunshades.

Christopher expected to find his family on the beach. His family lounged about on the beach. His father held a cone, eating up his fresh ice cream. Tara and Sebastian were occupied at making a big sandcastle. Mother and daughter sunbathed together next to each other. Jennifer and Mother were blissful and joyous at sunbathing in the paradisiacal surroundings of the golden beach, the pure gold sands. The fine sands thick and golden, the paradisiacal sceneries amazingly breathtaking.

Christopher stood away from his family some yards away. Christopher thought of Grandfather. Since his beloved grandfather passed away, his life had never ever been the same again. His fond memories of his grandfather made him feel so sad. Christopher was mournful, bereaved and regretful. He remained unable to come to terms with the loss of his grandfather.

Christopher remained unenthusiastic about going walking with his family. The rest of his family were uninterested at going for a walk. Christopher just wanted to relax in comfort and indulge in luxury, perhaps occupy his time taking a look at the sublime sunset or sunrise in his dreamy state of mind. He wanted to take delight in his fantasies and ecstasies.

Christopher decided to join his father to take a walk all the way up around the beach. They both walked a fair distance, finally reaching the café, harbour, bars and restaurants.

Along the route of their walk, there were also facilities for water sports.

Christopher and his father entered a bar. There was a choice of a few bars to choose from, including a luxury wine bar.

Christopher and his father sat outside the bar. During the daytime, it was crowded with people. They both sat down at a vacant table. As soon as the barmaid came to attend to them, they ordered their drinks. They both enjoyed the view of the scenic lagoon in the distance.

"This is a millionaire's paradise. The Spaniards are so happy here, aren't they?" said Father cheerfully.

From their observational impression, most of the inhabitants and locals who resided in these parts were Spaniards and Iberians. (Travellers from mainland Spain from Mallorca and Menorca go travelling down in this region.)

"It's as pretty as a postcard. It's just perfect with such a lovely view."

The barmaid came and served them with their beverages.

Christopher and his father quenched their thirst. They both gulped down their glassful of Coca Cola and beer. They were refreshed from drinking up their drink.

Christopher spilled some of his drink on his shorts.

"What do you think of Ibiza?" asked Christopher.

"Ibiza is a beautiful island. It's different from anywhere else I have been to on my holidays and my travel. This place is for nightclubbing and parties. It has lovely beaches, some of the finest ones," answered Father.

Christopher interrupted his father by saying that he took note of the cultural characteristic of Ibiza, especially predominantly night-clubbers. The night-clubbers' traits at Ibiza nightclubs. Christopher was inclined to be wistful, pensive and regenerated.

"I am too old for nightclubbing. All this decadence and hedonism. It certainly doesn't appeal to me anymore. Why on earth did I come here? I have no wish to return to Ibiza," grumbled Christopher.

"Son, I do feel the same way. I too no longer have an interest in Ibiza anymore. My wife loves it here. Sally raves about it. My daughter likes to go nightclubbing. She's a raver! Jennifer can't wait until she is eighteen. Jennifer doesn't want to miss out on the fun in Ibiza," grinned Father.

Christopher remained seated while his father went to the toilet. He sat while waiting for his father to pay the bill. The bar became more crowded with tourists and holidaymakers.

The restaurant nearby was full of diners outside who dined out. Christopher observed people, persons, in their groups. The countrymen and countrywomen Spaniards. The rest of the others seemed to be Europeans and Mediterranean.

The Shadow of the Daughter's Ring

Christopher got flustered in the presence of strangers and the company of Spaniards who stood together and toasted amongst themselves. All the revellers were exuberant and ecstatic.

Christopher got up, moving past persons as he made his way out. Christopher went out of the bar outdoors and stood waiting for his father. He admired the view of the beautiful lagoon, its stunning aquamarine waves. He marvelled at the stunning strikingness of the lagoon; its scenic invitingness was a great delight. The natural surroundings were scenic.

Christopher and his father turned back as soon as they finally reached the other end. They both walked down the beach, walking along the shore on the golden sands. Christopher breathed in the fresh air. The sultry sea-wind was cooler along the shore.

Christopher wore his sunglasses to conceal his eye expression and movement and to cover up his eyes. Christopher walked past suntanned figures and bodies everywhere along the beach. He ogled a buxom woman sunbathing. The sunbather's beautiful figure aroused the ogler. Everywhere and anywhere none of the sunbathers took any notice of either of them walking.

Christopher remained calm and cool whilst he fumed at the women. He failed to attract or impress anybody else lying down when sunbathing. Christopher was still unimpressionable at this present time. His trendy clothes Hawaiian.

Christopher fretted at being an undesirable male! Fretting in the presence of other sunbathers, while in the company of their female friends, girlfriends.

Walking back a distance, Christopher and his father rejoined their family, at that time taking pleasure from the enjoyment of relaxation, as their family intended to lounge around on the beach for hours longer.

Sebastian and Tara were still occupied at making their dream sandcastle. The other children helped them to make their sandcastle. The time it took to make the sandcastle. It took quicker to make because of the children helping them. Sebastian and Tara wanting help from them. They grovelled at those ones helping them, appreciating their help to make the sandcastle.

Within less than an hour, the dream sandcastle had been made. All the children were satisfied and pleased at their finished sandcastle.

Christopher was impressed at the finally finished sandcastle. He stood admiring the impressive sight of it. He congratulated all the children who joined in and made it, all the children's hard work and effort which they had all put in to make the sandcastle. Christopher regarded all the children as angels!

Christopher had forgotten to bring his camera. He regretted being unable to take photos of it. The photos could have reminded him of the angelic children. (Christopher enjoyed puritanical times with a few Spanish children, the inhabitants.)

Christopher reminded his father to take photographs, preferably those photographically scenic ones of great nature's beauty! (His father possessed a camera and was proficient in photography.) He also encouraged the rest of his family to take holiday snaps. Two of them were filled with enthusiasm to take photos. Additionally, this included the breathtaking sceneries of the natural impressiveness of the mountainous range.

Christopher spoke briefly to all his family before leaving them together by themselves.

The hot weather was sweltering. The heat becoming hotter and hotter from the scorching sun shining. Today the sunny day and the weather was the hottest of summer.

Christopher walked all the way back to the resort in the distance. His father accompanied his son!

Christopher entered in the entrance of the resort and walked past the reception and occupied receptionist on duty. On the ground floor, Christopher took a lift to his floor. He got out of a lift with a paying guest.

Going down the long corridor, he looked for his hotel room number, remembering the actual number of his hotel door. At the hotel door, Christopher slotted a card in it. The hotel door automatically unlocked. Christopher took the card from the slot. He entered his hotel room. He was too tired to bother to shower. His sweaty clothes stuck to his sticky sweat-soaked body. His body sweaty from perspiration. His anti-perspirant deodorant gave him soothing comfort.

Christopher lay down on his bed and rested. His tension eased as he relaxed in comfort in the peaceful silence. His saliva dribbled down deep onto a soft pillow.

From an open window, Christopher breathed in the fresh air. Half-awake, Christopher enjoyed the heavenly sensations of the Spanish climate. The Fahrenheit drop in temperature as a result of humidity. The weather was oppressive.

Christopher stayed in his hotel room. He avoided everybody else. Christopher wanted his own privacy. Keeping quiet. Christopher rested today.

Yesterday, the flight and travelling had been exhausting. He suffered with jet lag.

Since Christopher was alone in his hotel room, he wanted to rest in his bed. Christopher overindulged in the luxury comforts of his hotel room. Christopher ended up staying the rest of the long night in his hotel room.

Christopher declined to come down to the hotel and see his family who were expecting him to come to the bar.

***

The next day, after breakfast, Christopher, feeling tired and moody, went back to bed again. He rested until about noon.

Later in the afternoon, Christopher and his father went to the restaurant outdoors at the hotel. They sat down at a vacant table. At that time there were only a few diners present at the restaurant.

Christopher and his father waited a short time before the waiter came to serve them. The waiter served them first their drinks which they had ordered. Christopher drank a glassful of Coca Cola, and his father drank a coffee. They ate a bowlful of chips each and a fresh sandwich.

After about an hour later, Christopher got up from his chair. He left his father alone again.

Going out of the resort, Christopher strolled down to the beach. He expected to find his mother and sister sunbathing together in a secluded spot on the beach. Tara and Sebastian played happily together, and Sally and Jennifer were snoozing under a sunshade while lying down on a tartan blanket.

Jennifer and her mother were unaware of Christopher being present. He took immediate notice of their suntanned bodies becoming darkly tanned from exposure to the scorching sun. Jennifer looked ravishing. Her irresistibility caused wonder among oglers, lechers and starers. His sister's sensuousness was striking. Her figure quite curvaceous. The teenager's eroticism an obsession. Jennifer had an obsessional teenager's narcissism. The teenager's eroticism a narcissism. A teenage narcissistic pre-occupation.

Christopher went to the sea. He joined Sebastian and Tara in the ultramarine sea. The two children played and splashed water at each other.

Christopher cooled down while going in the water. He remained alert and wide awake. He was in a playful mood. By playing with the two children in the calm sea. He liked to see them happy. He wondered at how long they could stay that way without squabbling. He admired the good children. It was seldom that they misbehaved. One of the other children behaved badly. This boy had a tantrum at his mother. In a temper, the violent boy sulking stormed off.

Christopher splashed about in the sea with the two playful children also splashing in the waters. The three of them having fun. They certainly did enjoy their time spent together. None of the others intruded on their privacy.

Christopher's clothes were sopping wet in the deep sea. His hair wet and splashing water got in his eyes. He blinked, his eyesight and vision blurred. His eyes bloodshot.

Going out of the sea, Christopher used his unbuttoned shirt sleeve rolled up and tucked in to wipe his eyes. Christopher got out of the sea first, with the two children trailing behind in the sea. Christopher's bloodshot eyes were stinging in discomfort.

Christopher went walking back to the resort in the distance.

On the ground floor the lift at present was full up of people getting in the lift. Christopher was too impatient waiting to get in the vacant lift. He took the staircase to get up the flights of stairs.

Reaching his floor, he went down the very long corridor which had many numbered doors on both sides of the corridors. Christopher had gone the wrong way. His direction he had taken down the corridor was a different way. Christopher proceeded up the corridor. He was looking for the number of his hotel door. Eventually he found the right way through the corridor to get to his right numbered door of his hotel room. Christopher slotted in his card. The hotel door of his room unlocked itself. Christopher came into his hotel room. Christopher feeling tired had lie down on his bed to get rest.

***

In the afternoon, Christopher ate at the restaurant with his family. He relaxed until the evening.

Later, Christopher went back to his hotel room. He showered and dressed to go out to the wine bar that night.

He put gel on his hair and combed it. He also put on aftershave. Christopher stood and looked at himself in the mirror. He fretted. Christopher was aged in his late twenties. Tonight, Christopher desired a romance! He did wish for a date. He desired to get married! His unfulfilled dream of marriage a wishful thinking and a desire of fantasy. His romantic fantasies exciting. (All the current romance in women's fiction. Did he depict himself as a hero married to a heroine? The bride of his dreams!)

Christopher cherished his dream. His fantasy excited him. It was the only thing he thought of on that Spanish sultry night.

Christopher entered a wine bar. The bar was full of married couples smartly dressed. Christopher looked at the chic women drinking exotic cocktails.

Christopher took an interest in something interesting. He was interested in something else. A Caucasoid! Christopher ogled the voluptuous Brazilian woman appearing out of the crowd. The Brazilian came forward and queued up at the bar.

Christopher was aroused at taking a glimpse of the buxom Brazilian woman. Christopher at the sight of the woman's cleavage. Her beautiful breasts were so noticeable in direct closeness to persons standing.

Christopher smelled the scent of the woman's perfume. The gloriousness of this fragrance the finest of all perfumes!

Christopher stood waiting for his family to turn up. Christopher lined up as he joined the queue at the bar. Christopher bought a beer. He took his glass. He stepped away from the other persons standing together in groups.

Christopher gulped down the glassful of beer. He was refreshed from drinking the beer. A mouthful of froth around his mouth. Christopher felt a little tipsy.

Suddenly Christopher was startled as his sister touched him on his back. Jennifer standing behind her brother.

"Good evening!" smiled sister.

"Good evening!" replied brother.

"Aren't you going to treat me to a drink?"

"Yes of course. What would you like?"

Jennifer thought for a moment. She appeared to be undecided at making up her mind.

"A sangria. I'll have my usual."

Their mother came up to her son and daughter. Sally stood behind them, resting her hand on her son's shoulder.

"Get me a cocktail."

Christopher lined up while waiting at the bar. He gave his sister a sangria. He ordered a non-alcoholic cocktail for his mother. Sally drank the appetiser.

Jennifer was apologetic standing and facing her brother.

"I apologise if I have ignored you. I've been sunbathing these past few days. I must get that perfect tan."

Christopher accepted his sister's apology.

"Take it as a compliment. I am not exaggerating. My sweet dear! You really do look like a beauty queen."

Jennifer favoured her brother's compliment. She smiled, touching her brother on his shoulder.

"Thanks! I am glad you think so," said sister joyously.

Christopher glanced at everybody else standing around and seated at tables. Christopher hardly made an impression on anyone. With observation individuals took notice of his sister. A stunner! (A teenage photogenic model who was photographical in exotic backgrounds and paradisiacal locations, especially in Islands of Paradise.)

"No one is interested in me. I am with Miss World," exaggerated brother.

Jennifer fantasised about winning the pageant. Becoming a runner-up dissatisfied her. Jennifer assumed it caused her displeasure, frustration and discontentment and a feeling of failure because of losing.

"Let's be realistic, I am too young. I'd like to give it a go when I am older."

Christopher perked up at being with his sister. He enjoyed her company. He was tolerant of his sister's attitude. Her cynicism towards modelling clear. A model's career was short-lived! Going on the catwalk or major cities.

Christopher walked with his sister back to her hotel room. Jennifer and her brother entered in the hotel room. Jennifer was narcissistic of her suntan, of her suntanned body. Jennifer proudly showed her brother her suntan. Jennifer lifted up the hemline of her dress and flounced with unashamed lack of embarrassment. Jennifer showed her brother her bare legs which were beautifully tanned. Her sleeveless dress showed her exposed tanned arms.

Christopher admired his sister's beautiful suntan, her golden bronze tan. Christopher stood looking at Jennifer's tanned body admiringly. He whiffed in the air the scent of his sister's perfume. It was a ravishing, sensuous fragrance.

Christopher with admirable favour touched his sister's wavy hair.

Christopher came out of the hotel room, leaving his sister alone by herself.

Christopher walked down the corridor to his hotel room which was nearly at the very end of the long corridor. There, within reach of a fire extinguisher hinge on a wall.

Christopher went back in his hotel room. He stayed in his hotel room till early next morning. He intended to avoid his family for the rest of the night. A motivational intent of his. An intentional motive to be with his beloved sister at midnight. The mutual arrangement of brother and sister both meeting expected. A discretion!

***

The next day, Christopher and his parents and sister took a ferry to the mainland, followed by a boat trip to the island of Ibiza.

They reached a secluded beach uninhabited. It was one of the prettiest islands. It was an ideal spot and romantic location for sunworshippers, ravers, and nightclubbing.

They all strolled down the beach. They stopped somewhere on the beach. On the white sands they rested together, admiring the scenic natural paradise island.

They drank mouthfuls of still mineral water. They quenched their thirst. Jennifer refreshed herself. They realised that they would run out of water within the hour.

Christopher and his father wanted to explore the bays and coves. Jennifer and her mother seemed uninterested in setting out for a trek. They were unenthusiastic about exploring at this present time.

Christopher regretted not going to Valencia. He realised he made a bad decision. A bad choice of selecting a destination. The location of this island was naturally scenic.

Everyone persuaded Christopher to go to another destination somewhere else. Their preferences made him decisive. He had given in to peer pressure. Their influence a decisiveness. Christopher wondered as he reflected on his preferable choice of destination, location. Where would he see Iberian eyes as beautiful as the Spaniards! Theirs are the most beautiful! Those eyes of theirs.

They all lazed on the beach. They rested on the sands. They dehydrated in the blaze. The scorching heat was unbearable.

The Shadow of the Daughter's Ring

Christopher lay down on the sand while daydreaming. He covered his eyes with his fingers stretched out. Christopher was in his element on the beach, a daydreamer. The sublime azure and the stunning aquamarine sea striking in beauty.

Christopher fantasised and romanticised at the Balearic paradise!

In daytime, there were nobody else in sight anywhere. This beach appeared to be isolated. The island in seclusion. Christopher and his parents and sister were secluded at present.

They all lolled on the beach for quite a long time. They enjoyed their time together as a whole family! They marvelled at the paradisiacal island. They took joy in the nature and beauty of the paradise of the Mediterranean. They relished their quietude and the tranquillity of the scenic island. Their father was meditative as engaged in quietude.

After about an hour and three quarters. they turned back. They set off back to a boat which took them back on land. From there they all returned together to the continental resort.

***

At Gerald's villa, Christopher and members of his family were invited to spend a day.

Christopher sat on a lounge chair in a corner of a lounge. He browsed through a car magazine. He heard Gerald's friends talking. They may have been businessmen.

Christopher felt discontented at his lack of achievement. His unsuccessful endeavours humiliated him. Christopher felt humiliated and inferior, listening to a few businessmen.

Husband and wife joined in the conversation. Gerald and Trish invited their colleagues to come around for a drink. Christopher objected to their liberties. He disapproved of their intrusion. The businessmen intruding on him. Gerald took liberties of his affairs. Christopher agreed when Gerald had invited him and his family to their villa.

Christopher regretted the decision of coming to Gerald's villa today.

Listening to their conversation, Christopher was inclined to think Trish, Gerald's wife, a businesswoman, was pragmatic, arrogant and businesslike. Trish's husband was a property tycoon.

As Jennifer handed out the drinks to everybody, Michael, Jennifer's father, took the opportunity to introduce his daughter to make acquaintances.

The son objected to his mother's motive. Sally, a single parent, had approved of the invitation. Sally took the initiative of allowing her daughter to introduce oneself to the few businessmen.

Sally's unprovocative daughter attracted attention by dressing up like her great-grandmother! The oglers all had a fascination for the enigma! Jennifer had the same resemblance and likeness of her great-grandmother! (With great pride, Jennifer admired the portrait of her beautiful great-grandmother!)

"You're a bookworm, just like your father," remarked Trish.

"It runs in the family," grinned Christopher.

A while later, Christopher took a glass of rosé from his sister standing, holding a silver tray. The few businessmen seated joined in a toast. Christopher and his sister and his parents joined in with the toast. The family was in a celebrating mood. They all engaged in celebration. The revellers standing while raising their crystal glasses to toast. Sipping their rosé wine. Christopher gulped a mouthful of rosé. He was apathetic and sullen. All those invited approved of Jennifer. The businessmen respected the teenager by showing obvious interest in Jennifer regarding her aspirations and ambitions.

Gerald's friends revered Jennifer. They regarded Jennifer with great favour. Undoubtedly Jennifer was the prettiest brunette they had ever seen. It was certainly true that Jennifer had grown up to be lovelier than ever.

Christopher knew from his senses that they liked her. His sister made an admirable impression. The overwhelmed businessmen were captivated by the mystique. Jennifer possessed such fine manners, grace and etiquette.

Realising Jennifer would be leaving them, they hoped to meet Jennifer again!

The Shadow of the Daughter's Ring

Christopher was aware of the businessmen who changed the subject as they had each spoken about themselves. Every businessman was noncommittal about being involved in ventures at the Stock Exchange. They each had vested interests in properties abroad.

Christopher was uninterested in the businessmen's conversations, the businessmen's wives, voluptuous, jetsetters and multi-millionairesses. Two of the wives were wearing too much expensive jewellery and showing off their wealth. One of the wives was sly and pretentious. Another wife haughty and superior.

Christopher was desperate to leave the villa. He fidgeted with restlessness until he and his family were picked up and driven away.

***

A few days later, Christopher declined Gerald's invitation to a gathering. A beach party at Es Caná. Depending on his situation, Christopher refused to go. He loathed to drink with jetsetters, elite and rich.

On that occasion, Jennifer lived it up at Es Caná that sultry night without the company of her brother.

***

The following day, Christopher got up from bed at midday. He had a lie-in. Christopher showered and got dressed. He wore his smart clothes.

Christopher left his hotel room. He went through the corridor and made his way to the staircase which was halfway down the corridor. Christopher went down the flights of stairs. Expectedly, Christopher met his sister waiting in the courtyard. They both went out of the entrance of the resort. They walked together down to the beach. They stopped walking as they came somewhere along the beach, picking a spot far from the resort.

They basked in the sun, sitting down on the thick white sands.

Christopher wore trousers and a cotton shirt. Jennifer wore a black slinky sundress which revealed her exposed back, showing her glossy bronze tan.

Everywhere else on the beach there were sunbathers and families. Also, there were a small number of children on the beach today.

Christopher was sitting in a straight position on the beach. He was deeply contemplative while looking at the sea opposite. This was the first time Christopher had spent time alone with his sister on the beach. He did really enjoy his time together with his sister. He savoured this truly wonderful experience of his Spanish holiday. His wonderful days were unforgettable.

Christopher listened to the atmospheric sound of the electrifying sea. He felt cool and fresh in the sea-wind.

Jennifer looked prettier from being suntanned. Her big eyes, her fine eyelash with black mascara applied, glinted. Her cheeks reddened in the hot sun. Jennifer flushed.

Christopher lay down on the sand. He took comfort from lying down in a different position. He closed his eyes while dreaming of paradise! The stunning paradisiacal beauty of the Balearics. The tranquil paradise of the Mediterranean.

Jennifer moved nearer to her brother lying supine. Christopher sensed the presence of his sister. He smelled the glorious scent of her incredibly ravishing perfume and unscented body lotion.

Christopher and his sister stayed together for a long time. They both enjoyed their privacy together and quietude as well as the tranquillity of the beach. The scenic paradise!

About over an hour later, their father called out to his son and daughter. The brother and sister both disturbed by their father calling out at the top of his voice. Jennifer and Christopher were unresponsive in answering their father. Jennifer and Christopher both looked at their father standing still in front of them.

"There you are. I knew you'd be around here somewhere," said Father.

"I didn't think you would come," said daughter.

"Are you swimming?" asked son.

"Not today. Jennifer, did you sleep well last night?"

"Daddy, I did sleep, actually and with no hangover. I dreamt but I can't remember a thing," sighed daughter.

"What are your dreams?" asked Father.

The ambitious daughter had materialistic desires and dreams.

Jennifer blabbed out, "I would really like to have my own villa. To live in Spain. Mallorca or Menorca."

The father approved of his daughter's dream and ambition.

"That's a really good dream. It's an interesting one. This dream can come true. It is possible," grinned Father.

The son joined in the conversation.

"Me and my sister, we're both obsessed with Spain. Aren't we? It's an obsession of ours," said Christopher proudly.

Their father seemed pleased with it.

"We'll toast to that," gasped Father.

"Oh yippy! Can we? Can we make a toast?" said daughter childishly.

"Of course we can. We will make our toast," assured Father.

Christopher and Jennifer rose from the sand. Christopher rubbed off the dry sand from his creased-up clothes. The hot sand scorching from the heat.

All of them went back to the resort.

Reaching the resort, they stood together on the ground floor near the reception. At that present time, the receptionist attended to guests arriving who checked in for their reservation at reception.

"Meet us at the bar at 7.30 p.m.," reminded Father repeatedly.

"We'll be there," confirmed son assuredly.

All of them left each other. They all went off in different directions.

Christopher walked off and went to his hotel room. He was hot and sweaty. His black baggy shirt covered in sweat. His perspiration from his exertion of himself. His sweaty armpits shaven. He sprayed deodorant on his armpits. Christopher put on clean shirt and trousers. He felt dizzy and faint from dehydration. He felt perspiration all over his body.

Christopher opened the small fridge and decided to take out a bottle of still mineral water. Christopher was refreshed from drinking up some fresh mineral water. He felt refreshed with his thirst quenched.

In his hotel room, Christopher got into bed. He wearied at changing positions when lying in his bed as he tried to get some rest.

During the night, Christopher met Gerald and his parents and sister waiting for him in a crowded bar. His father bought a round of drinks.

Christopher was unenthusiastic as everyone else joined in a toast. They all stood together while facing each other. They each held a glass of champagne. The effervescent champagne bubbled. The froth spilled over every glass of champagne.

"To a villa and a life in Spain!"

Christopher and his sister disapproved of the gloater. Christopher thought Gerald patronised them. They both still had doubts about their dreams. They disbelieved their dreams would come true!

Christopher and Jennifer became unhappy, humiliated and frustrated at their unrealistic dream, at the unreality of their dream and fantasy! They both ha discontentment, dissatisfaction and misery. From their wish and dream! Their hope disappointing.

Christopher and Jennifer looked at each other with brotherly and sisterly love. They both had the same values, ideals and dreams and wishes.

Christopher felt irritated by all the babble in the bar. There in the bar was a lack of space to move about in. Everywhere there was claustrophobic with persons' bodies pressing against others. The people gathered together were either standing or seated. Those individuals suffering from claustrophobia. They ended up at staying in the bar for a longer time.

Jennifer took discomfort from standing up and being among holidaymakers and foreigners. Jennifer made an excuse to go and leave the bar at once. She groaned about having a migraine. Jennifer gave her explanatory reason why.

"I am going out to get some air. I've got a headache," moaned Jennifer.

Sally put her arm around her daughter, showing concern for her.

"So soon? Mind how you go," said Mother.

"See you back at the hotel," said Gerald.

Christopher and his sister expected a surprise visit from Gerald without his wife being present. The visitor popped in at the bar.

Christopher followed his sister out of the claustrophobic bar. It was becoming more and more crowded. At present it was overcrowded with many persons having a drink at the bar. From the air-conditioning. All the persons sitting at tables and those standing up around in their groups with their friends or members of their family. The bar was full up of people.

Jennifer left the bar while going past crowds of people and headed out of the bar.

Christopher decided to go. He followed his sister out of the claustrophobic bar.

Christopher and his sister came to the ground floor. Going out of the main entrance, they left the resort and went in the direction of the beach in the distance. This spa resort had the most popular beach. It was the favourite beach among holidaymakers and the jet-set. It remained one of the loveliest beaches in the Oceanic region of the Mediterranean.

They strolled down the beach, leaving an endless trail of footprints in the sand. Reaching somewhere secluded on the beach, they isolated themselves from everybody else who came out on the beach that day.

They lay down on the beach. They occupied a secluded spot. The hot sand was scorching and dry. There, further on the furthest end of the sands, toward the shore, it remained damp and wet. The sea-breeze was windy and cooler along the shore. This ended up being the second time Christopher spent time with his sister. He liked the company of his sister. Christopher felt calmer, peaceful and joyous at being together in the presence of his beloved sister.

Christopher lay down on his back. He faced upwards looking at the sky. Christopher closed his eyes and relaxed in a supine position. Christopher listened to the sound of the blowing wind and the waves. The tide. He felt electrified from the atmospheric sensations. He enjoyed the peace. He could have stayed there for hours enjoying the relaxation, dreaming of paradise, of the heavenly bliss of a paradisiacal nature. Resting with his eyes closed, he was oblivious of his paradisiacal surroundings and natural environment. The paradisiacal beach of a fine beauty. It's wondrous gloriousness naturally.

A considerable time later, Christopher finally awoke. He found that his sister had gone. Lying with his hands clasped behind his head, Christopher looked up at the azure sky. He daydreamed. Maybe he was having a reverie!

A short time later, Jennifer emerged from the sea, thrilling from the creation of natural paradise. Along the shore Christopher stood waiting for his sister to come out of the sea.

Jennifer rejoined her brother by heading back to the resort. Christopher accompanied his sister all the way back to her hotel room.

Reaching Jennifer's hotel room, Christopher decided to leave his sister to get back to his hotel room.

Alone in his hotel room, Christopher took banknotes out of his wallet. He had stolen money from his sister on purpose. Christopher retaliated. Obviously, Christopher felt pleased with himself! Christopher had been pent up with anger for some time.

Did Christopher have a guilty conscience? Did he show any remorse for what he had done by stealing money from his sister in retaliation? There had been times when his provocative sister had provoked him to anger!

Tomorrow he would confess! (At the confession box, he would make his confessions!) Christopher would repent of his sin indeed!

Christopher stayed the rest of his time in his hotel room for hours. At this time of day, it was quieter with far more privacy in his occupied hotel room.

Christopher feeling tired lay down on his bed to rest.

The blazing sun shone through the windows. The dazzling radiant sunrays blinding.

From the sun shining through the windows there were dazzling reflections. The radiance of the sunshine a resplendence!

Christopher cooled down in the shade. The hotel room was shady.

Christopher rested in his bed for over an hour, then he got up. (Customarily, the Spaniards have a siesta. It is a Spanish custom.)

Christopher followed suit!

***

On Thursday afternoon, Christopher and Jennifer went down to the beach again. At this time neither of them had eaten any lunch. As today's weather was far too hot, they had no appetite between them.

Christopher was uncertain what he wanted to do today. Christopher lacked interest in his negative unenthusiasm. His sister Jennifer had positive enthusiasm for doing recreation and leisure.

Christopher was uninterested at doing water sports. He was unenthusiastic about doing these activities. Christopher preferred to cycle or hike and walk. Christopher took to other activities which he took into consideration as well as engaging in leisure pursuits.

Christopher may have preferred to have gone sightseeing today. He appeared to have been undecided at making his decision. Again, Christopher was unenthusiastic and half-hearted as he finally decided on his option.

Today, Christopher was alone with his sister again. Since the morning, his family were on board a luxury coach. Today their family had gone on a day trip, on a guided tour to tourist attractions and places of interest which tourists and sightseers visited.

The coach stopped off at the Tourist Information Centre. The tourists and sightseers got off the coach.

The party entered at the front entrance. The sliding doors. At that time everyone gained the necessary required information. The tourists were informed by the assistance of the informative uniformed member of staff at Spain's National Tourism in the city. The advisor and her assistant also attending to the party of tourists who stopped by were rather impatient to get the required tourism information disclosed. (At present ready for disclosure.)

Christopher decided to join his sister by going down to the beach. His sister was enthusiastic about spending the day at the beach. They both strolled past lithe, voluptuous, petite and slim sunbathers who lolled everywhere on the beach. Enjoying their hot summer's day on the beach at summertime. These holidaymakers took a vacation at the High Season.

Christopher's temperament characteristically changed. Christopher acted in a theatrical way!

"My heart is broken!" gestured brother. "I will never love thee again!"

Jennifer was amused at her brother's theatricality.

"My dear brother! You're depressing me! You're a depressive!"

Christopher tried to explain himself.

"One day, Jennifer, you will fall in love. You'll get married. You won't want to know me anymore. You will get older, and you will forget about me," stammered brother.

Jennifer explained her true feelings towards her brother. Perhaps it was too personal to express herself concerning her brother's deep feelings. Jennifer may have been unfeeling towards her brother. Jennifer seemed unconcerned for her brother. Her brother's temperamental mood! Jennifer disregarded her brother's feelings.

Christopher and Jennifer stopped at their preferred spot, the most preferable to them. At this present time there was nobody around, not even any sunbathers there along these parts of the beach. Jennifer lay a thick blanket down on the hot sand. Christopher lay down beside his sister. He relaxed from the comfort of his position. He felt pacified by the peaceful quietness of the beach. Jennifer became calmer and cooler from her restful relaxation of her graceful figure.

Within about quarter of an hour, Christopher and Jennifer were surrounded by girls, virgins and young women. Christopher and Jennifer's privacy invaded by them surrounding the two loungers who were deeply pre-occupied.

The Shadow of the Daughter's Ring

Jennifer seemed intent on having her privacy. That all changed when they were intruded on by teenage girls and young women of Iberian and Spanish nationalities. Christopher preferred the presence of the Spaniards and Iberians which he welcomed invitingly and took joy in.

Christopher sat and took a glimpse behind him. He caught sight of a voluptuous sunbather and a curvaceous red head. These were luscious and sultry women. Two of them virgins, striking beauties. The other females were lithe and petite. Further on ahead, sunbathing, an unattractive sunbather lay a few yards ahead of them.

Christopher drew a Christian symbol in the thick sand, even though he did not really know what the symbol meant, the symbolism and the symbolic significance. He hoped it would deter any more intrusions from anybody else.

Earlier in the daytime, Christopher read the Holy Bible to please himself for about half an hour. Although he had the willingness and urge to do so, he also had the unenthusiasm to read the word of God. Christopher changed his mind, realising how crucial it was to read the scriptures. Christopher was aware of the constant danger of witchcraft. How it made him undesirable. He was used to it by now. This evidently made him a believer in the Christian faith. A Christian. He was enlightened and illuminated by his Christian illumination of Christianity. He became a believer because of it. The subsequent consequence. Showing his belief in Christianity. (Growing up, Christopher was sceptical of the Christian religion. From his life experiences he experienced and from his encounters, tragedies, miseries and disappointments, Christopher became a believer! Ultimately Christopher eventually became converted!)

Christopher looked at a daydreamer straight ahead, a teenage boy sitting with his mother who changed position, moving her body into a different position.

His sister Jennifer daydreamed. She fantasised from her fantasy. Jennifer dreamed of being a beauty queen! Winning a beauty contest!

Jennifer lay on the beach in the radiant sun. It shone in the blaze. Jennifer exposed her legs. Her tanned legs became an incredibly exquisite bronze tan. Her dark suntan so beautiful all over her body. The admirable teenager's figure was incredibly desirable, suntanned in the Mediterranean.

Christopher and Jennifer both got up. Jennifer picked up her blanket. They both went somewhere else. Strolling further and further down the beach, they reached a secluded part of the beach. They saw female sunbathers sunbathing. Their suntanned figures had a beautiful tan.

Christopher was aroused looking at a sunbather's beautiful breasts and buttocks. The eroticism of the female sexuality.

Reaching the end of the beach, they both turned back and made their way back down the long endless beach.

Jennifer and Christopher got back to their resort. Christopher left his sister somewhere along the narrow corridor. He went into his hotel room. Christopher undressed and showered. He got dressed. He met his father and sister down in the restaurant outdoors. The family was seated at the reserved table. Everybody was present except for Gerald who had left to take a continental flight in Europe.

The diners waited for the waiter to attend to them. They now already missed Gerald's company. Sally and Jennifer were pleased that they were both alone at last together with their family.

Christopher had enjoyed his time with Gerald, apart from his disappointing visit, time at Es Caná villa.

As the curvaceous Brazilian woman and her friend walked past Christopher, he was disappointed at Gerald's friends leaving the resort to get home. Christopher sulked. He knew he would probably never ever see the women again.

The diners ate their meal. The rest of them then stood up and made a toast. The revellers were merry and high-spirited.

"To health and prosperity. To our holiday in Mallorca. To our holiday homes. To Gerald, a generous man."

The Shadow of the Daughter's Ring

Except for Christopher, who was subdued and disappointed at the two women (Gerald's two female friends) who took an exit out of the resort by leaving sooner.

About an hour and a half later, Christopher got up and left the table. He was in an unsociable mood. He had thoughtlessness for his family. He left his family, going out of the restaurant.

Christopher went back to his hotel room. He stayed in his hotel room. He spent the rest of the summer night by watching a continental movie with subtitles. This foreign film was different from most contemporary films.

Christopher went to bed late that night, dreaming of the actress. He had an adoration for the attractive actress with long sandy hair in a cameo role.

***

The next day, Christopher stayed in bed until lunchtime, then he got dressed. He came out of his hotel room. He made his way down the flights of stairs. He went out to the poolside where sunbathers lay on sun-loungers surrounding the pool.

Christopher came closer to the swimming pool. He stood still somewhere. He spotted Jennifer in the swimming pool among the swimmers. Jennifer's graceful nymph-like figure appeared to be noticeable in the water. The conspicuousness of her figure a strikingness. A movement of grace as Jennifer swam. Her golden-bronze body glistening in the shimmering water which reflected in the light.

Jennifer occupied most of the swimming pool to herself. At this time only swimmers and virgins used the swimming pool. Perhaps the most privileged and favoured ones being allowed to use the swimming pool in preference to everybody else wanting to take pleasure in using it.

At present, Christopher avoided strangers he had unknown. He disliked being in the presence of strangers and members of their families.

Going to the poolside, Christopher lay down on a vacant sun-lounger. He used a vacant sun-lounger on the sun-drenched poolside scorching from the heat. One a sun-lounger next to his, there were his sister's belongings. a towel, sandals and bottle of still mineral water and a diary.

Christopher picked up his sister's diary. He flicked through the pages. He read Jennifer's last entry with interest.

It's another lovely day. This place is paradise. It really is. I must stay out in the sun to get my tan. As a teenager looking back, I was too young to really understand the true significance of it. I am enjoying the finer weather. My grandfather once said to me Mallorca, Spain, is a glorious paradise. At that age I was far more interested in having fun, playing with my friends. My grandfather said, in his profound words, paradise is like finding hidden treasures, at making a discovery!

Christopher tried to understand what his sister blabbed on about. What did his sister mean about a Spanish paradise? However, Christopher did think of his grandfather's profound sentiment. This may have been Grandfather's very last days alive. The very last time Grandfather spent with his beloved granddaughter.

Christopher experienced his delight of paradise mostly in the islands. Christopher's experience of an exciting adventurous exploration. It's something short-lived. This exotic island a paradise. A romantic location which was popular among holidaymakers, tourists and honeymooners.

Christopher stood still and watched with joy. A passionate mother cuddled her son who was seeking attention for his mother to comfort him.

The families lounged out in the sun and on the terrace. The sunbathers sunbathed around the poolside. The lithe one, the prettiest woman, female. A few children playing around the poolside. The children were well-behaved and on their best behaviour.

Christopher put back his sister's diary on the sun-lounger next to his.

Jennifer came up to her brother. He seemed at peace.

"Give it here!" grabbed sister.

Jennifer snatched it. She objected to her brother reading her personal entries of her diary.

Christopher kept calm. He was offended at his sister raising objection to her brother taking her diary without her permission and reading it.

Christopher encouraged his sister to keep a diary. He had been encouraging by making his remarks.

"It's a personal thing to keep a diary. It's private and intimate. It's really good that you make your entries every day. The reader may find it an interest at how the diarist makes her entry."

Christopher felt faint in the heat. A sweltering afternoon. The sun shone hotter. (One of the hottest days in summer.)

Christopher left his sister to go back into the resort. Christopher went to his hotel room. Christopher still felt tired and sleepy after staying up late last night. He lay on his bed and rested.

***

On Saturday, Christopher, his father, mother and sister spent the day sightseeing around Ibiza.

Finally, on their very last day at the resort, Christopher and his family embraced individuals whom they had befriended during the past week. It took several days for them to make their acquaintanceship.

They each exchanged their addresses and even the obliged and thoughtful au pair gave willingly her private address to those who asked for it.

The Staples family all felt too sad at leaving. Finally, they all said their goodbyes to everybody. As they parted from them. They all parted company.

On that hot afternoon, from the resort Christopher and members of his family took a taxi to the airport.

From the main airport, they flew back into Heathrow Airport.

From outside the crowded airport, they were pick up and driven home. The journey long through the motorway to Kent.

21

The English Rose

On a bank holiday Monday, Christopher and his sister walked around the garden. They both stopped at one of the flowerbeds. There were several rose bushes. Christopher and Jennifer admired the variety of beautiful roses.

Their father was occupied in doing gardening. He spent the afternoon gardening. He had a passion for gardening. Michael picked up the fallen withered rose petals etc. and debris off the soil of the dry ground. He put it in a sack. It was about a quarter of a sackful.

Michael's daughter, Jennifer, took a sniff at a rose. She took delight in the purely natural scent of a peach rose.

"This one is either Charlotte or Duchess. Actually, I forget which. Isn't it beautiful! There's none quite like it," marvelled Jennifer.

Standing at a rose bush, Christopher took a sniff of a rose.

"It is distinctive," remarked Christopher.

Christopher stepped away from a rose bush. Going back up to the lawn, Christopher sensed something deeply troubled his sister. Jennifer questioned her brother about theft. Her stolen money which had been taken in a situation when Jennifer been unaware.

"Did you take my money from my purse?"

Christopher hesitated in answering.

"I haven't taken your money," repeated brother fearfully.

"My mom won't ask me unless she is borrowing my money."

Christopher felt hardly any guilt about stealing from his sister! He did not have a bad conscience!

On a few times Christopher had conversational confrontation with his sister. Did Christopher steal his sister's money from out of a safe? Maybe in retaliation? Or because of revenge? Christopher mulled it over. He did realise how his hypocrisy caused double standards. A hypocrite!

Christopher must have retaliated in anger. He kept silent.

"Explain it. Where did my money go? If this continues to happen, I will go to the police," threatened sister.

Christopher feared being questioned by the police. Nor did he want to be subsequently detained!

"You should be more sensible with your money. You shouldn't be a spendthrift. Don't jump to conclusions," cautioned brother.

Jennifer scowled at her brother while she pointed her index finger at him.

"Chris, I do suspect it's you. Who else can it be? It must be you! You're acting suspiciously," accused sister.

Due to being fearful, Christopher said nothing else because of fear. Christopher was too afraid of his sister and how she intimidated him. Threatening and provoking her brother. His sister was provocative.

Christopher failed to protest his innocence and deny his sister's accusation.

Christopher reached out to stretch out his hand. He touched his sister on her shoulder. Jennifer was comforted by her brother's passionate touch. Jennifer took a deep breath. She calmed down. She changed the subject.

"How about us going to the flower show?" suggested sister.

Christopher showed enthusiasm. He was interested in admission to a flower show.

"Yeah. Why not. That's interesting," murmured Christopher.

"How about going to Kew Gardens? We could see the Botany. All the botanical things in the hot house. That typical sort of thing."

"I would like that very much. That will be a good day out," grinned brother.

Standing somewhere in the garden, the son and daughter watched their father prune the roses. All the budding rosebuds and rose petals were immaculate and perfect. Christopher stood admiring the surrounding lovely roses. All the deep colours of the roses. The raindrops sparkled on the wet roses.

"Does Father put fungicide and insecticide on the roses?" asked Christopher.

"I do expect my father does. The rose bushes have mulch as well."

"Mom has got green fingers. Isn't horticulture interesting?" breathed Christopher.

"Our father loves gardening."

"As far as I am concerned, gardening is far more than an interest. It's an obsession of my father's. A hobby."

Christopher admired the garden. In summer it was a lovelier garden. Christopher imagined the Garden of Dreams. It was the most beautiful garden Christopher could envisage. He visualised a garden paradise!

Christopher wished that summertime lasted. It was his most favourite time of the year. Coming towards the end of midsummer. The autumn soon comes.

Christopher avoided his sister on purpose as he feared his sister might report him to the police.

Christopher's bad conscience discomposed him and his guilt aroused suspicion. He trembled.

Christopher went indoors. He came into the lounge alone. He switched on the television and flicked through the channels. He began to watch a black and white film. A dashing film star who was a screen legend. Christopher watched the remainder of the old film. (Christopher had seen this film before. He had nostalgia watching the remains of the film till the very end.) Christopher was overcome with great emotion.

Christopher went upstairs alone to his bedroom. He stayed in his bedroom. He read a novelette. A mystery detective story. Sitting comfortably on an armchair, Christopher concentrated on reading. Christopher read for hours.

After he had finished reading, Christopher went straight to bed to get some rest.

The Shadow of the Daughter's Ring

During the night, Christopher woke up. He got up from his bed. He put on his slippers. He came out of his bedroom, leaving the bedroom door open to air out. Christopher went downstairs and into the kitchen. The venetian blinds were pulled up. He looked out of the kitchen window. There he saw his sister alone in the garden in the moonlit night. Christopher was half-awake moving unsteadily on his feet.

He joined his sister outside in the garden. Jennifer wore a black nightdress. Christopher stood beside his sister standing by a rose bush at one of the garden beds. Jennifer held a rose in her hand. She sniffed at the scent of the rose. The exquisite gloriousness of it.

Christopher looked at the romantic and dreamy teenage sister. A dreamer, romanticist.

"Shouldn't you be asleep?" yawned brother.

Jennifer straightened herself up. Her posture straight. Jennifer's poise was elegant.

"I just couldn't sleep. Isn't it a beautiful night! I just had to get out into the garden."

"You should go in. You'll catch a chill," said brother.

"I'll be alright. I want to catch my breath in the fresh air," gasped sister.

Christopher smelled the scent of the roses in the air. The exquisiteness of all the finest roses had quality.

Jennifer forgave her brother. She had forgiven him.

"I forgive you."

"Forgive me about what?" shrugged brother.

"Taking my money."

Christopher was agitated by his sister.

"Let's not accuse one another. Let's be reasonable."

Jennifer smiled and gestured. "We're family. We should love as happy families do."

"I think we should. Let's forgive and forget," gesticulated brother.

Jennifer nodded her head in agreement.

"If there's no love shown, then how can the love be mutual between us?"

Christopher in a dreamy state looked at the loveliest roses there near a tree which was towards the very front of the rear of the garden. Christopher was enchanted by the reflection of the moonshine. The moonshine reflected on the ground of the bigger flowerbeds rather than all the other smaller garden-beds everywhere else in the garden.

Jennifer held a stem of a rose. Jennifer twirled a rose in her hand. That deep red rose symbolised love. The rose that her brother had thoughtfully given her minutes earlier was a token of his love! A strong, passionate love!

The wind blew Jennifer's hair in her dark eyes. Jennifer moved the fringe from out of her eyes.

Christopher stepped closer to his sister. Standing behind his sister. Christopher ran his fingers down the back of his sister's straight hair cascading.

With the bright garden lights shining in the pitch dark, Christopher and Jennifer walked back together indoors.

Going in the dark house with a house light on, the brother and sister went upstairs. Christopher went up the stairs. Christopher stopped still on a stair. Standing on a stair, Christopher balanced himself.

Jennifer was going up the stairs ahead in front of her brother. Along the stairs towards the top of the staircase, Christopher saw his sister pull off rose petals from a rose. Jennifer threw every petal on the stairs by leaving a short trail of rose petals.

Reaching the top of the landing, they both left each other, Christopher going to the nearest bedroom while his sister went down along the corridor to get to her bedroom near the end of it.

They both went back to bed to get some sleep.

***

One Sunday afternoon, Christopher answered the front door as he was expecting his mother's friend (also a good friend of his sister's).

"I've come to do some gardening to help out," smiled Rosemary.

"Come in. My mom is out in the garden," greeted Christopher.

Christopher closed the front door. He walked a few steps ahead of Rosemary. Christopher pointed his finger and gestured. Christopher walked with Rosemary out into the garden.

Jennifer and her mother were waiting for Rosemary to come outdoors.

Mother and daughter hurried towards Rosemary coming out onto the lawn. Welcoming Rosemary with outstretched arms, the emotional greeters were affectionate.

"Our dear sweet friend!"

Rosemary was affectionate at embracing her two friends, showing her deep love as well as her expressive sentiment.

"You two are my dear sweet friends too. What would I do without you two? You're my best friends. You're the sweetest and dearest of all my friends," expressed Rosemary.

Jennifer and her mother both truly thought highly of their friend. Rosemary's touching sentiment was moving. The two of them had a deep respect for their friend Rosemary, and Christopher had a high regard for her.

Christopher and Jennifer watched Rosemary help their father to tend to the roses. Rosemary and her mother were professional florists at Interflora.

Today was the last day of midsummer and the garden looked quite beautiful today after they had finally finished doing gardening. Tomorrow would be the start of autumn. A few of these days might be sweltering, hot and sunny. Christopher knew this glorious weather would not last long.

Son, daughter and father and Rosemary walked up to another flowerbed and rose bed. They stood together while looking at the rose bushes which had grown quite big. They had been planted in memory of Federick Staples, their beloved grandfather!

In the whole garden these particular rose bushes with their roses were the most beautiful. They were proud of the blooms this year in summer. They took great delight in smelling the rose-scented air.

They cooled down from feeling the gentle breeze. They all went back indoors.

In one of the rooms, Christopher looked at the beautiful flower arrangement in vases and hanging baskets. Christopher thought of his mother, how she loved house plants and potted flowers. His mother had an interest in gardening. Nowadays, Christopher had seen less and less of his father. His father had separated from his mother.

Moments later, Jennifer came into the dining room. Jennifer put a tray of glasses on the dining table.

Christopher, Father, Mother and Rosemary each took a glass of appetiser. They gathered around while standing at the middle of the dining room. They each raised their glass and make a toast.

"To a lovely garden. To Rosemary, a fine florist."

Everybody drank a glassful of appetiser. They were refreshed from drinking it.

Afterwards, Rosemary left them, saying goodbye to Christopher and her friends, Jennifer and Mrs Staples when going out of the door. Rosemary had gone home.

Everyone else went out into the garden again. They all enjoyed the very last day of midsummer. Summer solstice!

Admiring the fine garden, they imagined how beautiful the garden could look next summer (the enthusiastic ones who did gardening).

The remaining members of the family stayed out in the peaceful garden until night, spending hours talking to one another. (Their father was a conversationalist who changed the subject to suit himself.)

Christopher, Jennifer and parents drank a cup of tea in the wondrous enchantment of the moonlit night.

***

One September night (these few autumn days were the loveliest hottest days), Christopher drove to Stella's house.

The Shadow of the Daughter's Ring

That evening Stella was having a party. All of Jennifer's best friends were personally invited.

Christopher parked his car in a reserved space in the front driveway. At that time there were another two cars parked there too.

Christopher sat in his car for a few minutes. He got out of his car. He locked his car door. He walked up to the detached house. He rang the doorbell. He stood by the front door. As he moved, he rang the doorbell again. Still, no one bothered to answer the front door. Christopher became impatient while standing and waiting.

One of Stella's friends answered the front door. A mystery guest, a student, Christopher recognised the guest, a stranger, Stella's friend.

Going out of the front door, Jennifer appeared. Christopher arrived just in time to come and pick up his sister to drive her home. Jennifer's flushed face beautifully complexioned with her make-up.

Jennifer said goodbye to her emotional friends affectionately, saying and waving goodbye. Jennifer's friends came out to the front door. They came out onto the front drive. Jennifer said goodbye to all her friends watching her get in a car.

Christopher reversed his car out of the drive before driving off at high speed down the road. Jennifer was unable to see Stella again until weeks later.

Christopher concentrated on driving. He looked in the rear-view mirror. He caught a glimpse of his sister looking beautiful dressed up.

"How was the party?" asked brother.

"Oh, I had a good time. It's a shame I was not at the party for longer. It's disappointing."

"Did you meet anyone nice?"

"I met thingumabob. We are good friends," breathed sister.

"Oh good! You have many friends."

Jennifer spoke about her exciting highlight.

"We danced and talked; my friend Jamie even played guitar. It was good. It really was."

Christopher sensed his sister felt amorous. Her expression was of amorousness.

"Is it love? Or is it a crush!"

"It's a good love. A friend's love which one has for a friend. I love all my friends. They are good to me. I get on well with everybody," said sister frankly.

After less than half an hour later, Christopher reached home.

Both brother and sister got out of the car parked in the front drive. Christopher inserted a key in the front door. Christopher and Jennifer entered the detached house.

They both entered the lounge.

Christopher stood still in front of Jennifer who was seated. Jennifer stretched out her hand. She proudly showed a sapphire ring set in a cluster of diamonds. (It used to be Jennifer's grandmother's ring which she gave to her beloved granddaughter on her birthday!)

Jennifer felt regretful and remorseful as she reflected on her grandmother. Jennifer was a tearful and sorrowful bereaved teenager.

"I truly miss my grandmother. I wish I had spent more time with my her. This is my grandmother's. I shall always remember her forever, with this ring of hers," said Jennifer reflectively.

Christopher stepped forward. He touched his sister's shoulder. He rested his hand on her shoulder. Christopher deeply sympathised with his sister. He had deep sympathy for his reflective and mournful sister.

Standing back, Christopher stood admiring his sister's diamond sapphire ring which sparkled in the light. With fond sentimentality, Jennifer took pride in it. It was her favourite jewellery. (With her jewels Jennifer possessed, it was her obsessive possession.)

22

Jennifer Fell Off her Horse

On a warm day Jennifer came out of the stables with her horse. Jennifer a rider trotted on horseback along a quiet country lane. From there the horsewoman reached the beautiful countryside. Jennifer rode on out into the countryside. At that time, she enjoyed her peace, freedom and quietude. It was peaceful, tranquil and she felt such languor.

The rider on horseback rode out somewhere remote in the countryside. Suddenly, Jennifer's horse bolted. The rider lost control of her horse. Suddenly, Jennifer fell off her horse. She had an accident. Jennifer's accident could have almost cost her her life!

With certainty a death which could have almost resulted in MISADVENTURE!

Jennifer's body remained lying on the dry ground which was scorched by the sun. In a daze, confused and confounded, Jennifer got up from the ground, shaken, bruised, dazed and injured. She was in pain and hurt from her fall. Naturally, from providence it was a miracle Jennifer was still alive!

Somehow miraculously, Jennifer got to her horse which neighed. She felt body and shoulder pain. She took the reins of her horse and walked back on foot all the way back to the stables which were located deep in the heart of the countryside. The ambience was natural, peaceful and scenic. There in that rural region it was remote, picturesque, charming, with solitude and quaint houses.

Somehow Jennifer out of breath and full of adrenaline, reached the stables and barnyard. It was within reach of the green fields and a paddock in the distance.

Jennifer expected to meet the stable boy waiting for her outside the stables. The stable boy was expecting her to come.

The stable boy showed concern for Jennifer.

"Are you alright?" he asked, concerned.

Jennifer felt shaken while staying up on her feet. Keeping her balance. She felt dazed, and confused, in pain and hurt.

"I fell. Nothing broken. I think I am alright."

Immediately the attentive stable boy attended to Jennifer's horse, a thoroughbred. Quickly he took the horse back to the stables, then going back outside, he attended to Jennifer who was injured and shaken.

The stable boy took hold of Jennifer and carried her back into a country-style farmhouse. He carried her into a varnished wooden room with a plain polished wooden floor. The Stable boy carried Jennifer to a chesterfield, and she slumped down on it to rest.

"Are you alright?" asked the stable boy.

"I'll be alright. You can go," groaned Jennifer.

Within seconds, the stable boy had gone. Jennifer was left alone indoors.

Struggling to stand up, Jennifer ached and was in pain. Jennifer left the room. She went upstairs to a girlish bedroom, a boudoir. Jennifer came to her bed. She was unable to walk and move. She threw herself down on the bed and lay down to rest for hours.

She looked pale and blanched, in a bad state. She remained bedridden for about a night and day.

Eventually, Jennifer recovered from a sustained injury. Jennifer had suffered a bad trauma.

Would this rider ever ride again?

Jennifer's obsessional passion for riding was seemingly now over!

23

Jennifer's Trauma

Jennifer was suffering from her trauma. Jennifer stayed at home to suit herself and to please herself.

In the lounge, Jennifer sat down on a armchair. She preferred to be alone today. She was introverted and felt discomfort and anguish. Her body ached. She was concerned about herself as usual. She bent down and looked at her beautiful legs. She fretted. (Yesterday at the G. P.'s, her doctor examined Jennifer a patient.)

Normally Jennifer was narcissistic about herself and her beauty. At this time, she lost her obsessive narcissism for herself. Usually, she was vain and conceited.

Jennifer took the actual time to lounge about and rest. On certain days she remained housebound, remaining indoors for days. (On other days during the week, she went to her best friend's house.)

Jennifer reflected on her accident. How suddenly, her horse bolted and she had fallen off her horse. Suddenly her parents came into the room. Jennifer felt irritated and annoyed at her parent's intrusion. Jennifer was irritable and fidgety.

"You're not worrying, are you? I don't want you to ride anymore. Not now," insisted Mother.

The traumatized daughter acknowledged her stern, unfeeling mother.

"Oh. I won't. That's for sure."

"N more riding. It's dangerous," cautioned Father.

The sulker suffered with a trauma. Jennifer recovered from her fall. Her injury sustained from the fall from her horse.

Jennifer obeyed her parents. She remained an obedient daughter, listening to her parent's caution and reprimand and obeying them.

"I can't ride. Not now. Not ever! I am traumatized. Can you not see! I just don't think I can ever ride again. It's unlikely now. I love riding. It's my passion," admitted Daughter.

The Mother stepped forward and kissed her daughter on the forehead.

"Oh, Sweetheart. We know."

The Father held tightly his daughter's hand.

"Do Rest. Take it easy. Do take care of yourself, " he insisted.

Both concerned parents left their dearly loved daughter. Going out of the terraced house to leave.

Jennifer, sitting all alone took her time to reflect on her life. Her trauma, miseries, happiness and joys. Also, her spirituality. Jennifer contemplated in silence.

She thought about her horse riding and Mr Harvey's stallion. Now this just seemed to be another phobia of hers experienced.

Jennifer did consider giving up her riding!

Jennifer was in a disturbed and distressed state.

(Due to her stubborn nature and frame of mind, Jennifer was determined to ride again!)

Jennifer felt tired, lethargic, sleepy and lackadaisical and tried to rest on the comfortable armchair. Within a short time, she dozed off. On the mantelpiece a brass carriage clock was ticking with its luminous numerals.

At The Beauty Parlour

On a hot day Jennifer and her mother went to a Beauty Parlour. Her mother had a massage from a masseur while Jennifer had a manicure. Her mother treated her daughter to a manicure. Although the daughter appeared to be ungrateful, she did like being pampered. Usually, her mother pampered her only daughter!

Jennifer was obsessed with beauty treatments. It was a natural obsession of hers.

Depending on Jennifer's mood, sometimes she would engage in a manicure, a massage or enjoy the pleasure of a luxury Spa and sauna at a private (Sports) Club.

24

Jennifer's Days of Being Housebound

Jennifer stayed at home either alone or in the company of her family. She took joy at their presence. Jennifer's family cared for her and looked after her. Her affectionate, possessive brother, Chris was sweet and her loving parents too.

Jennifer cherished family life and their deep love as well as parental love and their guidance. It was such a goodness, the way her own family were loving and caring towards her.

Usually, Jennifer sat in her bedroom alone.

A beautiful bedroom. A feminine pink colour. For hours she stayed seated while deeply contemplating. She rested herself and relaxed in silence. At times she avoided her family and friends. She eluded them. In preference for solitude. Preferring to be alone.

Jennifer was deeply contemplative. She engaged in religious contemplation.

In time Jennifer developed a deep spirituality and a good faith. She learned from her experience. Jennifer remained religious. (Her fall from her horse and how she suffered from a trauma and ordeal, subsequently made her become converted.

***

Jennifer liked her peace and quiet and freedom. It was such a precious and good thing!

Jennifer tended to stay indoors. She took that time to contemplate and reflect on her situation. Jennifer was deeply reflective and meditative, staying indoors. She preferred to be alone. At times, she did avoid and elude her friends and families.

Learning about love itself. The fundamental and essence of love. Jennifer realized just how precious family life is. Her bond with her intimate family was close. Her intimate closeness!

Day after day, Jennifer stayed at home until she fully recovered and recuperated. Jennifer coped with her ordeal, problems, failures and shortcomings. She was well-aware of having a relapse. But that didn't make her apprehensive, fearful, afraid or anxious in any way. Of course, Jennifer still had anxieties and anguish.

Jennifer grew strong in the Lord! From her beliefs and Christian faith and from being naturally religious.

25

Preliminary Rounds. Dressage. From Runner-up to Winner

On a hot sunny day, Christopher and Jennifer went to an arena to see the dressage. The spectators were sitting high in the stalls near the front rows. They both watched the dressage. Chris took notice of the miraculous transformational changes in his sister's life. A miracle!

His sister was cooler, calmer, spiritual, regenerated and laidback.

Jennifer had a natural interest in all things equestrian. A love for horses. Watching the dressage made her so happy, overexcited, and joyful. Jennifer was also calm, cool, peaceful and serene. With a peaceful nature.

Her obsessive love for dressage was quite evident when watching it. Jennifer became engrossed in watching the dressage. At watching every competitor compete.

***

Jennifer was a spectator seated next to her brother in the stalls. She admired every competitor in this competition, how they performed dressage. Performing beautifully well. The horsemen, horsewomen, riders doing technical movement on their horses. It was a phenomenal and sensational spectacle which was quite magnificent. It was truly amazing indeed, the riders' intuition and how they interacted with their horses. The winner of the dressage was a phenomenon.

Jennifer felt patriotic watching her own countrymen and countrywomen participating in dressage. This made Jennifer feel naturally proud. Jennifer was patriotic and proud of her country. Her nation!

Chris witnessed the great joy, thrill and excitement of his excitable sister. Jennifer rose to her feet. Raising her fists and punching the air. She cheered on the competitors who took part in the dressage in every round.

***

Chris looked at the pure joy on his sister's face. It made him feel so good and proud of her. Chris felt possessive and protective of his sister. He loved his sister.

Jennifer took far more pleasure from watching the dressage than her brother did. It had been an exciting and close competition. It had been a good day.

Later that summer evening, Chris was alone with his sister again. At that time, he just could not get a word in edgeways. As his sister rambled on about dressage again and again. Jennifer was obsessed with dressage and all things equestrian. Jennifer's interest was obsessional. She had an obsessive obsession for it!

The members of their family entered the room. They joined them and sat down together, listening to Jennifer's conversation about dressage and equestrian sport. It was a passion and interest of hers!

Jennifer was obsessed with it. Particularly the equestrian side, the horses (Palomino, Arabian and Stallions) and riding. Jennifer remained obsessional about it. Jennifer had a love for the sport!

26

Nobbs and Nells

(Tamley & Hedley)

Jennifer went to Nobbs and Nells late at night. A dark house in the shadowy darkness. It was the very last house at the very end of the road. Jennifer forced herself to go there. She dreaded it. She was reluctant to go there that night. Nobbs and Nells and the clan expected Jennifer to come. Jennifer kept her word. She came to avoid disappointment. Jennifer did not join them in an upstairs room at the top. She was feeling defiant with them. With refusal she avoided them. She didn't compromise with the dabblers. The clan followed Jennifer into another room. The clannish group of teenagers joined Jennifer in another room somewhere else in a dark room where there were shadows. They all stood together.

Jennifer spoke in a low tone of voice.

"Look! I can't do it! I can't join you tonight. I can't. I am a Christian now. I have my new beliefs. I do love you all. I have always loved you. Things now have got to change right now for me and us. I shan't come here again anymore. I make myself clear. I hope you all understand. I will not set foot here again, of that, I am sure. You are all a bad influence. I will not be led astray. I have seen the light. I must separate myself from all of you. That I must. I am set apart. I am no longer a witch like all of you. I am born again! I am free. I am a Christian," proclaimed Jennifer.

Standing together the group of female friends gathered, then realized the change in Jennifer's attitude and ethics in accordance with her beliefs and faith.

"What has driven you to this?" asked Sammy.

Jennifer looked at the glint in Sammy's big, dark eyes. Her pupils dilated in the light.

"I don't know. I really don't know. Since I had my accident, my life has changed. I have seen the light. I repeat myself. I am a Christian. I am proud of it. Things have changed. Now my life is different. Of course, everything about it. I can't compromise. What you lot are all doing! It's all bad and wrong. Living in darkness. I shall not come here anymore. It just has to stop. I have had enough. I will separate myself from all of you. I have no choice. I just have to. I cannot play with darkness. I am living in the light," said Jennifer indignantly.

"Oh. You are sanctimonious!" remarked Claire.

In the light, dark and shadows, they glared at Jennifer. "Goody-Goody." They tutted.

"Well. If that's your wish. Well, we will say our goodbyes," said Sammy rudely.

Jennifer loved her friends. She felt ambivalent towards all of them.

Dobbs and Nells objected to Jennifer's ways.

They disapproved of Jennifer. Jennifer regarded all of them with contempt, disregard and disrespect. Jennifer felt disgusted. Jennifer left Nobbs and Nells, never to return here ever again at this strange place, this house to attend a seance with a witch's coven.

From leaving them, Jennifer found such peace, joy and bliss at last. As a believer of the Christian faith. The darkness no longer affected Jennifer's life anymore, in any way.

There was a light in Jennifer's life!

A light that brightened and shined on…

***

Arriving back home at past midnight, Jennifer was expecting her sober mother to be staying up, waiting for her. Her son also waited for his sister to come home.

With affection Chris welcomed his sister.

Greeting his sister affectionately.

"Luv. How was it? Tell me. How are you feeling?" asked Mother.

The Shadow of the Daughter's Ring

Standing by the settee, Jennifer leaned on it gracefully. She stretched out her hand. Her sapphire diamond ring sparkled in the dazzling shining light.

"It's pretty bad. It's over between us," replied her daughter.

Chris interrupted them.

"Where have you been?" asked brother.

Jennifer admitted it, confirming,

"I have lost them. All of them," said Jennifer, sadly.

"Bad company. Keeping away from them does make sense. That's a good thing," said Mother assuredly.

Jennifer unashamedly admitted it.

"I have given up on my friends. That's for good," she confirmed.

"Aren't they your friends?" asked Brother.

"Well, they are. And they aren't."

Chris felt agitated by his sister for being too judgemental and critical of her friends.

"Aren't you being too judgemental?" he protested.

Jennifer nodded.

"Look! They are a bad lot. They are no good!" she said ashamedly.

Chris pressed for an answer, an immediate response.

"I confess I was bad. I had an accident. All that rehabilitation I took. It was beyond me. All that suffering. All that trauma. How on earth did I cope! I recovered. How I recovered. It's a miracle! I saw the light. I just did. I really did you know. It was glorious. It's such a glory! I became converted. Now things have got to change right now. They just have to. Right now, I cannot mix with idolators. Of course, you can have fellowship with Christians and sinners too. We are all sinners. We all fall short of the glory of Christ. One must repent of one's sins! Me, personally, I haven't looked back," said the Christian proudly.

Chris looked at his pure and angelic sister standing near a lampstand. There in the shining light, a lamp shone. In the brightened-up room there were shadows, moonshine and reflections.

Chris had such a regard and deep respect for his sister's Christian faith and beliefs. Chris was well-aware of his sister's spirituality. He realized his sister's miraculous transformation in her life!

A divine intervention!

Chris took much more interest in his sister than he had ever done before. At his sister's devotion and devotional faith. His sister Jennifer was devoted. A devout Christian!

Revival

At home at the long weekend, Jennifer found herself alone with her brother. Chris tried to talk to his insouciant and unsociable Sister. Jennifer ignored her brother on purpose. Chris had been tolerant of his spiteful, provocative and temperamental sister. He did have sympathy, understanding and patience for his beloved sister. At that present time, Chris was unable to confide in his moody sister and left the guest room. Jennifer stayed there by herself.

Jennifer had undergone a spiritual revival. A new Spiritual experience. A religious awakening. Jennifer knew she was now a follower of Christ!

A Christian believer!

Jennifer reflected on her circumstances. In previous months, Jennifer had undergone rehabilitation to recover from a fall she suffered, and she did recuperate from her fall. At present Jennifer stayed alone, isolated from everybody, in particular her friends and family. Jennifer liked her solitude and isolation. Jennifer remained protective of herself. She relaxed, restful and much happier, calmer and quieter. She was in a good mood. In her state she was calm, peaceful and naturally peaceable from being indurated, spiritual, regenerated and religious.

Jennifer's situation had been much more pleasant since she had freedom, peace, quietude and solitude at Christmas. Her nice time of loneliness was pleasant indeed. Jennifer desired to ride. She deemed it unwise due to her unfortunate situation. Instead, Jennifer preferred to relax herself in the self-indulgent comfort and luxury of her home. Jennifer took delight in her luxuries. She thrilled from her joy of relaxation and leisure. Also, in her quiet time, Jennifer was reading her scriptures and praying. Jennifer was prayerful and deeply contemplative.

At Christmas, on certain days, nights and times Jennifer kept away from her family when she and her family had been invited. Every time Jennifer declined an invitation at their nice homes. At her family's as well as friends. Jennifer stayed away from all of them.

Jennifer was enjoying her great bliss, pleasure, joy and ecstasy at being all alone at home. Personally, to Jennifer it made such a nice and lovely difference to her welfare and wellbeing, staying at home. She took the spiritual time to get redeemed, enlightened, illuminated and deeply spiritual in her religious outlook. Whilst everybody else, friends and family seemed to be worldly, materialistic and hedonistic.

Jennifer engaged in her religion. The religious aspects of her faith. Jennifer had a Christian faith! (In addition to this institution, this pupil had a good Catholic upbringing and a meaningful and profound spirituality.)

At Christmastime Jennifer sat alone again in a nice and luxurious room. She remained housebound in a lovely, cosy house.

Jennifer was uneasy and felt anguish and discomfort. She took narcissistic obsessive interest in herself. She bent down and rolled down her beautiful black stockings. Jennifer looked at her beautiful shapely legs. She saw a blemish on her leg. She fretted at the unpleasant sight of it. Jennifer felt uneasy at the sight of if. She again felt uneasy and discomfort at it. Jennifer shuddered. At present she seemed not to have any interest and further narcissism for herself!

Jennifer lost interest in her beauty, fretting, it caused her anguish, making her feel deeply psychotic and disturbed.

Normally, Jennifer had a natural self-love. Usually she was vain, narcissistic and conceited. At this time, Jennifer remained withdrawn again indoors.

As the day drew to a close, suddenly the light grew darker and darker. Jennifer was sitting and resting in comfort. Sitting in a nice position on the armchair which made her comfortable. She rested her head on a nice soft cushion. Suddenly Jennifer nodded off in the dark. Jennifer was lost in a deep beauty sleep. A Christmas one!

27

A Seasonal Peace at Christmas

At Christmastime Jennifer stayed away from her family deliberately. Including relatives and relations and extended families. To them she referred to it (her absence from all of them) as doctor's orders!

Preferring to be all alone. Jennifer took the time to spend time alone. She was an eluder, avoider and unsociable. Jennifer constantly kept away from all her family.

Jennifer cherished and enjoyed the peace and quiet on certain days at Christmas. On other days at Christmas, her family came over to her home. Spending Christmas together. A festivity and merriment.

On Christmas Eve, Jennifer, a shopper went Christmas shopping in the Shopping Centre in the High Street with her parents.

On Christmas Day, she spent Christmas with the family.

On the morning of Christmas Day, Jennifer and her family attended a Christmas service at the Cathedral.

Later at home, her family had Christmas dinner. Both daughter and mother ate a

vegetarian Christmas meal. Chris and her father ate a roast. Christmas was a merry, lovely time together with family. A seasonal festivity.

Today on Christmas Day, Jennifer liked to be with her family. It was a special seasonal time at Christmas!

Jennifer received really nice Christmas presents and gifts which she opened very early on Christmas day morning. At that time, Jennifer was overexcited like an excitable child!

Jennifer was feeling wonder and seasonal excitement at Christmas.

On Boxing Day, Jennifer stayed indoors. She enjoyed the peace and quiet and freedom of being alone at home. How she cherished and loved the peace! Since a beautiful child, Jennifer experienced Christmas to be an exciting time. A thrilling delight!

Jennifer got overexcited at Christmas. It was a lovely experience with such joyful thrilling encounters. (A sort of seasonal mystery at Christmastime!)

On other days at Christmas, Jennifer spent times and days with members of her family and extended family who called at her house to see their family.

Generally, there was love with their families, though unfortunately on this occasion a few of them did show resentment, bitterness and disrespect to Jennifer because of her being too selfish, inconsiderate, thoughtless, neglectful, uncaring, unloving and unreasonable. As usual Jennifer had a disregard for them by having a lack of consideration for them. Jennifer typically showed inconsiderateness towards her family. It was usually Jennifer's way.

On other days and at other times at Christmastime, Jennifer found herself all alone again indoors at home. She stayed indoors. Jennifer greatly enjoyed her great peace and quiet and her freedom at Christmas when she was all alone!

She likes to be lonely. She did rather like it!

It was an enjoyable seasonal experience of hers!

In a room Jennifer warmed herself by sitting in front of a luxury fireplace, a fire, enjoying the comfort of luxury. Jennifer took comfort from being nice and warm in a lovely warm room. Jennifer took time to reflect on her life. How reckless she had been at times! She thought of a few occasions as well as her unfortunate accident, when she had fallen off her horse when it had bolted suddenly. From this danger her life was endangered. It was a miracle how Jennifer survived and recovered and recuperated from the dangerous bad fall from her horse.

28

A Religious Talk

One day their mother came home late from work. The tired Parent entered the dining room. Her son and daughter sat on dining chairs on opposite sides of the dining table, facing each other.

As usual brother and sister were talking away.

"I See from your habits, that you two are talking. That does make a change," interrupted Mother.

Jennifer felt unease at being observed by her mother. Jennifer shrugged her shoulders.

"Why shouldn't that be?" groaned Daughter.

The mother did not answer. At once the worried parent left the dining room, leaving both her son and daughter alone together. At that time Jennifer and Chris preferred to be alone together without any intrusion between them. Jennifer and Chris felt laidback, restful, relaxed, calm and peaceful.

They both engaged in a religious conversation. (At that particular time there weren't any apologies from either of them. Nor any difference of opinion nor any disagreements between them.)

Both brother and sister agreed on the basic principles of religion, in this case Christianity!

"How about your faith?" asked Brother.

Jennifer answered with honesty.

"I am a believer in the Christian faith. When I was younger, I was once set in my ways. I was like everybody else. Exactly like my friends. I dabbled. We had big dreams and ideals. I did what everybody else did at the time. What on earth was I doing? It was something you did. You felt compelled to do. What your friends do. I just followed suit. It's a sin as I know. I guess I didn't know at the time. When I look back it was reminiscent of something that my family and ancestors did in past generations. Playing with darkness comes naturally to us. It's something of a family trait. Something that occurs. That always happens. We all do it! It's something we always do. Bless or curse, I don't know which? It's a sin! I remember one day when I rode, I fell off my bloody horse. Then everything changed for the better. My life changed. How it did I don't know. Your guess is as good as mine. I became converted. I just did! A born-again Christian! A follower of Christ. I have deserted all my witch friends and cronies. I just cannot compromise to their ways anymore. Their witchery and treachery. It's not on. It's not right. It's all wrong. I admit I was sinful. I confess. We all are. Falling off my horse and being injured made me change my ways. I became a Christian! I haven't looked back ever since," said Sister candidly.

"Do you have any regrets?" asked Brother.

"Oh! Yes! I may have. Then again, I have no regrets. It's the best thing I did. Surrendering! Repenting. Giving up my life of sin and darkness to follow Christ. That's the best way forward, isn't it! Moving forwards in a good and positive way. Having a good faith. Living that Christian life. It makes all the difference. For me it's what counts. That's what it's all about," admitted Sister.

"Are you regretful?" asked Brother.

"Yes. I should have been converted sooner. I admit I am remorseful. I do have regrets. Well, how about you?" she asked.

"I am not a believer. I do listen. My mother drags me to church. It's her way!" answered Brother.

"Did you know our funny mother was born in a barnyard!" chuckled Sister.

"That's just typical of Mom. We are no different, are we?" laughed Brother.

Jennifer burst out laughing. Jennifer was amused at her brother's wisecrack.

Suddenly Jennifer was hysterical. They both ended up in hysterics. Their hysteria was shrill.

Jennifer in hysterics nearly fell off her dining chair. She somehow kept herself balanced while seated gracefully on the dining chair. She balanced herself.

Jennifer was aware of her falling off the dining chair as a result of her hysteria. Chris was amused at his sister's hysterics!

Jennifer kept calm and cool. She cooled off. Jennifer reclined on the dining table gracefully. Jennifer sprawled. Keeping calm and quiet Jennifer rose from the dining chair.

She left the mahogany dining table. She came out of the spacious dining room and went upstairs to her bedroom alone. There she spent time alone to reflect on everything else which was on her mind at present.

Jennifer worried about general things. Then she became unconcerned about practically everything and she became impractical. Her purpose and function were to wise up, to be sensible, and stay healthy, religious, protective and last but not least, to stay safe! Those were the main concerns of hers! Generally, that was her wish!

29

Jennifer's Friends Call at Her House

A group of Jennifer's friends came to her house. Suddenly the doorbell chimed a few times. Jennifer sitting alone in the Lounge had got up and answered the front door. She had sort of expected her friends to arrive. On time usually their arrival punctual. Jennifer anticipated this to happen during the course of the weekend. Jennifer was already beautifully groomed and preened. She led her group of friends into the quiet lounge where they all sat down together.

Lucy was sitting in comfort, restful and relaxed. When seated, Lucy spoke about something else entirely different.

"Have you read anything lately?"

"Oh! Yes. It's something religious. It's miraculous," answered Jennifer.

"Well, what is it?" prompted Lucy.

"It's something I have read. It's of some spiritual profound meaning. Well, it's about a Leper in a Valley of Lepers. This Leper sees the light. He is cured of his leprosy. It's a miracle! The Leper is cleansed," replied Jennifer.

"Not Religion. It's not religious, is it?" They grumbled.

Sammy expressed her heartfelt sentiment.

"Don't you love us?"

"I do love you all. Why shouldn't I?" responded Jennifer.

They glared and glowered at Jennifer.

"You don't show it. Do you?" grumbled Claire.

"What will become of us?" asked Stacy.

"I expect we will still see each other. However, I can't compromise on any of your bad ways. I make that perfectly clear. Is that understood?" said Jennifer plainly.

Sammy took notice of Jennifer's ways.

"You do take your religion very seriously. That is clear. We do see that. That really shouldn't stop us from seeing each other," pointed out Sammy.

Jennifer raised objections.

"All of you. Your black arts have to stop now. I can't participate in it any longer. I advocate the light, Christianity. The feeling of darkness has no part and meaning in my life any longer. The sooner you all realize that, then that is the better."

"We don't know anything else. Do we?" they said.

"That is not the point. It has to stop. Now I don't want to see damnation. Your souls in damnation!" reprimanded Jennifer.

"You do preach. We do listen," said Lucy.

The others objected. They took a negative view. They disapproved, making a disapproving remark.

We won't bother!" they said disapprovingly.

"You all should still see me. I would really like that very much. I still do like you all. That won't change. It shan't. Damn it! You all being dabblers has to change and stop. There is nothing else for it. No more darkness. No more seances. If that's the case, I am afraid I have no other alternative but to break free from all of you," said Jennifer defiantly.

"We can see. You are religious," remarked Sammy.

"Yes. You Are. We can see that," perceived Claire.

Stacy put her fingers on her lips.

"What would the boys think? You are some kind of weirdo," retorted Stacy.

Jennifer stayed calm and cool. She repeated herself,

"Enough is enough. I cannot compromise. Not now. Never! It has to stop," said Jennifer repeatedly.

All of Jennifer's friends sitting together in the beautiful luxurious lounge rose to their feet. They all realized Jennifer's ambivalence, aggression and defiance towards them. All of them were unenthusiastic about talking further to their friend. They all decided to go. Going out of the lounge, Jennifer led them towards the front door and showed them all out of her house. All of Jennifer's friends had gone home. At that late mid-afternoon Jennifer decided to stay the rest of the day indoors to suit herself.

***

She sat down back in the lounge. She indulged in being comfortable. Sitting and resting in comfort in a position on a settee. She reflected on her nice friends.

As a follower of Christ, she advocated Christianity in a natural way of hers!

Jennifer stayed seated in comfort. She thought of her bad, charming friends. She contemplated and meditated in the silence of the room. Jennifer took such joy from all her peace, freedom and from such nice comfort in her home.

Jennifer contemplated. A religious contemplation. Jennifer was meditative and contemplative, wistful and pensive.

Jennifer shed a tear. She cried!

Jennifer had lost her friends. Losing her friends! Did they desert her?

30

Jennifer Stays at a Close Family Friend's

One day Jennifer and her mother were both doing their usual weekly housework at the weekend. As Jennifer used a clean duster to dust the mantelpiece thoroughly to clean it, she accidently knocked a fragile ornate vase off the mantelpiece. From moving along sidewards she was clumsy in her movement. The fallen vase was broken and damaged.

The Mother heard something break and smash. She burst into the room and saw a broken vase, smashed. The angry mother shouted at her nervous daughter, pointing a finger at her.

"You clumsy bitch! What have you done? You have broken a good vase!" she shouted.

With her bare hands, the daughter bent down and picked up all of the fragments of the broken vase and put them in a wastepaper bin. Jennifer apologised.

"I didn't mean it. It was an accident," she said nervously.

"It's bloody broken. I won't get a vase like that ever again!" said Mother angrily.

Jennifer flushed. She avoided her mother and stayed upstairs in her bedroom for hours and hours. Jennifer was standing by her bedroom window. She wanted peace and quiet. She sought it, that peace. Hoping to get a joyful wonder of peace!

She cheered up when her arrangement to stay at a retreat with a close family friend had been approved of and agreed!

Days and days of peace. She desired it! Jennifer satisfied her eager desire to go!

Jennifer, in a distressed state became much calmer, quieter, cooler and wiser. She withdrew, becoming sensible, wise and introverted. With extroverted tendencies with regards to her theatrics, her airs and graces. Jennifer recited. Jennifer planned to get away and therefore keep away from her unpleasant mother. For a few days Jennifer's mother was temperamental, angry and fuming.

Jennifer At a Retreat and Sanctuary

Jennifer stayed at a retreat. She had been invited to a country retreat. On that occasion Jennifer grovelled due to bad circumstances, an escape to a sanctuary.

A break and escape, Jennifer depended on her self-control and that good faith of hers!

Jennifer was ensconced at a sanctuary. She enjoyed staying a few days at a retreat. With a nice, and lovable family friend of hers!

Jennifer's nice invitation at a retreat was rather pleasant indeed, lovely and enjoyable. A good experience of hers!

For a change, Jennifer liked the peace, quietude, solitude and privacy at the retreat and sanctuary. She prayed and was prayerful and worshipful. She also took the time to read her scriptures too.

Nobody else intruded, obtruded and imposed on this well-favoured guest those days and nights.

Spending a few days at a retreat, she recovered and recuperated. For Jennifer staying at this retreat was a thrill of delight!

Jennifer would certainly like to return there again. Staying there Jennifer felt protected, safer and from certain individual family friends who were protective towards her.

31

Dream House

(A Beautiful Retreat)

Jennifer as an opportunist took her opportunity to stay at a retreat. A nice family friend of hers and her parents too.

Jennifer experienced peace and quiet here. It affected her mood. (Jennifer was no longer moody, miserable and depressed. Her mood change made her happier, more cheerful and exuberant.)

Jennifer was solicitous, peaceable, peaceful, calmer, cooler, quieter, restful and relaxed.

Jennifer indeed cherished her peaceful times staying at the country retreat which was located deep in the remote and lovely countryside.

As a believer in the Christian faith, she experienced great beatitude, joy and euphoria. At certain times, Jennifer felt blissful and euphoric, at times of rejoicing. "Hallelujah!" She praised and glorified Christ in a reverence.

Throughout the course of the long day, Jennifer had the pleasure and freedom to do what she wanted. She took the chance to explore the whole retreat to please and satisfy herself. Jennifer went into every room of the retreat. With wonder and curiosity, Jennifer was excited looking around at every room, big, small, large or spacious. Jennifer looked at the drawing room, reception rooms, cloakroom, a master bedroom and attic. There she found it to be invitingly exciting, entering all rooms that were either downstairs or upstairs. Of course, this was a place which was somewhere new and unusual, different and more or less strange.

Jennifer felt overwhelmed at seeing and looking at this lovely retreat. It took her breath away.

This too affected how she felt with their passion for Arts. Jennifer was in a joyful, happy and cheerful mood. She had seen and admired the art everywhere else.

Jennifer found herself neglected again and alone for a certain time. She liked to be lonely and alone. It made her feel alive and so good!

Experiencing the solitude, quietude and isolation and seclusion remained a peaceful joyful experience for Jennifer.

During the midafternoon, she played with the parents' son and daughter in the lovely country garden. Jennifer had such fun playing with the children. She enjoyed such thrills. It was a great delight!

Finding herself alone again by herself, Jennifer relaxed in a drawing room. About an hour later, she rose to her feet and left the drawing room. Jennifer was going somewhere else. She entered another room to please herself. She sat down on a leather upholstered armchair. She gratified herself with the comfort of luxury by resting herself on an armchair in a plush room.

Jennifer indulged in self-indulgence, sitting in front of a fire, a luxury fireplace. With nice comfort, Jennifer warmed herself up as the sybarite gratified herself with such comforts and luxury. (With added luxuries added on.)

Jennifer indulged in fine luxury. A sybaritic hedonism!

Jennifer liked the natural joys of peace naturally, quietude and solitude equally as well. She too experienced the sanctuary and the joyful delight of this really fine luxury retreat itself and what it had to offer by providing her with fine luxury. With a purposeful sense of pleasure, it was pleasure-loving and gratifying, indulging and pleasurable. With a gratification of overindulgence and self-indulgence and far more pleasure!

But instead, Jennifer overcame her overindulgence and self-indulgence of it, by being too mortified and disciplined. Jennifer too had resilience and buoyancy with her acts of self- mortification and self-discipline. Due to her religious faith (Christian) Jennifer applied her acts of self-discipline, disciplinary abstinence and self-mortification naturally of course.

The Shadow of the Daughter's Ring

Naturally, Jennifer enjoyed her freedom, peace and quiet, solitude, and quietude as well as her privacy. Jennifer liked and preferred to be free and all alone and to be isolated and secluded. She rounded off the day by having a nice conversation with good family friends. The husband, a loving father. His chic independent wife, a multi-millionairess, a jetsetter, a professional fashion designer.

Jennifer confided in her.

"I really do love it here. It's wonderful! It's been great! I have had a lovely time so far. I just can't get enough of it. I love it here. It's pretty different to most places I have been to. Coming here is a fine thing. This house is really lovely. I have only got good things to say about it. Looking around, you have such fine art, decor, furnishings, linen, antiques and ornaments. Yes, I do love your fine furniture too. It's a dream! There are so many rooms in this house. I just lose count of it all. The rooms are beautiful! Isn't it fascinating!

"Your portraits too make me interested. I love your paintings and pictures. Coming here today and staying here, I have experienced great things. It's amazing!

"I just love the peace and silence here. Isn't it great! Yes. I must come back. I really must," smiled Jennifer.

"I am glad you like it. I am pleased. You're always welcome to stay. We are pleased to have you here. You are our guest. Do make yourself at home. Next time if you like, you can choose your own room of your liking when you do decide next to come back here to stay," said the wife amiably.

With sweet charm and affection Jennifer expressed her gratitude.

"I am pleased. You have invited me. It's great! Thank you very much. You are so kind."

Jennifer appreciated both hosts' welcome, kindness and their warm hospitality.

"Well! That's settled. Do come back. You're welcome to stay." smiled the housewife.

32

Jennifer Visits a Gipsy Friend at a Caravan

Jennifer went to a caravan site where she visited a Gipsy's caravan. Jennifer paid a visit to a family friend at her cosy caravan. She wondered what it was like living in a luxury caravan. She thought living in a caravan must be a new and strange experience. A lovely one too!

This way of life must be rather unusual and quite different from the customary way of living.

Jennifer sat down at a table next to a vampiric, curvaceous Gipsy, a Romanian brunette.

The Gipsy laid her Tarot Cards down flat on the table, concentrating on her predictions made. Jennifer objected to the Gipsy reading her set of tarot cards while making predictions. The Gipsy predicted Jennifer's future. Jennifer was unconcerned and uninterested in the Gipsy's predictions. To an unconcerned Jennifer, this uninteresting course of events and present and future predictions were what would surely happen to Jennifer. As it was, Jennifer remained uninterested and unconcerned at her uninteresting predictions. Jennifer abhorred it! Naturally in her natural way!

***

"No!" she said. "That's not necessary. I don't wish to have my future predicted. It's not my way. If you don't mind. In a spiritual sense, one cannot play with darkness and light," she condemned.

The Gipsy respected Jennifer's decision.

"If that's your wish. How are you?" asked the Gipsy.

The Shadow of the Daughter's Ring

Jennifer did admit to how unwell she felt.

"I haven't been well lately. It's my periods!" groaned Jennifer.

"I know the feeling. I do hope you get well," empathised the Gipsy.

Jennifer shook her long, beautiful hair tumbling down to her shoulder, hip and back.

"Look! I have come to see you. You're a friend of ours. A good friend of mine. You're sweet. You do put yourself out for all of us! That's saying something. You aren't a pikey after all," said Jennifer pleasantly.

"That is nice," replied the Gipsy.

"How is life?" asked Jennifer.

"It's fine. I make my living from the occult as you know," said the Gipsy unashamedly.

"I know that it's bad practice. I condemn it. That's why I have broken free from all of my bad friends. I can no longer practise with practitioners and dark forces at work. This to me defeats the object!" stated Jennifer clearly.

"You have said," murmured the Gipsy.

Jennifer looked the Gipsy in the face. This witch-like Gipsy was handsome. Her rouged cheeks were flushed, and her powdered face made her uglier and uglier. Her red lipstick on her lips was smeared.

Jennifer objected to the experienced fortune teller doing her fortune telling. She abhorred her practice of it. Listening, she was appalled at the predictions which were being made by the fortune teller. Her fortune telling outraged her!

"Now what?"

Jennifer was watching the fortune teller intent on doing her predictions with the use of a crystal ball. Her beautiful black cat with green eyes was on the prowl!

"You will stay away from people. You will spend most of your time alone. You are happy and relieved to be free. At having your own freedom. Due to bad trauma, you will avoid everybody. Your friends and family. You will be withdrawn. You will find peace, joy and happiness at going to another new place in the nice country somewhere. Your life will change for the better. There you will find peace, joy, love and true happiness! Your faith will drive you onwards. You will seek your Lord. Your life will move forward in a more positive way. In the right direction. At last, you will find purpose. You will find it," predicted the Gipsy.

***

For Jennifer there did remain a good change of fortune. Jennifer no longer felt oppressed and suffering anymore with oppression. With any oppressive standards in living. Now Jennifer had freedom and approval to go to a Retreat whenever she wanted and fancied.

Jennifer reached for her handbag resting on her lap. She opened her black leather handbag. She took out a black leather purse which was trimmed with gold. She opened her purse. She took out a new ten-pound banknote and thoughtfully gave it to the Gipsy as a gesture of gratitude and goodwill.

Quickly, together they both left the nice caravan which was smelling of real leather and pot-pourri air freshener, fresh coffee and incense and a fragrance. The Gipsy went to a Bingo club somewhere on the outskirts of town to meet her mother and an elderly gentleman who was wearing a hat and carrying an umbrella. At that same time, Jennifer a pedestrian made her way back home. Jennifer was quite fit as she got back home safely.

33

Jennifer's Bitter Blues

Jennifer stayed indoors today. For the whole day. She suffered with a bout of depression as well as being bereaved. Did she fret because she was undesirable, thinking of herself as being undesirable and undesired? Was this a common reality of hers, what she now had to face?

Jennifer was sitting on the armchair feeling anguish. She bent down and looked at her leg. She disliked what she saw. She noticed there was a blemish on her leg, looking at both of her shapely and long legs, which were still tanned from the hot sun shining. Jennifer caught the sun. She had a natural tan and a glow. She had a rosy complexion with a suntan of a golden bronze.

***

Jennifer relaxed while she rested on the armchair. There in a library, waiting for Ann Stroud to come. On a Friday evening, Ann a family friend had turned up at her house. Ann was slender, graceful and elegant. She entered the library and sat down on the armchair in a comfortable way. She took comfort from her position, facing opposite in another leather armchair, a matching pair.

Ann, a teenager and a romance lover, picked up a hardcover from the table and began to read it.

"Spells, potions and magic?" she muttered.

Jennifer disapproved of Ann looking at a book of magic.

"You're not looking at that, are you? Put it down and read something else. There are plenty of other books to choose from," reprimanded Jennifer.

Ann, a pretty girl, obeyed. Ann was a witch who used to be with other witches her age from witch's covens. Ann appeared to be unafraid or was she just acting in a way which was cool and indifferent and nonchalant? She put her finger on her chin. In deep thought, Ann looked thoughtful.

"How do you protect yourself? How does one do that?" she asked.

"Haven't I told you that already? You should know that by now. It has been drummed into you time and time again," tutted Jennifer.

With impatience Ann prompted Jennifer. "Well, tell me. How do I? C'mon tell me."

"In its simplest terms by Christianity," blabbed Jennifer.

"Yes, you are knowledgeable, aren't you?" Remarked Ann.

Jennifer got up and walked towards Ann who was sitting on an armchair opposite, at an angle. Jennifer moved forward. Standing in front of Ann seated on the armchair. she held Ann's hand and squeezed it. Applying pressure playfully to Ann's hand by squeezing it firmly. Jennifer's blood pulsated through her veins and arteries. Her heart was beating faster.

Jennifer indeed had such sisterly love for Ann. Another family friend.

"Is that it?" asked Ann.

"Yes, that's it. Do remember Christianity and holy communion," advised Jennifer.

Jennifer's great love for Ann simply conquered Ann's fear. If of course Ann still had any fears. Ann became less and less afraid.as a fearless female teenager growing up. At this present time Jennifer took the opportunity whenever she was alone with Ann, to preach to a wayward, stubborn girl. Jennifer sounded very convincing when she preached to an apathetic Ann.

"You mustn't fall. Don't fall away. Don't be lead astray. Do take responsibility. Don't be led astray. Do take responsibility for your actions. Do what is right. Don't sin," cautioned Jennifer.

Ann gasped while staying seated. She listened to what Jennifer said. At this time Ann listened intently. Jennifer spoke with further religious convictions. She intervened to try and preach further to Ann again.

34

Jennifer Goes to the Stables to be Alone with her Horse

Jennifer truly hated her horse. She loathed it. She hadn't seen her horse for days and days. How many days she hadn't seen her horse she could not remember. She must have forgotten. At certain times and on certain days, Jennifer did wish to see her horse in the stables. She desired to be with her horse. Then again, she changed her mind, losing interest in seeing her horse. She bore a grudge against her horse time after time. Thinking of her horse again,

Jennifer wished and desired to see her horse alone in the stables. With her strong deep faith, Jennifer soon forgave her horse. One day, Jennifer went alone to the empty stables to be with her horse. She was reconciled with her horse. She forgave her horse. Jennifer felt emotional. She stood by her horse for a short time. Jennifer stroked and patted her horse. Jennifer loved her horse.

Jennifer remembered her fall from her horse. How she had fallen! She retraced and recalled it. Learning from this dreadful experience. Suffering with an ordeal and trauma.

She also remembered how this fall had completely changed her life for the better. Subsequently it converted her. Jennifer leaving the stables did not go back there until a few days ago. During that time, Jennifer cooled off. She spent time with her horse again!

Jennifer was reconciled at being with her horse again!

35

Jennifer's Family Friends Come to Her House

Jennifer's family and friends came to her house. They all came to see Jennifer's parents, especially with the motivational intention to see Jennifer as well.

Everybody gathered together in a furnished and refurbished living room. They all sat down together and talked away. Jennifer sitting amongst her family and family friends. The two chic women were jewellers. Both ladies wore fine, lovely dresses and were beautifully bejewelled.

Jennifer's female family friends were adorned with such fine jewellery and jewels. A brooch too. Looking so lovely indeed in their figure-hugging, slinky dresses and wearing the finest jewels and jewellery, ladies' watches, gold bangles, bracelets and necklaces. Everybody else talked while Jennifer kept quiet. She cherished her time with everybody. Her family friends and families. Jennifer, sitting gracefully, took comfort from her seated position. Jennifer compared her sapphire and diamond ring with theirs, their expensive and precious jewels and jewellery. Jennifer felt smug and great pride. She was so proud!

How she loved her precious ring. With her heart beating faster, her veins pulsating and her temples throbbing, Jennifer was perspiring. She took joy and pride from her ring. Jennifer treasured it from her heart, her ring!

She had such deep, sentimental pride!

That autumn day, Jennifer stayed with them for hours, sitting together with them in a relaxed and restful manner. Jennifer looked poised, graceful and dignified with such elegance and mannerisms.

36

Late Grandmother's Spirt in a Pretty Summer Garden

Jennifer roused from her sleep, her deep beauty sleep. Getting out of bed, she was up early in the morning. Jennifer was suntanned, with a golden bronze suntan. She was wearing a slinky black nightdress. She put on her black slippers and negligee. She tied it tightly around her waist. During the morning, Jennifer found she was the only one alone indoors again. At home, Jennifer made a mug of sweet tea. She relaxed alone in the nice lounge. Sitting on the armchair, her shapely legs emerged out of the slits of her negligee. Her beautiful tanned bare legs were suntanned. Jennifer was refreshed from drinking about a third of a mug of tea. This was her favourite black tea.

Jennifer stayed downstairs for about an hour before going back to bed again for more rest.

Later in the morning, Jennifer got up and got dressed and came back downstairs to the lounge again. Jennifer all alone enjoyed her peace, freedom and silence. She felt calm, quiet, peaceful and peaceable. She liked to spend time all alone. It was something she did more often to suit herself. At this time of the afternoon, Jennifer enjoyed her privacy as well as the delightful luxury and fine comfort of her home.

***

Jennifer doing nothing during the daytime, relaxed herself and was restful. (She enjoyed nice peaceful days alone at home.)

Jennifer was idle and lazy for a few hours. She spent most of her time staying indoors, remaining housebound.

Jennifer also enjoyed the pleasure and privilege of being a well-kept daughter, loved, favoured and pampered by her parents and family.

Hours later, Jennifer went outdoors. She came out of the back door and into the back garden alone. She liked to be lonely and alone. She took joy at her feeling of loneliness. She actually preferred it that way. Jennifer felt peaceful, happy, in high spirits and exhilarated.

Walking around the acres of the English country garden, Jennifer discerned that her grandmother's spirit remained in this pretty country garden. The light wind blew. Jennifer breathed in the cool fresh air. She felt calmer and cooler and in a good mood. Not going anywhere in particular, she came upon a border and flowerbed in the garden. That cool, shady spot was where the trees were.

Jennifer stopped at a bed. She admired all the roses there. Naturally, all the rose bushes were along some of the beds down there.

Jennifer stretched out her hand. She took moments to admire her shiny sapphire and diamond ring sparkling in the sunshiny daylight. There the radiant sunrays shone. All of the beams dazzled.

Thinking deeply of her beloved late grandmother, she felt mournful and sad. She treasured her lovely diamond ring. She cherished her happiest memories of her late grandmother.

Jennifer was elegant, chic and stylish. (Customarily Jennifer wore all sorts of fashion. She was obsessed with fashion. She was obsessive too about particular styles of fashion in a natural way. She had a passion for fashion, women's and females. Women's and females!

The daughter had natural panache, style and finesse like her chic, cultured and fashionable mother of course.

Jennifer was tanned and wearing a rather beautiful sundress. Her natural beautiful figure and body was naturally exposed. (Somewhat like a nude!)

Jennifer's natural suntan was quite beautiful indeed. (After a vacation abroad at a coastal Mediterranean Resort.)

Jennifer was naturally suntanned and beautifully complexioned. Her complexion peachy and rosy. She had a natural tan.

Jennifer enjoyed her peace and quiet and silence out in the beautiful garden alone during the course of the late midafternoon. At the time of the afterglow, Jennifer was tearful standing and holding a beautiful red rose. She stooped down and sniffed it. This rose scent itself was pure and exquisite. She breathed in and inhaled it. Stepping back, Jennifer admired with wonder the beautiful floribunda everywhere in the surrounding lovely garden.

At present Jennifer thought of her grandmother for the final time today. She was deeply pensive and wistful thinking of her grandmother. Jennifer reflected on her happier memories!

Dream Elements.

During the past fortnight there had been changes to the weather and season. (That included seasonal weather changes also.) The elements changed.

Today Jennifer stayed indoors. From day to day, night and day, she tended to elude and avoid her family and family friends with purposeful intent. All alone in the living room. Jennifer ended up staying in that room. Standing and facing the window. She looked at the window dreamily. She was lost in a dreamy daydream. The thick heavy raindrops splattered on the windowpanes, which were double-glazed. Outside it rained. Jennifer daydreamed. She was wool-gathering.

She was dreamy while lost in a daydream. In a state of a trance. She took an interest in the changes of the weather, in its elements. Eventually and suddenly, all the weather changed.

37

Jennifer's Request

A few days ago, Jennifer repeated her request to her mother.

"Please leave the photos on the table."

Her mother obeyed her emotional daughter, respecting her daughter's wishes. Days ago, the thoughtful mother put the old black and white photographs on the polished dining table as requested by her daughter!

The next day Jennifer came into the dining room. There she found a pile of black and white photographs of her deeply spiritual grandmother. Expecting this, Jennifer sat down on a dining chair, one of the matching set of dining chairs. She sat at the dining table and with curious interest and wonder looked at the old photographs of her late grandmother. Her grandmother was dowdy. She wore frocks. A handsome Wife. A religious one!

***

Looking at the backgrounds, Jennifer didn't know where they were taken, whether her grandmother was living in poverty or whether she was a well-off housewife. Jennifer felt confused, perplexed and baffled by this. A few of them were Christmas photographs with her son and daughter. Other ones were at Easter time. Others were just simply ordinary days in the eventful life of a grandmother. Another was an old, faded photograph.

Jennifer looked at all of them. She cried, blubbered and sobbed. Jennifer felt heartrendingly sad and upset. She cried like a sobbing little girl. She sobbed and sulked like a child!

38

Dream Rider

(Horseman Pride)

Jennifer stayed indoors all day long. She remained alone at her home. During the daytime, she did nothing that day. She was lackadaisical, sluggish, daydreamy, and lazy. Jennifer spent time looking at paintings all on the walls everywhere. She walked up to a painting on the opposite side of a room. There she saw a painting. A Rider Riding Out. This was a natural one. It was naturally good with an aesthetic appeal. A panorama of a natural Equestrian modern art. A panoramic natural landscape of the Countryside. (It was in walking distance of a picturesque village less than a few miles away.)

This may well have been Jennifer's most favourite painting.

Jennifer naturally admired the painting. She raised her finger at it. Her sapphire diamond ring sparkled. The daughter had empathy with this natural one. She empathised with how the rider, the horseman rode. The way the horseman had mastered the art of horsemanship.

Jennifer marvelled at it with great wonder and the rest of the collection of art. Standing in front of a wall in the sunshiny daylight where the sun shone, that same painting reflected in the light. Its radiant dazzling sunlight. Standing still, Jennifer was lost in a reverie while looking at it dreamily. Jennifer fantasised while lost in a dreamy fantasy and ecstasy. A dream rider rode out. Jennifer caught sight of a shadow and at how the light reflected on the painting, from the frame of a painting which gleamed in the light.

Jennifer was thrilled at a spell of enchantment. Jennifer was spellbound and mesmerised by it. She was in a state of trance. Jennifer caught a glimpse of her diamond ring sparkling in the light.

She daydreamed while standing in the shadows and reflections. Jennifer was a dreamy daydreamer lost in a dream!

Jennifer was once again daydreaming to her heart's content. Suddenly she was distracted as she caught sight of her luminous ladies' watch which glowed.

Jennifer came back to her bedroom alone. She ended up staying in her bedroom for some hours, sitting on her armchair, near a corner of a wall. In comfort, Jennifer rested.

Later at night, she came downstairs on an enchanting, dark, moonlit night. Jennifer stayed in a luxurious living room. She sat on a luxury Chesterfield and rested.

Jennifer was enchanted at the sight of the moonlight as well as the moonshine reflections. Jennifer felt wonderfully romantic, in a romantic mood!

With a charm of romance. Jennifer romanticised in the shadows. There the beams of light reflected on the wall, casting shadows. Jennifer stretched out her hand. Raising her hand, she pointed her finger directly at the wall opposite. There her sapphire and diamond ring made a shadow and reflection on the wall. In the light her diamond ring sparkled. It reflected on a shadowy wall. It made a shadow and reflection too. Jennifer was obsessed by her ring. To her it was like a charm! She felt deeply sentimental about it. Jennifer at the sight of her ring, admired it!

She had an obsessive sentimental love for it!

Her feminine obsession for it was a female obsessiveness!

Jennifer was greatly proud of her diamond ring. She treasured her ring with all her heart!

She remembered her grandmother with a wistful fondness. Jennifer was deeply pensive from her deep thoughts and memories.

In the moonlit shadows and reflections in an illuminated room.

Jennifer was sitting alone in the dark. She rested herself there indoors and outdoors. Outside the moonshine was making illuminations in the darkness. Jennifer was enchanted and spellbound by its natural illumination. Jennifer felt deliriously overexcited, delirious, rapturous and exhilarated. Jennifer with a thrill of joy was overwhelmed, overcome with emotion when thinking of her past memories.

Available worldwide from Amazon and all good bookstores

Michael Terence Publishing

www.mtp.agency

www.facebook.com/mtp.agency

@mtp_agency